Welcome to the war for the Gulf

The Biker Princess

Southern Devils Society

Book 1

Trigger Warnings

If you don't give a shit about triggers, boldly walk right into this war. I'll hold the door for you. I bet you love twisted surprises, don't you?

Trigger Warnings: Please take a moment to go over these if you are unsure about proceeding.

Explicit sexual language, Descriptive sexual acts, Vulgar language, Murder, Blood, Graphic Violence, Hitting women, Sex trafficking, Abduction, Gun usage, Torture, Family trauma/PTSD, Parental alienation, Parental emotional abuse, Loss of Mother, Breath play, Edge play, Somnophilia, Stalking, Power dynamics, Touch her and die, Possessive and Obsessive MMC who is also a Cinnamon Roll inside that tough exterior.

This is not an exhaustive list as specific triggers vary widely between each person.

ISBN-13: 979-8-9993028-0-9

ISBN-10: 1477123456

Cover design by: Collin Foster https://everythingfeathered.net/

Library of Congress Control Number: 018675309

Printed in the United States of America

French to English Translations

There are some French parts in the story since they are in the heart of the Bayou and New Orleans, and a good portion of the population speaks French in that geographical area. I have included translations for easy reference.

Chapter 13 - Ici - here

Chapter 13 - Tu m'as manqué - I missed you

Chapter 13 - Mon cœur – My heart

Chapter 13 - Je t'aime - I love you

Chapter 14 - Je suis l'homme parfait pour toi - I'm the perfect man for you

Chapter 14 - Pas aussi belle que toi - Not as beautiful as you

Chapter 14 - Je pense que tu es belle quand tu ri - I think you're beautiful when you laugh

Chapter 14 - Pas si mal toi non plus - You're not too bad either

Chapter 21 - Bon matin, mon amour – Good morning, My love

Chapter 21 - Ça va bien maintenant? - Are you ok now?

Chapter 21 - Tu vas faire une bonne belle-fille, chérie! – You're going to make a good daughter in law, honey

Chapter 21 - il va t'aimer jusqu'à la fin du monde. – He will love you until the end of the world

Sometimes good girls
are the villains

Dedication:

To my biker Daddy. Though he was an inspiration for the story, and he may not approve of the spicy parts being public, he would have giggled at being written into a book with his best friends. He may be gone, but he's never forgotten.

Chapter 1 - Linx

The night I found out about Noah

She purrs out a sigh when I walk over to the bed unbuttoning my cuffs and tell her, "Flip over, all fours." She does it with a hungry smile because she's a good little whore that will fuck anything. So, she does what she's told to get some high profile, rich dick. Just the type of women I like. If I can't have what I really want, these poor substitutes will have to do.

However, I'll be damned if I want to look in her eyes while I fuck the shit out of her in my anger. She's not the cause of it but she's here. She's going to get the cold, heartless part of me that's simmering hot in rage. I don't even remember what she said her name was. Not like I care. I don't even think I told her mine.

I don't give that much of a fuck.

I don't care who she calls for when she comes either. Fuck, I don't even really care if she comes.

I'm being an asshole tonight. The bourbon and broken heart aren't helping either.

I just want to get off tonight. Get lost, block out feelings. I finish off my bourbon tumbler and refill it. I'm being reckless but I can't stop myself. I hate to admit it, but it feels like my heart has cracked open in my chest and I'm bleeding to death.

This piece of ass gets to deal with the monster she never helped create. I picked up this fake as fuck little number in the hotel bar downstairs. She seemed easy enough when she walked in. Beautiful navy-blue satin wrap dress that was easy to fall to the floor, straight brown hair, and mahogany brown eyes. Under that dress was legs for days, tipped in shiny black stilettos.

I'm a sucker for a good-looking dark-haired woman. I prefer black as night goth girls, but a stuck-up dejected brunette will do tonight.

It was the hungry look of desperation as she perused the bar with those sharp, greedy eyes that tipped me off to the easy lay. She's looking to land the biggest catch she can. I pegged her at first glance as one of those sharks that hang out in places rich men frequent, just to land themselves a loaded man to take care of them for the rest of their vapid lives. Those men are just happy to land some beautiful pussy to be their arm candy to charity events.

I'm not that man.

Never will be that man.

I'm never getting married.

I'm the man that takes their nameless asses to bed and fucks them within an inch of their lives, then sets them free, never to contact them again.

No strings.

No contact.

No feelings. My heart belongs to another. This is just a means to an end, a release, since I can never have what I want. These bitches just occupy my time and provide the outlet. I will never love any of them.

Looking at her pussy, I laugh to myself, it will take a really special woman to make me trade in my hoe days for married days, especially if it's not married to my one true love.

I don't ever see that happening because the one I want is unattainable. Forbidden.

I so love me some easy women who are just as eager to fuck and move on as I am. They occupy my time when I need release. It's never as often as the rumor mill.

I quietly wine them and dine them; I bed them but never wed them. No matter how much my mother hints around about it. "Play with yourself," I order her.

She obediently begins fingering herself.

I finish unbuttoning my white dress shirt and toss it on the wingback chair by the window. The slurping sounds of her pussy fills the quiet space in the hotel suite.

Shucking off my pants and boxer briefs, I quietly bend to get these socks off. Can't give her fodder for gossip about fucking one of New Orleans' millionaire moguls with his socks on.

Rolling on the condom, because safety first, I crawl up the bed behind her. I don't trust any woman to tell me the truth to trap me. "You going to fuck me now, big boy?" she smoothly says like the lustful viper she is.

"I'm no boy. I'm going to fuck you like a man and you're going to be my good little fuckhole, aren't you?" I smirk from behind her.

I lightly run my hands down her hourglass curves. She's a looker, I'll give her that. But she's nothing to me and nothing compared to my girl. I don't even plan to take my time with her tonight, I can't, my heart is hurting. She's not getting the Mr. Danger that's on top of his game right now.

Tonight, I'm exhausted but just want to get off in some pussy. That's it. Anyone will do because I'm numb.

I pull her back up against me and she rests her head on my shoulder. My hands roam down the front of her, over her breasts, cupping them, caressing her nipples. Her soft moans are music to my ears. Means I'm doing my job right even if I'm being a bastard right now.

I may not give a fuck about these women, but I damn sure care if they enjoy it. I may be a cutthroat, cold businessman, but I pride myself on being an exceptional lover. But tonight, I'm half- ass caring. Tonight is a bad night for me.

Women been gossiping for years what it's like to fuck me. I'm not some playboy out screwing everything I can. I maybe take one lady a month to hotels, if that. I'm rich, that's what makes me so popular. That's what keeps me in the good graces of the New Orleans socialites and cutthroat single ladies club.

I wrap my large hand around her delicate neck and apply minimal pressure. I can feel her flighty pulse thumping against my thumb. Her breath catches and she whimpers.

My other hand slides lower and my fingertips reach her engorged clit, I whisper by the shell of her ear, "How bad do you want it?" "Please fill me up, I want it all, fuck me good," she pleads.

I release her, shoving her over onto the bed, face down, hair flying everywhere. "You want it," I notch the head of my cock to her entrance, "You're going to take it all too." I may not be the longest, but by golly, I got some girth.

I push into her warm hole, her slick wetness coating the condom as her needy cunt swallows me up.

Fuck, it feels amazing every time I sink into some hot pussy, and I see her face in my mind. The only thing that feels better is making money.

"Oh god, you're so big. I feel so full," she whimpers on a moan. I grunt, "You begged for it." I work my cock in and out of her, not caring if I'm rough. Not tonight.

Not with another woman on my mind.

Not with my dream woman taking up space in my thoughts.

Definitely not when my heart hurts.

This is more like an angry fuck.

Fuck you, Noah, you're on borrowed time.

The bar whore pushes back onto me, I don't even remember her name even after she told me again, not that it matters, and I force myself to the root and make her cry out in pleasure. There might be pain there too.

"Please, let me come. I'm so close."

Even better, I don't have to work as hard now.

Chapter 2 – Birdie

"What do you mean I'm not booked? Like at all today?"

What kind of madness is this? I've been booked solid for months. My only days off are Sunday and Monday and chances are, I'm working one of those days too. Like there's a waiting list and all. At least that's what my assistant tells me. A long one if I believe the rumors, even with my grueling schedule and traveling to conventions and guest appearances all over the world; there's still a waiting list here at home base. I only open my tattoo appointment books for three months at a time.

There's never any downtime for me. The tattoo studio I own stays extremely busy even with the other five artists.

I prefer it that way honestly. Gives me less time to think about being a disappointment to my mother, my father and the family cat. Plus, I'm sadly single and don't like going out to meet people. Staying in all day and doing something I love on one person at a time, yeah, I'll take that.

Mom died last year from cancer, but before she succumbed, she made sure to get in one last coherent directive to me, "It's time to stop playing around and take your place in the family. Enough with this coloring bullshit."

Which translates to find a rich man, have his heir and a few spares like a good little wife and daughter of one of the wealthiest men in America. It's an expectation. So far, I've only ever had three boyfriends, I don't even know how to land a husband. Not that I want one. It's utter bullshit the pressure my parents put on me.

Be the good little biker princess I was born to be.

Forge bloodlines.

Make empires.

Strengthen treaties.

Make men more powerful.

Over my dead body.

I'm truly surprised my dad didn't have an arranged marriage lined up for me.

There's no way in holy fuck I want to settle down right now, especially to the kind of man my mother would have picked. Stuffy, uptight, vanilla, habitual cheater, closet drunk, and all-around asshole.

No thanks. I'd rather get fucked in the ass with a cactus covered in hot sauce.

My mother had been salivating for years, dreaming of the type of man I will land for myself inside our circle of acquaintances and business partners. To her we are royalty, and I guess we are with Daddy's billions, but for me, this is my life, my passion, my freedom she was playing around with. I don't give a shit about being with a man like that.

It was bad enough; I barely got out of my parent's house when I was eighteen to go to art school. Daddy would have kept me under lock and key some more if I hadn't threatened to run away. They can take their princess position and shove it up their asses.

I'm in an excellent place in my art career as a world renowned, highly sought after tattoo artist. I've clawed my way to the top and I'm sitting pretty as a leading artist that people respect and want to take lessons from or wear my art proudly.

I make millions from creating one-of-a-kind art pieces on skin. I'll be damned if I throw all this hard work away to become someone's baby machine.

Besides, as Mother so eloquently put it, 'No respectable man will have you with all that whorish skin mutations you've done to yourself.'

There it is. My tattoos covering my body. My colorful pieces of art that inspire me to be a good person and leave color everywhere I go.

Mother said I can't possibly land someone by age twenty-eight who will overlook my 'transgressions of rebellion' and settle down with me in a respectable way. So, to her, it has to be all my badass tattoos keeping decent men away, and not that fact that I'm not interested in dating, marrying or living with anyone else. It's quite possibly my aura of 'go the fuck away.'

Not fucking interested in her lifestyle.

Snapping back from my trainwreck of a brain, "Jules made sure of it, Birdie, triple checked even. Your client canceled because of a death in their immediate family. You're free to roam around the French Quarter to your heart's content today, Princess," Pierre says and mockingly bows to me.

The only person in this entire studio that knows who I really am. Pierre has been my ride or die since freshman year of college, so his bow is indeed a personal mockery. He knows all the wretched history.

"Alright. I shall take my leave, kind sir." I flash a quick smile, and a curtsy, then step outside to the hustle and bustle that is the French Quarter in New Orleans.

Home.

Everywhere I go in this city, it's home to me.

When I'm away, I miss her terribly.

I step out and call one of my best friends, Zharia, while walking to a bench in Jackson Square.

"Hello, my darling."

"Hey Zhar, guess what?"

She giggles, "Chicken buuuuttttt!"

I chuckle at her silliness, "Almost. I have the day off somehow." Zharia's shocked gasp. "Do you want to hang out and go to lunch together?" I bite my thumb nail while waiting for her answer. I know how busy she is.

"Yass, girl!" We decide on a time and place and when we hang up, I continue my stroll through the Quarter. When I step out of the shade, I smile as the sun hits my face. Yeah, it's hot as Satan's balls, but I fully believe in the healing powers of the sun. In small doses. I don't want to wreck my tattoos.

I'm excited to see Zharia.

Zharia has been my best friend since my sophomore year of high school. Her father is some kind of Indian tech tycoon from India but moved here like thirty years ago. I met Zharia in our private Catholic girls' school here in the city. We were sisters at first sight. Inseparable since then.

Zhar's drop dead gorgeous with her Indian and Asian bloodlines. We both have almond shaped eyes, her dark chocolate and mine light sky blue. We have the same thick, jet-black hair, except mine is wavy whereas hers is board straight. We make a unique pair standing together, her darker skin next to my pale, almost translucent white skin, ha, in the patches of skin that are still left. There's mostly my legs, which I keep coloring on in any free time I get.

Zharia loves the French Quarter as much as I do. We've spent so much time here with our other best friend Tally. Man, I miss her. Times aren't the same for the Fab Four.

That's me, Zharia, Pierre and Tally. The best of friends and family by choice and fate.

Zharia and I have been friends the longest. Ever since I was a teenager sneaking out past guards to catch a ride down here to meet her.

Sure, the Quarter's turned into a tourist trap somewhat, but if you look under all that, look at the bones, listen to the heartbeat; you will see the Quarter is alive and rich culture still.

Those are the such places I'm going to today. These are the places I hang out in. I swing over to Royal Street and grab some beignets and a fresh coffee at Café Royal that has the best beignets, my favorite.

It's a beautiful morning and the scorching late June sun beats down relentlessly on everyone scurrying about. Nary a cloud in the sky for any reprieve from sunburn.

I'm still in shock about a day off. Even on my 'days off', Sundays and Mondays, I'm still drawing custom tattoos for clients and writing in my book on the tattooing skills of color realism that I've been working on for the past three months. So, I guess it's technically still working.

After I finish my breakfast, I toss my trash and head into an art gallery, where I find myself looking at expensive paintings of Paisely Cat, the city's icon. Once you've been through too many devastating hurricanes as we have, you must have a redemption mascot. Paisely Cat is ours.

We like to think he's the loving pet of Touchdown Jesus.

A few boutiques and a few dressing room try-ons later, I'm lugging around a few bags of goodies. I think my favorite might be the new lingerie shop on the corner. I may have gotten some new bras and panties in delicate lace and satin.

I snort to myself. *Who you gonna wear them for?*

For me. I deserve purdy things.

Walking into Miriam's restaurant, I spot Zharia and her exotic aura immediately. Goddamn, my best friend is beautiful, I think to myself as a big smile spreads across my face. She jumps up to hug me. It's been about two weeks since we've gotten to hang out.

We have something called Wine Wednesdays and Pierre comes over to my place, we video chat Tally in New York, and we stay friends. She's missed the past two weeks' get togethers. That's not like her. Something's up with her. That's a long time for us. We are at least once or twice a week kinda friends. A testament to how busy we've both been lately, I suppose.

"Sit, sit," she jiggles her hands in excitement. I would love to live life as carefree as Zharia does, not giving a shit about how people saw you, enabled to show so much emotion and drawing attention to herself. Instead, I'm paranoid, standoffish and always wondering if I'm doing the correct thing. Therapy says I get these mental issues from my mother and her over the top, sheltered, rigid upbringing. I gave up at twenty-three trying to impress her, or make her proud of me, even a teensy bit, and I was done a long time ago trying in vain to earn her approval.

She died still livid that I started tattooing at nineteen. I don't care anymore.

Once the waiter has taken our order and brought our wine, she can't resist, "Soo, tell me all about him?"

"Who?" I'm genuinely confused as I sip my sweet red.

"The guy keeping you busy." She nudges my arm with her brows wagging.

I chuckle, almost choking, "Oh, yeah, sorry to disappoint, but there's no one. I've truly been working long hours. Inking until midnight some nights."

"Bea," she tsks at me, and levels me a look. Oh shit, she's got her hardcore '*Mom*' look going. "That's no way to live life. You don't have to work that hard. Here I thought you were getting dicked down every night." She actually pouts.

I scoff, rolling my eyes and shaking my head at that ridiculousness. "I do it because I love the art. And I couldn't get lucky enough to be dicked down every night. I just love slinging ink, Zharia." My eyes seek out the inside of her wrist, where I put a small tattoo of a piece of bread, with peanut butter smeared all over it, complete with little arms and legs. We laughed and laughed because it looks like burnt toast against Zharia's medium skin tone. It was one of my first tattoos. She was the bravest one to let me practice.

She's the peanut butter to my jelly, which I have the matching piece of bread on the inside of my wrist. Mine is grape jelly because it's my favorite. She keeps me in check, has helped me through some pretty epic depressive episodes, especially after Noah left abruptly. In turn, I have been her rock and biggest supporter while she went to med school to be a surgeon, and I offer up my shoulder when she gets her heart broken at least once a week on fuckboys.

Currently she's dating one of my dad's 'associates' aka a club member, that she's been super secretive about. Actually, I have no idea if they are still dating. It's not like her to be this secretive. I have no idea his name and since I don't know any of my dad's members, I can't even guess. She confessed to me a few weeks ago now, at our weekly Wine Wednesday, that he was the best fuck of her life, and he treats her like a queen, but they have trust and attitude issues. Her father would have a shit fit if he knew she was dating a biker.

"I know, but I'm trying to knock out a few large pieces for a magazine spread I have coming up, that I didn't tell you about yet," I almost squeal with my big cheesy smile.

"Oh my god, Bea! That's so amazing! Headlining?"

I nod my head, "Yeah, main artist. Ink'dYouUp magazine interviewed me two weeks ago. Came to the shop and took pics and everything. I wanted to tell you in person."

"Wow," she breathes, "This is the best thing ever. I'm so proud of you, bestie. Well deserved, babe." She holds up her wine glass and I grab mine up and tap hers. "To awesome things happening for once," she says, "To my girl, may she get the recognition she deserves."

"Hear hear, hon." I echo back.

Our lunch conversation flows smoothly, and we make plans to have dinner next Tuesday night. We talk about going to visit Tally in New York in September and seeing if Seven will allow Pierre to come too.

Pierre's husband is a little weird but it's us girls, not another man. We all know Pierre is not coming near a vagina, even at gunpoint. Fuck, me, Zhar and Tally are the safest people for him, I laugh to myself. Damn, we've been friends since college, which seems so long ago, and never once has Pierre ever shown interest in a pussy or a woman.

"How's work?" I ask her.

"Learning new things all the time. There's so much I don't know yet, even with this big brain. But I've been told there will always be something to learn in medicine." She points to her temple and taps it.

Zharia is an academic phenom. Hands down the smartest person I know but you would never guess it. She received a full scholarship and has managed to graduate med school a year earlier than she was supposed to. She's in her third year of surgical residency at our big city hospital.

"So, what guy has your mind so busy? And don't try to deny it, I've watched you be twitterpated for months. Why is it a secret?" "I don't want to spoil it. It's new, plus if it doesn't work out, I won't be so embarrassed again. He's trying to make me settle down and I don't want that. So, we'll see." She shrugs while not meeting my eyes. If I didn't know better, I'd say she's met her match because clearly, she's fallen hard, even if she doesn't realize it. My bestie even looks different, it's a glow, an aura about her now. Zhar's found love. She's just trying to play it off.

I'm not buying it but I let her off the hook...for now.

Once we finish and she has to run back to her office, I wander haphazardly throughout the Quarter for the next few hours in and out of my favorite shops. Listening to the street performers is one of my favorite things to do. Big Pearl's blues singing is top notch.

You can find her belting out 'When the Saints Go Marching In' down by Rouse's most days.

God, it feels like forever since I've had the opportunity to walk with leisure around the community I love so much. I've got to have more work/life balance. Pfftt, now I sound like some corporate slave to the timeclock.

I stopped and talked to some neighbors, a few tourists asked me for directions, and I even got to pet a parrot who called me 'pretty girl.' Anything goes down here in the Quarter. Even dressing like a pirate and walking around with a real bird on your shoulders...that's shit down the back of your jacket.

It was cute though. I want a talking bird. Maybe. Wonder what it would be like to have someone, or a pet to come home to? I'd teach the bird to say 'Hello Mom, welcome home finally.' It's stirs up some of the loneliness I feel. A bird that tells me they missed me and coos when I pet them? Or a kitty cat that rubs up on my legs and purrs, happy to see me? Or a fierce dog who dances when I walk through the door?

I may never know. My schedule stays so hectic, no one would want to put up with my absence. It would be cruel to a pet to be missing so much from their lives by an absentee owner.

As for the human to come home to, been there, done that. Only for six weeks but it was enough. Not up to trying it again. Negative six out of ten, do not recommend cohabitating with a slobbish man who can't get his shit together to save his life.

I can't stay away from Big Pearl and The Clams stationed over on Royal Street today, "Pearl, as always, it's such a pleasure, beautiful." I drop the three crisp hundred-dollar bills in their coffee tin and head back towards my apartment.

For a cool $4.2 million you too could live in the Quarter, in an apartment with a balcony and nosy tourists. Actually, that's for the whole building that takes up a block. This apartment is my splurge and it's part of why I've worked so hard. Something that's truly mine.

I have a trust fund my dad set up for me when I was born that I rarely use because I make plenty slinging ink, but on this building, I used that Daddy Warbucks trust fund. I bought the entire block. The whole building and became landlord to all the shops below. My studio only takes up a third of the block, but it's enough to make your eyes pop when you pass it.

It's my dream come true. Six different artists, constantly booked, doing what they love and living their dream.

My phone rings as I get back to my studio and as I head up to my luxury apartment above it, I pull my phone out of my shoulder bag and see it's my dad's private line.

Answering with the pleasant voice he likes so much, "Hey, Daddy!"

"Heya, kiddo! What'cha got planned today?"

Thinking about what day it is, I remember it's St. John's Eve and he has a family tradition to uphold, one I'm expected to participate in for my Catholic upbringing. "Nothing much. Apparently, my client canceled, and I wasn't booked today so I've had a free day. What do you have planned today?"

"I wanted to see if I could take my beautiful daughter to Evangelina's for dinner tonight. If it's not too much trouble."

"Never any trouble for you, old man," I tease, "What time?"

"What time would you like? I'm on your schedule, Birdie."

"We both know that's a lie," I half snort half chuckle into the phone. This man works as much as I do; however, he always makes sure he has time for me, his only living heir and little girl. I've always been a Daddy's girl and since Mom died, he's been struggling. I have too. We may not have gotten along all the time, but I feel her absence in so many ways. There's no one to make me feel like shit anymore and I'm not sure how to cope with that. There's no one to keep raising the bar for standards and I'm not sure what goal to strive for to appease her. She was never flat out mean to me, but she wasn't kind either. But my dad hung the moon, and I always am available for him.

I wanted for nothing growing up. I ate the finest foods, went to the best schools, and mingled with some of the richest people on the planet. All because of who my father is. One of the east coast's heavy hitters. President and CEO of Rockwell Shipping and Receiving. My father is King of the Gulf and runs 80% of the ports along the Gulf and about 30% of the east coast ports. I'm sure he's into a lot more shit than I can ever imagine, but mostly I've been sheltered from it, so I have theories, but nothing confirmed.

"Seven o'clock sound good?" he asks.

"Yes, I'll be there, Dad."

"Excellent. I'll see you at seven, baby girl. I'll send a car. Love you lots, honeybee." And with that sign off, he's hanging up the phone.

In my kitchen, I noticed there's a note from my housekeeper. She instructs me on how to heat up the lasagna she's prepared for me. Glad to see she genuinely cares. I'd asked her for it last week, citing it's the best in the Quarter and I'm the luckiest girl who gets to eat it.

A little flattery will get you everywhere with Melda.

My day has been perfect so far. I'm excited to get dressed up and go out, even if it's with my dad. Wonder if Linx is going to be there? *We aren't thinking about him right now.*

Too late. His gorgeous eyes, sexy smile, and hot as fuck body makes my clit twitch. I've always had a small crush on my dad's second-in-command. Only problem, he's an asshole. Another problem, I'm off limits to any of Dad's people.

But that doesn't stop me from rubbing one out to memories of Linx's sexy ass. He's seriously calendar model beautiful. I can only imagine what it would be like to have a man like that inside of me and pounding away, giving me the greatest sex I've ever had. Rough, rugged, downright nasty is what I think it would be like. I'm here for the daydreams. The horny part of me pulls me over to my bed. The rational part says to stop and go get ready. Maybe just a quick rub. The devil on my shoulder does win a few battles.

I quickly undress and snag my pink vibe from the bedside drawer and hop up on my bed. I don't even bother to pull the covers back. I spit on the silicone and reach down, sliding the rotating rod inside of me. God, that makes me shudder. I turn the vibrating ears on and jerk at the sensations as it vibrates my clit. I love this fucking thing. If I want a quick O, this is the way to do it.

I picture Linx's smile, his body under his tight shirts, the cut of the dinner jacket over his jacked-up arms. He has the cutest butt, and I never thought legs would do it for me, but seeing his pumped-up thighs and calves one day while he was wearing running shorts, let's just say my heart thudded in my chest while my vagina screamed 'Ride 'em cowgirl.'

Pretty soon I'm writhing and moaning and daydreaming of Linx, imagining him as naked Linx. I want so bad to find out if that sizable bulge in his pants is as big as it looks. I want to run my tongue over his velvety soft crown and gobble up the rest of his cock, forcing him to the back of my throat, enough to make me gag and drool down my chin and boobs. I want it filthy. I want to feel his hot cum slide down my throat as he pumps into my mouth.

The mighty need I have to be choked by his cock is unreal. It's embarrassing.

I picture Linx between my legs as he licks me clit to ass and I finally find out what it's like to have a man eat me out. I want to know what it's like to come on a man's face. Linx strikes me as a man who would gladly stick his tongue in my pussy.

He'll make sure I'm not left wanting. Thinking of his tongue inside me and what it would be like to have him suck on my clit, rolling it around with his tongue, my juices smeared all over his face as I tell him what a good boy he is; that's what does it for me.

The orgasm rips through my body, firing through my veins, making my body stiffen and causing me to lose my breath. It's been a few days, so this one was a little more forceful than usual. I shut off the vibrator and catch my breath when the pulses of electricity fade away, just laying here spread eagle on my bed, blissed out. The beauty of living alone, I will never get caught masturbating.

After I take a long, relaxing hot bath, that was heavenly to soak in, I take care to touch up my eyebrows and make sure the jungle down under is cropped and tamed.

Out in front of my giant full-length mirror, I lotion up everything I just shaved. My legs look like I dipped them in oil, I'm so shiny. *Looking hot, B!*

Donning the silver-gray, shimmery cocktail dress and slipping on my silver heels, I face the mirror one last time. The shiny diamonds on my ears and the tennis bracelet on my wrist are the only jewelry I wear, both purchased by my father for my college graduation five years ago. They catch the light just as nicely as the shimmer of the silver threads of my dress. I must say, I look banging. Am I overtly sexy for a dinner with my father? Possibly. Or am I exuding confidence? Perhaps. Am I hoping every time I leave my apartment my one true love will land in my lap? Yeah. And I'm going to try to entice him to come to me any way I can, starting with looking good in this dress. Maybe my true love is at the restaurant tonight and sweeps me off my feet. My father would be positively tickled.

Either way, I'm dressed now, and I look fantastic. Sometimes it's good to get dressed up and feel sexy and beautiful. Remind yourself of your feminine power and I have the means to bring a man to his knees. If I can learn how to do it.

Even now, months after Noah, I'm still trying to get my groove back and feel sexy. Somedays it's hard. I mean, I've only ever had three boyfriends in my twenty-eight years in this lifetime, and none of them were all that serious. Well, I thought Noah was going that way.

As I'm getting ready to head out of the bedroom, Tally calls me. "Hey, girl, hey!" she says when I answer.

"Where have you been all my life, lovely?" I tease her with a laugh.

"Been ass deep in fabric and had my fingers tied together with stitching tape. How are you, fren?"

Putting the phone on speaker, I tell her, "I'm good. I'm getting ready for dinner with Dad. I had lunch with Zhar today and we were talking about you."

"Oh yeah? Was it all bad? I hope so because I've never been good a day in my life." I love her little tinkling laugh.

I bark out a laugh and reply, "Don't we know it, instigator, always keeping us in trouble. We were talking about how much we miss you and plotting to come see you in September."

"You know that's cutting it close for New York fashion week, right?" Talullah Belle Montellosi is a superstar in the fashion industry and made her debut four years ago. She's a highly sought-after designer for evening wear among high profile clients. She's also mine, Zharia's and Pierre's best friend from college and we routinely video chat with her on Wine Wednesdays. It's how we hang on to our friendship and I thank every deity around for giving us the gift of technology.

"Yes, we do, that's why we're asking if it's a good time for you well in advance."

"Can I think on it? I'm swamped right now with making dresses and pant suits. I only have roughly two months to get it all done for the show. Gah! I'm a mess already." I hear her exhaustion through the phone.

"Calm down, girl, it'll all be ok." I say as I check myself over once again.

My long jet-black hair falls in natural waves down my back and my ice blue stare makes some men tremble, others get hard. I get my natural resting bitch face from my mother. But these lips, oh I know I have nice, plump natural lips, they were made to suck cock, and I use every bit of this beauty to my advantage when I can. Or I should say, when I feel like it.

However, the main show is my tattoos being on full display in this slip of a dress. Arms, back and chest covered by color, murals of my life, paintings of my favorite things.

This is one of my new dresses I bought today. It flares mid-thigh and flows as I walk, shimmering and catching the lights as I walk. I feel like a model, although one wrong move and I'm flashing my gray thong to everyone. The halter style neckline comes up to my collarbone but drapes in front of me to give the barest hint of cleavage. I have those chicken fillet things on to cover my nipples. I can't remember what they're called but we all call them chicken cutlets. What a godsend, kudos to whoever invented them. Getting them off, ehh, that's not so comfortable, but it's the price we pay for beauty.

The crisscross satin ties holding this dress onto my body were a pain in the ass to get tied. I may have a tiny waist, but it doesn't match my more than a handful of boobs and my thick thighs that lead to a bubble butt. I'm not one for flaunting it, matter of fact, you can find me most days, not all of them, in some cut-off jeans shorts and a funny quote or band t-shirt, but tonight I decided to show out a little bit.

I wanted to be seen and sexy out in the public. Out where I might meet the love of my life. I don't know why, just felt like being cute. Maybe because I've had a really great day. God, I sound desperate but lately I've started feeling my age and my biological clock ticking. I don't want to be alone anymore so I vowed to Zhar and Pierre, I would put myself out there. Tonight is a perfect night to start.

After I get off the phone with Tally, who is team Zharia and Pierre for dating again, I step out into Jackson Square. The car my father sent is idling at the curb, right beside the row of mule drawn carriages. I turn the heads of the people milling about as I walk to the blacked-out parked Rolls-Royce with Jonesy standing by the back passenger door, in his crisp black uniform, waiting on my arrival.

"Hey, Jonesy, glad to see you again," I say to the driver, whom I've known since I was a child.

I slide into the buttery soft leather in my father's Rolls Royce and smell the familiar cigar and leather scent that always reminds me of my dad. The car is over the top, just like him. I would have taken a rideshare and he knows this, hence the flashy car fetching me.

"Hello, Miss Birdie, always a pleasure to see you, *chile*. You are looking beautiful as always," he says as I get situated and he shuts the door. His thick Haitian accent washes over me and reminds me of the summer vacations our family spent in the Caribbean, sunning, learning local culture and the bulk of my time spent sketching by the pool.

Jonesy maneuvers us through the Quarter's horrible traffic up to the less traveled road where the restaurant named after me is located. It's one of my father's pride and joys, besides his shipping and receiving empire in the Gulf and me.

My father runs his business out of the New Orleans port mainly. Every port along the Gulf, except for Texas, is dominated by his ships and men. Nothing gets in nor out without him knowing about it. Actually, he runs most of the entire southeastern part of the United States. Who am I kidding; he's a worldwide powerhouse.

Who also just so happens to be reigning Regional President of the Southern Devils Society, a large motorcycle club that's ruthless and territorial, their name synonymous with lethal, cunning, and vindictive. They own all of Louisiana and the surrounding ten states, except for Texas…They refuse to give up their footing, even for a peaceful resolution and merger with my father's empire or sign a treaty.

Their peaceful solution was to have me marry their President of the Lone Star Saints as soon as I turned eighteen. My pussy was the peace offering. I flat refused much to my mother's dismay, who not surprisingly, wanted to marry me off to the highest bidder, no matter how sick and twisted they were. My father stood by my side and rescinded his offer of peace immediately and told them to get fucked, royally.

It's been bad blood ever since. Ten years later and there's still beef.

Lone Star Saints control all the Texas ports on the Gulf of Mexico. Houston is their home base and that's where they ship out for their sex trafficking ring.

LSS wants to control the entire Gulf, by any means necessary. They're the leaders in human trafficking across the nation and they are trying everything they can to take over every port on the Gulf. Bloodshed along the Gulf has leaked to the water's edge and war is almost here. They will stop at nothing to get these ports.

One thing stands in their way: my father.

Every port along the Gulf from the Texas/Louisiana state line on down to the Bahamas, Cuba, and more, my father controls with his associates, who are also mostly bikers in his motorcycle club. From what I know about the family business, it's lots of guns, lots of drugs, and lots of precious gems from diamond mines our family owns. The only reason I knew this is because my mother told me that much.

Dear ole Daddy is one of the richest men in the world.

And I am the only child born from the King of the Gulf.

The Biker Princess my mother never wanted.

Chapter 3 – Linx

'Why are people so fucking stupid?' I think to myself.

"I dunno, boss."

Well shit. I must have said that aloud then. Not one fuck given though.

This operation has been shit since its inception. Half my team of guys are green, and they've never seen action. All I needed was warm and breathing bodies that could watch, use a walkie talkie and shoot at a moving target.

There's not much more use for these guys other than that. I hope they never procreate.

Word on the street is Lone Star Saints has a shipment of underage girls being dropped at the Port of Lake Charles at ten in the freaking morning. It's close to their home base in Houston. The dealer refused to bring them any further, even though Houston is literally right there.

We have inside intel that says these are Asian girls between ten and fourteen, being auctioned off tomorrow night to people that are obviously pedophiles.

These are children to be sold as sex workers to the elite, twisted and fucked up rich. They're being transferred and trafficked within Louisiana territory.

Not on my fucking watch.

So far, we've seen about six men outside guarding the perimeter and standing by the idling transport van with blacked out windows. I'm sure there's more fuckheads we need to worry about that will be escorting the girls off the boat.

Won't be an issue.

Except we're doing this in broad daylight….where anyone and the cops can see. The cameras at this dock have been disabled for this mission. Good thing we own the dock too, so we can do whatever we want without evidence. The cops know not to come sniffing around any dock or port along the water line.

There are never cops involved. They know better. And if there were, we own them too. All over the state, down the Gulf. They are just as eager as us to disband LSS and stop their transports.

These LSS men down there are dead and don't even know it yet. Up on the roof of this warehouse, Travares takes the right flank and Gunney takes left. Both are excellent sharpshooters, almost as good as me. All three of us have been special forces in the Army with extensive combat training. We're basically ninjas with guns. When we have on our fatigues and black balaclavas over our faces, you can't tell us apart. We all have the same rugged build, broad shoulders, chiseled muscles, each topping at least six foot and over. We are muscled machines, and no one fucks with us.

I know for a fact Gunney has his own spicy video site people subscribe to. He says he does it for fun and it's not about the money, but that money part is really nice too.

Travares just got patched in a little over a year ago and he's already proving to be a superstar. He's a masked bandit on Instagram with a motorcycle and a helmet and a shit ton of followers. If only the girls knew he had a scar down his cheek, they would go ga-ga even more than they already do.

But the real guy to watch out for after me is Shadow. The man was a legit spy, torturer, and Navy SEAL. Like me, he prefers the private security sector lifestyle by being a bodyguard to Rock's family and protector of the small and weak. We don't mind getting paid well to kill evil men. Or as we like to say- biker associates conducting club business.

Shadow joined our riding club eight years ago but didn't really start working up in the ranks until a few years ago. He became third in command a little over a year ago at twenty-eight. He has excelled at his role as Sergeant-At-Arms and handling disputes and keeping order.

He's helped us intercept numerous shipments of underage girls headed for Texas out of the Caribbean and Florida. Everyone wants an island girl it seems, or a sweet little blond virgin with pitiful, doe eyes.

These fuckers have to pass right by our territory to get their 'merch' delivered to the waiting handlers. They finally stopped driving them over the state lines like idiots and just started shipping straight from Florida or wherever their drop points are now, across the Gulf to Texas.

We have a few Florida chapters that do the same thing we do here in Louisiana, and they are quietly bringing girls home every day.

Can you imagine intercepting human traffickers every single damn day? What a depressing job. But I imagine it's rewarding too.

Thankfully, we have safe houses set up everywhere to house the victims. We have systems in place to get the kids back home, or if they can't or won't go back, we have processes in place for them to enter foster care. We have our own caseworkers that vet the foster parents and do random check-ins in person. A lot of us know how horrible foster care can be, therefore we work hard to weed those people out.

The adults or older teens, there's a process to facilitate a new life for them in any of our reigning states. They will be given housing for six months, a job and five thousand dollars on a debit card if they so choose.

We're out here doing the Lord's work (I snort at that thought) saving one person at a time. Or trying to. Bikers doing something nice to fight evil? I thought they were evil, the pearl clutching old biddies think. They think we are straight up gutter trash—The very same people whose husbands are out here buying children for sex in the underground black market.

My boss, Mr. Jaques Chavanet, (Sha-Vah-nay) or 'Rock' as he's called, rules the world around here and practically everywhere else. That man has his hands in everything it seems. He wants to personally put a stop to any human trafficking in the United States and with the chapters we have throughout the country, it's starting to make a huge dent in their operations. Dealers are feeling the pressure and heat. Handlers are dying. People are being saved.

Business is bad for the Lone Star Saints. I imagine they're getting desperate. And we all know, desperate men do dumb shit.

They should know by now we aren't going to stand for this type of fucked up shit in our front yard.

My helmet crackles and Gunney comes through, "Danger, I've not seen anyone else come up this way, I think we have them all surrounded. It's our team of fifteen against their, maybe 10. Cross hairs on each one. Waiting on the boat to unload and further instructions."

"Copy, Gunney. Stand down until the last girl is off the boat and into the back of the van. Wait for my signal. No one is to shoot at or near the van regardless of what happens. Repeat to the team, no one is to shoot at or near the fucking van."

Their obedience is expected and it's mandatory to show it. They will get to prove themselves when this mission gets the green light from me.

To stay a Devil, you have to continuously earn it. It's a privilege to be a brother in arms, not an entitled right. Not every Devil is a Ringman. That's what we call the band of brothers who take on these missions of saving people.

Every man down this line is waiting on my command as I sit on top of this building with binoculars, trained on the boat entrance. The first two girls, who look no more than twelve, are already being shoved into the back of the van. Two more take their place and so forth.

Our informant said there were ten girls in total for this trip.

As the boat is quickly pulling away, the last two are unceremoniously thrown into the back of the van with the rest of the girls and the doors slammed shut.

I key my mic, "Green green go."

It's over in seconds. I knew it would be, that's why I brought these couyons, they needed a taste of blood and to get their hands dirty. Besides me, Travares and Gunney, all these men are newly sworn in Devils after they've spent their year as probate.

I see my men below are already running to the van to drive it to the recovery compound.

Their men dropped like sacks of potatoes, left dead on the pavement. Kill shot to the head. One and done. Now the cleanup crew moves in.

This place will be tip top and back to normal in ten minutes. We have to move fast and within eight minutes the whole operation is just wrapping up and cleanup is almost done power washing the concrete, the van is enroute, and I'm heading back to my truck to drive the three hours back home.

Travares is from around here and he's driving the van to the recovery compound and will see that everyone gets settled in. It's just outside of the city, and it's a large six-bedroom house that sleeps up to fifteen. It's ran by a Catholic church Rock utilizes.

It's more like a safe house. One of dozens in the underground network that is Southern Devils Society. We sponsor freedom. We offer safety.

Never judge a book by its cover.

Some of us have hearts of gold under these black souls.

Chapter 4 – Birdie

Jonesy stops about ten yards from the restaurant and rests at the curb in traffic.

"I can walk the rest of the way, Jonesy." I can see the front of the restaurant from here; it shouldn't take me long to get there. Besides, my father's guards are always watching me. They think I don't know but I've always known they were one step behind me. "Miss Birdie, I cannot allow you to walk alone."

…Even though I just walked all over this Quarter today by myself. No please, babysit me now. Insufferable, stupid archaic bullshit.

I open the back door while he's stopped in this long line of traffic. As I step my foot out, I say, "I got it from here. Thanks for the ride, Jonesy." Before he can protest, I've shut the door on his stuttering with a smile and a wave.

I square my shoulders and with my clutch in hand, I strut my way to my restaurant.

Evangelina's.

One of the finest restaurants in all of New Orleans.

Named after me, Beatrix Evangelina Chavanet.

Just the thought of going in there gives me warm fuzzies. My father opened this restaurant when I was a baby, and it's turned into one of the most famous and exclusive places to eat.

There are so many patrons standing out in front already, most likely waiting on a table to open up. There's always a line. It's some of the best cooked meals that I've ever tasted, and it's handcrafted from scratch right in the kitchen.

I nod at the people I pass out front when I walk by them for the door. I always feel bad when I can skip the line. As my arm reaches for the handle of the door, a warm, strong hand wraps firmly around my forearm and the owner's baritone voice says, "Beatrix."

No one calls me that.

Absolutely no one.

Hardly anyone knows my government name.

My eyes jerk from the tattooed hand on my arm to the hazel-brown eyes that belong to none other than my dad's second in command, The Right Hand of God, Lincoln LaFleur.

"Linx?" I use his pet name I gave him years ago instead of his handle or road name of Danger. We both play a game with names. "I need you to come with me, Princess." The way he says it is so urgent the hair on my arms stand up. It makes fear coil in my belly. I hate this reaction right now. Linx has never used this tone with me, and it gives me goosebumps.

"No, let go of me, Linx, I'm meeting Dad here." I try hard to pry his fingers off my body, but he refuses to budge, gripping my arm so hard I wonder if I'll bruise.

He's closer now, looking over my shoulder. I smell his signature cologne, and it makes me sway a little. Quietly by my ear, shivers racing down my spine for another reason entirely, he softly says, "Do you see your father's men by this door?"

I quickly look around. They aren't here. Which means my father isn't here.

"Get in the car, Trixie." He pushes me towards a sleek black car. "Now." He says with enough deadly force to lay out a whole army. I comply willingly since he put it that way. He yanks my arm enough to get me moving. I numbly walk to his car by the curb, trying not to trip in my heels. He still doesn't let go of my arm until I'm at the car door.

When Linx uses that authoritative tone, he means business. Of all my father's associates, as he calls them, Linx is the only one I've been allowed around. He's the only one allowed to touch me like this. Sometimes Shadow, third-in-command, is allowed around me too.

Linx has been around since I was eighteen. I fancied myself as his girlfriend on many, many occasions. He attends parties at my father's Garden District residence with business investors and anywhere else business is conducted behind closed doors. He's at all the charity events, fundraisers, boring political dinners rich snobs go to that I get dragged to and he never misses the opportunity to make me dance with him.

One day in the past, I would have killed for that, but not currently.

We're kinda in this weird stage right now where I really don't like him, but I fantasize about him when I finger myself. I tell myself it's because he's gorgeous and that's all. I know, I'm fucked up. As long as he never opens his mouth and just stands there looking pretty, I can get along with him. But that's an impossible feat for him. He never shuts his mouth around me.

Lately though it's merely been witty banter between us because that's all I'll tolerate. When he starts his dreadful teasing and snide comments, I nope out of the event or avoid him at all costs. Everywhere he goes in the party, he watches me with that knowing smirk and it infuriates me. Enough to make me detest him and his whole personality.

My dad has deemed him no threat to me though and continues to allow him around me when I've repeatedly asked him not to. It's like I can't fucking escape the big dumb ox.

He is the only man allowed this close to me; therefore, I should shut up and deal with it.

And if he's here right now to fetch me, something is seriously wrong. Like bad bad. My dad wouldn't dispatch the Right Hand of God for just any silly reason.

All his bikers were always off limits to me. They aren't even allowed to talk to me.

Except this big, goofy one that frays my nerves with one look. Ugh. Why does he have to be so hot? Can I just glue his lips shut while I ride him. No, I want my titties sucked too bad for that.

Jesus, Birdie.

He opens the door and drops me into the Porsche nonchalantly. Everything is happening too quickly to process. Linx gets into the car, that was still running and zooms away from the curb.

"Linx, what's happening?" Trying to maintain some decorum here is really hard. I just want to scream from panic. That was a really intense kidnapping on his part. I've never seen Linx that riled up.

Don't get me wrong, he looked cool as a cucumber on the outside, but the vibe he gave off when he touched me was anything but.

His broody stare moves from the road beyond the windshield to my eyes, to stare into my soul with his relentless gaze. He looks back at the road while we travel away from the Quarter.

"Lincoln LaFleur, you better tell me what's going on right now!" I burst out.

"I'm not sure how much I can tell you, Princess," is his controlled reply.

"Ugh, enough with the princess already."

"Ok, Trixie."

"Jesus on a tire iron, you know my fucking name, *Lincoln*."

"Beatrix Evangelina Chavanet," insert my dramatic eye roll here, "your father is holed up at the mansion in the Graden District on lockdown. You are the main objective and priority. I was dispatched to retrieve you by any means necessary. We're going to the compound. There's been a threat. You know the drill."

No, no, I don't remember the drill because we've never drilled the drill in all the drilling years he's been around. I frantically search my brain for the drill instructions.

My lips part and I'm stunned. I'm never allowed at the compound. And a threat? Is it to me? Argh! What's happening!?!? The last time I was at the clubhouse I was nineteen and it was because my father wanted them all to see my face, to know who they were annihilating the enemy for, to know what I looked like if they ever saw anyone taking me against my will. Because that's exactly what the LSS had threatened.

Linx had just come on board the year before, working for my father, and leaving the Army behind. At one point in my very early twenties, I thought I had a crush on Mr. Tall-Dark-and-Broody. I thought maybe he liked me back. Turns out Mr. Danger is an asshole and likes to tease 'kids' into hating them, because he made it clear that's what I was to him, just a kid, ten years his junior.

I'm sure my father had something to do with that too, just as I got 'a talkin' to' *again* about not fraternizing with his associates.

I gave him what Daddy wanted. My cold shoulder. It's been cold ever since. I attempt to ignore Linx as much as I can, while watching his every move.

Alright, I'm fascinated by him. He is so effortlessly smooth. I don't get it, and it makes me so angry. I catch myself wondering what a ride on Mr. Danger would be like.

I hate that he gets to me but would love to be under him. I loathe his mocking laugh but love how tight his pants are across his sculpted ass. I hate his knowing winks but fantasize about kissing him til he's quiet.

It's truly a mindfucking. I do this shit to myself, I'm the problem. And goddammit, I get so angry at myself for reacting that way towards him. Every. Fucking. Time. I'm near him.

I can never decide if I want to be the bigger person or be the bigger problem for him.

The worst part is, I think he knows all about my silly crush I had. Like he can read every last sordid detail lurking in my mind.

Occasionally I'm required to go to some charity gala or dinner with my dad, more so when I was a teenager. Thankfully, it's dwindled down some in my twenties, but here lately I've had to go to more than my fair share in my mother's place, and I always drag Zharia with me when I can. It's like two or three things a month. And Linx is always there, in the background, mingling, dancing, eating, and drinking, like he doesn't have a care in the world, and giving me a wink each time my eyes would stray to him.

Which is often, because unfortunately my eyes and brain are on two different memos because he catches me doing it damn near every time.

Just taunting me, letting me know he notices my gaze on him. I guess it's a game between us, how much can he annoy the fuck out of me, and how much can I ignore him and give him frostbite.

I haven't seen him in about three weeks. Mercifully. Hmm, I think that's when I was last at Dad's house and Linx was there, of course. He gave me his killer smile and winked at me. My pussy flushed hot, and my stomach turned as I mentally told my traitorous body to simmer down. He makes me feel lovely and flushed and hot. Like a bad case of diarrhea—just know, I thought that last part sarcastically.

Before that, last thing we did was the three, or was it four art galas, I believe it was May, wait, maybe it was earlier this month. Fuck, I've seen him so much in the last year I can't keep up.

It was at one of those events where he insulted me, I wasn't in the mood, and I just simply said my goodbyes to the host, thanked them, and merely left. I never looked at him again as I walked out. I received a text from Linx that read: *I saved a dance for you, Princess.*

I mentally flipped him off. I hope he felt it.

Mixed in there were a few charity events, a Senator's dinner, a handful of small fundraisers, two museum dedications; all since January, mind you.

Ya know, all the social shit I don't want to do. Now that it's the end of June, I'm hoping it lets up and Daddy doesn't expect me to do anymore. I paid my dues and did my fair share, now let me be in peace. Last thing I want to do is put on a nice cocktail dress and heels while staring longingly at my e-reader and bed.

Oh, and then there was the Christmas thingy for the shipyard last year. What a shitshow that was. He asked me to dance; after telling me my red dress made me look like Jessica Rabbit and he liked the swell of my bosom, (who fucking says that to someone), and I told him to get fucked. He said, 'Only if you're offering.' The audacity of this man, I swear to god.

My dad loves him so much, I doubt telling my dad about all the raunchy shit Linx says to me would make him get rid of Linx, but I do it anyways, and he just laughs it off 'Oh, Honeybee, you'll have that' or some other bullshit brushing me off. I've been wondering for years what it will take to axe Linx out of my life.

"I can't go to the compound looking like this." Not on a Saturday night. Everyone will be there. Dressed like this in a biker's clubhouse is not my idea of a fun time. So many guys leering at my body. It wasn't just that, it will be the way they go about it and the things they will say.

This was not the confident and sexy display I had planned on. I'm shook. A restaurant with other woman dressed this way is one thing, a biker clubhouse with Penthouse centerfolds on the walls is another.

You'll have to excuse me sir, this is my first kidnapping.

"Relax Princess, I'll be with you. I'm not going to leave a pair of stunning legs like that wander off."

He thinks my legs are stunning?

I don't know why this makes my stomach flip when in actuality I can't stand him. He's an arrogant fuck, a womanizer to the highest degree that has done nothing but get under my skin for the past few years. Every fucking chance he gets.

On the flip side, I live for pissing him off.

I look over at him driving with his haughty little smirk, "I really don't think you should be looking at my legs. Stunning or not."

I should never have said that. In the next moment he slaps his large, tattooed hand on my thigh, which is tightly pressed against the other one. I momentarily freeze. No air to be had, the whole car void of air. He has never touched me like this.

I marvel at his hand on my thigh. I always thought my thighs were too big, but his hand on them makes them look smaller.

"I would love to do more than look but you're the forbidden fruit all of us dream about."

What in the actual fuck? My face heats up, yet he doesn't move his hand.

I grab his hand and pry it off my person and cooly reply, "It'll be a cold day in hell before I ever let you between these thighs. Don't touch me again."

He laughs. This fucker has the audacity to laugh at me. After his humorous guffawing, he goes silent.

Soon, we're pulling up to the clubhouse gates and the armed guards, looking straight out of a movie in tactical gear, lets him right in. We drive to the paved parking lot and the very second space is reserved for him. Of course it is. The first one being for my father.

He opens the passenger door and offers his hand. I think for a minute about how to maneuver this, so I don't flash him the lady bits getting out of his low ass sports car. I didn't really think of that when I plopped down in here, not by choice. This is not really the time to be self-conscience about flashing people. Apparently,

there's been a threat, and I need to eventually get out of this car.
"Will it help if I turn my head?"

"Yes," I practically hiss at him.

Once I see him looking off into the distance, away from me, I grab his hand and lift myself out of the car, knowing full well that would be a flash of my crotch. I could have been more graceful, but these are heels, stilettos with a thin, skinny heel. Plus, it's hard to be graceful when your legs are shaking.

Linx is too close to me when he looks me in the eye and says, "If you change your mind about spreading them lickable thighs, all you have to do is let me know, Trixie. I can have you laid out buffet style on any surface in no time flat. Call it lickity split if you want, Trix."

I hate it when he calls me that. He's the only person who does and I've told him repeatedly over the years not to call me that. It's no use telling this man what to do—unless you're my dad. About seven years ago, I gave up. In turn, I call him Linx to needle his nerves because he too hates his pet nickname I've bestowed on him. I can do petty as good as nice.

I straighten my shoulders and calmly, as much as I can muster anyways, retort, "Over my dead body, Mr. Danger. Let's get this over with, shall we."

His dark eyes roam my face and down my body and back up one last time before he chuckles and darkly says, "Yes, milady." I feel stripped naked, like he can see straight through my clothes and he's hungry for more. I take a moment to glow under his attention. Even though his smile is feral, and I know how lethal he is, having those pearly teeth flash at me sends shivers down my spine where they nest right inside my needy vag. Whether it's from fear or arousal, I have no idea at this point. My betraying body thinks it's a little bit of both, but I absolutely refuse to let him see.

I can hear the party from out here and I just know there's going to be a crowd with how jam-packed this parking lot is. My heart races with nervousness. I've never been allowed around the bikers my dad commands.

Sure, I've heard stories of bikers here and there at my studio and obviously I've watched shows and movies, but as for real life, I've got no clue.

I'm a sheep walking into the wolf's den.

Chapter 5 – Linx

I open the clubhouse door for her, and she breezes right on through like she owns the place, head held high. But I know there's an underlying nervousness, fear of this place, thrumming through her veins. She's scared and she's pissed she has to do this. What makes her even more mad is she has to depend on me right now and she'd rather spit venom in my face than ask me for help.

Beatrix Chavanet has been sheltered her entire life. Daddy may be the badass head biker in charge, but his little princess was never allowed to slum it with us. She went to fancy schools, fancy college, and had fancy apartments. Nah, she doesn't know about struggle.

She stands just inside the main door, in the small foyer that leads into the main area. She's curious, her eyes dart around the foyer and into the main area. Curiosity kills the cat as she takes a small step up to the open doorway into the clubhouse while I talk to the guards, Slim Jim and T-Bone. These two take any chance they can to goad me into a sparring conversation.

"Where did you pick up that beautiful piece of ass?" Slim asks with his Santa Claus bearded smile, practically drooling.

I point my finger in his face after I look over to make sure Birdie didn't hear him, quietly I tell him, "That's Rock's daughter. LSS threat. Drill is activated, make sure you know everyone coming through these doors. And stop staring at her legs." I snap my fingers in front of Slim's old, weathered face. "Tell no one who she is."

"Son, let an old man have his fill, ok. I'm not hurting anyone. I got it." T-Bone has already come over to hear what I've said to Slim. "You got anything to add?" I ask T.

"Nope, all good, Boss."

I swing my gaze over to her. Goddamn she's so beautiful. I can tell she isn't sure what to do. The way she fidgets with her clutch, her fingers wrapped around its bottom and tapping against her material covered thigh. That's the only thing that gives her nervousness away. She could play it off as tapping to the beat of the music, but I know her better than that.

I know plenty about her, more than she could ever imagine. I know her nervous tics, her tells, her facial expressions. I think I'm going to enjoy watching her squirm.

Placing my hand on her lower back, I guide her into the main area and quickly scan for Twilla, the clubhouse mom, who I think is as old as the club itself. She's a wrinkled, crass, wizened old woman who takes no shit off anyone. She's watched Birdie grow up and has had a gentle hand at being Birdie's babysitter on occasions when needed.

She can be a babysitter tonight, too. I have business to attend to. Although, I do take notice of the momentary lapse of people talking. People are definitely going to be whispering and questioning who she is, especially since she came in with me, who never brings anyone here. Let them question. I don't have time to deal with it.

Finding Twilla in the kitchen, I deposit Birdie and tell Twilla not to let her out of her sight and don't tell anyone who she is. Twilla nods and knows not to question why Birdie's here.

Twilla's aware of how the drill works.

The clubhouse is in full raucous mode tonight. There're half naked women dancing on tables, alcohol is everywhere, the smell of weed's in the air, and I guarantee there are lines of some kind of substance being snorted off a passaround's ass or tits somewhere in this building. There's a pretty big crowd tonight and it looks like the bar is doing good for itself. I notice there's an influx in the number of feisty women to pass around too.

The clubhouse is a huge open warehouse with a stage up front and an upstairs. It's mostly open concept on the lower half. In the back of the Great Room is a locked office, two bathrooms and lockers.

Off to the top left of this Great Room is the kitchen. Restaurant quality. The stairs leading up to the ten bedrooms is along the right wall, by the front door. There's a fully stocked bar on the bottom floor.

It smells like the kitchen has been cooking up some orders. Right now, it smells like pizza and makes my stomach growl. The upstairs ten bedrooms has its own kitchen and three bathrooms. At any given time, a member may need a place to sleep. The compound offers temporary housing to those associates in need.

Further into the room, there's pool tables, dart boards, there's even a space for axe throwing. Tables and chairs dot the center of the room. Looks like they are all full. There must be over a hundred people here tonight.

Can't forget the one lonely air hockey table pushed against the wall back there. These fuckers are continuously losing the puck. The office sits in the back right corner of the building and that's where I'm headed now. I have to report to Rock that his daughter is safe at the compound.

As I walk through the clubhouse, I shake a few hands but keep walking. Plenty of greetings to the tune of 'Hey, Danger' to 'Fuck, Danger's here tonight.'

I'm not sure why it's a shock to them. I'm here almost every weekend. But probates are like that. Apparently, I'm an enigma to the probies.

The probies are our probates. Not officially initiated but definitely pledged to the club and down to do whatever we ask. They also know my reputation and how hard I am on probies. Prove your worth to me.

I swipe to call Rock's private line. He answers immediately. "Is she safe?"

"Yes, sir. She's here at the clubhouse and I've left her with Twilla in the kitchen while I make this call. She's not been alerted to the danger she was in. I haven't told her about the LSS threat. She just knows there's been a threat and protocol was activated."

"Very good, son, I'm happy to hear that."

It makes my chest puff up when he calls me son. I know I'm not his real son, but I'm the closest thing he's got to one, and seeing as how I never had a father growing up, it makes it seem like I made a father figure proud of me. I tamp down that feeling and trudge onto more business.

"What do you want done with her? Where's she going after this?" If she's around me too much more in that skimpy ass dress, I may not be able to keep my hands off of her. Of course I don't tell him that.

Birdie has grown into a gorgeous woman and she's no longer that awkward barely eighteen-year-old kid who gave me puppy dog eyes. Who my heart tripped over, and every woman's beauty is compared to. No siree, my Trixie has blossomed into this fine specimen of a woman and turned out sexy as fuck. Cute as a kitten to sleek as a panther. She makes my heart pound hard every time I think of her. She also makes something else on me hard too.

I've spent years following her around, at her dad's request. I'm always one step behind her and one step ahead. She has no idea I've been her shadow everywhere she goes for the past few years. I'm paid to be her stalker. Obsessed stalker.

She also has no idea Pierre is my stepbrother and lets me have free reign of Birdie's booking schedule, so I know where she is at all times. As long as she's at the shop or with him, I know she's safe. He is the only one at her studio that knows her lineage and her importance.

Birdie wanted to maintain a normal-ish life. One where bodyguards don't stand around and people are not trying to assassinate her whole family at every turn.

She doesn't trust easily, so it's a good thing they've become close, and she trusts him, much to my envy. He helps protect her every day when I'm not around.

"I'm not sure. The compound is secure but it's one of the first places they'll look besides her apartment and my place. I guess I could send her away, she won't like it at all," Rock muses.

I grimace at the thought of sending her out of state. "No, sir. She didn't want to leave with me and tried to fight me at first outside the restaurant."

Rock chuckles at that, "Of course she did. That's my little spitfire."

An idea forms in my head. Probably a horrible idea but it will keep her safe and no one will know where to look for her. "I think I know of a place."

"Go on."

"My family has a camp, down by Grand Isle, out in the bayou, where no one's around. No one can trace it back to me or my family. It's in a corporation's name; one I made up but untraceable to me. I can take her there and lay low with her until a solution with Grim has been reached."

Grim Reaper, the leader of the LSS, has basically declared war by planning to kidnap Birdie and essentially sell her to the highest bidder to get back at her father. They were tracking her, and they were stealthy about it. I'm kicking myself in the ass I didn't realize she was being watched and her moves cataloged.

Our informant contacted Rock earlier this evening to let him know the abduction was planned for tonight and she was being tailed. He said the directive came down from the top; procure Birdie, unharmed, and bring her to Grim. Grim isn't the smartest man, but he's had enough common sense to get him by in LSS as leader for the past twenty years. Quite frankly I believe they need a change in regime because that old fucker is going to get them all killed one way or another.

"That sounds solid. I don't think she'll go for it at all, but she won't have a choice." He goes silent for a moment. "Did you see the tail?"

"Yes sir, I did, he was far enough away I was able to get her out of there but close enough for me to spot him. It was sloppy work on their part." This guy was no match to my six foot three, built like a brick shithouse frame. I'ma bulky motherfucker. But he moved gracefully enough that he melded right into the other tourists walking about seamlessly. Hiding in plain sight.

"Take her to your camp tonight then. I want a tracker in her, pronto. Then await my word for the all-clear. Check in when you arrive, no matter the time."

"Yes, sir. Will do."

"One other thing, don't touch her, Lincoln. She's still hands off, even for you."

If I ever had thoughts of seducing Trix, it just went right out the window with this order and made my dick shrivel.

"Yes, sir."

"Good. Wait on my order, son." He hangs up and I'm left feeling unsettled about this whole situation.

I make a quick call to my mother and arrange for us to use the camp. She's delighted I want to take a woman there with me. She thought it was a romantic getaway until I explained this is a mission I'm on and it's the boss's daughter. She knew it was serious then.

For the record, I've never brought a woman home to meet her.

I check my text messages and see I have one from Pierre. Not only is he close to Birdie, but he's my best friend along with being my stepbrother. My mom found his dad about six years ago and we instantly got along. Weird, because I knew of him from being Birdie's best friend in college. After a year of dating, Mom married Pierre's dad, solidifying our brotherhood.

Pierre: Word on the streets is you took my woman.

Me: The rumors are true, little brother.

I really wasn't expecting an answer back so quickly, yet here were the chat bubbles bouncing.

Pierre: Dare I ask what made you snatch her in broad daylight?
Me: She had a tail. Verified threat has come in. LSS was going to abduct her tonight at Evangelina's, selling her into sex ring. I got there just in time. It was a close call, man. I could have lost her.

Pierre: FUCK, man. Does she know?

Me: Yes and no, she's shook up about it, I can tell. She's quieter than normal. Paranoid now. She knows no details.

Pierre: texting her now. Will be vague. She's prolly scared.

Pierre: Can you tell me where you're going?

Me: On this phone, all I'm saying is we're going to the place we swam as kids.

Pierre: Good idea. If you need me...

ME: Roger that

We both grew up within twenty miles of each other but had never met until our parents started dating. This bayou is his home too. The camp we're in is the one I grew up in. When Mom married

Bret, Pierre's dad, they lived in the camp house, and he fixed it up nicely with the money I sent them to rebuild with. They live in a large brick home in a lovely HOA now. I wasn't about to let my momma stay in a camp when I could finally buy her a mansion. Now we use this when I come in for the weekend and drag Pierre home with me. We stay at camp instead of under Mom and Bret's noses.

However, that woman is trying everything to get me married off. Pierre's already married, and his life is a joke most of the time. He's in love with his husband but sometimes I don't think the feeling is mutual with Seven. He's an odd bird.

Pierre: Do you need anything?

Me: Watch the shop. Everyone coming in, anyone standing outside for too long. I'll have men stationed outside and you have access to the cameras in the shop. Anyone staring in the windows that creep you out, call me. I'm tapped into the cameras in the studio too, so I can monitor too.

Pierre: Copy that, big bro.

Pierre: Don't fuck my girl.

Me: She's off limits. Daddy's rule.

Pierre: Her dad is smart then.

Pierre and Shadow are the only people who have any clue about my crush on Birdie. I confide in Pierre. We come up to camp with a few bottles of bourbon and confess our hearts out. Like where he pretends to be so in love but he's really hurting because of Seven's bi-polarism. Feigning love makes Seven stay calm and happy. I don't know why he has to keep Seven happy but I sure as hell don't. I don't really care for him, but they've been dating, then married since college. They just celebrated eight years together.

With me, I'm not even sure it's a crush at this point. Over the past few years, it's evolved to an obsession. I yearn for her. Any way I can get her. I can't get enough of her, and I go out of my mind if I can't see her.

Three years ago, I offered myself to be in charge of her security. Her father trusts no one else with it but me. There is round the clock security on her and her place of business, even inside her apartment, that only I have access to.

Leaving the office and coming around the corner of the bar, I hear before I fully see, "What do we have here, boys, looks like a fine piece of ass just dropped into our laps."

I see red when his hands reach under Trix's dress to caress the back of her thighs lewdly.

I grab him by his ponytail, pulling his head back and I wrench his arm behind his back. He cries out in pain, but I don't give a shit. This probie needs to know his place.

The music stops. The voices stop chatting. The entire clubhouse goes silent, except for his painful yelps.

I growl at him from beside his face, looking right at Trix in all her sexy glory, "Bow to her."

His terrified eyes try to look over at me, but I have his scalp pulled so tight it's almost impossible.

"I'm not bowing to no bitch," he spits out to me.

I kick his knee out from behind him, and he falls to one knee. "I won't order it again."

He slowly lowers his other leg and looks up at her.

Her stunned face goes from mine to his. Her lips parted in shock and her knuckles grow white around the beer bottle she's gripping. No matter the emotion, she looks beautiful.

I let go of him, shoving him to the floor amidst his grunts of pain. I stand beside her, looking out into the room. All eyes are on me. Good, as they should be.

Very loudly, and very clearly to get my point across, I say, "Take a very good look at this woman. Know her face. Know her name. This is Birdie Chavanet. Some of you know who her father is, for the ones that don't, or can't remember why it sounds familiar, this is your Princess. This is Rock's only daughter and his most valuable possession. Which now means she is your most valuable possession and you will protect her with your life. Is that understood?"

A murmur of understanding and agreement ripples through the crowd.

The probie on the floor stares up at her slack-jawed and wide-eyed. He knows, at this very moment, he could have had his hands cut off for such a grievous error.

"I'm sorry, I didn't know, I'm so sorry, please forgive me, miss," his pathetic whimpers turn my stomach. He could have lost his life with this transgression.

She looks down and tells him, "It's ok, I accept." She holds out her hand to help him up and I grab her hand.

"No, it's not ok. He needs a lesson in manners and how we do things around here. We respect women. We don't manhandle someone against their will, especially without their consent." More than a few cheers go up from across the room.

"If this is how you're going to act towards the females in this clubhouse, I suggest you turn in your probie patch and merrily walk the fuck out," I say as I stare him down.

"No, I swear, I'm drunk and a little high, it won't happen again, I swear it." He looks at her again and says, "I'm so sorry."

She just nods at him down at her feet, but her eyes quickly flit over to mine.

"You swore allegiance to this club and for all it stands for," I tell the room, "There has been a threat to Birdie, and we must be the eyes and ears on the streets to nullify the threat."

More murmurs in the building waft over to us. Concerned whispers penetrate my anger.

In my peripheral vision, I see her eyes narrow at me and her mouth snap shut. She's pissed I didn't tell her she was in danger. *Another time, sweetheart.*

If she only knew how much danger I've kept her out of over the years, she'd shit a brick. Too many men like to follow my Trix, and I keep the hounds at bay. She has no idea about the stalker I took care of two months ago for her. I like to keep her in her own blissful world, wrapped in her bubble of ignorance.

That's why she has a shadow like me.

Beatrix Evangelina is my obsession, not theirs, and I will protect her with my life.

"Danger? Is she going to be staying here?" Twilla asks from the other side of Birdie.

"No, I'm leaving with her right now, Twilla. Business as usual here unless orders come down before I return in a week or so." Little Birdie's mouth pops open again to argue with me, and I growl at her. *Not here, little one, do not usurp me in my own house.*

She very smartly shuts her mouth, but she does send me a lively death glare. Her love language is mean looks. I can take all the glares you can give, sweetheart, but you're still coming with me, for as long as it takes.

"Danger?"

"Yeah, Bam?"

"Are you taking any of us with you?"

I shake my head, "No one is leaving with me except Birdie."

I see them all looking between themselves, wondering where I'm going and what I'm going to do with her. They must think I'm going on a weeklong vacation with the boss's daughter, and essentially, I kinda am.

"Where ya going?" another member calls out.

"That's classified." My tone brooks no argument nor any more questions.

"Alright, behave and I'll be in touch." I take Birdie's beer bottle and put it on the table beside the couch she's near and settle my arm around her waist, resting on her lower back, leading her out of the clubhouse.

I'm waiting for it. She's going to blow her top. We reach the door, and I open it for her-

3

2

Shutting the door behind me.

1

She rounds on me, "Who the fuck do you think you are? There's *NOOOO* fucking way I'm holing up with you somewhere for *ANY* amount of time! Do you hear me?"

Hands on her hips, puffing like a bull ready to spear me with her horns. If she could kill me with a look, I'd be a pile of ash right now. Man, she looks glorious when she's pissed. Her whole body comes alive with her fury. Flames actually dance in her icy blue eyes.

Whoowee. Fire in the hole! I settle the smirk on my face when I step up to her.

"I know I'm the one taking you to safety. I know you *are* going to come along nicely, or I can not-so-nicely take you. Your choice." She backs up and starts digging in her purse. She whips her phone out, hands shaking as she unlocks it and then calls someone. I bet I know who.

I hear his deep voice greet her.

She immediately starts in, "I'm not going with Lincoln, Daddy. I can't, I'm booked solid. I don't want to leave with him except to take me back to my apartment."

"Now Birdie, you must know he's doing this on my orders."

"Well then, un-order him. I'm not going. And he just threatened me." She's really trying to tattle on me; I laugh to myself. Precious.

I hear Rock sigh loudly. He normally doesn't get frustrated at his stubborn, willful daughter, but I can feel it through the phone.

"Beatrix, cancel your appointments and go with Danger. Now."
The tone he uses snaps her spine straight and her eyes get huge.
Rarely is her father so gruff with her. He never orders her
around. I can see where it's shocking to her.

Meanwhile, I'm just standing here, running my thumb over my
lips to keep silent.

She bites her bottom lip, which does wicked things to me, and
lets loose a deep shaky breath, then softly says, "Yes, Daddy."
That answer also did something weird to my innards.

She knows not to argue with him. She can argue with everyone in
the whole wide world, but not him. Ever.

"But what am I going to do about clothes? I can't go dressed like
this. I'm in a cocktail dress and heels, Dad."

Personally, I wouldn't mind if she dressed like this for our
extended stay alone together, but the situation will get real dicey
quickly since I'm not allowed to touch her.

And I want to touch her right now. I want to touch her
everywhere, all over. I want to be the one running my hands up
those smooth, creamy thighs. Up to where she keeps her treasure
locked far away from men like me.

"I will permit you five minutes in your apartment. Grab what you
can. Five minutes, Beatrix."

"Ok, I can do that. Can you tell me what's happening? Why am I
leaving? What's the threat?"

Rock pauses before he speaks to her. Seconds tick by. It has to
be hard for him. He doesn't usually hide things from her.

"Grim was planning to abduct you. Tonight. They were following
you when Lincoln came for you."

I watch the color drain from her beautiful face in the stark,
unforgiving security light.

Her horrified eyes swing to mine, and I nod my head, affirming
her nightmare.

Chapter 6 – Birdie

The world just tilted around me but magically I stayed standing upright.

I almost don't believe it. I shudder at the thought of the nightmare my life would have turned into if Grim had gotten his claws into me.

My eyes are still glued to Linx's face after hanging up with my dad. At least he's lost his smirk and has on his business-as-usual face, with his steely eyes and lips pressed into a thin line. He actually looks concerned. God, why does he always have to look so distractingly good.

Now IS NOT the time to be thinking that shit. WE ARE IN TROUBLE.

I'm the business now. I'm his main business. All the years of being kept away and now I'm the business. The priority. Tonight, I would have been taken if it weren't for Linx.

"Thank you, Linx, for saving me," I acknowledge his heroics, as halting and broken as my voice sounds. Nothing like being told you're about to get abducted and sold into sex slavery to humble a girl. Brought me down a few pegs, it did. I promise myself right here that I'm going to try to be nicer to Linx, even if it kills me. He just saved my life.

My dad's words knocked the fight left in me right out of the ballpark. I'm stunned. I'd cry if I was a crier. I just feel slightly sick and a little numb. Linx dips his chin to me, and I can tell it's not his usual mock bow.

"Shall we go get your things, Princess?"

"Yeah," I say, absently nodding and woodenly walking to his car. I'm still so mad but I'm too shook up to fight. Sliding into his luxury car while he holds the door is a blur. The drive to the Quarter, all a blur. Lights just zinging by as I stare out of the window.

Linx didn't pry, didn't rub it in that I had to leave, and that my refusal was overturned by Dad. He allowed me space to process, and for that, I'm grateful. I texted Pierre on the way home and let him know how dreadfully sorry I was but please rebook all my clients for the next week and I'll be out of the area. I'll work on Sundays and Mondays to catch up. Offer them a 15% discount. I have the compassion to understand some of these clients have been waiting weeks, even months, to get their tattoos but staying and doing them is not an option any longer.

I unlock the door to my apartment and start up the stairs to my apartment. I don't even care right now that he can see up my skirt. I'm numb all over. The thought keeps tickling my brain that I should be crying, maybe even hyperventilating, ya know, like a normal person. I mean, that might still happen when it fully sinks in that someone tried to fucking *steal* me.

Linx's never been in my personal space. Not that I know of anyways. This fucking guy's like a ninja. I don't know how I feel about having him in my apartment. God, I hope I didn't leave it a mess. Just one more thing to worry about. *Gee Linx, thanks for stopping by, don't mind that vibrator over yonder, or that other one, seeing as how I can't keep anyone interested in me and get laid.*

As soon as we reach the top landing, I put my finger on the print scanner on the front door. Linx holds his hand up and pulls a gun from under his shirt.

He enters my apartment, and I just stand out here trying not to panic. I stare into the fading light, trying to make out any shapes. Moments later, Linx comes back and tells me it's all clear.

Immediately, I'm kicking off heels. Fuck all of this shit. He stands with his feet apart just inside the door, he starts a timer on his watch, looks at me and says, "Five minutes, Trixie."

This spurs me into action. If anything, I know Linx doesn't play around.

I run to my bedroom and grab a big duffel bag. More bags fall on my head. I yelp and dodge, no time. I gotta be fast as fuck.

I had done laundry earlier, but I still hadn't folded it and put it away. I take the whole laundry basket and dump it in the bag. Next, I throw open my panties drawer and just grab at anything. I snag some bras too. I know my new lingerie is drying on the rack in the bathroom, so I run in there and grab them right quick.

What? I want to feel pretty. *Right.*

Running to my closet I frantically snatch down t-shirts and sun dresses. I don't know where I'm going. Mother always said, 'Bring a nice dress to wear wherever you stay.' So, I bring a dress.

I dump it all in the bag. Next, I open a drawer and grab shorts. I snag a few bathing suits, you never know. After that, my pajamas. I'm filling this bag completely full; I don't give a shit how heavy it is either. I don't know how long I'll actually be gone.

I must look comical to anyone spying on me as I run around in a panic, literally waving my arms like a lunatic, just grabbing at things.

It's like that show my mom used to watch, where they send you into a grocery store with a buggy and tell you grab what you can within three minutes, and you can keep it. And then everyone races for the meats. My meats are comfortable clothes; I throw them all in the bag.

This is going to sound awful, but I sure as shit don't want to be kidnapped wearing a dress.

In my bathroom, I load my arms down with toiletries. And just in case, I grab a roll of toilet paper. Once again, I don't know where I'm going. Grab Benadryl too! Don't forget your birth control pills!! Don't forget the razor!

Fuck! Shoes!

I run to the closet and grab some sandals, my favorite pair of Crocs, and a pair of sneakers. Into the bag it all goes. I wish I knew where I was going, this would make packing so much easier.

My time might be up, but I'm definitely changing out of this dress. My confidence and cool demeanor left me when I found out about the situation I find myself in. I'd put on a chastity belt if it meant those assholes couldn't get to me.

I quickly untie it in the back and let it flutter to the floor.

Of course, this is the exact moment Linx wants to stick his head in the door.

"Hey, we have one…oh holy fuck."

Thank whatever higher power, I was turned away from the door and I had enough time to cross my arms over my ample boobs…that still have the chicken cutlets attached to them. "LINCOLN!"

"Jesus fuck, Trix, why are you naked?"

Looking over my shoulder at him, he's simply standing there staring at my backside. Why wouldn't the manwhore be looking? "Hey, hey!" I yell at him. His gaze rises to mine, "Please leave, I'm trying to change my fucking clothes, Linx." I try my damndest to growl at him now. If he can do it to me, I can dish it right back.

His jaw flexes and he turns on his heel, walking away.

Normally I would get some type of shit for this, or some flirty comment, or even some kind of insult. I'm confused when I'm met with silence. Confused, but grateful.

No time to dwell, I'm running out of time.

After I throw on a Rolling Stones crop top and cotton shorts, I hurry to my bedside and grab all my chargers and my iPad.

I'm yanking the bag off the bed when I remember something. Dropping the bag, I run to the closet and grab a briefcase—my traveling tattoo kit.

It has two cordless guns, plenty of clean needles, gloves, salve, cups, cleaning solution, and of course, ink. It has anything and all I need to do tattoos in a safe environment.

I still have a whole leg that I can work on. Mine.

Dragging the bag to the door, I kill the light and heft the bag over my shoulder. AHH! The fucking thing weighs as much as I do. Linx is standing by the front door, fingers massaging the space between his eyes. He hears me come out of the room and rushes to take my bag.

"Everything in here?"

I nod while saying, "I believe so." I grab my over-the-shoulder sling-bag off the kitchen island where I left it. I swap out my wallet from the clutch to the bag and grab my reading glasses off the catch-all dish on the counter.

"What's that?" He nods to my briefcase.

"Tattooing kit."

I take a deep breath and close my eyes to let it out. I shake out my arms and wiggle my fingers. When I open them, I'm less shaky, but Linx is close to me, making my breath hitch.

"Are you ready now, Princess?"

I gulp past the lump in my throat. You've got to be fucking kidding me. I have to be ovulating if this man, of all peoples of the world, is having an effect on me in my panicked state of mind. This realization irritates me because I've been having fantasies lately and I'm a royal hypocrite. I lie to myself as a hobby. I'm an expert at it now.

Everything's fine.

Me, calmly telling my ovaries to sit down and shut the absolute fuck up.

Immediately I shove that 'Oh how is Linx in bed' bullshit down and square my shoulders. I'm going crazy, that's what's happening. It's finally the moment my mind breaks. Should have gotten laid before this. "Yep. Let's go." I can't even look him in the eyes as my face heats up again.

I hope he knows I don't plan on putting up with his bullshit either. My plan is to try and avoid him.

I can barely stand putting up with my own bullshit right now but seeing him make a man bow to me as he stared intensely at me, made me entirely too wet and flushed for my liking.

I've never been one for alpha-holes, but it definitely made my body have a strong reaction and my traitorous pussy throbbed in glee at the taste of violence.

"So where are we going?" I ask as I buckle into his slick as shit sports coupe.

"My apartment."

Please god no. Just no.

"Oh ok. I'll just wait in the car." Play it cool.

"I don't think so."

"Uh, I know so." Wow, B, that came out uber childish. Maybe that's why he's smirking.

Tactic change.

"How far away is this place you are taking me to and hopefully just dropping me off by myself?" I smile and blink my lashes at him.

His chest rumbles with a chuckle, "It's about two hours or so outside the city." He looks over at me then, "And I'm going to be with you."

Fuck.

I contemplate this. What's in a two-hour radius from home? "Will you tell me where we are going?" I pause for a moment then be sure to add a "please" to the end.

"I'm taking you home. To my home, where I grew up. We're staying at my family's camp." I notice the way his muscles cord on his forearm when he flexes his hand on the steering wheel and how the dark dusting of hair catches the streetlights as we cruise through the French Quarter. Traffic is always a nightmare here, but I can sense he's on edge.

Like Grim and his goons are going to rush the vehicle and steal me. Shit, they might. I don't know how fucked up these guys are. I'm trusting Linx's word on this.

While Linx sits with his face propped in his palm, I try to study him without looking. I'm a master at this by now.

Linx decided to go extra dangerous tonight and wear a ball cap and jeans with an entirely too tight black shirt. He can't possibly breathe in that get up.

This is criminal the way he's doing me. He has to know he's every woman's wet dream and he's out here in the wild just showing out.

I can't even look at him without thinking he's on Instagram somewhere with a mask on, I just know it. I don't even know what he looks like without clothes on, but I imagine it's pretty rock solid under there judging by the defined ridges and curves of hard muscle lovingly covering his man titties.

Man titties I could lick chocolate off of. Oh god, and how his thighs look in those tight pants.

I never knew I was attracted to a set of thighs on a man, yet here I am clenching vaginal walls to get any reprieve.

I can sit here and lie, saying I've never fantasized about him naked. I mean, those biceps are pretty hard not to notice.

I did notice the bulge in front of his jeans. I guess you could say it was average.

See, lying again. It's a problem for me.

Linx apparently carries an anaconda around in his pants. What super sucks is I have no idea where home is for him, currently or in the past. I'm a little shocked when we cross over Canal Street and roll up to a parking garage in the Central Business District. Canal street is the divider between the French Quarter and the CBD. This means he doesn't live far from me. Five minutes by car.

Suspiciously close to me.

Nahh, couldn't be a twist of fate.

I'm not sure how I feel about this.

There's no way he could have gotten closer except live in the Quarter beside me. Instead, he went one street out of the Quarter. I wonder if my father told him where to live.

Looking around the parking garage while he punches in a code, I begin to doubt the size of the parking garage and how we're fitting his big ass ego in here. Definitely small dick energy rolling up in his sporty black Porsche.

We head around the bend, and he pulls into the very first parking space. I think, how does he get so fucking lucky all the time? Then I see the plaque, 'Reserved for Lincoln LaFleur,' screwed to a pole in front of us.

Jesus fuck. No wonder this guy's so full of himself. Next thing you know he'll be saying he's got the penthouse. As if.

Sure 'nuff, we get into the elevator, and he presses the PH button. I just stand here shaking my head on the ride up. I don't even raise my eyes because the damn elevator is mirrored on all the walls, and I know he's staring at me. I can feel it. My entire body is heating up under his stare.

I just stand here lamely and stare at the floor instead of looking at him. He has on a nice pair of shoes. Practical. Great for a soldier. No scuff marks or anything. I'd whistle a tune if it meant this ride would end sooner.

Finally, the ding. I look up and my eyes meet his in the reflection before the doors open to reveal a giant of a man standing by what looks like a front door to a house. There's a wreath on it that says 'Unwelcome' in a girly sort of font.

I can't help but crack a smile at the wreath. Big, bad, macho man decorates his front door.

He scans his thumb into this fancy looking pad and the door unlocks. Oh, a high-tech macho man, I taunt him in my head. I'm losing my mind.

Linx leads me through the door into his home. The lights are low, but you can tell by the dim light this is a place of opulence. I expected nothing less, honestly.

He's stuck-up enough to have white carpets.

He's arrogant enough to own the penthouse. Fuck, for all I know, he owns the whole building. I mean, I can't really pass judgement here, I own the whole building at my place too. But the difference is I'm not a raging dickhead.

I'm a raging hypocrite instead. I'm an even bigger problem now. I'm not sure what to do but the first thing I do is take my Crocs off by the front door. I step further into the living room, onto the white tiled floor, and it's nothing but floor to ceiling windows all the way around the open concept. My breath catches in my chest and my heart swells then my eyes fill with tears at the beautiful sight beyond the wall of glass.

I rush over to the windows and take my fill. His living room overlooks the French Quarter.

All the lights. The twinkling fairy lights spread all over the Quarter. It's beautiful. I've never seen it from this angle or lit up like this. I can't stop the smile that comes across my lips.

I feel Linx come up behind me, he whispers right by my ear, "I think of you every time I look out these windows and see the Quarter below."

I snap out of the spell that the view put me under and turn my head to him. He's right there, so close. Too close.

You hate him, whispers through my mind.

I sidestep, looking down while wiping my eyes. I hurry and cross my arms because I realized on the ride over, with all the potholes and bumpy roads, I forgot to put a bra on. When I look back up at him, he's tossing his hat on the coffee table.

"It's beautiful from up here," I politely tell him. It's one of the most magical moments of my life, but I don't want him to know. It's more breathtaking than I imagined.

"Not as beautiful as our Princess. Long may she reign." I know he's teasing me, but he sounds so serious. I'm glad the lights are low so he can't see me blushing. He's extra saucy and flirty tonight and I'm not entirely sure how to cope with it or how to relax around him since the clubhouse.

"What's the plan here?" I get right to the point, even though there's a slight shake to my voice.

"I'm going to pack me a bag, change and then we head out. Feel free to grab you something to eat from the fridge. I know you missed dinner tonight." He almost winces while saying that, as if he's thinking about snatching me from in front of my restaurant on an empty stomach. A turnabout and he starts walking away, calling over his shoulder, "I'll be right back."

Alright. In turn, I call after him, pledging in a mostly pleasant voice, "I'll try not to barge in on you naked, I'll give you the privacy and respect you deserve as a human being for such an intimate and personal moment that you're having in your own bedroom."

Yep, I feel him flipping me off from here, through the walls.

Chapter 7 – Linx

I'm never going to survive a day, let alone a week or longer. I can't be in the same room as her and not think about her lips wrapped around my cock, or my face buried between those exquisite thighs or fucking hell, that perfect peach ass I got a great look at. I want to pull my fucking hair out. It's maddening. The only way Pierre can be around her so much is because he's gay, it has to be that because I'm not sure how long I can last without touching her…with my tongue.

And now, oh now, I know for a fact what she's always hiding under the clothes she wears. Jesus. I've never gotten so hard so fast in my miserable life. Curves for days, man. The perfect heart ass. Those shapely long legs. Long black hair falling down her back to her waist. I silently begged her to turn around.

I blow out a long breath and run my fingers through my hair. I'll never forget that sight as long as I live.

Grabbing my tactical duffel off the top shelf of the closet, I set to work filling my bag. I'm not sure what to expect so I grab some riding gear, jeans, shorts, t-shirts, and a few button ups. I make sure to stuff my flip-flops in a pocket and I grab my riding boots and shove them in for good measure too.

Toiletries obtained and dumped into the bag. I snag my phone charger from beside the bed. And I stand there for a moment, eyes landing on the bedside drawer. There's a whole box of condoms in there.

The desperate urge to dig them out and throw them in my bag for later…

Fuckity fuck fuck.

You can't touch her, Linc.

I look at the drawer in the nightstand again but drop my shoulders in a pout and grab my bag, grumbling to myself about keeping my dick to myself and she's just an assignment. Keep her in that zone, knowing damn well the love of my life is not just some assignment.

When I reach the kitchen, she's bouncing up and down, doing some kind of shimmy and shoving cheese slices into her mouth. I think she's doing a food dance.

"Do you really think you should be eating all that cheese with your gut issues?"

She stops chewing, with her mouth open. "H-How do you know about that?"

I wink at her and reply, "There's lots I know about you, Princess." She swallows and takes a drink of wine, straight from the bottle. *Fuck it, girl, chug that $600 wine.*

"Yeah? Like what?" she goads me.

As I move around my penthouse, grabbing this and that, such as my favorite books, my extra riding gear stashed in another duffel, and finally, a sealed bottle of bourbon. On second thought, I grab another bottle too, can't have too many if I need to deal with her.

"Are you going to answer me?" she asks.

I start shoving things into my bag pockets while talking to her, "I know you like your coffee with heavy cream and two pumps of vanilla flavoring with a bit of chocolate syrup but come October you turn into a basic pumpkin bitch. You take your steak medium rare. Your favorite band is The Rolling Stones. You're secretly a

Swiftie. You take pepperoni and green olives on your pizza. You're allergic to latex and Bactrim. Should I keep going?" I look up with a gleam in my eye, eyebrows raised.

"Why? Why do you know all this?" she whispers. She shakes her head and says, "Fuck! *How* do you know all this? I'm scared to even know."

"It's my job to know, Princess."

"So, what, am I your job?"

"Essentially? Yes. I've been assigned to you." She doesn't need to know it's been that way for the past three years. Back when rumblings of a bloodbath floated across the Gulf to our ears again.

I can't even spare her a look. It has to be this way. There can never be anything between us. Her daddy would never allow it. I could have all the money in the world, but because I'm pledged as a member, I can't ever have her. She's off limits and only one member, me, is allowed around her, until tonight at the clubhouse.

Seeing her in the clubhouse made me hard. Fuck, everything about her makes me hard, even when she's defiant and argumentative. Seeing her lips part and her chest rise when I made that dipshit probie bow to her, almost made me abandon my oath right then and there. She liked it though. I could have run my fingers over her pussy lips and guaranteed they were glistening with arousal.

I walk over to the wall and push an invisible button and the wall slides over. Inside this alcove are guns and ammunition. The bonus side of being an arms dealer is you get pick of the litter; therefore, I have a very nice gun collection.

"Whoa, are you fucking kidding me right now? What in the Batman hell is happening?"

Ignoring her for once, I pull out the briefcase that is Styrofoam lined for numerous guns to fit into. Picking out about four pistols, I grab the ammo from below. I bring all this over and set it with my bag.

Walking back over to the alcove, I grab the GPS tracking kit. This is going to royally piss her off.

"Trix, I'm under orders to put a tracker in you."

Her face goes blank before the horrified expression takes over as my words truly sink in. Her voice shakes, "No, I can't allow that. Absolutely not." She starts backing behind the island, away from me.

I bring it over to the front of the island and start opening the sterile tools and baggie with the tracker inside of it. "Your dad has ordered it. It would be easier if I didn't have to hold you down." "No, Linx," she tries to be firmer, but her revulsion is masking it. False bravado all the way.

I try to deflect and give her a shit eating grin, "I won't mind running my hands all over that lush body and pinning you to the floor to get this done."

I see the fury working in her eyes once again. There's my girl, thought I'd lost her back there to fear. It's just a tracker. She won't feel but a pinch.

"It's for your own good. Only I can track its location."

Her bottom lip trembles and her chin wobbles. "Is it going to hurt?"

"Probably. And there's nothing I can do to take away the pain of it or I would, Trix. If they manage to get to you, I can find you." My voice rough, "I'll stop at nothing to find you. I promise, Trixie."

I watch her shoulders slump as she comes to terms with it. She has no choice. I really will hold her down to follow orders and she knows this. This will also make my job a lot easier.

Pulling out the piercing gun and the tiny tracker, I sync it up to my phone and upload its location to the untraceable cloud. No matter if I lose my phone, I can log in anywhere on a secure connection and find her.

"Com'mere."

Birdie comes around the corner of the island and looks so small and scared standing in front of me. So helpless and vulnerable. I know she's afraid and I'm doing everything I can to assure her I can keep her safe.

"Turn around and hold your hair off your neck," I ask nicely. Calmly.

Her chin wobbles some more and something in my cold, dead soul stirs in the place reserved just for her. The only place in my life that's bright. "Please," I add.

I watch her slowly turn around and gather her long black hair over her shoulder. Fuck me, I catch a whiff of her shampoo, sweatpants were a bad idea. She bows her head.

"It will be over before you know it," I say as I put the device to her skin and press the trigger. I don't even give her to the count of three. It would have made her more nervous if I had.

She yelps and goes up to her tip toes in pain. "Is it done?" "Yeah." Her hand that's wound tight in her hair starts to relax and her shoulders ease back down. "Go into my bedroom and let me see if it will calculate range."

She spins around to face me, eyes full of unshed tears, and hoarsely whispers, "I'm not going into your bedroom."

"I need to calibrate, Trix." I point to the door at the top of the stairs. Putting a little more bite in my tone, "Go."

Her body jerks into motion and she numbly walks to the stairs. If I had a heart I might be moved by her pain, instead it reminds me of how fragile she is and how much she needs protecting. Life as she knows it is being stripped away right in front of her. Layers of lies and betrayal from her parents are being peeled back and she's realizing how much was kept from her, how dangerous the real world she was born into is.

She may never forgive me.

I just took her freedom.

It's for her own good.

Looking up from the app on my phone, I see her going up the stairs, she's halfway up, then I realize I can see her under boob from the bottom of her crop top as she gets higher and higher. No bra.

Fucking hell, woman.

It's official, I'm going to die, and it will be all her fault.

Chapter 8 – Birdie

Upon entering his room, the first thing I notice is the overwhelming smell of *him*. Everything that makes up Linx. His scent clings everywhere, to everything. He's worn the same cologne since I've known him, and it's ingrained into this room, into every fiber, into my memory and secret fantasies. I would know his smell anywhere. I imagine he could move out and the smell would still linger for weeks.

Sometimes I swear I can smell it in my apartment when I come home at night. Of course, I know it's my imagination, but it always makes me think of him. Deep in my psyche, I knew two years ago there was something inherently wrong with me when I started masturbating to memories and fantasies of Linx. He's a very good-looking man is the excuse I use.

He has god like beauty. It's hard as hell not to be attracted to Lincoln LaFleur.

But as long as he stays pretty and shuts up, I could possibly see me fucking him. With him gagged and bound. Now that's the spirit! But we all know that's never going to happen because he just can't keep his purdy mouth shut around me.

Standing here in his intimate space, looking around at his black satin comforter on a giant bed, and black curtains that are open to the view of the Quarter, my heart slams inside my chest, rocking back and forth, flirting with disaster. I'm a cologne girl. It's overwhelming in here. Smelling a man wearing a good cologne does it for me. Hell, I even liked Axe Body Sprays back in the day.

This is torture.

Pure torture.

If it was anyone but him...Literally anyone. I'd even settle for Satan himself over it being Linx.

I feel my sex grow heavy and that familiar flush come over me, which embarrasses me to no end. I cannot have him come in here and see me like this, I'll never hear the end of it.

It's such a shame someone so annoying must be so sexy and good looking. Life's unfair. I'm sure there's a woman out there willing to put up with his moody ass enough to enjoy the sex with him or even live with him. I'm not the one.

"Shut the door and walk into my bathroom," Linx calls from down below. He's on my last fucking nerve already. I had hoped like hell he was just going to be taking me somewhere and dropping me off, with orders for me not to leave.

It just gets worse when I enter his bathroom, I'm taken aback by the other strong male scents. In here the scents clash together, aftershave, soap, and deodorant. It all mixes together to make up his unique scent. I wonder what it smells like warm, right up against the curve of his neck, as my lips trail over his skin so very softly. My breathing goes a little haywire thinking of this.

No, no, no bitch, we ain't going there. Shake them dimwitted thoughts from your head.

At this rate, I'm going to be throwing myself at him by the end of the week, hate be damned.

I should have gotten laid sooner and not been so picky. It's been a while since I've had any dick, and I must be ovulating is what I'm telling myself is the excuse for these confusing as fuck reactions to him tonight. I'm pissed at him, but I want him, I don't want him near me, but I'd like him on top of me. Yep, definitely should have gotten laid. My last fuck was with Noah eight months ago, and he wasn't anything special. It was honestly quite boring.

But I wouldn't know really good sex because I've only been with three partners. Maybe sex is supposed to be boring in real life. Maybe porn set me up for failure. Maybe romance books are lying.

I bet Linx fucks like a god though.

Beatrix Evangelina! We hate him. He's done nothing but be a dick to us. All my personalities are in agreement, except my pussy, who is trying to throw a hat into the ring for fucking him.

No, absolutely not. Flying under Linx's radar is for the best right now. Just continue to be bitchy towards him and maybe he'll leave you alone this week.

Yeah, 'cause that's always worked out. It just spurs him on harder, and you know it.

My eyes roam over the items on the counter, to his drying towel by the large glass shower room, the one that's covered his naked body and rubbed up against all those muscles. The smooth rounds of muscles that's bound to be under his suits, dress shirts, t-shirts and tactical gear. I've never seen him shirtless, but I bet it's a sight to behold. The man knows he damn well should be on the front of a calendar for lonely, thirsty ladies.

There's an urge to open his medicine cabinet, rifle through his linen closet, find any secrets about him. Maybe he secretly has hemorrhoids. I don't know why I care. I'm deranged. Why do I need to know anything about him?

Because he knows too much about you somehow.

I scoff and shake my head at my idiocy.

Still, it smells heavenly enough to make me press my thighs together. Zharia will forever tease me for this when I tell her about it.

About the time I wrangle my needy, damp impulses back under control, the bathroom doorway is darkening with his presence behind me.

My shoulders tense and I feel trapped but I'm not afraid of him. Linx would rather die than hurt me, this I do know without it ever being said. This man would die to protect me, not harm me.

Because I'm his assignment. I'm Daddy's most valuable asset. Stick to the script, B.

Bitterness washes over me and steels my spine. I have no idea why that bothers me. It shouldn't matter seeing as how I detest his whole personality. It would be nice if he saw me as a person and not just some mission.

"Are we done here?" I muster as much dismay as I can into that one question, directed at him behind me, as I watch him in the large mirror in front of me.

He steps up behind me, looking into my eyes in the mirror, he leans down by the shell of my ear, "Do you want us to be done here?" his husky voice wraps around me, sending a small shiver over my skin as I turn around and face him with a death glare. I have to lay some kind of boundary.

He backs up to the doorway with a chuckle, but he's leaning on the doorframe, one arm resting overhead, muscles on display, biting his bottom lip. And fuck, there's no denying Linx is fucking sexy, and I'm entirely too attracted to him for my own good.

Maintain mean face!

I know he pulls pussy, but I've never seen him try. I have no idea what his game is like. Any time I've ever been around him, his focus has always been on protecting me or annoying the shit out of me. What snide comment he can come up with next, what thing can he tease me about this time, what inappropriate comment can he slide in to make me blush. Goddamn my fair skin. It gives me away too easily. He makes me blush hard every time.

I've watched women fall over themselves to get his attention, but he kindly nods and lets them down most of the time that I see. Maybe he does his dallying off the clock because when he's around me or my dad, he's working.

"I'm really tired and I'd like to get to wherever we're going two hours away." I speak truthfully even if it sounds bitchy. My day has been pretty full of adventure, and I'm not used to that. I live a fairly quiet, predictable, charming little life away from biker gangs and sex predators. And that's saying something since I live in the Quarter, one of the craziest places on Earth.

He drops his arm down beside him and says, "Come on, it works. We need to get going anyways." He promptly tuns on his heel and storms off. Moody, remember?

He cranks the diesel truck over and my stomach bounces. Gone is the sophistication of the Porsche, here we have the rough and rugged country boy from the bayou.

God fucking help me and my ovaries.

You despise this man, Birdie!

Keep telling yourself that.

Fast cars, loud bikes, big tattoos and loud lovers are my addictions, and this truck is a sweet ass ride. I knew he would have a small dick energy truck.

We rumble out of the private garage and out into the muggy night air, on to somewhere foreign to me, but home to him.

We must be going to a circus.

"So, where are we going again?"

"Grand Isle."

"What? You're taking me to the swamps?"

"Is there something wrong with the swamps, Princess?"

I grind my molars at his bullshit. Why the fuck couldn't I have holed up in a five-star hotel with room service? Gah. Why do I have to sound so spoiled?

I whine in my head because I am a spoiled bitch and I'm not being grateful. It's just, I finally get a vacation, and I have to take it with him of all people and just to top it off, it's in a swamp ass bayou.

This makes me hate him even more. I feel robbed of a great time. "No, there's nothing wrong with it. I just thought we'd be going to a hotel, where I could have my own room."

"Don't worry, where we're going, you'll have your own room." I don't like the dark sound of his chuckle. Like he's mocking me in some way, which wouldn't surprise me one bit coming from him. This guy lives to annoy the piss out of me.

I cross my arms in front of me because the AC is too cold blasting at me. For Christ's sake, my nipples can cut glass now and I'll be damned if I give him anymore fodder for his spank bank. "Is there a particular reason we're going to Grand Isle?"

He notices my coldness and drops the air down a couple notches so it's not full blast on me. "That's where I'm from. I know the layout of the land. I have a camp there we can stay at. We'll be there soon, Princess, don't worry."

Be grateful, Birdie

I try not to wrinkle my nose while thinking we'll be staying in some dusty, dirty and musty camp house on stilts in a swamp somewhere. Mosquitoes are going to carry me off before Grim ever finds me. Camps're notorious for not having electricity or water, just primitive lodging, mainly used for fishing trips, so why have anything luxurious? My heart sinks as my dreams of comfort turn to ash and float away on the humid night air.

I pick up my phone to text Zharia. When I tell her what's happening, she immediately sent a barrage of questions,

ZBaddie: OMG a whole week ALONE with Mr. Danger <eggplant emoji> = <pacifier emoji> Be safe girl!

Me: Whoa! It is NOT like that!!!!!

ZBaddie: LOL sure it's not. Keep telling yourself that, girl <laughing face emoji> I can't wait for deets! Stay safe and keep me updated!! xoxo love you #TeamDanger

Well, fuck her then. I text Tally next and tell her what's going on.

Tally: God, your life is so exciting. I'm jelly. Not that someone wants to kidnap you and basically sell you into slavery, but the forced proximity to the steamy, grumpy devil <sweating face emoji> That man is drool worthy and totally fuckable. I bet he fucks like a demon too. You should totally find out finally. Daddy doesn't have to know. Then let the rest of us know.

Me: You're no help either. All Zhar can think about is me fucking him too.

Tally: Yeah, well you know her, she's addicted to cock.

I snort at that because it's so true. Her goals include fucking her way across the greater New Orleans area and sampling every flavor that's being offered. Tally isn't wrong. Zhar is a free spirit and believes in redefining double standards. She has rules, never get serious, don't get attached, no feelings.

Me: I needed that laugh.

Tally: We all know it's true, no matter how much she tries to deny it.

Tally: Tell me how you're feeling.

Me: Scared. Grateful. On high alert. Hungry (for food)

Tally: Sounds like all the normal feelings under the circumstances. Is there anything I can do from here?

Me: No I don't think so but I appreciate you offering. imu ilu

Tally: I love and miss you too <blue heart emoji> Let me know how that first night goes. You're so gorgeous, he's gotta be a saint to resist your beauty <smiling devil emoji> let me know how many times he 'accidentally' touches you lol

I get so flustered by her remarks; I put my phone away and just stare out the window as night slowly engulfs the daylight. Houses with lights shining from within whizz past the truck while my thoughts whirl around in my sleepy head.

"Thank you, Lincoln," I tell him through the silence between us. The radio plays old rock softly in the background over the hum of the engine. Every once in a while, I hear him sigh.

He clears his throat and asks, "For what?"

"Saving me, protecting me. I know I'm your job, but I can still be grateful."

He seems to mull that over before speaking, "You're welcome, Birdie."

The absence of his pet name for me leaves me hollow, an ache of loss, of something so familiar while my mind whirls. I know he's establishing the distance between us, but I feel like I did something wrong. I didn't realize I'd miss it. He's never called me Birdie, and he's only ever called me Beatrix that one time, earlier today to get my attention urgently.

It's never escaped my attention that I've been highly sexually attracted to him since I met him at a fresh young age of eighteen. I was still a virgin, and he was intimidating. He's all muscle, authority, danger and sex appeal. How could a woman not want to hop on that and take a ride?

I can tell you how; his personality is shit. He's gruff, moody, condescending, and sometimes he's flat out rude and crude. A pretty mouth that bullshit flies from. Beautiful on the outside, rotten on the inside. Don't be fooled by those lovely, lush lips that could lay fire to your skin, or the wicked tongue that sucks his teeth before he strikes. His large hands could raise you up while his muscled, corded arms lay you down gently, then he plows into you with a victory hiss. Gawd dayum.

This is the kind of man Lincoln LaFleur is. Oh, I've heard the stories. There's pictures of him online, not a lot, with these beautiful women on dates. He's a millionaire bachelor, why shouldn't he date models or socialites? He's a very wealthy man and women flock to him. He doesn't strike me as the type to settle down. He's usually off somewhere for my father, on a job or at some charity event the motorcycle club is hosting or seeing how far he can push me.

I've given Daddy the idea to create a half-naked calendar of bikers and their bikes, and they'd sell like hotcakes to the fuckton of women who love sexy bikers. He still hasn't done it. He's sitting on a gold mine of delicious looking men.

I mean, look at his top four guys. Linx we've established is too good looking for his own good. The third in charge is Shadow. Let me tell you, that man has this mysterious air about him. Lethal, even more dangerous than Danger. He has this calculated possessive vibe that makes women weak in the knees. He has long black hair, tan skin and dark eyes. His Native American heritage is hard to miss, and he works it to his advantage.

Then you have Gunney and Travares. Both of them are cute as a button and drip sex appeal. I've seen them in the house when I've visited my dad. They've never spoken to me, but I feel their eyes tracking me and I've even caught Travares grinning at me. They are hard to miss, with being so easy on the eyes. Those two definitely are online thirst traps. You can just tell. If they aren't they really should be.

I make a mental note to ask Linx for their socials. Hopefully it gets my traitorous mind off Linx.

I sneak a glance over at him. Brown close cropped hair tapers to a longer style on top. Hair that he loves to run his fingers through when I see him. It's one of his nervous tells. I can tell when I fluster him because he automatically reaches for his waves and walks away. It isn't often I get to see it, but the times it's happened makes my evil little heart sing. It's one of the very rare things I've picked up on him after all these years. Besides his assholishness. But it's those golden-brown hazel eyes that get me every time. I've never seen anything else like them. Green splashes with honey-colored accents, with rays of milk chocolate streaking through. There's so much going on with his eyes that it's distracting when looking at him. They make the ladies' knees weak. You have to watch out for Linx when he gives you his smoldering gaze. He knows what he's doing. Those eyes will suck you right in.

Framed by beautiful, dark, long lashes that any woman would envy with all their jealous little heart, his eyes speak of sex and mischievous secrets that he'll never tell. I could only imagine lying under him while looking into those starburst eyes.

Of course, with my hand over his mouth for good measure.

At the Christmas party last year, Zharia kept giggling because she kept catching him looking at me. 'He looks like he wants to bend you over one of these tables and lick you from clit to ass.' I remember blushing furiously, the heat of my face burning me alive as it traveled down my chest.

Zharia giggled some more and then said, 'Now he wonders what was said to make you this lovely, shade of pink rose.' I looked up at him right then and saw the half smile, with his dimple peeking out, his eyes dancing with curiosity, eyebrows raised. He knew we were talking about him. It was almost my undoing when he straightened up and tilted his head back slightly, like he was groaning, then bit his plump bottom lip between those pearly white teeth.

I knew exactly what he was thinking about. I was thinking the same thing about him.

I stared curiously at him while Zharia whispered in my ear, 'Oh, yes, Mr. Deep-Drink-of-Water wants to see how deep he can get into you. I guarantee that, Bea. If he wasn't enamored by you, I think I would try to climb that and see where he takes me.'

Jealousy and rage bubbled up in me at her words and I cut my eyes over to her. She simply smiles and quietly chides, "See, you hate the thought of someone else with him."

I pushed it out of my mind because that's just asinine for one, and two, I don't even like him that much, no matter how much my clit tingled at his hot look. Case in point, he came up to me later and told me I had toilet paper on my heel. He walked off when I looked down to see nothing. Like who does such childish shit? And why is it so fucking annoying?

Before I left for the evening, Linx insisted on walking me to one of my father's cars that was waiting for me outside of the restaurant. The car pulled up and he opened the door, leaned in, his lips barely off my collarbone. Blocking me from getting in, he took a big inhale, 'Mmm, Trix, if I didn't know better, I'd say you rolled in cotton candy before coming here.' His voice rolled through me. It made goosebumps spread from his breath on my skin.

I blinked up at him, waiting for the 'but' and then something insulting.

His face got closer to mine and I could smell the cinnamon candy he was eating, 'I just love how cotton candy melts on my tongue.'

I rolled my eyes at him and slid into the backseat under his arms. Outside the open door, he bowed, and his parting words were, 'Always a pleasure, Princess Trixie, think of me later while you work that clit,' then he gently shut the door and rapped his knuckles on the roof. As the car pulled away, I chanced a look back at him as he stood there with his hands in his pockets, watching the car drive away. He's getting mighty bold in his advances.

I'm no prude, but the fucking things he says to me. God. Damn. This past spring was the French Quarter Festival, and I sponsored a local gallery with local art. Some of their art are my own pieces. I helped them hold a fashionable gala and sale, with a side order of a fundraiser for a local dog rescue. Surprisingly,

Linx came in and bought up numerous pieces, some of them I saw displayed back in his penthouse. They were all my pieces. He saw me across the gallery. When I felt him staring, more like when I felt as if a warm hand was caressing my chest and the top swell of my breasts in that short, red strapless dress that showed off my killer legs; I looked up at him. Our eyes locked and he winked at me.

I simply looked back down at the super rich little old lady telling me a riveting story about her grandson who is looking to settle down. So far, I know his astrological sign, his bad habit of oversleeping and how much money he has. Trust fund baby like me. But sounds much more pompous about it.

'If I can get your number from you, dear, I'll give it to him so he can ask you on a date.'

I felt the firm hand caress across my lower back to wrap around my hip, as his smooth as good whiskey voice washed over us, 'That won't be necessary, ma'am, she's spoken for.' It made my heart skip a beat and my vagina flutter. She's a traitorous bitch.

'Oh, I see. Well, it was nice speaking to you, dear.' Then she trotted off while I stared after her trying to figure out what just happened.

Suddenly, Linx is everywhere, arms caging me in, too close in my personal space while he whispers in my ear, 'Just me, out here doing the Lord's work, saving young men from your cold, viper personality.' I stiffened in his arms and brought my hands up to push his chest away from me. God, I had needed air so bad. And not his cinnamon flavored air either. His scent was all around me; no way was I allowing it to cloud my mind.

Once he let me loose and stood back with his smirk, I narrowed my eyes, raised my chin, and walked away to find my father. Fuck Linx.

That was one of the last times I'd seen him before today, when he stepped up to me, touching me, out of the blue. Poof, there he was. It's like Linx appears from a mist into solid form. I don't know how he does it. He's not there one moment, the next he appears. Any event I'm at, he's always within a safe distance to get to me if needed and it makes me feel silly, because it makes me feel safe and important. There's never a time I can look up and not see him looking at me.

Because I'm just his job.

And you hate him.

Really tired of reminding myself of this.

Chapter 9 – Linx

Here I am gently shaking her awake before I get out of the truck while she drools on my seatbelt, "Trix, wake up sweetheart, we're home." I try to shake her lightly again. "Trixie, wakey wakey." She's out like a light.

I hop out of the truck and the interior light above shows me her raised crop top, under boob peeking out as she clings to her pillow, arms up by her head, sound asleep, leaning up against the truck door. I know she's been putting in some heavy-duty hours at the studio, but I wasn't aware she was this exhausted. She's actually snoring softly. Sounds like a purring kitten over there.

I walk around to her side and slowly open the door, shoving my hand in to catch her slumped form before she tumbles out onto the gravel driveway. I grab her pillow with my other hand, tossing it back over to the driver's side. Before I can even lay her back, she throws her arms around me and presses her tits to my face to mumble by my ear, 'Ok, Linxy' in her sleep, but it comes out as a soft purr.

My whole body feels like it's electrocuted. Dick instantly stiff. Fuck me, it's too much. This is how I die. Stick a fork in me.

I tuck her further down, so she doesn't rest her gorgeous titties on my cheeks, not that I would ever complain, but it gives me the ick to do it without her consent. My arms come to rest on her waist, on her sides…on her bare skin, and for one stolen moment, I let her sleep on me, I let her lush body press up against mine. I let her feel like mine. I relish the feel of her so near, finally in my arms. I know this isn't real, but my god, my body feels like it's on fire and my cock grows harder behind my zipper in no time at all. Fuck, to have my dream girl wrapped around me. My cock throbs to be released at the contact. The desire to claim her overwhelms me when I'm near her.

God, her perfume. It fills the humid air around us. She's worn the same cotton candy, sweet smelling perfume that I've never found on anyone else for years. It's her, uniquely her. It drives me wild every time it hits my nose. I started eating cotton candy because of her.

Every single fucking time I smell her and this damn perfume; my dick reacts and twitches. For years, fucking years, man.

Intrusive thoughts win. A desperate man's desire spurring me on, I lean down and smell her perfume directly off her silky-smooth neck and my knees damn near buckle with my groan. Why the fuck did I just do that? So many stolen moments right now that could get me gutted and hanged. But fucckk, I want so much more.

Trying my hardest to keep it together and not growl at her, I whisper by her ear, more like quietly plead, "Hey, Trixie, wake up, babe." I pull her off me and set her back in the seat, tapping her cheeks lightly, "Trixie," I croon at her.

"Linx," her breathy, sleepy voice sighs and my cock surges. Jesus fuck. This is my last week on Earth, I just know it, because if she doesn't kill me, her daddy sure as fuck will for touching her like this. I won't be able to stop if she ever gives me the green light. There will be no control if this woman ever submits to me.

It'll be the best day of my life.

"Yes, baby girl, wake up." I unbuckle her seat belt just in time for her to sleepily launch herself out of the truck, right into my surprised arms. She uses the truck's step side and the front of me to climb down to the ground, rubbing herself on the whole length of my body on the way down. Shirt sliding up further and further. Fuck, man.

Not my inner devil trying to act saintly and pray.

One hand gripping the door frame, white knuckling it for some semblance of control and the other splayed on her back as she slides.

Thank fuck she's much too sleepy to notice my rock hard cock pressing onto her. Me however, I'm woke as fuck right now with her luscious, curvy body sliding all over me.

Dreams really do come true. I'll take what I can get.

I take a deep breath, then another as her crop top rides up dangerously high, like over those gorgeous tits. I just know her nipples are pressed against the front of my shirt. *Eyes up, Linc.* Lucky ass shirt. There's nothing I want more right now than to sink into her hot little pussy, but I fucking took an oath. And she detests me, so there's that. I hiss out a deep breath as every ounce of willpower is tested.

From the motion light, I can tell her eyes aren't even open as she stands here with her head thrown back, face upturned, lips parted. Her beautiful, beautiful face, and lips right there, upturned and ripe for kissing.

I groan again.

"Where's my bag, I'll get it," she says in her perfectly sleepy sex kitten voice. Today has been absolute torture for me, I swear to god, I can't take much more.

"Trix." I put a little more umph into it and she seems to rouse more. "Trixie." A little more firmness.

Her eyes snap open and it takes her a few blinks to realize she's pressed up against me, more like splattered on my front really. She quickly snaps awake and shoves off my chest, taking a few steps back. My hand slides off her as her warmth leaves my body. Thank fuck her shirt drops down immediately.

"W-What's happening?" She wraps her arms around herself and shifts from one foot to the other.

"I helped you out of the truck and this is where you landed. I swear it, little bird, no funny business is going on."

My words take hold finally. Her eyes don't look so frightened or panicked now. I know she wakes up slowly, and she's usually disoriented in the mornings. She's a cup of coffee immediately kinda girl after fumbling into the kitchen, half alive moaning like a zombie. Ask me how I know.

"Let me help you into the house and into bed, then I'll come get our bags." I hold my hand out to her, "Come on, Trixie."

She doesn't hesitate when she places her hand in mine. That's when it settles in my chest, she actually trusts me.

I've watched her keep everyone except Pierre, Tally and Zharia, at arm's length, letting in very few to her personal life. She likes to read romance novels and draw, paint and spend her free time lying in her king-size bed or on the comfy couch in the living room watching murder documentaries. She also loves animal planet documentaries, and I love the smiles she gets watching them.

My Trix likes her quiet alone time. She loves listening to old rock or country and dancing around her apartment with the music loud...in damn near no clothing, might I add.

When I think it can't get any better, she likes making herself come, laying in the middle of her big, empty king-sized bed. I always wish I could see her face when she comes on her favorite pink vibrator.

Yet again, ask me how I know.

I pull my keys back out of my pocket when we get up the stairs to the small porch. When the door's unlocked I go in first and turn on the lamp by the front door. The room is bathed in a soft yellow glow, enough to make out the furniture and kitchenette.

Birdie comes in after me, her hair all over the place, my hand twitching to run my fingers through it and pull. Her eyes take in the place and then are directed right back at me, "Come on, I'll show you to your room."

Heading more into the camp house and turning to the right, I present two doors, one on either side of the small hallway. The rooms are furnished with beds and dressers. I'm giving her the king size bed, maybe she'll feel more at home in it.

I gesture into the room and turn the light on, "This will be your room." I walk over by the Jack-and-Jill bathroom that connects both our rooms and point, "This is our shared bathroom, I'll try my best not to walk in on you or leave the toilet seat up." I smile a little at the memory of her stunning body.

Walking back out into the hall, I point to the door right across from her room, "I'm in here. I'll go get our bags now." I turn and walk away from her before I try and push her up against the wall and I rut on her like a wild animal. Her being in my safe space is kicking up a primal reaction in me.

"I can help, Linx," she says as she follows me back into the living area.

I turn back to her, holding herself like she's cold. I see my mother was over here earlier and turned on the air conditioning. Or maybe it's just the stress of the day that has her holding herself.

Most likely Mom's stocked the fridge too. "I got it. Do me a favor, fix you something to eat. And if you find something in there for me, I won't turn it away," I smile at her and wink.

She smiles back and says, "I think I can do that."

God, she's so pretty when she smiles but I must remember I'm not here to think with my dick and the moment I allow her to distract me is the moment they find a weakness and strike.

Chapter 10 – Birdie

This is far from the picture I had in my head as a camp. This is like a full-on, nice two-bedroom home on stilts. The decorations are a little dated, but you can tell it's well taken care of, and people love this little home. And thank god, there's electricity and air conditioning.

I walk over into the little kitchen area and open the refrigerator. I'm surprised to see it full. Or am I? This is definitely something Linx could have somehow had done before we arrived. But he would have to trust someone enough not to give away our hiding spot. Now my curiosity is piqued; who does Linx trust that much?

He comes back into the front door and continues down the small hallway to our rooms, depositing bags. I see he's a bring-every-bag-in-one-trip kinda guy. If I had arms like that I probably would too. Not that I'm noticing the nice shape of his arms right now in my exhausted state.

"Where did all this food come from?" I turn to face him, nosiness getting the better of me.

"My mom."

His mother. I'm deep in his personal life now. Deeper than I care to admit. I didn't think his mother would be by. Oh god, am I going to meet her? Something tells me this time together is going to be much deeper than rooting through his medicine cabinet. I'm going to see the real Lincoln, what he is at heart.

I'm excited in my deranged sort of way. Best to know your enemy well.

Pulling out lunch meats and condiments, I set to making us a quick sandwich. He's done a lot today and the least I can do is make him something to eat. I don't mind honestly, even if it's that sexist cliché of a woman in the kitchen making a man a sandwich. I'll survive the blow to my feminism because gratitude took its place.

We sit at the table eating. His open briefcase full of guns is on the small four-seater eating table beside him. Of course, being the daughter of who I am, I'm used to seeing men with guns, with all the armed guards my dad had at home.

"Do you remember how to shoot a gun, Trix?" he asks then takes a bite.

"I do, but it's been many years since I've shot. You should know, you taught me. I own a gun but I'm kinda iffy on aim."

"It doesn't mean you retained the knowledge. As long as you aren't gun shy, I'll take you over to my cousin's gun range and practice with you this week."

"Linx, is there something you're not telling me?"

"I've told you everything I can."

I snort at him, shaking my head, "That's the most deflective answer, I swear."

I watch him look at me, examining me, testing himself. Just when I think it's useless to ask any more questions, he sits back and he makes up his mind to tell me, "You came very close to getting stolen tonight. Another few minutes and you would've been gone. I got to you just in time." He clears his throat. "Closer than I care to admit. Thank you for not putting up an even bigger fight than you did. I was out of time."

I've never heard him admit things like this. Mr. Danger is always so perfect. This could have all went to complete shit if I had stood there and made a scene. I gulp past the invisible vice grip crushing my throat, choking me. I realize now how urgent the situation was. Giant doses of reality suck.

LSS steals people and sells them, never hearing from those victims again. They're rumored to sell children to pedophiles as long as they pay the highest amount. They have no morals, no compassion. Just ruthless savagery. Human life means dollar signs to them.

If they were going to steal me, it wouldn't have been to give me a good life, not as their rival's daughter. Oh no, it would have been living hell. I would have had a world of hurt and pain in store for me, praying to whatever god to just let me die.

"I'm not supposed to tell you, but he was fifteen feet behind you and closing in." Linx stays staring into my eyes, into my soul, pleading with me to understand the severity of the circumstances. "They almost had you, Trix."

Chills run over my exposed arms and down my spine. My stomach clenches, thankfully I'm finished with my sandwich. I owe Linx so much.

Fully waking me up is the fact that someone was following me, and I had no clue. It turns my blood ice cold. My legs start shaking and thank fuck I'm already sitting down. There's no way I could stand up right now, I'm in shock. Fear courses through my veins, cold, jagged, stabbing fear.

"We aren't sure how they were going to do it. We were thinking there were others in the restaurant waiting. Shadow is reviewing the camera footage from outside and inside Evangelina's. So far, he has seen three other men casually standing around outside the restaurant that he's not sure were there to eat."

My restaurant, my favorite place to eat, has been tainted by their evil. Their ruthless pursuit of innocent women, earning them one of the most feared reputations across the south. It makes me sick.

When people go missing, you immediately think of Lone Star Saints.

"Linx," he looks up at me from his paper plate full of crumbs, "T-Thank you," emotions choking the sound out of me. I try really hard to suppress the shudder and tears, but my eyes well up anyway.

"Anytime, Trixie, anytime."

He makes the feeling of safety settle in my chest and for the first time in hours, I let myself relax. I'm safe. I know with him here with me, nothing is going to get to me. There's no one on the planet who can protect me better than Linx. He was born to be a soldier.

He's my soldier. My white knight, my shiny armor, my fierce protector. Goddamn it, I have to be nicer to him now. The first crack in my façade is happening, I can feel it. It's really hard to hate the man who's being nice to you, for once, and saves your life.

Leave it up to fate to fuck me over.

Rising to throw my plate away, I ask him, "Is it ok if I take a shower right now?" I feel the need to cry away from him.

"Of course. I'll stay out here. I've got to call your dad anyways." "Thank you. I won't be long." I hurry off before I break down in front of him.

After gathering my things and taking it all to the bathroom, I wash myself and my hair in the small square shower. It gets the job done, that's the most important thing, I reckon. Not sure how he's going to fit his manly frame in here.

My mind drifts to Linx. The way we've dodged each other for years to come together for this week, alone together. I'm so confused about the past few hours.

He's making it really fucking hard to continue hating him. Hate is strong, how about strongly dislike. I want to fight, goddamn I want to fight him, but the fight is being knocked out of me every time I learn how nice he is. I'm so confused about my feelings for him now. Why do I even want to fight anymore?

I was all prepared to remain neutral towards him this week, stay out of his space, and focus on my books or drawing. Now curiosity is going to kill the cat, so to say. I want inside his head.

Sure, there was always the extreme attraction to him, and fuck, maybe that's why I fought him so hard, maybe I couldn't admit I liked him. I don't fucking know anymore. The 'No Linx' area in my heart is losing some of its sharp edges.

I remember that twitterpated eighteen-year-old girl he first met. The girl that lost her heart to a tall, dark and beautiful stranger.

I allow my heart to think about a life with Linx, like a boyfriend, if I get over myself and my anger at him. What would he be like? What if my father would allow it? It's so easy to picture, which confuses me even more. How much do I really know about Linx? It's not like we've sat around having deep discussions about ourselves. So how the fuck does he know so much about me?

My father must have people watching me all the time and I don't even know it. That's the only explanation I can come up with. It's a little off-putting to think people have been following and watching my every move and I've been unaware. Perhaps it's because I've been used to it my whole life, but I had thought my dad backed off when I went to college, and now since I have my own place.

If anything, Linx spouting all the Birdie facts he knows shows me Linx knows me on a much deeper level than I realize and it's most likely my father's doing.

Drying off I look at myself in the mirror above the small vanity. I'm a colorful display of lines and shading, forming all my favorite things. My soul is written on my skin for all to see. Some of the best artists in the world have 'colored' on me.

I have a feeling I'm finally going to get to see where all that ink ends on Linx's body. If I get so lucky.

Stop thinking about him! It does no good.

Dad would never allow me to date one of his associates. I wouldn't get so far as going to the restaurant before my father called and told me to go home. I would show up to the movie theater to be turned away at the door by his other associates he sent to intercept.

I never thought bikers would be my thing, or my type, but some of the ones I saw last night. Damn. Hot. H-O-T. When did bikers become so fucking sexy?

Is it just his second in command I can't have? Or is it all of them? Not me sitting here wondering if they might be off limits for a fuck, not dating. I should ask dear ole daddy next time I talk to him.

But the one who gives me the strongest reaction and makes my skin prickle and burn is out in the living room of this small house we are to share for the week. That's the one who evokes the strongest reaction out of me. No other man has ever gotten under my skin this much.

I'm going to end up liking him, aren't I? I groan to myself.

Chapter 11 – Linx

"Yes, sir, safe."

Understandably, Rock is worried for his only offspring. Her safety is his top-notch priority right now. After losing his wife, his focus on Birdie's safety has doubled, tripled.

Sometimes I feel creepy watching her so much but then I remind myself it's for her own good. Her dad has enemies. And I'm obsessed.

I have enemies too; that's just another good reason she can't be with me.

"We've checked the camera footage from inside and outside Evangelina's. There were three of them we know for certain. We could tell by their body language and them communicating amongst themselves in earpieces. Bastards looked like they were talking to themselves. I've forwarded the videos to your encrypted cloud."

"Thank you, Rock. I'll look at them as soon as we get off the phone and I unpack the laptop."

"Do it first thing in the morning, son. She's safe for now, get some rest. I need you well rested. It's been a long day and I'm sure she's pestered you with questions you can't answer and plenty of attitude." His dark chuckle matches my dark mood. I'm glad he can find this humorous, but as far as he knows, she despises me. I think her hard shell is crumbling though.

"Yeah, she is." Much to my annoyance. I want to express how much danger she's truly in, but her dad and I agreed, it will just make her panic.

She doesn't need to know Grim has already taken bids on her on the black market.

Our informant came through an hour ago and said Grim's plans have changed. He says he's going to marry his enemy's most precious person, and then he's going to tie her down and let the highest bidders have an hour with her. He wants them to rape her until she bleeds, the informant says those are his exact words.

I want to strangle this motherfucker with my bare hands. Skin him alive and it still wouldn't be enough. No one talks of my baby girl like that. As much as I want to be out there hunting him down to kill him, I know my best place is here with her.

"Just keep stressing the seriousness of the matter without giving too much away that will cause her to flip the fuck out. Last thing we need is her freaking out and running from us," Rock says. "She's smart. She knows there's nowhere she can run that I won't come after her and find her."

"So, the tracker is in then?"

Of course, he thought I meant the tracker. *Watch yourself, LaFleur, lest you give yourself away.*

"Yes, it's in. Minimal fight." Sorta.

He laughs, "Something tells me it wasn't minimal, but I'll believe you. I know what a firecracker my daughter can be. By the way, I'll expect her call tomorrow bitching about you. If I didn't know better, I'd think all the time she spends complaining about you is a hobby of hers now." He laughs more at my expense.

She complains about me? What does she say?

"Like what?"

"Oh boy, you get under her skin and set her blood on fire faster than anything," he can't help but keep laughing. "She has asked me repeatedly not to have you come to functions where she's required to go. She told me if I didn't, she would move away. Like that's ever happening. Now, I know she isn't going to be quiet at this latest development, so I'll ask you to only keep her on a need-to-know basis and as far as I'm concerned, she don't need to know. I do wish you good luck, son. I'll talk to you later today." With that, he hangs up, his laughter still ringing in my head.

My little bird spends time complaining about me, but that means she's thinking about me, and that makes my blood thrum hot through my body. Another win for me! She notices, oh god, she's noticed every advance and every wink and smirk, and it really does penetrate her fake bravado she tries to show me.

My Trixie needs someone like me to grab her and show her who's in charge. Fuck the brat out of her. She silently begs me for it with every heated glance, every lip bite, every blush. At every event she side-eyes me, every glare shot my way, every time her chest rises sharply as my words caress over her skin. I see it in the widening of her eyes when I whisper sweet and sexy inappropriate comments to her.

I get to her.

A lot apparently.

She will never admit to it but now that I'm armed with even more confirmation she thinks of me; my own bravado surrounding me inside surges forward and I smile to myself wickedly. Oh, little bird. I could break her by the end of the week, that haughty, pissed off attitude she gives me will melt away under my touch. I would love nothing more than the thrill of the chase with her, but no matter how much her siren's song calls to me; her daddy is my boss and President, and she's off limits.

I never thought I'd grow up to find my wife only for her to be off-limits. It makes my chest ache.

I won't stop at one time, ten times or one night, I want her for the rest of my life. She's mine for eternity. I won't give her up to anyone. I'll step in before I allow another fuckshow like Noah near her again. I'ma greedy motherfucker when it comes to her.

Her dad sent me on a mission that was to last three months but ended up being five and a half. In the time I was gone, Birdie went and got herself a boyfriend. I had managed to run everyone off before him and he slipped in while my back was turned.

She met him right after I left and had been together the entire five months I'd been gone. Even moved him in with her. I was having none of that. If I can't have her, I don't want anyone else to either. She's mine.

I almost went out of my mind with jealousy. Pierre could barely stand me.

She's been mine since I saw the most beautiful woman at the barely legal age of eighteen looking up at me with the most stunning clear blue eyes. My twenty-eight-year-old heart tripped and fell. All while standing beside her daddy, who would never let me have his daughter, never in a million years. My heart shattered before she could even break it.

That's the moment Beatrix Chavanet became my obsession and sealed her fate. I've watched her grow into the most amazing woman, my dream woman, and I have fantasized every day what it would be like to have her truly be mine.

So, Pierre and I followed that shitcicle, who was supposed to be 'going out with the guys' to this Tulane frat party. We saw him pounding away at some little blond number, needless to say, his and Birdie's relationship didn't last much longer. Like an hour later.

Mainly because Pierre and I caught him walking home from the party and whipped his ass, but we didn't hurt pretty boy's face. He went right home with a few broken ribs and bruised torso to Birdie's apartment and packed a bag and left. He sent a friend for the rest of his shit two days later.

The fallout was me watching her heartbreak in the aftermath from afar, not being able to hold her, or wipe her tears away. Her hurt, hurt me too but not enough to have remorse for getting rid of him. Fuck that piece of shit.

She can do better. Fuck, she can do better than me, but I won't allow it. Since he left eight months ago, I've made sure she doesn't get another boyfriend. Not that she's been trying. She doesn't go out and when she does, I'm either in the background watching or my tails have eyes on her.

My little bird is always within reach of me one way or another and she can't fly fast enough to escape it.

A shuffle catches my attention as she comes out of her room. I wasn't ready to see her in a pair of skimpy shorts and a tank top, with one of those built in bra thingies, that is struggling to hold in her ample tits. Christ I can see her nipples.

Fuck, I'm going to die.

Her face is scrubbed and free of the make-up she always wears. This is the first time I've seen her up close with no make-up, not a lick of it on and I prefer it.

She's even more beautiful. Don't get me wrong, Birdie is stunning every day, but her freshly showered face is breathtaking. This is my favorite version. Wet hair hanging down her back, skin glowing, crystal clear blue diamond eyes watching me as she walks up to the table. She looks like my wet dreams.

"You're making it hard to hate you, ya know."

I drag my gaze up her voluptuous body to settle on her face as I rise, crowding into her space, "Good," I gruffly reply.

"Why's that good?" her forehead wrinkles as she frowns. "Because one day you're going to beg me to slip between those gorgeous thighs and make you feel good. I'd prefer it if you'd like me, even a little bit, when I sink into you."

Her breath hitches in her throat and her nipples harden under her shirt. I love getting to her. God, I love it so much.

"Good night, Trixie." I let my arm rub on hers as I slide by slowly. It's taking everything in me to walk away and shut this bedroom door on her.

For fuck's sake, this is going to be the most difficult week of my life, and I've done tours in the middle east and been in worse situations than this. Surviving Birdie will be the ultimate test.

Once I hear her go into her room, I take my shower. Bad idea. The entire bathroom now smells like her girly soaps and lotions. It's everything I can do to stop myself from roaring my frustration. I hate her dad right now.

My cock instantly hardens at the first smell of her. This fucking shower isn't big enough to turn around in let alone jack off in.

Doesn't stop me from doing it though.

I know how thin these walls are, and I know she'll hear and maybe I want her to. I need her to. She should know how much I want her.

I mean, I've never missed an opportunity to flirt with her.

I remember Thanksgiving was heartbreaking for me to watch her, and I didn't even try to mess with her. She was barely a month away from dipshit's abrupt departure in her life. She wasn't her usual vibrant, fiery self towards me, instead she was numb and indifferent to everything.

While she was alone on the back porch, I walked up to her as she stared out over the pool and the Grecian statues spotting the landscaped yard.

"He never deserved your attention."

She took a deep, shuddering breath before facing me, softly telling me, "I'm destined to be alone because there's something fundamentally wrong with me deep down, and the darkness will be my only friend until the day it suffocates me under the guise of love."

My heart cracked.

It's for her own good. That's the excuse that keeps me going. "I'm sorry, Trixie. However, I stand by my opinion. He never deserved you."

I left her there staring after me.

I did turn around before I went into the house and met her beautiful, sad eyes and said, "You look beautiful today, by the way." I meant every syllable. I gently closed the door and went back to the dining room with her dad.

It was the first time she spoke to me without her usual venom in fuck, I don't know how long. She didn't glare at me, and she showed me rare, raw emotion for once. I'm not one for kicking people when they're down. I merely wanted her to know I acknowledged the shift in her mood and why.

Her dad hated the guy, so he was his jolly good self about it for the entire dinner. Finally got rid of the pest that took up too much space in his daughter's life. I'm sure he would have given me the assignment to get rid of him eventually, but I couldn't wait that long. I took matters into my own hands.

Noah is alive because Pierre wouldn't let me kill him with my bare hands.

Speaking of those hands, they're currently trying to strangle my cock with her shampoo as lube. All I have to do is remember her smiling face, or one of her feisty glares, or the newest, greatest thing, her standing in the middle of her bedroom gloriously naked.

That's what does it, I grunt and hiss through my teeth when cum erupts from my dick to slide down the shower wall. I just lay my forehead on the smooth wall and catch my breath.

Sweet dreams, baby bird.

Chapter 12 – Linx

As soon as I open my eyes, my gaze sees through my open doorway, into her room, where she has her door wide open. She's facing away from me, on her side, with her leg bent up outside the covers, and her hiked up shorts revealing the curves of her half naked ass.

Christ, not as if I'm not already rock hard waking up anyways, I gotta deal with this vision. What a good fucking sight to wake up to though. Filed it away in my spank bank.

I swallow thickly and lay here looking at her like a creeper until I groan to myself and I roll over to my back, looking up at the ceiling.

What's your life come to, Lincoln?

Pining after the one thing I want most but never touching. My life is pure torture.

Might as well start this torment and get up.

This is a hostile work environment until that little brat has her coffee.

Once my teeth are brushed and I'm cleaned up, I wander into the kitchen with only my pajama pants hanging off my hips. I don't even care how ratty and thin my pajama pants are. They're my favorite and I happen to know they make my package look big.

I'm sipping on my coffee at the stove, cooking us eggs and bacon when I feel her at my back, her eyes burning a trail across my skin. *Yes, baby bird, look your fill.*

I'm nothing like her scrawny ex-boyfriend whom I ran off. I'm built like a tank with a broad chest and shoulders, a muscular back that tapers into trim hips and flares to muscular legs. I spend my spare time in a gym making sure I'm in tip top shape to protect her.

I know exactly what I look like to women. I'm their wet dreams. "You don't have to stand there and stare, sweetness, you can come touch me." I twist around and look at her with a grin.

Her sleepy bedroom eyes are in full fuck me mode right now. Fuuck. Her hair is up in her satin sleeping bonnet and she looks adorable with that big bow on top of her head.

"Jesus, Linx, why don't you have any clothes on?" she says while running her hands down her face. Glad to see I affect her.

I turn fully around so she can get the complete devastating effect. I want her to work hard at hating me.

I sip my coffee over the rim of my cup while watching her practically cream her shorts right here, right now in this small kitchen. When I lower my cup I retort, "I could say the same thing about your barely there ensemble, little bird."

"I have shorts and a tank top on." She gestures wildly up and down herself with her hands.

"Oh please, I can see the whole bottom half of your ass cheeks jiggle when you walk, and your nipples are hard as fuck standing there looking your fill of me finally. Do you like what you see, Princess?" I cock my eyebrow at her.

Her mouth snaps shut, and her eyes bug out. How dare I call her out like this, I smirk to the point I almost giggle. This may not be my first time seeing her half nude, but this is the first time she's seen me this undressed. Them there nipples are the perfect indication she likes what she sees, a lot.

"I can't do this with you so early in the fucking morning." She sighs, "I'll be mad about it later. Right now, I need coffee, nipples be damned." She moves beside me, closer than I thought she would get to me. She almost drops the coffee mug, that's how flustered she is.

I chuckle deep in my chest, "I like your nipples though."

"Stop Linx. Just stop. I can't even think straight right now at this ungodly hour, the last thing I need is you in my head," she says while stirring in her favorite creamer that I had my mom pick up. "You realize it's eight in the morning, right? It's not five AM when I'm usually waking up. This is like a vacation for me too. I got to sleep in for the first time in years."

I reach across to the cabinet above her and pull down the Ghirardelli chocolate sauce and quietly place it beside her coffee mug. She just gives me a bleary stare, shrugs to herself while shaking her head, then proceeds to put the chocolate in her cup, stirring it in.

She pulls the steaming mug up to her lips and as soon as the sugary drink hits her tongue, she moans so low and so long my dick wakes up and jerks. That fucking moan, it runs a shiver over my skin. How much I'd love to hear more moans like that.

She makes her way over to the table and sits facing me in the kitchen area. "Soo, Linxy, what's the grand plan for today?"

I thought it was too early in the morning for bullshit? Linxy. Hmph.

"Well, you can have your pick. You can either go swimming or go for a ride."

Her eyes pop open, "A ride?" she breathes.

Cocking an eyebrow at her in question, "Yes, a ride."

"What kind of ride?" Instantly suspicious.

"A bike ride, with me, on my motorcycle."

"Your bike is here?"

"I have one at my mom's house. I think I'd like to go for a ride to clear my head and would like if you went with me."

"I've never been on a bike before," she rushes out much to my astonishment.

"What do you mean, never?"

"I've sat on bikes, but I was never allowed to ride on one, not even with my dad. It's too dangerous. I've always wanted to know if it feels as free as I imagine it to be. Is it like flying?"

My lips curl up, "I'll be happy to pop your riding cherry, Trixie."

"Ugh. I can't do sexual innuendos with you at," she looks at her smart watch and wrinkles her nose, "8:24 in the morning."

"Let me just have one more- I can't wait to feel your legs wrapped around me."

"Ugh. Alright dammit! I change my mind; I want the swim, take me swimming." She rolls her eyes while taking a sip of her sweet concoction.

"Ohh, a bikini then. I'm down with that too, just so you know." I wink at her while I plate our food.

I slide her plate in front of her and head to the fridge. "While you're in there, can you get—"

I place the ketchup in front of her without a word and turn back around to get my cottage cheese. "Do you want some?" I ask her. "No thank you, I'm not a big breakfast person."

No matter how much I wanted to say yes, I know, I refrained. I know she prefers bagels and English muffins and all other sorts of carby goodness. This is why today she's starting off with a real breakfast of bacon and eggs around me.

"We'll leave in an hour, ok?"

She nods with her mouth full. She looks so cute eating the food I prepared for her. She's much more at ease when she's sleepy.

"I will meet your mom?" she quietly questions.

"Yes."

"Isn't that too personal for you?"

"No, why would it be?"

"Cause you know, it's your mother. Men usually only bring home women to dear old Mom if they're serious about them. You shouldn't get her hopes up."

I stop chewing and look at her, "Who says I'm not serious?" Birdie cocks her head and looks at me like I've gone nuts, "Because I'm your job, Linx, I'm not the girl you're going to marry." She couldn't have kicked me in the stomach harder. Does she really think that's all she is to me?

I grind my molars together at her words. She has no idea how much I hate my assignment right now, since it's preventing me from finally making her mine.

I run my hand over my face and groan. When I open my eyes and look at her, she's staring wide eyed at me, a horrified look on her face.

"Lincoln," she breathes out with her hands up by her mouth, "I never thought to ask, are you secretly married? Am I pulling you away from a girlfriend?" She pulls her hands up to her chest.

Oh, how I want to tell her yes to see her jealousy, but I opt for honesty. "No, I don't have anyone."

Her eyebrows raise, "And why not?" She gulps and says, "Oh god, I'm sorry, that was really personal, you don't have to answer." Sitting back in my chair, I let my eyes roam over her. She's absolutely beautiful first thing in the morning. I've wished so many times to sit and have breakfast with her after spending the night together. I didn't see it being like this, but I'll take it. "Because the only woman I've ever wanted to bring home to momma, doesn't like me back and I don't want anyone else. One hour, Trix." I rise to throw away my paper plate and go dig through bags for riding gear.

Chapter 13 – Birdie

 Goddamn, it's hot already and I'm starting to sweat in these riding pants that Linx left on my bed while I got ready in the bathroom. I have my boots on, the pants, and a tight spandex tank top showing way too much of my oversized cleavage for my liking. Of course, he picked these out and of course, they happen to be my size, fitting perfectly. My hair is down for now, but I plan to pull it aside and braid it once we get to his mom's. I hate my hair up in ponytails.

 Linx grabs the door handle and just walks right into his mom's house like he owns it. Actually, I don't know if that may be true. I know Linx is a very rich man, and he strikes me as the kind of guy who'd buy his momma a house. It doesn't matter to me either way.

 "Bonjour, maman!"

 A female voice in the back of the house yells back, "Ici!"

I follow him to a beautiful white and marble kitchen done in tasteful farmhouse decor. He walks over to wrap his mom up in his arms. He softly says, "Tu m'as manqué."

Huh, Linx knows French. Color me impressed. I mean, he's a Cajun man from the bayou after all, complete with a sexy accent, why wouldn't he speak French when most the people in this area do?

He releases and turns to me, holding out his arm to me, "Momma, this is Birdie, Rock's daughter."

I see where Linx gets his gorgeous eyes from. She smiles at me from her tan face with hardly any wrinkles, "Bonjour, honey, it's so good to finally meet you. I've heard so many good things about you." She holds out her tiny hand while I cock an eyebrow at Linx. She's slightly shorter than my five foot eight, and she looks like a small hobbit next to her hulking six-three son.

A takeaway from this conversation is he's been talking to his momma about me.

I take her hand in mine and with a big southern smile and say, "It's a pleasure to meet you, ma'am. Thank you for my coffee creamer and chocolate syrup."

Her eyes twinkle back at mine, "You're welcome, honey, but please call me Collette." She has such a warm smile. Nodding, I pull my hand back and clasp them in front of me while I stand here in this brand new, personal experience trying to figure out what to do. As an introvert, I hate social situations and meeting new people, but this is his momma we are talking about, and I try to simmer down and relax.

However, this is my very first meet-the-parents. I didn't even meet Noah's because they lived out of state. Any boyfriend I've had, or just a person I went on a few dates with, was never serious enough to get to that step. My dating game is non-existent and I'm just not putting myself out there, much to Pierre, Tally and Zharia's dismay, so I never had to prepare to meet the parents.

At this point, I think my eggs are drying up and I'm never going to find a husband.

"I'm going to take Trixie on a ride through the bayou; I came to get Sampson."

"You know where he is."

He turns to me with a blinding smile, and it lights up his face with boyish happiness. I can't help it, it's contagious, I smile back. He says, "I'll go get him ready, meet me outside in a few minutes, ok?"

I nod at him and wonder how long I should wait. It's not like I know how any of this works. I mean, I'm not stupid, I can figure it out from watching tv. I'm rambling in my head while his mom stands here watching me with a knowing smile.

After a few moments of standing here awkwardly while she looks me over and I braid my hair, I face Collette and ask, "Does he come home often?"

I feel like an idiot because I don't know much about him.

"He comes home about once a month and stays at the camp. Sometimes he comes with his brother, or his best friend, other times, it's just him. He loves to ride his bike through the bayou and eat his momma's gumbo."

"Oh, I guess I didn't realize he had a brother."

"Well, stepbrother actually, but they became the best of friends when Bret and I eloped. Brotherhood at first sight you could say."

"Does he bring all his girls here to ride bikes?"

"No ma'am, you're the first and only." This takes me by surprise. I would have thought for sure Linx would have women beating down the door.

Linx pokes his head in the back door at that moment, "Ready Trix?"

"Yeah." I turn to his mother, "Thank you, for everything."

"Shh, sha, anytime." She jerks her thumb towards the door, "Now go have some fun with my boy, yeah."

That hunk of a man is far from a boy, but I don't remind her. I walk to the back door where Linx is waiting on me, excitedly bouncing, "Come on."

The bike is beautiful. A Harley-Davidson Street Glide, painted in the perfect shade of pearl white with gold pin-stripping.

White leather saddlebags grace the sides, and the shiny chrome is everywhere. There are glitter flecks in the paint job that catches the eye and sparkles in the sunlight and I fucking love it.

Looking closer, between his legs, on the gas tank, "Is that one of my drawings?"

It's a crow, not just any crow either. This one is proud to wear a sparkly crown and show off her pretty bluish-purple feathers. It sits on a wreath of pastel flowers and says, 'Come home, little birdie.' It's shocking as it's not something a big, burly biker would get on their bike.

My heart is racing in my chest. Where did he get this from? Am I the birdie to him?

"Yes. I got it off your Instagram page. I loved it at first sight."

He has my art on his bike. He loves my art. It's even in his home. *Birdie, you have got to stop letting this man get to you, we hate him, remember?*

Oh, shut up.

It's getting harder and harder to hate him. Who knew under that hot/cold, badass exterior that Linx was a good guy. This other side of him is really intriguing.

"Hop on the back, Trixie." He's rolled his bike out to the driveway, kickstand down and is tying on a baby blue bandana over his hair, straddling the metal beast.

I stand here like a dummy as his mom looks on from the garage. I'm sure she's confused why I haven't moved.

He turns to look back at me, "What's wrong?"

Honesty is best with Linx, if not, he'll badger me until he gets to the root of it.

"I'm excited, but I'm scared."

He hops off the motorcycle and steps in front of me, flipping his riding shades up on his forehead. He puts his hands on my upper arms, looks down at me with his gorgeous tri-colored eyes and says, "I've never wrecked a bike. I'm a good driver and don't take unnecessary risks. I even have a helmet for you to wear. I would never intentionally hurt you.”

I look up at his eyes, they remind me of a sunburst of fall colors. They speak to me sincerely and truthfully. He wouldn't lie to me about this. Then and there I decide that I could either chicken out or get on the damn bike with the only man I trust and have the ride I've always dreamed of.

“I know,” I say softly, “but I don't know how to ride with you. I don't even know how to get on.”

“I've got you, little bird. Let's go over a few basic things.” He walks me closer to the bike, “Don't touch this pipe right here, keep your feet on the pedals, lean with me not against me on curves and turns, and try not to fidget or make any sudden movements. Climb on behind me, putting your foot here and swing over your leg, using my shoulders if you have to.” Then he gets a really big grin, “My favorite part, wrap your thighs around me and put your arms around my waist, and hang on.” The heat of his eyes are scorching on my skin.

Just so we are on the same page, Linx never misses an opportunity to say something sexual to me. It's like the man can't help it. It's a hobby of his he's trying to master. I wonder if it's the same kind of shit he tells all the other women.

“What can I say, I don't know if my thighs can spread that wide to accommodate your huge ass and even bigger ego.” I smirk at him.

He barks out laughter and so does his mother. Their laughter floods the space around us, echoing in the garage. “She's got you right there, mon cœur.”

“Come on, little birdie, I'm going to teach you how to fly,” he promises. Twin flames watch my heady reaction, and I melt under his gaze. I tap my fingers against each other and excitedly rise up on the balls of my feet.

He ushers me over to the bike and hands me the helmet. He helps me fastens it and before he flips down the visor, he says, “This has a Bluetooth communication system in it. I'll be able to talk to you while we ride, and you can talk to me. Any time you need to get down to walk or use the bathroom, let me know." He flips the visor down and puts on his own helmet.

Collette calls over to me, "Cher, did you put on sunblock?"

In fact, I did not. It completely slipped my mind. I shake my head at her because I don't know if she can hear me through the helmet.

"One second, mon cœur, let me fix your girl up before she burns alive." Before I can correct her, she disappears back into the house. Wait, she thinks I'm with her son? Does she not understand who I am and what's happening? Has he told her I'm not allowed to date him? Does she know I don't even like her son? That tidbit probably slipped his mind when he was talking about me oh so much.

Through his helmet, he pins me with a molten stare that makes my pussy quiver with need. But it's him.

I inhale a ragged breath. Also, I'm not sure how I feel about being all up on Linx like this. Riding with my pussy plastered to his ass is a little too intimate and personal. I didn't even consider that until I was standing here trying to figure out logistically how to get on the bike.

I didn't want to look like a fucking idiot in front of them. Flipping my visor up as Collette comes back, she has me turn around when she reaches me. His mom slathers sunblock all down my arms and on top of my shoulders, then hands me the sunblock, "Depending on how long y'all are out there, you'll need to reapply in a few hours."

"Thank you, Collette, I really appreciate it." Linx takes the lotion and puts it in a saddlebag for later.

"Now go have fun!" she says and steps back from the bike with a smile on her face and blows a kiss on a wave.

I get on the back of the bike exactly how Linx showed me, and I settle in behind him. Even through the helmet, and over the coconut smell of the sunblock, I can still smell him, and it makes my body tingle. My pussy settles right up next to him too and I inwardly moan softly at how good it feels. Yep, I should have gotten laid within the past eight months before leading up to this. If I find my enemy enticing, I must be desperate.

"Can you hear me, Trix?" Linx's smooth voice sounds in my head.

"Yep," I reply. Realizing he just heard me moan as I slid my crotch right up to his ass.

"Good. I'm going to turn on my music, remember let me know if you want off."

"Je t'aime, Lincoln! Be careful with your toot toot!" His mother calls.

"Je t'aime, momma."

Toot toot?

He starts up the bike and it's a loud rumble that fills up the neighborhood and reverberates off the other houses. It makes me smile. There are vibrations slithering up my body, causing my nipples to harden and my vagina to clench. Oh, damn! Just turning the beast on feels good. The sensation makes my ole girl clench down there. God, I hope he can't feel that through his jeans.

His low chuckle makes me suspicious he heard.

But damn, oh, I likey these vibrations. It's like using a whole-body vibrator. It's arousing. It's stimulating. It's amazing. No wonder so many women like bikers. I see the allure now; they're in it for the bike rides. I see your sly smiles, girls. I love when I get to be part of an inside secret.

He waves one last time to his mom and we are tooling down the driveway. I throw a hand up and wave to her as he gets on the street and hits the gas. I quickly lurch forward and wrap my arms around him for dear life right before we speed off. Jesus, I can't get my arms all the way around him. There's just too much of him. I think I have my hands spread on his man boobs. *Get it together, girl.*

I feel his chest rumble as he laughs. He covers one of my hands and moves it down to his stomach. I move my other hand down and can finally clasp my hands together and I immediately feel safer.

He does not remove his hand off mine and I have to admit, I like it there.

Although, I have always wondered what he felt like under all those clothes; feeling it is sliding me into another dimension. Today started off with seeing, now we're on to feeling. Later tonight can we be on to tasting?

Your mind is straight gutter trash.

I've never been one to be a daredevil and this might be the most thrilling thing I've done yet, but I'm willing to throw aside my fear and anxiety to try it. Throw caution to the wind. Literally.

Also, facing the conflicting feelings about me willingly and easily wrapping myself around the man I find most annoying, so that I don't fall off this monster and die. Can't forget the old-new feelings about liking him instead of killing him.

If I fuck him to satisfy my sick curiosity, does my dad have to find out?

Linx taps his big hand over my clasped hands on his stomach, and I feel his chest rumble as he chuckles low.

"What's so funny?" I ask.

"You."

"What did I do?"

"Nothing, Princess, you're safe. Just sit back and enjoy the ride."

After riding for about twenty minutes, I loosened up my grip. Every turn or curve he puts his big hand on my thigh and keeps me steady. Part of me thinks he's doing it just to touch me. They aren't accidental like Tally predicted. These are very intentional touches. The other part of me has no idea if these are normal actions for motorcycling riding. I'm not going to complain because I like the attention.

For a girl who was her daddy's pride and joy, I grew up lacking attention from my parents and I and my therapist believe that led me to a self-destructive path in my early twenties in college and leads me to dating awful guys who are no good for me.

I don't think there's ever going to be a man who loves all the broken, dark pieces of me that are scattered everywhere in my soul. I suffer from depression and take medicine for it. I doubt Linx knows that. But sometimes I'm not a nice person, and sometimes I'm just sad for no reason.

I get in these scary moods, for days, where I become a sad little bundle of darkness and don't want to eat or be social. My thoughts are horrendous and sometimes I feel like hurting myself. I drown myself in work and music. After two or three days, I'm back to normal. Happens every few months since I was a teenager.

"So, you speak French?" I ask him after a while.

"Yeah, don't you?"

"Not as good as you apparently. I took it in high school and barely got through it."

"My family speaks it, sometimes slipping into a more Cajun French, which is harder to decipher unless you know basic French."

"What's a toot toot?"

He laughs and hesitates, "Google that shit. It's a girl, in this case." He gives no other explanation. I remind myself to look that up when we get back. Looks like I'll be googling a lot of things he might say.

"I think it's really nice you told your mom 'I love you' before we left. I'm glad you're secure in that, not like most dudes. Almost like you're human."

"My momma is my world. She raised me as a single mom, working hard and making sure I had everything I needed. In turn, I make sure my mom is well taken care of now."

"That's sweet. I really mean that."

"I made my first million at thirty after working two years for your dad. He paid me handsomely and I invested everything I could. At thirty-two I started Legacy Security, where we provided bodyguards to the rich and we install security systems at corporate offices and anywhere else really. Then there's the technology I've invented for security purposes. I used to do technical warfare and IT communications in the Army, and I used my skills for developing better, more advanced instruments for surveillance and security that the Army and your dad uses now." "I had no idea Linx. Congratulations to you. That's some accomplishment." That's pretty cool actually. Brains and brawn. "Thanks. It was just me fooling around with things. What about you? Did you always want to be an artist? Why tattooing?"

As I sit back and let the air tickle my skin, we roar down the road surrounded by water. I relax and begin to open up to him, "Well, I always wanted to be an artist in some capacity. I used to draw on everything. Napkins when I would go out to dinner with my parents, any scrap paper I found lying around, some walls much to my mother's dismay," I chuckle at the memory, "Then she bought me a sketch book, so that put a stop to the doodles on shit." I remember her shoving that first book at me.

I continue, "I love tattooing because people can get a permanent piece of my art. They can proudly display it and know it's a one-of-a-kind piece we cooked up together. I'm a color specialist in realism and I couldn't imagine me doing anything else but what I do."

"Your work is beautiful, Trix, maybe you can tattoo me while we're here."

I hesitate, "I'm not really a good black and gray artist." I had noticed that's mainly what's on his body, his obnoxiously fit and muscular body is truly a work of art. His black and gray tattoos are perfection. *Stop drooling over this fool.*

"Then make my world colorful and fill in some of these blank spaces, I'd be honored."

I smile to myself, "Ok, I can do that." I involuntarily clench my thighs and dammit, I know he felt that because he reaches back and puts his glove covered hand on the outside of my thigh.

We ride in silence at times, occasionally he would point out things and give me a story of his youth. We played twenty questions. I explained some things he saw in our house growing up, example, the relationship I had with my mother. After a few hours I asked to stop and use the restroom and get something to drink.

He pulls into a mom-and-pop diner—my favorite kinds of places. I love the atmosphere of these little dives. They make you feel at home and their food ends up being amazing. I hope they have cherry pie inside.

Anywhere I go to eat, I always look at the dessert menu first. It's the most important part of the meal.

Once we're seated and our order taken, he looks at me across the table from him. He's got a sexy, lazy grin and the heat in his eyes makes my stomach flutter.

Jesus-tap-dancing-Christ. This is getting ridiculous.

"Yes, Linx?" I barely contain my own grin.

He leans his elbows on the table and speaks to me in his delicious gravelly tone, "Tell me how horny it made you to have that machine under you, vibrating your body and the thrill of flying through the air."

I lean forward with my own wicked smile, eyes alight. Close to his face, I whisper, "I'll never tell you."

He leans back and laughs, clapping his hands. I don't recall ever seeing Linx laugh so much as I have today. He's so at ease and not his usual uptight, dickish self. It's a nice change. Real nice.

"Fair enough, but one day, it might sneak up on you and the orgasm will steal your breath." This fucker has the audacity to wink at me after a remark like that. "Or so I hear." Oh yeah, I bet he's heard.

"If that happens it just might be the best lay I'll ever have because it doesn't involve a man but a mighty, fierce, rumbling metal beast." I end with a pretty smile and some dancing eyes. His smile falters and I see the muscle work in his jaw as he clenches. I love when my words affect him, and he has to hold back. Ohh, I know he wants to fire off more of his sexual bullshit and I've decided to spar right back with him. I feel a little feisty today and I love pushing his buttons.

"Tell me, how many girls have you taken on day trips on your
bikes."

"Why, are you jealous?"

"No, I was just curious."

"You're the first girl on any of my bikes, besides my mother."

"I think you're lying to me," I hedge him.

"Believe what you want, but my mom has been the only woman
on my bikes. Every year for Mother's Day she asks for me to take
her on a spin through the neighborhood. I, being the perfect son
that I am, oblige her request. She loves to piss off her HOA."

I mull this interesting information around in my head. This is a
completely different Linx than I know, or more like barely know,
but I'm starting to like it.

Son of a biscuit. It's starting to happen.

His phone rings and he looks up from the screen to tell me, "I'll
be right back, it's your dad." He gets up and walks out to the
parking lot, walking in a back-and-forth line while talking with his
hands.

I look over at the servers behind the counter and their eyes are
glued to Linx. He cuts a mouth-watering picture with his fitted
white t-shirt and snug blue jeans and riding boots. I get a spark of
jealousy in my chest, and it surprises me. He's not mine and I
don't know where that feeling came from. Let them look all they
want. He is some pretty tasty eye candy, after all.

Checking my phone, I see I have a few missed texts from Zharia
and Pierre. I answer Zharia first.

ZBaddie: Are you still alive or in a sex coma? Plz say sex coma.
That man is fine as fuck. You'd be a bird brain not to fuck him.

ZBaddie: I'm hilarious

I roll my eyes. She is the cheesiest, Dad-joke loving woman I
know. Punchlines are not her strong suite. All that brain and she
has the comedic personality of a clam.

Me: No sex coma. We're out riding on his bike today thru the bayou.

ZBaddie: God, how romantic

ZBaddie: You can't tell me this isn't making you wet. This is straight up fantasy shit right here, Bea, and you're one lucky bitch. Recognize!

Me: I decline to comment.

ZBaddie: I knew it!!! <licking face emoji><eggplant emoji><Cat emoji>

Me: You're awful. I can't believe I put up with your horny ass. It's bad enough I have him slinging sexual innuendos every chance he gets….

ZBaddie: I'm telling ya girl, that will be the ride of a lifetime and Big Daddy doesn't need to find out. Get some girl! Danger looks like he could make you come seven different ways and that still wouldn't be enough for him. He's got pleasure dom vibes for sure. Fuck him for research purposes, beautiful lololol

ZBaddie: seriously tho B, if you don't want him after this week, you need to turn him loose. He's so in love with you it's unfathomable how your dad hasn't picked up on it already. Or you too for that matter. Literally everyone can see it, from far away even. Danger is yours and he has been since you met him that day we moved. He's just waiting for you. Either claim him or let him down gently.

Gulp.
Shit.
Double shit.

Me: Understood

I don't want to let him go just yet. I'm curious now and want to know him. I'm still a little leery and peeved at him but still curious.

She has a good point about fucking him, but that means I have to like him to let him put his cock inside of me and I don't know if

I'm there yet. Today's been nice, but not nice enough that I drop the attitude right alongside my panties. There's a lot of abrasive history there. It's starting to seem like it's only one-sided though. Once again, I'm the problem.

He thrives on goading me and trying to piss me off. Has this been his way of flirting the entire time? O.M.G. Is being an asshole his love language? Like an elementary boy picking on the girl he likes at recess? That's ridiculous.

Do guys really do that shit?

If I didn't know better, I'd say he's just trying to get into the boss's daughter's pants. I can't let that happen.

But for research purposes, I want to know what it'd be like. He's the kind of guy that makes a woman want to worship cock and become dickmatized, and I'm not ready to be that woman. I want to be that woman, but I don't know if I'm brave enough.

Over the years there have been rumors that have made their way to me. I've seen pictures online of him at other events my father goes to without me and Linx isn't pictured with other women too much. I thought all bikers were dirty womanizers but if Linx is, he's hiding it well. He looks very respectable with all the women he's photographed with, and I wonder if he sleeps with them all.

You don't care.

But I feel like I do.

He's always at my father's beck and call, and I doubt he has time to date. It seems like every time I go over to my dad's, Linx is there. He's always in the background, silently judging me or winking at me with a sultry smile just to put me on edge.

I snap a quick pic of Linx next to his bike and hastily send it to Zharia to put in her spank bank. Sometimes I think she's obsessed with my nonexistent relationship with Linx. God forbid I take her to a function with me, and she does not spend part of the evening raving on about #TeamLinx and whispering stupid shit in my ear.

Zharia's always my plus one, and I'm hers, and I wouldn't be surprised if society thought we were lesbian lovers. I bet that rumors out there somewhere. If they only knew, Tally is the lesbian of the Fab Four, not us.

I don't give a shit. I've never cared about my reputation in the high society scene that my parents frequent and tried to push me in. No thanks. Now, as an artist, I give a shit. A big shit.

I care about the people I tattoo, and I hope they know they can trust me. I've worked diligently for years to establish myself and learn all the evolving techniques I can. I've spent hours practicing, even now, I still practice on pig skin and synthetic skin. It's important to me to stay up to date with modern techniques.

I believe the mix between old school and modern is what makes a lot of artists stand out among their peers. I enjoy a fine line and a big splash of color. I'm known for vibrant pieces that pop.

I switch over to Pierre's text. I smile super big as I change his contact's name. In case anyone ever ninja peeks at my phone.

BigDickEnergy: Yo, B, how're you doin?
Me: I'm still alive

I set my phone down and wait for either of my friends to respond while I look out the window at Linx. I must look like a swooning schoolgirl with my head resting in the palm of my propped hand. "Please don't take this the wrong way, but the girls and I think you're one lucky lady."

I startle and turn to look at the older server I'd seen behind the counter. Her interruption to my musings is welcome. I didn't like the direction my thoughts were going.

"Is that so?" I smile kindly at her. I know she meant no offense; I take none.

"He comes in here once or twice a month and he's always alone. I'm happy to see him bring in someone that makes him smile like that."

Linx hangs up his phone and starts heading back into the diner. She says, "I just wanted to say that. I'll have your food out in a jiffy, honey."

"I took no offense. Thank you." There's no reason I should take offense, he's not mine. Women can look all they want. He's a fine specimen after all, he's worth looking at.

God knows I spent the better part of the past ten years rubbing one out to him every chance I could. Until he became a dick to me. Well, even afterwards because I'm a glutton for punishment. Then I just pictured him with duct tape over his mouth. Sucking on tatas be damned.

He scoots into the booth, and I ask, "Is everything ok?"

"Yeah, Princess, it's all good. We still can't go back though."

I nod my head and look down at the chipped Formica table. A jukebox plays tunes in the background and the sound of a busy kitchen pours out into the general dining area.

"Hey beautiful, don't look so sad that you're stuck with me some more."

I blink up at him, "It's not that." I look out into the parking lot, past to the expansive flat land. *You will not cry!!* I look back at him, "There's worse people I could be stuck with, I suppose," I say as I give him a weak smile through my unshed tears, because it's true. I know truly deep down, Linx is a good guy. He may kill people and torture them for my father, but he's solid.

"Then what is it? Anything I can fix?"

How much truth to say to him is too much? I can't be like *'I'm conflicted inside because you're turning out to be a really nice guy that I could see myself with, but I want to hate you because you've been an annoying dick to me.'* Definitely can't say *'I'd like to ride your cock like a bull and hang on for dear life.'*

This is insane. This is Linx.

You don't have to love 'em to fuck 'em.

SIT the FUCK *down vagina!*

If I said some shit like that right now, even playing around, knowing him he'd bend me over this table and rip my pants down, right here, slamming dick into me as the plates crash to the floor. Not a fuck given.

The more I get to know him and I'm around him; I'm finding it hard to remember why I hated him so badly. I can see myself hanging out with a guy like Linx and that terrifies me.

"You're not what I thought you were." I rest my hands in my lap so I can pick at my cuticles in peace.

This surprises him, as it should. I bet he didn't expect me to say that.

Linx puts one hand to his chest in a mock heart attack, "It's the big one! Is Trixie changing her mind about hating me?"

He makes me giggle and roll my eyes at his silliness, "You're so dramatic, I swear." There he goes, making me smile again.

"I knew once you got to know me, you'd fall in love. I'm that good of a catch. You should be happy I'm on your leash." His eyebrows wag at me while he puts his tongue out and pants like a dog at me. "Jesus, does your ego know no bounds, man?"

He laughs at that. "No, it sure doesn't, not where you're concerned."

Just then the server brings out food and we begin to eat in silence. It's not an uncomfortable silence, thank fuck. It feels natural, that's more than I can say for our other interactions this year. This isn't good, but before I can say anything he speaks.

He stops chewing about halfway through his bite. "It's my turn to ask the personal question now."

My eyes pop up to him. I sit back in the booth and grab my sweet tea. "Ok, shoot."

"Why aren't you out trying to date? Are you even looking for a boyfriend?"

I swallow the giant pill of reality he just shoved down my throat. I'm not even sure what to say to this.

"Uhh. Well. I don't know." I cock my head at him with a blank look, "Honestly, I don't think I'm pretty enough and I-I don't know, I think I'm unlovable."

That's a hard truth for me and I've never uttered those words out loud. I'm not even sure why I said them to him of all people.

He scoffs at me and sits back abruptly. "Are you fucking kidding me right now?"

I frantically look around the near empty restaurant and put my hand up to him and whisper-yell, "Shh, you're so loud."

He leans in on his forearms and whisper-yells right back at me, "Are you fucking kidding? What's there not to love? Trixie, I gotta tell ya, you are seriously flawed on your perception of yourself." He shakes his head in bewilderment.

"Oh yeah, then why can't I find someone? Where's all the good guys who don't mind a passive aggressive, sarcastic, introverted girl that spends her free time reading or drawing or slinging ink on strangers? The ones who will tell me I'm pretty, rub my back with no expectations, and make me feel like an actual princess." I shake my head some more, "Those guys don't exist, Linx."

He's still shaking his head, and he looks like he's getting annoyed. Matter of fact, he's getting madder by the second and each word that I speak. His face is a lovely shade of red.

"And furthermore, it doesn't matter how much I like someone, my father will see to it that you or someone else will run them off because no one, absolutely no one, is going to be good enough for his little girl, so I'm destined to be alone. Do you know how many men ghost me? At this point all I can do is laugh, because crying about it sure hasn't fucking worked."

Chapter 14 – Linx

There aren't enough cuss words in my extensive vocabulary to express how angered I am by her words. I want to scream at her, *'I'm a good guy and I'm standing right here, no one, absolutely no one will love you as much as me or treat you better.'*

God, fuck, damn, I really hate her dad right now. Loathe.

"Then we can be alone together." That's the only thing I can say without blowing my top. She has no idea how true that is though. I fuck a woman about every few months lately but my Trixie's always at the forefront of my mind. They're all her, I never see their faces, it's forever her face I see when I fuck someone else. It's my brain's pathetic attempt to pacify my heart.

There's no way I can move on and give a fair chance to someone else. She consumes my waking thoughts and dreams at night. I don't give a damn about settling down with anyone who isn't her. My soul is set on her. It's been that way for years. I'm never going to fall out of love with her.

I rub my chest because it physically pains me to hear her talk this way of herself.

"Since we're personal at the moment, why doesn't your crush like you? What have you done to her?" I almost choke on a French fry. She levels me a smirky look with her eyebrow cocked. I know how persistent she can be.

Looking in her eyes, I picture Birdie drooling after this tall, built bomb of a businessman, she hangs on his arm like candy at rich guy functions. Just the kind of person her mom wanted her with. I just can't see it.

That's who her dad expects too. Not me. Not a man that kills for money and is duty bound to serve. It sends a pang to my heart.

But I can also see her settling down with some man who will live in a camp with her or a mansion and give her a ton of baby LaFleurs down here in the bayou.

I clear my throat and sit back against this rickety booth, looking out the window beside us, all of a sudden uncomfortable. My throat works as I swallow all the lies I want to tell her.

So, I just shrug and say, "I-I don't know."

"What do you mean you don't know? Have you even talked to her?"

This is getting so difficult.

"No. Her parents are traditional and don't want me for their daughter." There, that should be the end of it.

"That's a big load of horseshit and you know it. Who can stand in the way of love?" she demands.

Uhh, your daddy for one, Princess.

Of course it's not the end of it for her. She continues on, playing with her braid resting on her boob, being super distracting, "I'm sure if you just talk to her or her parents you could make it work. You never know until you ask, Linx. You shouldn't have to miss out in life." She throws her braid over her shoulder and crouches down to whisper to me, "I'm going to talk to my dad tonight." And she winks at me.

My heart just kicked into overdrive. "Oh yeah? About what?" I sit back chewing my coleslaw and my eyes are glued to her mouth, but my heart is racing faster than Dale Earnhardt.

There's a mischievous twinkle in her eye that I haven't seen in a while, and quite frankly, I don't trust that look, "Seeing as how that was my first time around a bunch of bikers, I happened to notice there's a lot of good-looking bikers I could potentially be dating."

I grip the fork so hard it bends, but she prattles on not noticing, "I mean, I don't get it, what's so bad about bikers? He's one. Is he saying he's not a good man?"

No, Princess, your dear old daddy is not a good man. Neither am I, nor were most of the eligible men that was in the clubhouse last night.

Over my dead body would I allow any of them to touch her and she has no idea that I laid claim to her last night in front of at least sixty bikers and women. I'm sure tongues are wagging and word traveled fast as fuck that I'm here with her and speculating on what we're doing.

There's not one of them that will willingly cross me and date her. They won't lay a hand on her now or they face my wrath and I'm not a nice pissed off person. I break bones and snap necks.

"It's just so stupid. I think it was all my mother, ya know? Any way she could make my life hell, she did it. And he just went right along with it." She puts her nose in the air and imitates her mother in a nasally voice, "Beatrix, don't slouch, men don't like curved backs, Beatrix, stop fidgeting with your hair. Beatrix don't stare at his tattoos. Beatrix, are you listening to me?... Err fuck, constant shit, man." She slumps in her booth shaking her head and looking outside.

I knew Trixie and her mother had issues, but I wasn't aware she felt this way. Her mother was a harpy and constantly belittled Trix in her teens and twenties and on the ride here Trix confirmed a lot of my suspicions about her mother. I heard some of her mother's shit with my own ears. I never wanted to hit a woman more.

It's like she never got over that Birdie abandoned the high life to live in a French Quarter apartment, even though said apartment cost a huge chunk of money. It was never good enough for her mother.

Birdie was twenty-three when she graduated from art school here in New Orleans, top of her class. I don't know what I would have done if she had left to go somewhere else out of state. Gone insane?

She was then still required to go to events with her parents. Her dad may be a biker king, but he's still a billionaire and part of the upper crust of society here in New Orleans. Everyone wants a piece of Jaques Chavanet.

Three years ago, when she moved into her own apartment above her studio, and out of the one she shared with Zharia, I became her permanent shadow. There isn't a measure of security I didn't put on her, besides that tracker thingy, and I would have done it earlier if asked.

The past three years have been spent getting to see her off and on for various reasons on a frequent basis. I would dance with her at galas because it looked good and was expected of me. Sure, that's what I tell them. But to me it's a dance in a room alone with my woman. I look forward to every one of those dances.

I've watched her eat champagne soaked strawberries while talking to the mayor's wife. This same wonderful, sexy, smart woman laid on a bar top on Bourbon Street and let the little goth bartender do body shots off her.

She's passed sly looks my way when she thought I wasn't looking or when Zharia said something to her. Oh, I noticed, baby girl. They were always followed up by her signature glare. I didn't care, she still looked beautiful and that meant her attention was on me and no one else.

Her and Zharia would make their rounds, talking to who they knew mattered, and then they would scurry home when they had spent a dutiful amount of time at the event to appease her mom and dad.

I always dipped out after she left, with her dad's blessing, so I could follow her or watch her phone tracker I secretly uploaded to her iPhone. Birdie has no idea how safe I make her in a very dangerous world.

"I wasn't aware the relationship you had with your mother was so troubling for you."

She lets out a sigh of disgust and shakes her head. "It doesn't matter how many art contests I win, how much money I make tattooing, or how many magazines interview me and put me as centerfold, or how many people stand in line at conventions to meet me; it was never enough for her. I was a failure and a disappointment to her."

Unfortunately, I was in the room when her mother passed. I was taken off Birdie detail near the end and placed at her mom's door until her mom succumbed to her breast cancer.

I know some of her mom's last words for her was to settle down and let a man take care of her, if she could find someone willing enough at this late age and how she looked. Harsh, it was foul of a mother to say that to their only child.

It was hard to stand there and listen to it and see it hit its mark inside Birdie. Her shoulders dropped lower, and her eyes filled with angry tears. How bad I wanted to carry her out of there and wipe her tears, reassuring her she's amazing. Thankfully, Zharia was there to hold a crying Birdie.

I can't argue with Birdie on this. She's right. Her mother never approved of her daughter being an artist and doing 'white trash' 'starving artist' stuff for a living. She never considered it a 'real job' or an honest living.

Birdie got where she is by being the best in her business and the one person she wanted approval from died never uttering a nice word about it to her.

That's how Antionette Chavanet treated her only daughter.

"I've got nothing good to say to that. No argument here." She perks up a bit, and gives me an amused grin, "I see you weren't a big fan of my mother, too."

"Promise you won't tell your dad?"

She crosses her heart with her finger. "Promise."

"Your mom was a bitch and none of us liked her. And when she said those awful things to you on her deathbed, I wanted to pick you up and carry you out of the room, far away from her vile tongue. We hated her."

She throws her head back and laughs with delight. I'm happy to see her laughing.

When she comes back down from her laughter high, she says, "Add another point to the pros column of reasons Linx ain't so bad."

"Je suis l'homme parfait pour toi," I say to her with my own grin. Her eyes get big, "I don't know what you said, but it sounded beautiful."

"Pas aussi belle que toi."

Birdie tilts her head and looks at me through her lashes, "Why do I feel like you're telling me secrets and not making fun of me this time?"

"I guess you'll never know."

She picks her phone up and says, "A-ha! No! Say it again and I can translate it."

I laugh at her persistence, "No, moment's gone. You're going to have to remember it and translate for yourself."

She pinches her lips and wrinkles her nose, and my breath gets caught in my chest. Goddamn, she's so adorable.

She tries to repeat what I said and she's butchering it horrendously. I can't help but laugh at her attempts and Siri answering her with a 'What? I didn't quite catch that.'

The death glare she sends me reaffirms I got to her. My job is done here, folks.

"Ready for another?" She nods and faces her phone to me, "Je pense que tu es belle quand tu ri."

She turns the phone quickly to look at it, her eyes go wide. I see her signature blush creeping up on her fair skin.

She looks up and gives me a shit eating grin with her eyes narrowed. She's typing something on her phone. She hits play and it's Siri speaking French.

"Pas si mal toi non plus."

Now it's my turn to smile. "Thanks, little bird."

She replies, "Thank you, too."

"Are you ready to go back now?"

"Yeah, let me use the restroom right quick." At least she has some bounce in her step when she struts off. The conversation got a little bit heavy there for a moment.

I stand up and reach for my wallet. Her phone flashes on the table with a preview of a text from Zharia,

ZBaddie: #TeamDanger I hope you brought condoms, ya prudey bitch <eggplant emoji><squirting water emoji>

I'm fucking shook. Is my little bird talking about me to her best friend? About fucking me? I'm blown away.

Her phone lights up again and it's from BigDickEnergy. Now that pisses me off, who the fuck is this guy?

BigDickEnergy: Oh babycakes, I miss you already. When you get back, let's get dirty & you can make me bleed xoxo <red heart emoji>

Who in the royal FUCK is this guy? My nostrils flare and my molars grind. There's no way.

Birdie comes back to the table in her nonchalant way and picks up her phone. I tell her, "You got a text from BigDickEnergy." Her eyes dart over to me and then she bites her bottom lip to keep from smiling. I groan inwardly. She eyes me up and cocks her head, "Are you jealous, Linxy-poo?"

Yes.

"No, I want to know if I need to watch someone new and do a background check on them."

She lazily shakes her head with a smile, "Nahh, that's not it. You're jealous. You're mad I don't have you in my phone as BigDickEnergy."

"Don't deflect. Who is BigDickEnergy?"

"Nope, I don't think I shall be handing out that info to you, sir," she retorts with a big smile. I think I'm going to lose my fucking mind dealing with her.

"Ok then, what am I under on your phone?"

She winks at me and says, "Siri, call Linx." No fucking way. Just no.

"Calling LinxSmallDickEnergy," Birdie's phone says, and my phone starts ringing. After my initial scoff, I crack up laughing and turn my phone to show her my screen, where it says MyIcePrincess is calling.

She grabs her stomach and starts laughing loudly. "That's epic Linx. I love it."

I love seeing her like this. This is the version I never get, the version I crave to get close to. I've seen her with her friends, and she knows how to joke around. She's quite cynical. She loves to sit around and tell stupid stories and laugh with Pierre and Zharia and sometimes they tag Tally in on a phone call. They have a great time at Wine Wednesdays, held at Birdie's apartment where they get plastered, play games, or watch a movie. Mostly romcoms or shit that makes them cry.

I pay and leave a nice tip of a couple hundred dollars on the table. I always tip nicely to the ladies that work here. This is the kind of job my mom had while I was growing up and trying to make ends meet.

I hand her the helmet, but she says, "Hold on, I have to text BigDickEnergy back." She sniggers while burying her face into her phone.

"I swear to fucking god, Princess, get your hot ass on my bike." Before I put my helmet on, she steps up beside me and holds her phone out for a selfie.

"Just need to send the Fab Four proof I'm alive." She pockets her phone and takes the helmet. Laughing while she puts it on, taunting me in a sing-song voice, "Linxy-poo's got his panties in a twist over another man, ha ha."

We pull out of the diner and head back to camp, her laughter up in my head. After a few miles, Birdie stretches her arms out, like she's flying as Sampson eats up the miles, roaring through the bayou. I hear her sigh happily inside my helmet. "I love flying. Thank you, Lincoln," she whispers, husky, low, sexy. A voice tone never used with me.

In the hot June sun, I got shivers.

Chapter 15 – Birdie

"No, you're not making sense, this is stupid. It was a fucking bike ride and I'm going to do what I want." I damn near yell at my dad through the phone. I don't give a fuck if I act like a petulant child. I feel like I'm fighting for my life here. My freedom to choose.

Having an argument with my dad about dating bikers is not my idea of having fun at seven at night, but here I am. I'm fucking twenty-eight!

Linx steps out onto the back deck as my dad says, "I'm not even considering this, Birdie. The only, I stress *only* really fucking hard, associate of mine I would *even* slightly, small sliver of a chance, entertain and consider you dating, is Danger and you hate him, so that solves that problem, doesn't it? Are we done here, daughter?"

"No, we aren't. I'm going to the clubhouse and have my pick of the litter when I get back. You've been warned."

"Over my dead fucking body you will," Linx growls.

My father quickly talks over him, "As of right now you are barred from the clubhouse. Good luck getting in. I believe we're done here now. Have a lovely night, Beatrix, I love you." Just like that my dad is off the phone and onto other business. Business that doesn't involve me.

Linx's phone beeps, most likely with a text from my dad to each one of his members, letting them know their precious princess has been barred from coming into their clubhouse. It's maddening.

My eyes never leave Linx. My chest is heaving with anger. There's some sadness there too. "I don't know if I want to cry or scream," I hotly whisper to him. So conflicted but I can't stop the tears. Big, scorching, angry tears slide down my cheeks.

"Oh god, Trixie, please don't cry," his voice cracks.

"Tonight," I nod with a purpose, "Tonight, I start planning to leave New Orleans and move as far away from here as possible. I have connections everywhere. I can go wherever I want. Perhaps I'll even leave the country." My tears continue to fall as he looks at me, horrified, my voice grows hoarser, "I can't do this anymore, Linx, I have to get away, I have to get out from under his thumb." "No, don't leave," Linx pleads, his voice husky with emotion too. "Thank you for today. Thank you for showing me all kinds of things I've been missing and sheltered from my whole life." I bring my hands up to my heart, "Thank you for letting me ride Sampson and teaching me to fly with you."

Looks like Linx doesn't handle crying women well, seeing as how he's rooted to one spot and mouth agape staring at me with a hurt expression.

"Please don't leave. Don't make me follow you across the country or somewhere else. I rather like it here."

I blow my hair out of my face. It's sticking to my sweaty skin in the hot, muggy evening air. "You'll never find me. I'll leave in the middle of the night. I know you sleep."

"I'll follow the tracker."

Beyond annoyed, I snap, "I'll cut it out of my fucking neck right before I walk out of my apartment and leave it in a puddle of my blood, so help me fucking god." My voice rises and I blink the tears out of my eyes, swiping my cheeks with my hands. With my voice wavering from emotion, "I hate it here. I hate being his daughter."

My fists are balled up and I just want to punch something, anything. I close my eyes and inhale through my nose. I'm not normally a physically violent person but tonight I could fuck some shit up. *Just breathe*. I try really hard not to crack my teeth as I clench my jaw.

But I look back over to him, and I see him in the light of the dying sun, he's beautiful. My constant shadow who makes me feel safe right now. My shoulders and jaw relax, and I take a deep, even breath. I have to calm down.

I can't help but think, when did his presence start comforting me? My mind is spinning as it is.

"From what I've gotten to see down here in this area, I love it down here. It's so beautiful. You were lucky to grow up here, Lincoln, and not in one of the busiest and dirtiest cities in the world. Do you think if I move down here that's far enough away my dad won't bother me?"

Linx is still staring at me, he releases a pent-up breath, it drops his chest like a deflated balloon. "No, Princess, this isn't far enough." His voice is low and raspy and does something inside me.

I just bite my upper lip and nod my head as it hangs. "Yepp," my lips pop. I raise my defeated head and my eyes meet Linx's. He looks so sad. Is he sad for me?

"Why are you so sad, Linx?" I ask him softly, not sure if he even heard me.

I see him struggle, his fists clench. "I don't like seeing you cry and being helpless to fix it," he says in a low, hard voice that holds emotion.

"It's not your job to fix it, Lincoln."

His throat works when he turns his head and looks out over the water. He nods his head and says, "Ok. Ok then."

Running a hand down his face he looks back over to me, "I was coming to tell you I was taking a quick shower while our food cooks." He drops my gaze, hanging his head, he walks into the house, leaving me out here by myself with all kinds of fucked up thoughts.

Something's shifted between me and Linx in the past twenty-four hours and I don't know what to make of it. I have weird flutters in my stomach about him sometimes. I don't know if I like that. I don't feel like being bitchy to him anymore. Quite honestly, it makes me feel bad about being bitchy before. It's like I see a whole different man now.

Being around him the past night and day, I've learned he really is a good guy at heart. He has a teenager sense of humor but that's part of his charm. He's a serial flirter and shows off his body every chance he gets. He could very well charm any woman out of her panties with that dimple. And he loves his momma.

I can't even believe you're entertaining this idea, the purity angel on my shoulder hisses.

The angel of sin on the other shoulder smoothly replies, "*Oh, we're entertaining so much more.*"

More of that wall crumbles.

I finally drag myself back inside after firing off a few texts to the group chat between the Fab Four. Gah, being welcomed back to the folds of civilization and air conditioning is orgasmic after being out in the humid air. On the kitchen table is a bottle of bourbon and two highball glasses filled halfway. That has to be like three shots in there.

Another point in the Pros column.

I pick up the bottle and about lose my tongue at the label. Does he realize how expensive this is? Eagle Rare 25 is like thirty grand a bottle. And he's opened it; I groan to myself. I'm such a lightweight but I plan to drink this whole fucking glass because that's his peace offering and I need it.

I close my eyes and take a sip. I tilt my head back and let it slide around in my mouth. The sweetness, mixed with that little hint of a sting, makes me moan deep in my throat loudly, as I keep the bit of whiskey on my tongue, then open my throat and pour the whole glass down into my empty stomach.

Chapter 16 – Linx

I hear the back door close and pop my head out of my bedroom door, with my towel wrapped around my waist, I lean out and watch her. She closes her eyes and takes a drink of the bourbon I bought for our first night together, if we ever got one. I know it's technically the second night but last night was a fuckshow, ok.

I bought this bottle at Thanksgiving.

Her delicate throat bobs up and down as she savors the flavors. A low moan rumbles in her chest, up through her throat and fills all the cracks in the room with her sultry tone. It sets my blood on fire.

Fucking hell.

She shoots the entire glass of bourbon.

Oh shit. I've not gotten the pleasure of drunk Birdie yet.

Her head lowers and she opens her eyes, right into mine. A thousand thoughts rush my mind, but none stand out as loud as *she's perfect*.

She pours more into her glass and lifts it in the air.

She watches me over the rim and takes another healthy drink, moaning again. We stand there assessing each other for a moment.

"You have good taste, Linxy."

"Only the best for my princess." I'm fighting here. Fighting so hard. I deserve a war metal for my restraint.

Birdie takes a gulp and knocks it back like she's an everyday drinker…which she certainly is not. I know for a fact she's got nothing on that stomach of hers, and she's already been emotional tonight. Fuck. Shit. Damn. Maybe my peace offering wasn't such a good idea.

From my 'research' I have deduced she's a lightweight of epic proportions. She's passing out soon. Meh, maybe that's what my baby girl needs. I need to get food in her.

Oh shit, she's walking over here, leaving her glass on the table with the bottom empty.

She crooks her finger at me. I'll play her game. I grin and bend down to hear her while she puts her hand on my bare chest. "Can I wrap my thighs around you again tomorrow sometime?" I smell the whiskey on her breath, as smooth as her husky voice, and it smells so good. Warm whiskey, oh god, my body shivers and my heart trips up. I'm already doing a piss poor job of hiding this erection. I want to slide my tongue in her mouth and drink the whiskey off her tongue and lips.

Her glassy eyes twinkle as she smiles. Yeah, the bourbon's went to her head, quickly. My Trixie isn't this forward.

"Baby, you can wrap your thighs around me anytime."

Her lips curl and she bites that fucking bottom lip again.

"What if I said right now? Would you break Daddy's rule for a bit of pussy?"

My hand slams around her throat and I push her back into her closed bedroom door with a thud. Instead of being thrilled, her eyes dilate, and her breath catches in her throat—that drunken Cheshire smile still on her face. Not even an ounce of fear. Nose to nose, I growl into her mouth, so close I feel her pants on my lips, "So help me god, little bird, I only have so much restraint." Instead of scaring her, my actions turned her on, her nostrils flare and she whimpers, never losing that grin.

"What's wrong big guy? You can dish it, but you can't take it?" "Don't tempt me, Trixie." My muscles all over my body are taunt from holding back.

Her tongue darts out and licks her top lip, dangerously close her tongue barely grazes my bottom lip. I feel a ghost of a touch of her hands on my ribs. I breathe her in, and she smells like sunshine, fine bourbon and sex appeal.

"You'll have to beg me for it before I'll break my oath to your dad." We're so close I know she can feel her lips on mine when I talk. If she even moves a little…I don't know if I can keep my tongue out of her mouth. I'll turn savage.

She scoffs, "I'll never beg a man to fuck me. Not gonna happen." She pushes at my chest.

"We'll see," I growl as I lick the side of her neck, across her sensitive skin. She's whimpering and wiggling under me, and I love that her ice queen façade is fading. I know she can feel the evidence of my arousal.

If I come in this towel standing here, I'll never live it down. Lightly, I run my nose right by her ear and whisper, "I promise you, you'll beg me to fuck you, mon amour. You'll want this cock so bad you'll do anything for it." After kissing her earlobe, I step back, dropping my hand off her throat and turning into my room. The last thing I see before shutting the door is her pressed up against her bedroom door, chest heaving and thighs squished together.

Yes, baby, just like that.

Chapter 17 – Birdie

Linx is not in the bathroom when I wake up. He's also not in his room. Or in the house at all.

I peek through the blinds, down to the parking area and I see him pacing back and forth with his hand flying through his wavy hair. I see he's already agitated this morning. Most likely about me, as usual.

He looks like he's got whatever that is handled, I think as I scurry back to my bedroom and shut the door quickly, making sure it's locked. I'm almost frantic when I throw myself across the bed and stick my fingers in my eager, starving pussy. I let out a low moan and immediately clamp my hand over my mouth.

My clit is on a livewire right now. Anything will set it off. I've been so worked up the entire time I've been with him, but last night was the tipping point. He manhandled me and I fucking loved it. I wanted him inside me so bad, but I'm not going to beg. I had to quietly get myself off last night because of it.

A flash of an image of me on my knees in front of him and his cock tapping my lips whilst he begs me to open my mouth.

The first tingles of orgasm gathers in my core. The flurry of my fingers across my clit speeds it along. One last flash across the back of my eyes is Linx holding me up against that wall and impaling me on that anaconda I saw forming under that towel. My breath leaves my body as fireworks shoot off from my pussy and spreads throughout my body. I can't stop the squeaks that are trapped in my throat, riding the wave of euphoria.

Once I come back down, I go to the bathroom to splash cold water on my heated face. My freaking legs feel like jelly. Unfortunately, that only took a small edge off. I want more. I *need* more. I growl out my frustration and shuffle into the kitchen area and grab a coffee cup. I look at my smart watch and groan. I usually don't get up until ten. Why is my body now insisting on getting up at eight?

I'm taking my first sip when the front door opens and Linx waltzes through making my heart skip a beat. He gets five feet into the room before he shucks off his shoes and just looks at me. Like he didn't just try to choke me last night. Like he didn't set his lips on mine and turn my blood to lava.

Like we didn't eat a meal in silence and go to bed, mumbling good night to each other.

He had to of known what he was doing to me last night. I'm sure my moans gave away my arousal and if he would have touched me, he would have found me drenched.

The throb is still pulsing through my whole reproductive system along with the throb in my head. Who authorized me to drink so much?

I've never been choked. Matter of fact, no one has ever manhandled me, not like that. Not outside of self-defense training and then it didn't feel sexual. I must say I was surprised when his hand wrapped around my throat, but I also loved it. It was thrilling, made my pussy jolt and I want some more of that. I could've come if he would have touched me down there.

I silently begged him like a wanton whore as I was plastered up against my bedroom door. Mentally thanking myself for shutting it when I had walked out. Also, thank fucking god one of us came to our senses before I could open my mouth to beg out loud.

Now I get to face him like nothing happened, or I can confront it.

"Everything ok?"

"Yeah, just talking to my brother, I didn't want to wake you. Are you wearing any bottoms with that?"

I look down at my oversized Harley Davidson t-shirt that I know for a fact covers my cooch. He's just being a fucking prude this morning. It's long enough to be a nightgown.

"Nope," popping the P like the brat I am. "Why? Are you gonna punish me if it's just lace panties? Maybe choke me up against a door again?" I cock one eyebrow up at him, amusement snaking through my tone. I like the look of Linxy squirming. He puts me on the hotplate enough.

He takes a deep inhale, drops his chin in shame, and pushes out the breath. Looking up at me, nodding, "About that, I'm sorry Birdie. I had no right to lay hands on you." Nope, don't like when he calls me Birdie. I always feel like it means he's mad at me.

"I'm not complaining." The memory of his hands on me makes fire blaze across my belly, heating up my core.

He gives me a puzzled look and shifts his weight. I love how he's contemplating what I mean exactly. He never makes it all the way over to me, so touching me again is not going to happen from way over there. It's one big open room; he could definitely take a few strides and have me up against a counter in no time. My nipples peak thinking of all the possibilities.

This wasn't planned but I'm gonna roll with it.

I'm choosing violence today. Fuck yes, I am.

"Matter of fact, I wouldn't mind if you did it again. Except this time follow through."

Yep, kill shot fired.

The air wooshes from his lungs.

He fucking staggers.

"That can't happen again." His voice sounds so strained.

Oh yes, big guy is holding back.

BEATRIX!

This fucking brain I tell ya.

Look bitch, we do not hate him, not anymore, let me have this hunk of a man. He's got redeeming qualities now. He's becoming the hero of the story.

I lick my teeth and nod slowly at him, "Sure. Ok." I bring up my coffee and take a long, nice drink, watching him the entire time over the rim knowing damn well it's going to happen again.

"Do you want to go to a pool with me today? My mom has an inground pool and she said we could come over while she's gone." He looks so cute, like he's asking me out on a date.

Shucks, maybe he is.

"Yes, I would love that."

Still choosing violence. I can't wait to drive him insane today with a string bikini. Evil Mojo Jojo laugh overpowering my brain functions.

My dad thought bitching was my favorite hobby concerning Linx, but this is by far more fun. I should have been fighting back like this the entire time.

Note to self: Always choose violence, Birdie.

Watching him unravel that impeccable control is like sugar to my tongue. It's a mighty need.

My new hobby is breaking Linxy.

Linx hands me the sunblock he retrieved from the saddlebags in the garage. I hand it over to his momma, who is insisting I be slathered with it. She done told me she would like to dip me in it and throw on some Tony's Cajun seasoning if she had proof it would stop me from burning, because the sun is going to eat me alive today, so she says.

I came with a swimming robe over my suit, but I can see Linx is already having issues. His jerky motions and covert glances my way tell me about how nervous he is. I've never seen him so flustered. He's in for a treat.

Their swimming pool is gorgeous, and I tell Collette so. It's got a waterfall built into it that you can swim behind. She has all kinds of ferns sitting around in planters and lounge chairs and tables placed here and there. Thankfully, it appears she has a large privacy fence too.

She leans in and whispers, "Do you want him to put it on instead?" And she fucking winks at me while wagging her brows. Danger's momma lives a little dangerously herself. I like her.

I take it out of her hand with a sweet smile and quietly say thank you.

This lady understands choosing violence.

"I'll be back in a few hours." She blows her son kisses and grabs me in a hug while mumbling, "Good luck." It makes me stiffen at first. I'm not used to being showered with affection from people who are not dad or the Fab Four. It's such a sweet gesture; I genuinely hug her back and it makes my heart happy. She squeezes me one last time and trots off, almost whistling with glee, she's so perky today.

Once I hear the door close behind her, I steel my nerves. It's now or never. It's so unlike me to behave this way but this is payback for everything he's done or said to me. I'm fighting fire with fire and there's no one going to stop me. Fuck the purity angel.

I'm letting the little demon be in charge now.

I walk over to the lounger next to the one he's sitting on. He's casually looking at his phone, or more like pretending to be interested in what's on the screen as he sneaks glances at me. Oh, he is very aware of what I'm doing. I imagine he's counting down the seconds until I drop this robe off my shoulders.

I plop my stuff in the chair beside him. One more glace and he's jittery. I slowly untie my robe, and his eyes snap to my body.

I almost whimper at the anticipation. There's a delicious zing that goes through my body when I hold his attention now.

I watch his face as I open the robe and let it fall to the ground. Underneath the robe, there's a hot pink and black string bikini that leaves little to the imagination. The naughty bits are covered in hot pink sparkles and the outline strings are black, but it just might be something a stripper wears on stage—if she's feeling modest.

When we bought it, Zharia begged me to buy it for Linx. She said it would make him have a coronary. By the looks of it, she was one hundred and ten percent correct.

"NO! Fuck no. Jesus Christ, Birdie, no. What the fuck?" his hoarse voice echoes in the backyard. He jumps up out of the lounger and makes to reach for me.

I throw my finger up, wagging it back and forth, dodging him, "Ut uh, no touchy, remember?"

"You're so fucking lucky my stepdad is at work and my brother's gay. *WHAT* are you wearing?"

"As you know, I didn't have but five minutes to pack for, might I remind you, no clue where I was headed, and I just blindly grabbed for clothes. This happens to be one of the swimsuits I snatched from my drawer."

Linx stares blankly at me, not moving his eyes from my face, even though I know he's totally taking a good look at the rest of me. Suddenly, he storms past me and slams into the house through the back door. As soon as the door is closed, he roars, 'GODDAMNIT," at the top of his lungs. I can hear it out here. I'm pretty sure the whole neighborhood heard it. Space Station heard it. I'm going to say he likes the bikini.

Revenge kinda tastes sweet as I roll it around on my tongue. For all the times you annoyed the fuck out of me, Lincoln LaFleur. Mentally I flip him off.

What? My triangles cover the naughty bits, like I said but there's still a portion of my more-than-a-handful boobies not covered on the sides and cleavage. Even the back has some coverage over the ass. It could be much worse. He should be happy I didn't bring the teal and black one, it's just a piece of floss up my ass crack and a small triangle at the top of my crack.

Zharia was right, this bikini looks sexy as fuck on me and by his reaction, it reached the goal.

Whatever, he can go pout. Piling all my waist length hair in a bun on top of my head, I shove chopsticks through it to hold it in place, and I start putting sunblock on my body. I'm starting to believe there's not enough in the tube to cover all my fair skin and protect my tattoos. I practically glowed in the dark when my skin wasn't inked.

I get it from my mother. She had jet back hair, vibrant blue eyes, and pale skin. Dad's always said I'm my mother's replica. I don't mind really because my mom was beautiful, she was just mean on the inside.

I know with my full, curvaceous body I could land so many men but that means I have to put myself out there. I've tried; it's no use. I'm starting to accept I'm never going to be a size small, and I shouldn't hide who I am. Zharia's been helping with the small case of body dysmorphia I have. She's been putting me in short skirts and going to concerts or clubs and making me show off all these curves. It's a start to being proud of them. Her daily affirmations she gave me, and my weekly self-care sessions help too.

Most every guy that talks to me or dances with me ghosts me by the end of the night. I'm left hanging to go home alone. This is why I feel like I'm destined to be alone. No one wants to stick around. Hell, the only other constant man in my life besides my dad and Pierre is Linx, I snort to myself at the irony.

It's so fucking hot out I don't wait for Linx to finish his temper tantrum. He's probably inside jacking off. Which turns me on immensely, if I care to admit. Lucky him, I can't get a decent diddle session in to save my life without him hearing in that tiny house. I have to settle for quick bean flicks and choke on my own air when I come. This morning was a treat, but it wasn't enough. I need to make myself come until I'm a sweaty mess and just pass out. I need something inside me to fill me up. But there's no damn way I'm doing that here. I draw the line at that.

After what seems like forever, Linx comes back outside and says, "I'm sorry, I shouldn't have yelled at you."

"You're fine, Linx. I take it you don't get much time around women while working for my father."

He pinches the bridge of his nose, frustration creasing his brow. "I spend the most time with you."

"And that's hardly fun." He stands there looking at me with his hands on his hips, "Tell me, do you enjoy going to those events and galas? Getting dressed up and schmoozing with the rich folks?"

"I don't mind it. I get to annoy you and give you something to complain about to your dad."

"You think I complain?"

"He tells me."

"Geez. Is there no one I can trust?" I roll my eyes behind my sunglasses.

"You can trust me."

"I've always trusted you," I rush out, because it's true. I've always known Linx would never hurt me.

"I should be the only man you trust."

Something in the way he says it. Sweet promises of something special if I trust him, rewards if I only orbit around him.

Feeling my fingers start to wrinkle, I tell him, "I'm about to get out of this pool if you don't want to see me."

I swim my way over to the stairs and walk up them, water sliding down my body in rivulets.

Linx sits down at the end of his lounger, watching me like a hawk. I come closer and he says in a restrained tone, "It's never about not wanting to see you, it's about not being able to do a damn thing about it."

"What's stopping you?" I ask as I lay back in the lounger, half under an umbrella, while he sits back with the sun on his chest.

What must it be like to lay in the sun and bask in its glorious light without burning to ash and blisters? Lucky tan bitches.

Linx rises and towers over me, "Look, I took an oath to my club and that included keeping a promise to never hurt you or hook up with you. To be here with you should tell you how much your father trusts me. Members aren't allowed around you, your father's order. It's to keep the temptation at bay. I'm the only one, and somedays you make it so goddamn hard. Just so you know, it has nothing to do with who you are as a person, you're beautiful and amazing; it's what we can do to you he doesn't like. No one touches his little girl."

Linx leans down and puts his hands on the lounger edges beside my hips. As he gets closer, he all but growls, "I want to ruin you so bad, I want you to crave my cock when any other man dares to try and take my place. I want my marks over those patches of porcelain skin so no one can mistake that you are taken and you're mine. But you are the forbidden fruit in the garden of Eden, Trixie. We can look but never touch. And I've spent a lot of fucking time looking while dying to touch."

My heart is lurching in my chest and I'm breathing erratically at his gruff tone. The little bird that lives in my chest is frantically flapping around. I'm embarrassingly growing wetter and wetter. Thank fuck my swimsuit is black and he can't tell.

His words hit right into my core and unfurls a feral need deep inside of me. I want a man who will ruin me. Devastate me. Destroy me. It's always been my fantasy. To lose myself in the moment and switch on all primal reactions. I'm dying inside missing something I crave that I don't even know what it is. What if I told him? What if he knew I wanted a man like him? What if he knew I wanted to fuck him? I'm playing with fire and Linx is already on edge.

Fuck it, violence.

"What if I said it's always been my fantasy to have a man utterly ruin me?"

His head drops and hangs before he mutters, "Jesus fuck, Trixie, are you trying to kill me? 'Cause that's what's happening."

"I'm just trying to figure you out." I smile sweetly at him, hoping he'll see things my way.

I get to wander around the living room while his mom fixes us something to eat in her beautiful kitchen. She refused to allow us to do it ourselves, saying it's not often she gets to cater to others, and it makes her feel needed.

I've donned my robe again lest he have another coronary.

I look at the pictures on the mantle. "Oh, hey, that's weird, there's uh, pictures of Pierre here?" I say, confused as fuck. I look up at Linx and his face is blank. I look back at the pictures, really looking this time, comprehending the scene. His mom and stepdad. Linx standing beside his mother and Pierre standing by what I assume is his father. It's a family photo. Family.

His stepbrother.

Best friend.

Suddenly a conversation with Pierre snaps to the forefront of my memory,

'Want to go see a band with me tonight?'

"No, I can't, I'm meeting my brother, can't bail, he's not having a good day."

"Oh no, what's wrong?"

"He's really hung up on a girl, like in love love, and there's nothing there. She hates him but he loves her."

She hates him.

"You've both lied to me." It comes out gruffly, husky with hurt and feelings of betrayal.

Is Pierre even my friend? Or is he someone conveniently placed in my life to keep closer tabs on me on Daddy's payroll? God, I'm so stupid.

I'm going to be sick.

"You both played me. Oh god, I trusted Pierre."

Linx's stricken face. I can't even look at him. Rage tears fill my eyes. All this time…I'm so fucking blind.

"I-I need to get out of here. I need away from you."

"I'll take you back to camp."

Chapter 18 – Linx

Pierre's told me he talks about me in code to Birdie. It's like a soap opera for her. He's made his brother out to be a lovesick, hopeless, fool for a girl that hates him, so he burns through women to find one to replace her, never having found one. Birdie's invested in Pierre's brother's lady drama.

Standing here looking into her eyes, my stomach drops. She knows who Pierre's brother is now. And I'm pretty sure she can piece together who the girl is.

My cat is out of the bag, so to speak.

Or one better, the shit hath hitteth the faneth.

"Don't bother, I don't want to be around you right now. I can't. I'll ask your mother to take me."

My hand circles her wrist as she tries to push past me. Her angry and hurt narrowed eyes fly down to my hand on her arm before she hisses, "Stop touching me, Lincoln." She pries my fingers off of her, throwing them back at me, like my touch is burning her skin. It can't be as bad as her clawing my heart out of my chest right now.

"Trixie," my voice breaks on her name.

She cuts her hand in the air as her tears fall and firmly says, "MY name is Birdie, MR. DANGER." She tilts her chin up and walks out of the living room, through the archway to the kitchen.

I've royally fucked up.

When Mom gets back, she quietly asks, "Do you want to talk about it?"

I don't know, do I?

"What's there to talk about? It's a no-win situation."

"Let's talk about how you're madly in love with your boss's daughter."

"Mom…"

"Mon cœur, it's written all over your face when you look at her. I'm not sure how her father hasn't picked up on it, or her for that matter." My mom knows most all of how I feel about Birdie.

I give a harsh laugh, "She's too busy hating me."

I push out the air in my lungs on a forceful exhale trying to calm my nerves. This is all a mess. I should never have let her leave without me. All my mind can think of is her by herself in the camp house, upset, at me. I can't wait for the lovely phone call from Pierre telling me how much of an asshole I am.

I want to punch things.

"I don't think she hates you as much as she lets on, son. At least not anymore."

I cut a bewildered look at my mom sitting in the lounger next to me. "What do you mean?"

"I mean her face softens around you. She relaxes and you can tell she is conflicted about finding out who you really are. She's spent a fair amount of time disliking you and your teasing attempts at flirting."

"There can only be this flirting. That's all I'm allowed to do with her."

"Would it be so bad to lose her father to gain her love?" Mom asks.

"I took an oath, maman. I'm not a man who breaks his promises."

"Hmm, I see."

"What's that supposed to mean?"

"You're either going to have to get away from her and find a life without her, or cave and indulge your heart then face the consequences. You've pined away for years after her, someone who is so off limits; this trip is a very rare treat for you, Lincoln." She sits up to face me and leans over to put her hand over top of mine. "I'm sorry, son, either leave her and her father, or show her real love, but you can no longer do nothing to fulfill your heart, it's eating away at your soul. Shit or get off the pot, mon cœur."

She pats my hand a few times and rises. "You should go to camp and talk to her. She's had time to calm down. I imagine it was a shock to see her best friend's brother is her enemy, who I remind you that she's forced to be locked up with for the week. I reckon she's done called and bitched Pierre out, rightly so," she says on a throaty laugh.

My mother is straight forward, no beating around the bush. As she walks back into her house, I gather the rest of our things and follow her in. I hug her goodbye and promise to try and explain myself.

When I arrive back at camp and walk through the door, the house is silent. I almost don't think she's here until I hear her sniffle in her room behind the closed door. Fuck me, she's crying again.

It rips my soul out every time she does it and what's even worse is it's because of me this time.

Knowing I'd be the last person she wants to see right now, like she'd rather see Pierre's lying ass than me right now, I turn on the Bluetooth speaker he insisted on bringing here and let music fill the void. Old rock drifts through the small house and gives me a small comfort in this clusterfuck of a mess I've made.

I take one last look at her closed bedroom door before I walk into mine and go take a shower. I can smell her soap as soon as I open the bathroom door, and it sends a pang straight to my heart.

I'm fixing dinner listening to some blues rock and Whiskey Myers sings on about losing a girl. How fucking fitting. My mood is straight shit.

Birdie hasn't come out of her room since I got home a couple hours ago. Either she's fallen asleep or she's dreaming up ways to kill me in my sleep.

Is this too far gone? Have I blown it? I should just ask to be reassigned.

I'm not sure how to salvage this. What is there to even salvage? I feel like my biggest secret that was hidden in plain sight has been jerked to the light and I'm reeling in the exposure.

Life is like a dagger. It gives all these tiny cuts up until the moment it pierces your heart and I'm a million tiny papercuts in, slowly bleeding to death.

Sweet, sweet little bird, I should leave you alone.

I should have Shadow come and take over, but I can't bear the thought of one of my brothers in arms taking care of her, not like I should. I sure as fuck don't want him around her in those skimpy outfits she's always wearing around here. What the fuck happened to her baggy shirts and cargo pants?

Granted, she does throw on tight crop tops and short skirts or shorts every once in a while, but it's like she's deliberately trying to kill me here. Possibly it's that I'm so close to her right now that my mind zeros in on every little thing.

And the fucking swimsuit. Duct tape would have had more coverage. But motherfuck, I loved seeing her in it.

These past few days have been like a dream come true for me.

I rub my chest to ease the ache in it but it's no use. I'm going to lose her. It's most likely for the best. I live a life of torture and that's no way to live. She stays wrapped up in my thoughts and it's getting to the point it's affecting my everyday life. I'm almost obsessive with checking the cameras I placed in her apartment, without her knowledge. Or the ones in her shop that she does know about.

It's for her own good. And I don't have them in her bedroom or bathroom. I'm not a total stalkerish perv.

How brutal will my punishment be if I give in and have my sweet little bird? What will Rock do to me if I defile his little princess? Am I willing to risk it?

At this point, I'm ready to beg on my knees.

Chapter 19 – Birdie

So many thoughts running through my head I can't keep track of them. Memories flooding me alongside the new revelations. All of it makes my heart pound in my chest. Flashes of conversations with Pierre about his love-struck brother. Interactions between me and Linx replay in my head as I analyze everything with a different eye.

Linx is in love with me and has been for quite some time. Talk about a mindfuck.

I've sat here and analyzed every interaction between us the past few days, even the past few years. All the looks, the brief touches, the sexual comments. It was there all along. He was there in plain sight. He showed me repeatedly, not once popping up on my dad's radar.

How stupid was I for not seeing it for what it is.

Zharia saw it. Zhar called it out. Numerous times. She pushed for it. She used to beg me to use Linx's body to forget life and climb him like a mountain, then making the ground shake with the violent attraction we have between us. She's one of the only people who know how sexually attracted I am to Linx on the downlow. Until, well, feelings happened, and they weren't good ones.

When I called her crying and confused earlier, she told me there's only one thing to do if I wanted to explore with Linx; defy my father and finally be with Linx.

Defy him? Easier said than done. You don't just defy Jaques Chavanet.

Could I even do that? I've never done that before. I've always been Daddy's perfect little angel and did as he wanted. He placated me to be a submissive daughter. His theory is how could anyone who gets whatever they want show defiance?

If I want to be with Linx in any capacity, I'll have to fight for it. I mean, I've learned in a few short days Linx would actually be perfect for me. There's been no harsh words, and we have actually been getting along.

Right now, I'm iffy on something long term. For the time being, I'd settle on mountain climbing to squat on his dick and ride that thing until I passed out. He has me so fucked up at this point. I'm mad and hurt, but I'm dying to see where it would lead.

If this is the real Lincoln, the one he's shown me the past couple of days, I can totally see myself falling for him. Easily. However, I think it's already happening. Especially if I'm considering letting him stick a cock in me. He said he wanted me to like him in order to do that and meh, he's not so bad.

So many times, I've wondered what's wrong with me and now I believe it's been Linx in the background the whole time, working to keep me his. I bet the night Noah left was due to Linx's interference somehow. In a way I'm mad at that too, but also, I recognize Noah was not good for me. His leaving was too abrupt for him not to have been spooked, but I was so caught up in my feels, I never questioned it.

The phone call with Pierre after the initial texting with him was a little more strained than the call with Zharia.

Me: How could you lie to me? Hiding the fact Linx is your brother. Who coincidently is in love with a girl that hates him and that girl is me? I'm so mad and hurt and confused.

BigDickEnergy: I'm sorry, Birdie. I swore to him I'd never tell you. He's my brother.

Me: I feel like a fool

BigDickEnergy: Not a fool. Please don't think that. You're his whole world. His love for you is his biggest secret. He's never going to step out and break your dad's number one rule. He'd rather see you from afar than not at all. I imagine he's a wreck right now. Not that I'm trying to gaslight you.

Me: That's no way to live

Me: Can you come get me? Please

BigDickEnergy: Sorry, babe, I can't. He'd kill me. He'll kill anyone who comes near you. You have no idea how protective of you he truly is, or the things he's done to keep you safe.

I'm starting to get a good picture.

Me: Is he why I can't keep a guy interested?

BigDickEnergy: Maybe

Me: I swear to god I want to rip his arms off and stick them in his eye sockets

BigDickEnergy: I know you don't know much about him yet, but that's foreplay for him sweetie lol Not trying to scare you, but Linc has a dark side, and he indulges it under your father's reign.

Me: I'm not afraid of him. He'll never hurt me. Unlike you. Fucking liar face McLiarPants. I hope your pants catch on fire and blisters your dick.

BigDickEnergy: LOL You're caught in a tragic love story and didn't even know it. How poetic. I lied to protect you from your father

Me: I don't hate Linx anymore

BigDickEnergy: But he still can't ever have you, princess. He worships the ground you walk on. I've never seen a man so far

gone over a girl. It's so unfortunate. Linc is a really great guy and I guarantee you will never find anyone as devoted to you as he is.
Me: I'm calling you now

Pierre apologized profusely about hurting my feelings but said he wasn't sorry about hiding it from me. He's quite loyal to his brother. Also, found out Collette knows too. The pieces are all starting to fall into place. Her interactions with me make sense.

I'm not sure what to say anymore and eventually I have to face Linx. That's going to be awkward as fuck. 'Hey, thanks for loving me and hiding it from me because of my fucking father.'

A soft knock on my door startles me and Linx's gutted voice lets me know dinner is ready. God, I don't want to do this anymore.

I can't go out there in a see-through tank and panties, so I throw on a pair of cut-off jean shorts and a cutoff t-shirt that hangs off one shoulder. I don't even care anymore if I have a bra on or not. It's not like he's going to complain.

Revenge has turned to rot in my blood. It feels like poison is coursing through my blood making it curdle. Shame burns through my skin at how I've treated him. How I taunted him. How I most likely ripped his heart out.

Empathy fills me with sorrow at the impasse we find ourselves at.

In the few quiet moments after Collette dropped me off to this empty house, all my plans for payback turned to ash and now there's just an angry sadness replacing that need.

I like Linx. Like a lot now that I've gotten to know him. Is he this perfect for everyone? Or is it just me? Is this the Linx reserved just for me?

When I step out of the bedroom, I take a few steps into the living room when he turns around from the stove and watches me through his lowered brow. His forehead furrows conflicted with how he should handle me now that his secret is out.

"Birdie." His tone denotes his personal anguish. One word spoken is all it takes for me to understand his pain. He takes two steps towards me.

I hold my hand up, stopping him.

"Why didn't you tell me?"

He shrugs and shakes his head, looking off to the side of the room with a sardonic smile. When his gaze locks in on mine again, he licks his lips and says, "Would it have mattered?"

He has a point. Before now, before this trip, before his assignment, it wouldn't have mattered. I was too much of a stuck-up blind bitch to see his actions as affection.

Well, maybe if he would have said something a long time ago, I wouldn't have been so bitchy.

"It matters to me now."

He scoffs at my remark. "Yeah, well, there isn't much we can do about it anyways."

I chew on my bottom lip and prepare to shoot my shot, because I want him. I've made up my mind. I can't get him out of my mind and the way I react to him, no one else has ever made me feel like that. I want everything he's offering to me. Somehow, he's needled under my skin in this super short time we've been together, and he sets my insides on fire in a completely different way than anyone else has ever done.

Damn him for being a great guy.

Damn me for paying attention.

Damn him for being everything I ever wanted.

And damn my dad for his stupid fucking rules.

"Am I more than just an assignment to you?"

He holds his hands out in frustration. "You're fucking kidding, right? You're my whole world and not because of a job either. It was because of this job that I met you. My heart skipped a beat the moment when I met a vivacious, excited eighteen-year-old who was headed to college, ready to take on the world. You had your whole life ahead of you. You didn't need some guy ten years your senior putting the demands of a relationship on you. Not like

I could have had you back then either." His troubled eyes never leave my face.

Ten years. Linx has harbored these feelings for ten years.

"What if I want to do something about it?" I lay it out between us. His eyes blow wide, dilating in his desire, and he takes a sharp inhale, putting a hand on his chest, rubbing it with his knuckles. "I can't take anymore. Seriously. What do you mean, Birdie?" he asks tentatively.

"What if we don't tell him? What if we can have this week?" He takes a step towards me but holds back. His restraint is legendary. He's much stronger than me because I'm ready to wrap my legs around him again, sing his praises and get off, only this time he'll be inside me.

"He'll find out," Linx says with a deadly calm and quiet warning.

"Are you afraid of the punishment, because I'm not."

"He'll send me away, if he doesn't kill me."

"I'll follow you."

He takes another hesitant step. Now he's six feet from me, six feet from betraying my father. Six feet to his dreams coming true. Six feet is way too much.

I'm ready. I want this. He's proven what kind of man he is with me. He broke every barrier and blew up every wall I erected. I take a step forward. Every nerve ending in my body lighting up.

"I want you, Lincoln," I breathe out. "Please touch me, please fuck me, please take me in one of these rooms and give me the ride of my life. Please do everything you've ever dreamed of. Just do something." I shrug and take another step forward, "If we're going to die for it, make it the best night I've ever had."

He's barely hanging on. I've pushed him too far. He shakes his head and painfully says, "I can't."

"Yes, you can. Please, Linx."

"Oh my god, you're making this unbearable for me." He growls loudly and covers his face with his hands. With his face still covered, he weakly tells me, "You have no idea," his voice cracks, "no fucking idea how I've died a million times inside wanting to hear you say that. I never dreamed it would happen. Goddamnit!" he curses with his fists clenched. Frustration and lust ooze off him, spreading that energy around the room.

There's only one thing left for me to do. I tried begging, I tried asking nicely. Now I just take it.

Ruthlessness is in my blood, and I come by it honestly. This is the part of choosing violence I'm here for.

Walking up to Linx with all my bravery and determination, I pull his arms down. He helplessly looks down at me with anguished eyes, "Please, Birdie, oh god." His vulnerability is showing.

Choosing redemption, before I chicken out, I quickly reach up and wrap my arms around his neck, and right before I jump onto his body, I say, "Catch me, Linx."

I launch myself up at him, as his arms come around to cup my ass, I finish climbing this tall, dark, drink of water like I'm a dying woman out in the desert.

My lips crash into his and I take, and take, and break the cardinal rule. Birdie is taking back her life and sin never tasted so good. It feels amazing. Like electricity running over my pebbled skin. Lightning flows through my blood and I know deep down I'll never be satisfied with just this kiss.

His tongue meets mine in a hot, fiery kiss that sears my soul. I had no idea kissing him would be such a spiritual experience. My chest explodes with something I can't even explain right now. He moans deep in his throat and squeezes me to him. Our heavy breathing echoes in the tiny house.

Losing my mind, my body ignites under his touch. I run my fingers through his hair, across his scalp and moan my own noises at this clashing of wills. Let's call it what it is, Linx's moral integrity crumbling while he breaks his oath. I shouldn't be testing his loyalty to my father but I'm not thinking of my father's hypocritical bullshit right now.

I'm thinking of me.

And Linx.

And what we want.

I feverishly lay claim to the Right Hand of God and blur all lines laid out. I open the floodgates of my heart to the only man who's ever stayed by me and protected me, loved me for me, expected nothing from me. There's no one else out there that would treat me better. He's treated me like a queen since I stopped fighting him every step of the way.

God, how the fall off my high horse came swiftly and my ass hurts from hitting the ground so hard.

He breaks our kiss and pulls back, moving hair out of my face, "Birdie," he says breathlessly.

Equally as breathless I tell him, "Don't call me that." I kiss his jawline with featherlight urgent kisses. I wiggle in his arms, wrapped all the way around him, hanging on.

"Trixie," he whispers kissing up my jaw.

"Mhmm," I hum into his neck as I kiss him there.

"You're everything I've ever wanted and can't have."

"Please, Lincoln, this is me begging, I need you, I want you."

He growls and marches into my room and throws me on the bed. He whips his shirt off over his head and tosses it.

He climbs on top of me, reigning kisses on every inch of skin peeking out of my clothes. "Fuck, you're so beautiful," he breathes across my exposed skin sending shivers across my flesh. His gaze roams over me beneath him, committing this sight to memory.

I spread my legs and wrap them around him as he settles into the cradle of my hips. His hot, hard cock rubs up on my equally hot sex through all these clothes in the way. I want him inside me so bad.

He braces himself over me, looking down then dips down to nip along my neck, "I've waited so long."

"I'm yours, Linx, take me. Claim me."

Chapter 20 – Linx

I've longed to hear those sweet words. I'm teetering on the edge of oblivion.

My forehead rests on hers, "If I'm about to break my vow to your father, at least tell me you like me finally."

She giggles lightly while running her nails across my scalp. God, it feels so good.

"Yes, I like you. Maybe even more than a little bit." She smiles and wrinkles her nose, teasing me.

"Well, that only makes me feel slightly better about betraying him."

"Do you really love me, Lincoln?" she asks quietly.

I pull back enough to look into her sky-blue eyes, "More than my own life, Trixie."

Her eyes well with tears, "I'm so sorry."

"Hey, baby, don't cry. We're here now, ok?"

"Fuck me like you love me. Show me, Linx. Please show me. Show me everything I've been missing."

I kiss her with every ounce of love I have for her. Her mouth opens to me, and I meet her tongue, swirling it around in a sexy, languid pace. She moans her pleasure into my mouth, and it's like music to my fucking ears. I grind my cock into her, smearing precum all inside my shorts. I feel the heat radiating off her sex and it's driving me wild. I bet if I reached down there right now, she'd be drenched.

What a wonderful idea.

I pull away from her and sit back on my calves. I unbutton her shorts, pulling them off her perfect legs. My first look at her pussy leaves me breathless. Her small patch of black hair is perfect, and her lips are the prettiest puffy pink.

"Trixie," I say in awe. I spread her legs wide. I see her sex glistening with her desire. The first look is heaven. I've died and this is heaven. "Baby, you're stunning." It's like looking at something you know is holy and you shouldn't really touch it, but the intrusive thoughts win. You touch it and you're immediately consumed by desire, lust, fire, red hot heat; everything all at once. I'd gladly burn down just to touch her.

My body hangs off the end of the bed as I lay between her luscious thighs. Wrapping my arms around her thighs, I pull her hips up to my lips like it's my last supper, I'm not waiting anymore. I lower my head, taking in a deep breath of her arousal. She smells amazing. Dipping my head to get my first taste of heaven, I throw away ten years of trust.

It's the sweetest nectar I've ever had. There's been nothing like her. The wait was worth it. *Finally*, I sigh. The forbidden fruit is the sweetest addiction in the making. One time and I'm hooked. Her pussy is more addictive than heroin. There's no way anyone else will ever compare to her.

In one lick, she's ruined me.

I open my mouth wide and swirl my tongue all over her spread pussy, stopping long enough to suck on her clit. In the back of my head, I try to convince myself to stop, it's still reversable. I try to rationalize my punishment and slip further into my bubble of denial. Rock will accept us once he sees how happy I can make her. I continue to lie to myself as I flatten my tongue on her lovely bundle of nerves.

Her hand brushes my hair on the top of my head. "Lincoln," her breathless moan calling my name undoes me. I'll never forget the sound of it. Forever committed to memory.

"Baby, my name sounds so beautiful falling from your lips." Angels can't sing as good as that sounded, listening to it from between her legs.

"Linx, I want to come so bad with you, please let me come."

Her begging sounds almost as good as her moaning my name.

I look up and urge her, "If I'm going to fuck the Devil's daughter and fight all the demons of hell to keep her, make it worth it for me Trixie, yell my name as loud as you can, baby."

I resume eating her pussy like my life depends on it, because technically it does and I'm going to enjoy my last days loving on the woman of my dreams. I insert one finger, give a few pumps, then push in another. She feels like silk around me. She's almost too tight for two. Holy fuck.

Birdie's back arches and she lifts her arms to grab the pillow behind her. She digs her heels into the bed pushing her gyrating hips up to my greedy mouth. Oh god, these are the moans I would have sold my soul to hear, fuck, to be the one making her sound like this.

"Lincoln, oh god...so close," she pants.

I flatten my tongue and swirl, making her unravel under me as she throws her head back. She doesn't disappoint me as she cries my name to the heavens, loudly with such force. She's coming so hard and choking the life from my fingers. Her body shaking, one arm above her clawing the pillow, and the other hand gripping the back of my head while she holds me between her thighs, is one of the best sights I've ever seen.

This is better than my dreams.

I can't wait anymore. I have to have her, I gotta be inside of her finally. I have to make my death worth it.

I stand up, dropping my board shorts. I grip my cock while growling, "Trixie." I stand at the foot of her bed stroking my dick, precum glistening off the tip, dripping onto the blanket.

She stares at my cock, licking her lips, and then spreads her legs wider, holding out her arms to me. Fire crackles across my skin because this is the moment. I've fantasized about this moment for years.

My breath catches in my throat.

She's still panting and spread wide, and so very wet. My pulse roars in my ears while I stare between her sweet thighs.

'Ride' by Chase Rice plays in the living room. It's on my playlist I made of songs that make me think of her.

This fucking moment is burned into my brain. Seared there for eternity. I hope when I get old and gray, I still have my memories, and I never forget her.

I met her eyes, "This is your last chance to say no," I gruffly warn her as I cup my balls with my other hand. I swipe the precum off the crown and swirl it around the head of my cock.

She's still out of breath. "Lincoln, yes, so much yes, come fuck me, if you dare." She grins while crooking her finger at me.

Her body beckons me to throw away everything I've worked for in the past ten years.

I see how women became the fall of man.

I see how easy it is to fall to your knees for them.

Because I would do anything for her. Even betray her father and my brothers.

I climb onto the bed and kiss her, drinking her in. A low growl escapes my throat. Her arms wrap around my neck and her legs slide up my body to lock on my hips, pulling me close. I kiss her neck and up her jawbone. I keep telling myself to slow down.

She turns her head and licks up the column of my neck, stopping at my few days' growth beard. The heat of her mouth, the wetness of her tongue on my skin shivers down my spine.

She kisses her way to the shell of my ear and whispers to me, "Fuck me, Linxy. Let's burn in hell together, baby."

Father forgive me.

I reach between us and notch my crown at her entrance, "Oh my fucking god, Trix, you're burning up." I press into her and she's so goddamn tight. "So fucking wet."

A few good slow thrusts, slow and sensual, coating my cock with her hot lubrication, all while she accepts my size into her. She makes the sweetest sounds under me. I hit bottom, and my girl gets louder when I start moving deep in her. "Oh god, fuck, Lincoln! More, I want more." She locks her heels on my ass, pulling me into her greedy pussy more, and she rubs her clit on my pubic bone. Fuck, it feels so good. She's everything I ever dreamed of and more.

"My little bird feels like heaven, my god Trix. You're so fucking perfect."

I fuck her harder, pistoning my hips as she cries out and digs her nails into my biceps.

"Lincoln, oh...oh oh."

Running my splayed hand up her ribcage, up to her breasts, I dig my fingertips into her fleshy tits. I roll her nipple between my thumb and forefinger causing her to clamp down on my cock.

I hiss out my pleasure at her tightness. "You're strangling my cock, baby."

I reach down and pull her leg further up on my hip and sink deeper into her. God, I love her moans.

Moving my hand upwards, I come to rest on her throat. Her breath catches in her throat and her eyes get a little wider. She surprises me when she leans up, applying pressure to her own throat with my hand, "Give me everything I've been missing. Fuck me wild, Linx."

Fuck, my baby wants this so bad. She knows what she wants; she just needs the right man to give it to her. A man she trusts. I'm the only man to do it.

I work my hips into her and apply pressure to her throat. Breathing heavily, "Trixie, fuck, I've loved you for so long." I hiss through the overwhelming tingles from the best fuck of my life.

She's destroyed me in the best possible way. "Come for me, baby, give it to me." I lay down over her, angling my hips up, slamming into her, rubbing her just right, "I want it, it's all mine, you're all mine, aren't you baby? Say it."

I ease up on her neck, "I'm yours, Lincoln, all yours," is her breathy reply.

We share a look so hot it could melt the sun. She's so fucking close. She nods her head, her lips parted as she tries to pull in more air. Any second she's going to tumble headfirst. Her brow furrows as sweat breaks out. Panic flashes in her eyes. "I've got you, baby girl," I lean down and kiss her lips, nipping at her bottom lip.

Her thighs tremble and I thrust harder and growl to her, "All mine, Trixie, every bit of you. Come for me, Trix. Come all over your cock. Make no mistake, baby, I'm all yours, every bit of me, heart and soul. I love you so much. I'm going to fill you so full of my cum. Come for me, Princess."

Her eyes roll back as she stiffens, hips arching up, coming hard, so very tightly around my steel hard cock. I release the pressure on her throat, and she begins sobbing my name very loudly over and over on her first deep breaths.

Watching her unravel and cry my name sends my heart into overdrive, straight to my balls and my orgasm pulls my soul out of me into her. I see stars, the universe, infinity as the most intense orgasm I've ever had crashes over me.

Fuck me if I didn't roar as I came inside her, calling for my little bird as I watch her face while she shatters all over my cock. I have never come that hard in my life. It's almost painful. But fuck, shit, goddamn, it felt amazing.

No fantasy prepared me for the real thing. I can't even remember my own name I'm so shook.

Birdie losing herself in the throes of passion is the single most beautiful thing I've ever seen.

Rock could kill me now and it'd be worth it.

I slide my arm behind her and pull her down harder, just to get the last little bit of her quivers.

I peer down at her with a big smile. She gives me a goofy ass grin in return.

I lean down and kiss her as we catch our breaths in ragged pants, chests heaving. Laying my forehead on hers, I breathe her in, "I love you Beatrix Evangelina Chavanet and you don't have to love me back right now, it's ok, one day I hope, but I'm just happy you like me now." I chuckle. "I just want you to know finally, I love you, Trixie and I always have." I kiss her softly and slide my tongue in gently, lazily sliding along hers.

I pull back to see her tears slip down her temple to the hair covering her pillow. "Hey, what's wrong?"

She shakes her head back and forth, with her quivering chin, she bites her lower lip, "I've looked for you, I search inside of every single man I've ever met that ghosted me, in every fantasy where I wished I had a partner, a bestest friend, a person to call my own. You were right in front of me the entire time, waiting for me to wake up and see you. I see you now, Linx, I see you so much. I know what you just sacrificed, and I want you to know I'll gladly suffer the consequences with you because that wasn't a mistake or an accident, I won't lie, that was the most connected I've ever been to a person and the best sex I've ever had in my entire life. I regret zero percent of it," she finishes with a triumphant smile through her tears.

She's my treasure. I'd give up every dollar I have to keep her. I'd take however many lashings Rock's going to dish out...if he doesn't kill me instead.

Birdie runs the palm of her hand over my scruff, "I don't know if I love you yet, Linx, but I'm not far from it I think. You're pretty amazing and I'm really glad I had to run off with you and got a chance to get to know the real you. Now, I get to spend the rest of the week fucking your brains out."

"Alright, fair enough," I chuckle, "I'm good with that. Can we eat supper now though? I'm starving after that."

Chapter 21 – Birdie

Dinner was eaten with sly glances and a couple of giggles. I've never felt like this before. I've never known pleasure like that.

He had me wear one of his motorcycle print t-shirts with no panties on. He said something about a fantasy of his. Personally I think he wanted to keep running his fingers up my slit to feel his cum leaking out.

After dinner we went to his bedroom and did all the good stuff all over again until we both were out of breath and couldn't move.

When we got to his bed, he slipped the t-shirt off of me while I straddled his hips. My hair fell around us like a curtain as I lifted up and then sat back ever so slowly on his cock.

BEST RIDE OF MY LIFE.

Linxy knows how to fuck a woman. From his hands all over me to his filthy, dirty mouth that makes me cream his cock even more. Now, near midnight, we're laying in my bed, because it's bigger than his, tangled up in each other and blankets. He's twirling a lock of my hair around on his finger and I can feel his contentment. It mirrors my own.

"I probably should have asked about this hours ago, about birth control and I'm really sorry I didn't use a condom. I'm clean, I swear."

"Yeah, I got the birth control covered. About that other thing, me too. I've never had sex without one. I didn't even think about it with you."

"Me either. I don't regret it though. It definitely feels better without. You feel amazing. Best pussy by far."

I slap his chest playfully, "Stop lying."

He lays facing me and his smile is so genuine when he says, "Not lying. Best day of my life. Better than my wildest dreams. Cross my heart." He X's over his heart then kisses his fingers. "You mean we could have been doing this for the past few years?"

He nods and whispers, "I know, crazy right?"

I snuggle further into the blanket next to him. "It makes me sad." "Don't be sad, princess. We're here now. We have right now. If this is all we get, then I had the time of my life, ok? Let's not dwell on the past. We know what we have going forward. And that's going to be a shitstorm."

"Yeah, about that too, after this week, if we get home and you choose your club over me, just know it will shatter my heart. I expect you to do that as soon as my dad finds out. He'll make you choose and I'm not going to say I'll understand why you would pick them, but I can say I'll be pissed and most likely will never forgive you."

"Oh, little birdie of little faith. I just signed my death warrant, baby. There won't be a choice. I'm a dead man walking right now and there's nothing you can do to stop it, so use your time with me well. I will always choose you." he says, not kidding around anymore.

"I'll just talk to him."

He rolls to his back with his arm over his face, "If I ever had any doubts that you don't know what kind of man your dad really is, that moment is very clear to me now, you have no idea." He rolls back towards me and caresses my cheek lovingly, "I'm not trying to scare you, but your dad is an evil man. *I'm* an evil man. My days are numbered now, and I want to spend those last few with you, right like this. I have to tell him, Trix, I'm not hiding my love for you anymore, not after this. I have to be a man about it, and I won't lie. I'm not sneaking around like some lying teenager. There's only one choice for me, it's you, always you, but choosing you is death. No regrets. Com'mere, baby." He holds his arm up with the blanket tenting while I scoot closer and snuggle into him. He smells so good, and it makes me sad for a second but my happy heart flutters.

Minute by minute I feel like Lincoln LaFleur was made for me. Word by word of his that I heard on the back of a bike, I fell harder. The words he said while inside me make me smile and fall harder. He's perfect for me. I see his teasing was harmless. If I hadn't of gotten involved with another asshole, I might have seen his teasing was actually flirting.

From his chest, where my head is nestled into, with a hardness to my tone I whisper up to him, "I'll kill my father if he hurts you. I'll burn the world for you too, Linx."

"Bon matin, mon amour."

Linx wakes me up by kissing his way up the nape of my neck and rubbing my hip with his big, warm hand. I sigh in contentment while he gently shakes me awake, making my ample ass jiggle. I wanna be woke up like this every morning- hands and lips all over me.

His hand slips into my panties and his fingers find my needy and sore clit. "This is the very last time you're wearing panties to bed. I need access twenty-four seven. I want my DNA smeared all over those luscious thighs when it leaks out of you." He uses his magic fingers to arouse me until I'm practically panting for him. Good goddamn, I do love his hands.

"Get up little birdie, breakfast is ready, sleepy head." He pulls his hand out of my panties, making me whine, and I feel his weight lift off the bed. *The fucking nerve of this man.* His lips smack behind me, *I'm finger licking good.* "Mmm, you taste delicious, baby. My favorite kind of breakfast. Wake up, sleepyhead." He rips the blankets off me and smacks me on the ass.

I roll to my back and flip him off.

"Come on, Trix, it's already after eleven."

I grumble, "Sorry I'm not a morning person like you are apparently. You shouldn't have spent all night fucking me if you didn't want me sleeping so late." I sit up on the side of the bed and wince, it's a little tender down there.

"Are you sore?"

"Yeah, you aren't exactly small there Mr. Danger."

He lifts his hands to rest on the trim at the top of the door and leans in, showing off his immaculate body that makes me drool, "Trixie," in an over-the-top sultry voice, feigning shock, "are you saying I gotta big cock?"

It's too early in the morning for him. For fuck's sake, make him stop.

"Gah, you *are* the big cock for waking me up. Why didn't you let me sleep?" I halfheartedly whine. I'm so sleepy, it's all his fault too for keeping me up half the night fucking me. I'm not going to complain about it, but I have to remember he doesn't know what a bear I am in the mornings. I've been on my best behavior here. Sorta. Yesterday was a little much, I admit. I'm trying for him. But it still doesn't stop my murderous thoughts when I first wake up.

He laughs out loud, "I want to take you somewhere, so get up and get ready, grumpy ass."

"Coffee," I croak.

"It's on the counter, ready to go for you, Princess."

"One of these days you're gonna have to tell me how you know everything about me."

Just then an alarm starts beeping a warning from out in the common area.

He jerks to attention and says, "Fuck!" and takes off.

"What is it?" I ask, but he's already gone, his footfalls urgently racing to the kitchen table.

I quickly follow him out as he drops into the chair and logs into his laptop. I'm wide awake now. I slide in to stand behind him along the wall and see numerous boxes flickering to life on his screen. All of them are rooms of my apartment.

"What the fuck, Linx? Why are there cameras in my apartment? Goddamnit, man."

"For this very reason." He clicks on the living room camera and two men, dressed in black, looking like henchmen, are searching my apartment. This looks like a cheesy low budget movie with these two clowns moving about.

However, I still lose my breath because this is my fucking house. It's really real. Someone's broken in and disturbing my peace. I feel dizzy. My precious sanctuary. Anger, deep and hot, spirals in my core. How dare they.

"What are they doing?" I breathe out.

"Looking for you, babe."

My blood runs cold. This is a helluva wake up call.

A little over an hour later, I'm buckled into the truck, and we are headed east to his mom's house. I'm nervous to see her again because let's face it, I didn't leave off on a good note yesterday when she last saw me.

Linx sees me fidgeting and reaches over and takes my hand. "What's wrong, princess?"

"You know, every time you called me princess, I thought it was an insult, like being condescending to me. I didn't know what it really meant." I look over and give him a small smile, still feeling like an idiot for not seeing it.

"Technically you are my princess, but you're *my* princess, if that makes sense."

"Yeah, it does."

"So, what's got your brain on overdrive."

"This is a lot, ya know, this is no shock to you, but I was sheltered from all this. My quiet life was disrupted and I'm not sure how I feel about it yet. Then there's you and all of whatever is going on now. And then I didn't handle yesterday at your mom's well before she took me back to camp. I'm nervous being around her again." That unfamiliar feeling coming over me is shame. I try hard not to do shameful things but here I am being bad.

Linx squeezes my hand and reassures me, "My mom actually loves you. She's been so sad you won't ever be her daughter-in-law. She knows all about you. I'm pretty close to my momma and I tell her damn near everything. Pierre and Shadow know too."

"I'm not sure how to handle any of this," I tell him quietly. "I'm not sure what I'm supposed to do."

"You're doing great. I never intended for you to find out but I'm glad you did. I should have been the one to tell you, not let you figure it out in my mother's house, but I'm happy you know now and we're having these moments. You're just supposed to be you, keep being you, that's the woman I love." He gives my hand a shake and reassuring squeeze to send his words home. They hit me in my chest, and I settle a little bit, because they're sincere.

I'm still mad at myself that we could have been like this for years. We could have been happy sooner because as much as I don't want to admit it, these past few days with him, I've been happier than I have in a very long time. He brings it out of me. I've never laughed so hard. It's fun to be around him. We have the same jokes, we talk about all kinds of things we are passionate about or just love doing, and I feel so comfortable with him now.

And it's crazy to me like just last week, he annoyed the piss out of me; now, not so much. It was truly the elementary school playground shit; the boy will pester you and tease you until you give in. The old adage of 'He must like you if he's teasing you.' That's Linx's love language to me. When I look back at the interactions between us, he was trying to say it in the only way he could.

I would have laughed in his face if he had come to me and told me last week that he was wildly in love with me. I would have been a bitch about it. But fear and him pushing me out of my carefully built box into this ball of nerves I am now, has made me wake up and look at life a different way.

I kick myself in the ass.

We're here now, as he keeps reminding me. He's got the patience of a fucking saint, I tell ya.

When we walk into his mom's house, she greets us and looks between us, and her face softens, and she smiles so big.

"Your toot toot is glowing, mon cœur," she happily chirps at him.

I googled that term yesterday.

A lop-sided grin spreads across my face, "Yes, I'm his *willing* toot toot now." I'm his main girl, his crush, his sweetheart, is what it means. I'm all that.

Collette winks at me and coos, "I'm so pleased." She envelops me in a warm, comforting hug and all is right between us. So, this is what mothers are supposed to be like.

She looks over to Linx, a conspiratory look, and asks, "What are you two off to do today?"

He grins over at me in his excitement, "It's a surprise but we're going over to Puppy's and see what we can get into."

"Oh, that sounds like fun."

"We're going to take Sampson and ride over. We shouldn't be but a few hours."

She hands me a tube of sunblock, "I picked you up some more. Lord above, you have some of the prettiest, palest skin I've ever seen, even with the colors, and I don't want it to burn." I don't know how, but she's found some pale skin. I may have some blank space in the back still but the majority of me is covered in colors. I'll take her word for it.

Slyly looking over to Linx with a questioning eye, Collette says, "Ça va bien maintenant?"

"Mom, you know it's rude to speak in a different language around people who don't know it."

She gestures vaguely in the air with her hand. "How come you don't know French, cher?"

"Honestly, I failed out of it. I can ask where the bathroom is and where is my sock."

Collette giggles with amusement at my revelation. Even Linx chuckles.

"Mon cœur, you teach her, yeah?"

"I'll try, but until then she tries to use her phone to translate."

"That's a good idea. Show me."

I whip out my phone and nod to her. She says, "Tu vas faire une bonne belle-fille, chérie!"

My phone says, "You're going to make a good daughter-in-law, honey."

There's a strange flutter happening in my chest and I feel the blush come over my cheeks.

Shyly I reply, "Thank you."

She reaches up to pat my cheek, "il va t'aimer jusqu'à la fin du monde."

Siri beeps awake and says, "He will love you until the end of the world."

It makes my eyes tear up and I can only nod as I'm choked up with emotion. One more word and I'm losing my shit. I take in a deep breath and give her a smile, trying not to be sad. I try not to think about losing him, about my father taking him away from me, about losing this promise of happiness with him, about the threat to me weighing us down and stuck between us. So many things fighting against us.

My gaze swings over to him and he puts his arms around me, "Pour l'éternité."

My phone says, "For eternity."

I drop my head to his chest and the first tear falls. He puts his fingers under my chin and tilts my head up to face him, "It'll be ok, we're here now." I nod while my lips press into a line with worry. "I'm taking you somewhere fun, it's too heavy in here right now. Damn."

I release the breath caught in my chest with a strained chuckle at him diffusing the atmosphere. "I don't know, I like when you speak French to me." I give him my most knockout, sexy grin. I think I do anyways. I could look like a total creep for all I know, snotty and red-nosed now.

God, I'm so sick of my own shit. How the hell has he put up with me for so long? I'm awful at being sexy. Feeling sexy, feeling beautiful. But I want to try now, with him. Movies make it look so easy.

"Thanks, momma, I'm taking my girl now. We'll see you in a few hours." I'm ushered to the garage to hop onto the back of Sampson again for my next flying lesson.

Chapter 22 – Linx

I love seeing Birdie throwing her hands out to the sides like a flying bird as we cruise down the road. I hear her in the headset giggle occasionally and it sounds like a tinkle of a dainty windchime on a spring breeze. I love it. My heart is so happy.

We come up on things off on the side of the road, buildings, businesses, old houses, camps, and she points them out and I tell her all about them. She's so curious about the area and a few times I pictured us living out here every time she ohhs and ahhs at one of the big plantation houses.

She asked me to speak more French to her, so I told her all about how much I love her, all the things I love about her and how beautiful she is as we zip down the mostly empty road. Then I had to translate it all, and then she would sigh with happiness. When I was finished, she wrapped her arms around my middle and hugged me tightly.

We arrive at Puppy's and get down from the bike. It's a business on the side of the road, a one room office that houses his receipts and waivers. That's the only office work he'll do. The rest is spent out on the water.

He comes out to meet me and we shake hands, then he hugs me joyfully. I haven't seen him for a few months. I've always been close to my uncle; we would go fishing for hours when I was growing up. He always felt like he had to be a father figure to me since mine had run off when I was two.

"Hey Uncle Pup! This is my girl, Birdie." I gesture to my uncle and say, "This is my mom's brother. We call him Puppy."

Birdie reaches out her hand to Uncle Puppy and he grips it, using it to yank her into a hug. She stiffens and looks over to me for help. His Cajun French accent so bayou thick when he tells her we don't shake around here, we hug.

Unfortunately, I know my Trix is not used to so much affection and she doesn't know how to accept the touch of someone else, because she was severely lacking it her whole life. I'll teach her. I'll show her what it's like to be wanted, to be cherished, to be loved. She'll love being loved the right way and passionately.

Pup looks over at me and questions, "We all set?"

"Sure are. She still doesn't know where we're going."

"Whooweee, this will be fun, yeah! Just you wait and see where Pup's taking you."

He walks us to the back of his building where his air boat awaits us.

Birdie's wide eyes swing over to me as he starts up the big engine, "We're going on a boat ride?" she yells over the giant fan spinning at the back of the boat.

I nod my head enthusiastically while I use my fingers to close her open mouth, then I gesture for her to step up into the boat with a big smile. I make sure she doesn't fall, and I hop in after her. I've been riding in one of his boats since I was a baby. Once she's seated and has the seat belt fastened, I hand her the headset.

I yell and tell her, "This is like the bike helmets." She nods her understanding with a thumbs up and puts the headset on. Looking over to her, "Can you hear me?" She smiles and nods.

I throw a thumbs up to Puppy and he slowly maneuvers us away from shore out into the big open waters of the Jean Lafitte National Historical Preserve. It's 23,000 acres of Louisiana wetlands as far as the eye can see and it's gorgeous. It sings to my Cajun heart and it's one of my favorite things to do when I come back home.

I'm thrilled to bring Trixie out here.

I key my mic, "This is where I find peace. Welcome to Elmer's Island Refuge." Her wild smile matches the sparkle in her eyes as she takes in the breathtaking landscape. She takes my hand to hold in her lap and absently rubs her other hand on top of our entwined fingers. Her wide eyes try to take in everything at once. My heart is so full right now. Her smile says it all.

The wait was worth every second I can call her mine.

We spent the afternoon watching wildlife and feeding gators marshmallows. Uncle Puppy has a master's degree in Coastal Marine and Wetland Studies. He's got a big brain filled with all kinds of water life knowledge and is one of the leading experts in this area of gator expertise.

Pup took us to the public beach and let us off for a while. We walked the beach looking at seashells and holding hands. Almost like a real couple who doesn't have the weight of the world on their shoulders.

Now, we sit on the beach watching the waves lap at the shore and she lays her head on my arm. "This is where you grew up too?"

"Yeah. Uncle Pup's ran a boat tour business for as long as I can remember. I booked him for the entire afternoon to take you here. He's always happy to come out on the water and hey, he loves me, so he was happy to do it." I hold her tiny hand in mine and rub the back of her hand with my thumb, kissing her dainty knuckles. "Thank you, Linx, it's beautiful out here. I've never seen this part of Louisiana."

"Anytime, Trix. There's lots of places you haven't seen that I plan on showing you when we have time," I promise her.

"I'd love that. I love this place. The solitude, the quiet and it doesn't smell like piss and vomit like the French Quarter," she says on a laugh.

"Thank god for that! I don't understand how you can live there. It's filthy," I tell her with a shudder. I really don't get the allure of the Quarter. So many people, so many foul smells.

She shrugs, "Tourists clammer for Bourbon Street, bypassing all the other streets, whereas it's the shops and little out of the way places that have my heart on Royal Street. It's the little tucked away book nooks and small boutiques scattered about the Quarter that lures me in. As a local, I hate dodging tourists, but I recognize it's a must if the Quarter is to thrive. And the restaurants! God, how I'd love some crawfish étouffée from Evangelina's right about now."

"Funny you should say that, because that's what my mom is making us for dinner. I told her it's your favorite."

"Oh my god! Thank you! However, that's just another thing you know about me, and I don't know shit about you. What's your favorite?"

"I'm easy, seafood gumbo. My mom's particularly."

"Do you know how to cook?" she asks.

Do I ever. "Yes, I do. My mom made it a point to teach me how to cook proper Cajun meals. Whatever you want, Princess, I can make it for you."

"That's fucking amazing," she squeals in awe and excitement, "I burn toast," she laughs. "I'm awful at cooking. No one ever showed me how and I never took the time to learn with so many places to eat around me. I don't know how I'm not as big as a house already from all the food delivery I order."

"Don't worry, mon amour, I can teach you and take care of you. I won't let you starve. Who do you think keeps your fridge stocked? It's not your housekeeper."

Birdie playfully slaps my arm, "What the hell? How do you get in?"

"I have my ways."

So, I do smell him there!

"Honestly, I should be more upset but I'm not. It's kinda scary how ok I am with shit right now." Shaking her head, she puts her head back down on my shoulder, and then pops it back up, like she thought of something she forgot, "And why is there cameras in my house? We ain't forgetting about that shit, Lincoln. Like how long have they been there?" She sucks in air sharply, "Oh my god, are they in my bathrooms? Are you watching me take shits, ya weirdo?"

At this point I'm laughing; I can't help it. She has every right to know why I invaded her privacy.

"No, Trix," I catch a breath, "I'm not watching you shit. There are no cameras in your bedrooms or bathrooms. There are four in the living room slash open kitchen area, one at the front door, two on the balcony, and one facing down the hall. I should tell you one of the living room cameras can see into your bedroom, but it just shows part of the bed, and I could see you sleeping." My voice dips lower, "And do other things."

"I can't believe you would watch me diddle with myself. Ya know what, nevermind, yes, I can totally believe it. My stalker's my boyfriend now. Jesus." She shakes her head with a rueful chuckle. I hold my hands up in mock defense, "Hey, I did it for your own good. And some of my own good too. It definitely made my job easier, that's for sure. Do you want cameras in my penthouse so you can watch me?"

"Actually, that's not a bad idea." The playful look she's giving me melts my heart. "Be a good boy and get on that A-SAP. I can't wait to watch you jack off in the shower." I love this side of her. It's a side I never thought I'd see. At least never directed at me.

"Done. We should get back; it's going to take a while to get back to Pup's."

"Ok." She stands up and brushes the sand off her bottom, "Too bad I couldn't fuck you right here, that would have been perfect."

"Who says you can't?"

She looks around to the deserted beach with her hands out, like I can't see the area surrounding us, "We're out in public, Linx."

"So? There's no one here," I tell her, waving my arms around with a grin. I'm down to get into more of that every chance I get.

"What about your uncle?"

Jerking my thumb back behind me, "Oh, the guy on the other side of the island…that I guarantee is taking a nap? Where he gets his nickname because he takes more naps than a puppy? That guy?" I shake my head at her. "He can't see us through the shrubbery. If you wanted dick, all you had to do was say something, princess; I'll oblige you anytime, baby." I give her a suggestive wink that makes her grin right back at me.

"You're incorrigible, you know that, right?"

"Aren't all the best men?" I reply, flashing her my dimple. "Seriously, Princess, do you want sand in your who-ha, or can I take you somewhere else for a little fun before we go to mom's?"

"Good point, Linx, we have no blanket," she wipes her hands off on her pants and dusts off her butt again, "Ok, lead me back to the boat then." She holds out her hand waiting for me to take it.

Gripping it in mine, I silently vow, I will always hold her hand, as long as she will allow it. Fuck, her touch rights my world so much.

"Thanks, Pup," I say as I shake my uncle's hand, and he pulls me in for another embrace. Next, he turns to Birdie and says, "Tout pour la belle dame," with outstretched arms and a huge smile. He wraps her up as she tentatively raises her arms to hug him back. "Thank you very much for the ride and all the cool information. I never knew alligators liked marshmallows," she steps back by my side and puts her arm around my waist. I'm tickled pink Birdie is just headfirst into this relationship thing with me. It's a dream come true.

Eventually I'm going to wake up though. And so is she but for now, we have the present and we are making the most of it.

As we were walking away, she asks, "What'd he say to me?" Slowly I look over as we walk up to Sampson, grinning at her, I reply, "Anything for the beautiful lady." I hand her helmet to her, "I think he likes you."

I go to put my helmet on, and she grabs my arm and says, "Waitwaitwait."

"Yeah, babe?" my slow sexy smile must be having an effect on her.

She steps closer to me, putting her arms up around me and says, "I wanted to kiss you before you put that on."

I quickly set the helmet down on my seat, and when her arms are around me, I scoop her up and kiss her while spinning her around. She starts giggling and I know within every fiber of my soul, Beatrix Chavanet was meant to be my wife. I've waited thirty-eight years for her.

Now, I just have to survive her dad to keep her.

On the ride home, I pull off onto a deserted camp road, far enough back off the main road no one can see us, and I kill the engine.

"What are we doing?" she asks in the headset as she taps my shoulder.

I pull my helmet off and hang it off the handlebar. Hers comes off next and I hang it off the other one. "We're here so I can break in Sampson."

"We're going to fuck on a motorcycle?" she exclaims excitedly while jumping down to the hard, sandy ground with a shocked smile. At least she's excited.

"Yep, strip."

"Out here?"

"Yep. Right now."

She looks around.

"No one's here, Trix. This camp has been abandoned for years. No one's back here. Now, give me a show, little bird."

Something in her eyes gives her nervousness away while she stands there chewing her lip. If I recall correctly, I've never seen Birdie flirt, and to some degree, I don't think she knows how. "Don't make me ask again, Trixie. You're sexy without even trying." Time to teach her about her own power.

This seems to motivate her, and she starts seductively taking her top off. Her beautiful C cups bounce out of the built in sports bra on her tank top and it has me drooling. Already her nipples are hardening.

Fuck, she's so sexy.

She watches me through her lashes as she unlaces her boots and shucks them off. She's like a siren, beckoning me to my demise. Next, she unbuttons her pants and those come off too and she tosses them on the saddlebags along with everything else of hers. My breath grips my chest at the sight of her.

She stands beside me gloriously naked with her hands on her hips and I drool like a caveman. I'll never get enough of seeing her naked.

I rip my shirt off and toss it over the handlebars. I unbuckle my belt, shimmy my jeans down a bit and open the front of my jeans for her. I'm already hard. I've been hard for her practically all day. Who am I kidding, I stay painfully hard around her.

I pull my cock out and immediately precum glistens on the end. My head is fat and red, waiting on what's mine. I can't wait to be inside my little bird.

She was so beautiful on the air boat and so animated seeing the sights, all the sights I love. It made my sore heart happy to see her so happy. I've never seen Birdie look so happy and all it took was an airboat ride and some attention. And a healthy dose of dick.

I hold out my arms to her and say, "Com'mere, baby."

I love when she comes to me when I call. Never in a million years did I think any of this would happen.

As I help her up onto my lap, she adjusts herself and seats herself over my jeans. Her heat could blister my dick her pussy's so hot right now.

"Now I'm going to drive you wild, and you don't get dick until I say you do."

"Can the bike be running for this? I like the feel and sound of it." "Yes, it can," my heart does little flips. She loves my bike! I start Sampson with a smile and give a few good revs to make her happy. The chrome pipes rumble out their power and I watch her close her eyes and take a deep inhale, absorbing the rumble.

Oh god, my heart. She's beautiful with her head thrown back, eyes closed, absorbing the vibrations from Sampson.

My hands tangle in her loose braid while I bring her down to kiss her hard, tongues clashing, hearts pumping. Our breaths grow heavy and louder, and she forgets her inhibitions about being outside when she moans into my mouth, grinding herself down on my dick making it slick with her juices.

"Be a good girl and give me what I want."

"What do you want?" she asks breathlessly.

"You, baby, always you. I want you to yell as loud as you can. There's no one around but us."

I lift her up slightly so I can take her boobs in my hands and lather my tongue all over them. I suck a nipple in and swirl my tongue around the pink bud.

I feel her pussy clench as she slowly slides her slippery lips over my cock.

I move to the other one, lightly rubbing across her beaded nipple, making her jerk but lean into me.

"Ohh, my good girl wants it so much, how bad, baby? How bad do you want this cock inside you?" She smashes her chest into my hands with a resounding answer, "Oh god, I want it, I want it all, fill me up Linx."

I've learned the way to her wetness is through her nipples, so I pay extra attention to them. I push her tits together and suck both her nipples into my mouth at one time, sucking with the right amount of pressure.

The moan starts deep in her chest and her hips start swiveling on my lap.

A hedonistic haze of lust consumes me. With my hand I lower it to her clit and gently brush across it, making her hiss and moan deep in her throat. She mewls by my neck as she seeks out my hand again with her needy clit.

"Linxy, stop teasing me," she pleads.

Circling her clit with my fingers, I kiss up her chest, across her collarbone, nipping at her neck, "I love fucking you, Trixie, I love everything about you, but I want you to be my dirty girl right now. Oh, baby, be my dirty little slut for me. You want to be my dirty girl?"

Her hips rub her wet slit on my engorged cock harder, and it feels amazing.

"Yes, Linx, anything for you."

"I want my cock inside you while you ride it and scream my name when you come, do you think you can do that for me?" Circling a little firmer to drive her crazy, "Fill up the world with your cries, baby. You'll do that for me right here?" Her hips remind me of a belly dancer, gyrating and wiggling, impatient as ever as I strum her clit teasingly.

She's already trying to get me inside her, running her slickness up and down my shaft and growing frustrated with me. I love that my dirty birdie wants me so bad. My fingers don't leave her clit, and she continues humping my hand, getting herself closer to the edge.

"Yes, Linx," she pants out, squirming around, needing release. I've teased her so much, she's almost feral. "Please, I need you inside of me."

"Say put your cock in me Lincoln."

She's breathless, just the way I like her, going out of her mind with arousal. With a velvety, low tone she says, "Put your cock in me, Lincoln, please."

God, I love to hear her voice like this.

I lift her up, and while she hovers over my dick, I line up to her entrance, I tell her while staring into her deep, fathomless blue eyes, "Tell me who you belong to."

She sinks down slowly, taking me inch by inch, coating me in her wetness, moaning out, "You, all you, Lincoln."

Fuck all, I will never get used to her tightness. I push up into her as I hook her shoulders and pull her down, seating her on the only throne she will ever know from here on out. Her head falls back on a gasp. Her nails dig into my shoulders she has clutched in her hands for leverage. She looks like a goddess on top of me, grinding her pussy down on me, and whimpering.

I would be lying if I said I never had this fantasy with her. I've always wanted to fuck her on one of my bikes.

"Mine, all mine," I growl into her neck, nipping and kissing, as my hands roam all over her making her core tighten around me. Her soft skin's begging to be used and gripped and rubbed roughly. She moans and whimpers my name so prettily, begging so sweetly to let her come on my cock as she undulates her hips on me.

Her striking blue eyes are glazed over with lust and desire, "I want you so bad, my body is on fire. Please Linx."

I grab her ass and haul her body closer to mine. I lean back a little so she can catch the friction on my bone. "Oh god, Linx, right there, oh my god…"

"Is this what you want? You want my cock filling you up and hitting bottom in there? You were made for me. Feel how good you take my cock? You're such a good girl, Trixie," I murmur into her neck.

With my hands cupping her ass, gripping her into position, I slam her over and over and over hard on my dick. I can't get enough. Fuck me, I love the way she's bearing down on my cock.

It's driving her wild and soon her cries fill up the desolate, empty camp, keening out my name, bouncing off the water and coming back to sing in my ears. Wave after wave of pleasure unhinges inside her and screams into the camp.

When I circle my hand around her throat, she willingly lifts her chin to surrender herself to me.

She starts shouting, "LINCOLN! Fuck. Come inside me, baby, come please, I want it all! Oh god, fill me up."

I feel her pussy walls tighten on me when I pull her close to kiss her and she drops her forehead to mine, hands on the side of my face, furiously working her body over mine, breaths mingling as our chests combust with need. It's the most beautiful thing to watch her throw her head back in ecstasy and yell my name to the sky, coming all over my cock deep inside her.

"That's my good girl, yes, baby," I gruffly tell her through her orgasm. I don't let her stop. "Don't stop, Trix, give me another one, baby. Come again for me."

She whimpers and I pull her harder to rub on my pubic bone. I feel her pussy quiver right as she wraps herself around me, nose to nose, and cries out with her release. When I can't hold back anymore, my balls tighten and my spine shivers, I feel the power to come inside her pull up from my toes, goddamn, I fill her with everything I have, yelling her name over the roar of the bike and her cries, holding her with everything I have.

Fuck yeah.

Chapter 23 – Birdie

I'm so full I could barely waddle up the steps to the camp. Collette's food is a-fucking-mazing, even better than Evangelina's, and that's saying something coming from me. And to think, Linx says he can cook like that. I'm going to gain weight so quickly around him. I can already tell I need to watch it, or I'll be buying a new wardrobe.

Drying my long hair with a towel, I come into the kitchen where he's on his laptop typing away. I'm impressed he can type so fast. I totally expected the hen pecking most guys do.

"Whatcha doin'?" I ask him while twisting my long locks in the towel.

Since he loves to see me in his oversized Harley shirt, I put it on after my shower. I'm lotioned up and thanks to Collette's diligence, I've not burned at all while here.

"You smell amazing. I've always loved your cotton candy scent. Ya know, I started eating cotton candy because of you."

"Really? That's sweet. Pun intended." I give him a cheesy smile.

He chuckles at my ridiculousness, then sits back, gesturing to the laptop, "I'm typing up a reply to Shadow. He's in charge of hunting down Grim while we're here fucking the days away," he says while giving me a sexy wink. I can tell there's some underlying stress he's trying to smooth over for me.

"And Shadow is Dad's third in command, correct?"

"Yes, he is the Sergeant-At-Arms. He's also dating your best friend."

That came as a small shock. I snap my fingers and exclaim, "Soo, that's the one. Zharia has been a little too secretive about him with me. I've not met her new man, but I guess I have in a way. Hmph." I sit down across from him as his phone rings.

He looks at the screen, then looks up at me. I see my dad's name sitting there between us.

"I have to take this Trix, away from you, I'm sorry. I'll go out on the deck."

"I understand." I do but I don't. I know there are club things that are none of my business, but I feel like my safety is my business. Like I'm not helpless. I may not be strong, or quick, or in shape, but, alright, spelled out like that, I suck at my own safety and need someone like Linx. *Point proven, brain.*

No matter how badass I feel, I will never be able to defend myself against Grim or any of his men if they attack me with more than one. I used to take down Linx on the training mat, but that was almost ten years ago. I didn't keep up with training or staying in shape. If I had to run away, they're catching me within a hundred feet, and I'll just wheeze in their faces. No wonder my dad sent me away from this mess. I'd just get in the way.

Nevertheless, my father is on my last nerves with not including me on my own life plans. Like why can't I know what's happening? Where is Grim and his men? How long am I going to have to stay here with Linx in our little utopia? Not that I'm complaining, but what are they not telling me? I still have a life to live outside of this camp.

Linx comes in and his jaw is clenched, face hard. It must have been bad news. My heart starts to sink.

"Please don't keep things from me that concern me." I walk up to him and lay my hand on his bare chest, feeling his heartbeat under my palm. I trace my fingers over his eagle tattoo that takes up his entire chest with its impressive wingspan. The detail on the wings is phenomenal. It does make me wonder why he never came to me for art.

I guarantee my dad has something to do with it.

"I can only tell you so much, princess," he tells me gently, rubbing my upper arms like he's warming me up. "I may have broken my vows, but I still have loyalty to my patch until I'm stripped of it." I hear the hurt in his words.

It weighs heavily on me that he broke his oath because of me. I mean, I was the little tart with my wanton ways who tempted him out of his mind. Once again, I'm the problem, but it turned out to be a very desirable problem.

Linx worked his way up to VP, playing by my dad's rules, being savage to our enemies, only he wears his signature boyish grin on his face as he kills bad men. Yes, I've heard the stories of my dad's ruthless, vicious Right Hand of God.

Of course, I've never seen that side of him, and I hope I never do, but I get the side none of them see, I'm sure of it. I get carefree laughter and joking, boyish smiles, dimples, and gentle hands.

Am I willing to stand in front of the firing squad my dad points at him for us being together? I helped him break those vows. I totally urged him on and maybe that was a little unfair. Why shouldn't I help pay the price? *Isn't that love, Birdie?*

Is it? I kinda feel like he professes to love me without really knowing me intimately. Like he knows *A LOT* already, but what about the stuff I doubt he knows of. Maybe I'm a bear to live with. Maybe I snore too loud. Maybe he doesn't like my hair portraits I draw on the shower wall with all my tresses that fall out while washing it.

Although, he seems to really love my pussy. I can't keep him out of it. He always has to have his hands on me now.

However, a thought, I have no idea what real love is, so I'm not exactly sure what to base these feelings on. I feel like I've been treated to a stoic version of love from my mother, I feel like my father gave me adoration with constraints. Linx loves me for me, so he says. For all my accomplishments, my hard work, for the good I do in the world. For my softness, and caring nature.

I believe Tally, Zharia and Pierre love me unconditionally too. They are my best friends, and we have a super tight bond, but that's not the same kind of love though. This feels different.

There's no way I could fall in love in a matter of days. Right? Insane. I'm too much of a realist. That shit doesn't happen; I mentally laugh at myself. Fuck, I just started *liking* him, for fuck's sake. But deep down, right in the core where the butterflies play, he stokes a fire in my soul, and if I want to be truly honest, he's always occupied that space inside me. No one else can touch it. There's always been an undeniable pull to Linx and that flame inside me, next to the little bird in my chest, is shining so bright right now.

If I'm completely honest with myself, I fell for Lincoln when I first saw him at eighteen. That boyish charm sucked me in when he was teaching me self-defense, when he was dancing with me, when he had to survive another family Thanksgiving sitting next to me between the ice queen and king. Core memories, and lots of them involve him. We used to laugh and be friendly. His constant presence in my life has been ebbing and flowing to this pinnacle point in our lives. It's about fucking time, right?

As much as I hated him up until a few days ago, which I'm seriously starting to doubt that was even hate, uh, more like me fighting my attraction to my tormentor and then not comparing him to another asshole; through all that, I still got butterflies around him, and I still admired him from afar. And I was so goddamn curious about him. I still went home and diddled on the clittle to his smile and voice, his scent, his nearness that made me tingle, and his hands, my god his tattooed hands. I thought about what it would be like to have his hands all over me, passionately fucking me, and telling me all the filthy things I read in books.

Every time he led me around, grazing my body with his hands, I flushed every time wondering what it would be like to have those warm fingers inside me. What would it be like to have his undivided attention and affection. There's not one thing sexually I haven't imagined Linx doing to me.

The naughtiest thoughts for someone who supposedly hated him.

The past few days have been a whirlwind of fun with him and even though there's like this movie worthy plot happening in my life and scaring the absolute fuck out of me, I still feel happy. Oh, and I found out so much about him!

I've never known such happiness. I wish my brain would catch up; it still has some reservations about falling so fast. But then again, love has no timeline. It happens when it happens.

I think I love Linx.

And I think I'm crazy. Certifiably. This shit only happens in movies and books. I mean come on. Was it there all along and I just couldn't recognize it? The butterflies have intensified a fuckton, my little chest bird is soaring in my rib cage. The little things are magnified now.

No, I know I love him in my own special way.

Or do I love the idea of him? No, I've seen the person he is. He is the one who captivated my heart and every ounce of attention.

He's a good man, it's all him. He's the only man that makes me feel safe. I love him for being that person for me. In a world where I have been running blind, Linx is my safety net. I think I've secretly hidden the affection I have for him under a mask of hatred. It was easier to keep him at a distance. Because as much as I feel physically safe with him, there were zero feelings of my heart being safe with him. He's reassured me the entire time I've been with him that he's devoted to me.

It's in every time I catch him looking at me like he'll eat me alive or drop to the ground at my feet, it's in every brush of his strong hands across my body, it's in the way he runs his fingers through my hair to comfort me. It's in the way he kisses me and loves me unconditionally. It's the patience he has with me, because I do be testing his nerves at times.

No one else has ever loved me this much and I can actually feel it. My parents showered me with gifts, not attention. I can't really say that about my dad wholeheartedly. He loved spending time with me as a kid but when I hit my teens, he kind of backed off, but I truly believed my mother had something to do with that. I also know business was booming and that took the majority of his focus, when meanwhile, I became a young woman learning how to be a rich wife.

A thought just occurred to me. "Linx? You sent me all the flowers on my birthdays. It was you, wasn't it?"

By his blush and his slow smile, he's exactly who my mystery person has been. Zharia and I have been trying for years to find out who sends me large floral bouquets full of colorful flowers every year on my birthday to the shop. The florist won't come off with a name. We've even debated breaking into the shop and finding the order, seeing who paid for it.

The flowers are very beautiful, and I always appreciate them. I have a lot of them dried and hanging around the apartment. It always arrives with a simple card that only says, 'I love you.' Zharia has repeatedly said it's an admirer, someone who's secretly in love with me. She always ribs me and says it's Linx, just to needle me. Shit. I'll never hear the end of this. She's going to love being right.

"Yeah. That's me." Nailed it.

"Thank you so much. I look forward to those flowers so much every year. You have no idea." I choke up at the end. "Those flowers reminded me that somewhere out there, someone loved me enough to send me flowers."

Linx's strong arms wrap around me, he whispers by my ear, "Dance with me, Princess."

"There's no music," I reply.

Linx starts humming something slowly deep in his throat, swaying me with his body. Slow, lazy rocking back and forth. His chest vibrates as my cheek lays on it. My arms slink up around his neck. This is the type of safety and peace I was missing, what I was yearning for.

Closing my eyes, I commit to memory what it's like to be with him. I won't let my dad or anyone else take him from me. He's mine.

After a snack and his shower, he asked me to tattoo him, so I set up an area at the small kitchen table after disinfecting everything in reach. Pierre will never let me live this down if he finds out I did tattoos at a kitchen table, considering he knows how much I don't like tattoos done outside of a licensed shop. Except the ones I do to myself.

This is the first time I've had a really good look at his tattoos. He's covered in black and gray, with spots open to bare flesh, like they forgot to put something there. He explains, "Those are for you. Put whatever you want in there, that's what they were saved for."

It's not very often you have a client say do whatever and completely trusts you to not fuck up their skin. Linx trusts me this much. I could put a dick with wings on it, and I bet he'd wear it with pride because I inked it on him.

I snicker to myself because now part of me low-key wants to do that to him. *Behave, Birdie.*

He settles himself in the chair before me and I prepare his skin for my design. This will be freehanded because that's what he's asked for. There's a clear spot on the underside of his arm, almost the entire underside of his left forearm is blank. Said it was my spot he's been saving. He asked me to put something there, knowing damn well people will see it and it will stick out like a sore thumb against all the black and gray.

As I'm drawing on the design with a marker, Linx speaks, "You know the guy who came in to install the security system at your studio?"

"Hmm, yes. Fuck. Let me guess, it's not really security."

He chuckles and it slightly shakes the flimsy table his arm is resting on, "Well, it is, but I get all the alerts from the security system. It was done by a probie who works for my security company."

"And you watch me there too?" I ask while drawing.

"Sometimes."

"What's a probie, again?"

"Someone trying to prove their worth to the organization before we allow them to take an oath and get patched."

"Interesting." I look up at him, hand poised over my doodles, "Ok, well, since it's Linx's romantic truth time, did you have something to do with Noah leaving?" I don't even need him to speak; the truth is written all over his instantly disgusted face. Noah did something, and Linx found out it wasn't good. I need him to say it though. I need to hear it from Linx.

"You know, mon amour, he slipped in while I was away on a mission for your dad. You were never supposed to have dated him." "What's that supposed to mean?" Immediately raising my hackles, what in the fuck, I can't believe this load of horse shit. "You've been mine far longer than you know of."

My temper flares up and I jerk back, angry because I know he meddled, but he snatches my forearm firmly, keeping me rooted in my chair between his legs.

Staring him in the eyes, I let the hammer drop, "Did you keep guys away from me, Linx? Do you know how lonely I've been?" He continues holding my arm, swirling small circles on the inside of my wrist, "Yes, I do but I couldn't bear to see you with anyone else."

"And Noah?" I ask, highly irritated.

"Pierre and I followed him to a frat party where we found him fucking some blond bitch. It was a mutual agreement he would leave New Orleans as soon as possible."

As the floor swallows me up, and the wind is ripped from my temper tantrum sails, my eyes go blurry. Linx pulls me over to his lap, cradling me while I absorb this latest dose of reality. I was with Noah for five months, not a lot in the grand scheme of things but enough that it made an impact on my sheltered little life. He left me with some trauma and a lot of questions. Was he cheating the entire time?

I'm shocked but am I really? Noah was decent to be around, but I didn't love him. "He was cheating on me?" Each word feels like it's being wrenched from my hurt heart. I feel like such a fool. I was so broken hearted over him. What an idiot.

"Yeah, and I wasn't letting that slide." He lifts my chin so I can gaze into his eyes, letting my damp hair sway behind me. "I don't regret sending him packing."

"Pierre knew?" He's making it hard to stay mad when he's wrapped his hand around my throat gently caressing it, and brings me over so he can smell me and kiss up my neck.

"He got in a few good punches for you, little bird," he supplies as he kisses across my cheek, taking the tears with him, then back to nuzzling in my neck, trying to distract me. "Pierre is who sent him away. I voted to kill him."

What has my life come to? Fuck that, do I even know what's happening in my own goddamn life? How could I not see the shit that was right in my face? Dude, I'm a complete idiot. Am I really this ignorant of the shit going on around me?

Deep breath. Calm, Calm, Calm.

"Ok. Alright. Good riddance then. I guess a thank you is in order, so thanks for getting rid of him." He nibbles my earlobe and gives me a sexy Mhmm. *Stay focused. You're kinda mad on the downlow.*

With one last shudder, I move back over to my chair, or else we'll never get anything done except fucking like rabbits. Sitting down with his hand in mine, I take a deep breath and sigh, "We're coloring here, ok, gimme your arm." He flops his arm on the table like a dead fish just to annoy me. Glad to see some things never change.

I scrunch up my nose and ask him, "Also, why haven't you come to me to get tattooed before?" I want to know. It's a mighty need to find out at this point. Years of wondering. If he has my art on his bike, why not his body.

"We aren't allowed to."

I go still and ask, "What? A rule of my father's?" No fucking wonder I've never seen any of them in my shop, not that I would recognize them individually, but I'd recognize the patch on their leather vests.

"Yes. Pierre's done all of mine." Pierre is a black and gray expert, no wonder Linx's tattoos look precise; he's brothers with the best. "Is this where Pierre disappears to about every three to four months for his 'self-care' long weekends?" I make sure I use the air quotes.

Linx huffs out a laugh, "Yeah, more like his brother's self-care weekends to get over his girl problems." He sheepishly shrugs. "He'd come tattoo me, right here in this very spot, just like you're about to do."

"I'll be damned," I breathe out.

Linx laughs and says," Yeah, I know all about how much you dislike at-home scratchers. Which clearly you and him are not, but right now, you kinda are, ya hypocrite." He snickers behind his other hand.

I shove his shoulder and tell him, "Oh yeah? Well, just for that I'm tattooing my original idea of a dick with wings on you." I follow that threat up with the meanest face I can muster.

He grabs his side, laughing and says, "There's my girl. Fuck, I love when you get riled up." He reaches down between his legs and adjusts himself, "Makes me hard as fuck to see them eyes light up."

"Jesus," I mutter under my breath. "Stop acting like a fool and get over here," I pick up his arm and yank it back on the table, "Did you truly want me to put some color on you, or did you just say that to make me feel better?"

Linx cups my face and softly says, "I'd be honored to wear your art, Trixie. I'm not sure if the colors will pop on my tan skin but I'm willing to give it a shot. Let's get this done, baby, I can't wait to see it."

Chapter 24 – Lynx

It's well after midnight when Birdie finishes up my tattoo. The Rolling Stones played in the background as we've sat for a few hours talking while she worked.

I've fallen in love with her giggle and the way her nose and eyes crinkle when she belly laughs. I love how animated she gets when she talks about the things she loves. I love her wicked sense of humor and how she can get sassy. Getting to know each other has been some of the best times of my life.

I want to be her everything so bad. I can't take my eyes off of her. The more I learn about her on an intimate level, the more I fall in love with her.

I've tried really hard not to look at the tattoo while she's doing it. Trusting the process here. I want to be surprised.

Quickly, I did make sure it's not a dick with wings though.

Birdie can be one of those silently petty girls. She used to prank her mom and dad all the time as retaliation, so she's well versed in psychological warfare.

Five and a half hours after getting home, Birdie says, "Let me clean it up and then you can take a look." She sprays my arm and wipes it off with a paper towel. Goddamnit, I hate that part. It fucking stings.

"Ok, all set. Have a look-see."

My eyes trail down from her beautiful face to my arm. She's marked me with a portrait of herself, plain as day, clearly her. Complete with her cute, upturned nose, her long black hair with a flower crown and deer antlers. There's her crystal-clear blue eyes that I love looking into, she captured her likeness down to the pout of her full lips perfectly.

She tattooed herself on me. My fucking heart.

On my forearm she's standing with her arm up and bent and there's a little blue bird perched on her finger, singing. There are these cute little musical notes above their heads, and in Birdie's other hand is a paint palette full of colors. The background is muted, splashed watercolors, barely noticeable they're so light. It's gorgeous and my new favorite tattoo.

"It's perfect. I love it, Trix."

She blushes and looks into my eyes with her head cocked, "You seriously love it?"

"Yeah, I do. It's you. What's not to love? Thank you, little bird. You knew exactly what I would want." I lean over to kiss her while she rubs me down with some goo from her briefcase.

"Do you want me to do anymore on you while we're here? Like tomorrow? What do we have planned?"

"I've got nothing planned, baby, I got all day for you to turn me on with pain."

She grins playfully, "Oh, so you're one of them types."

"Every time I've gotten tattooed, I think of you. Pierre even tells me to keep my hard-on to a minimum," I laugh. He argues with me every time to keep my dick under control and stop thinking about her naked. It always ends in me adjusting myself half a dozen times and him going, "Eww."

"That's so romantic," she snorts.

I watch her clean up her area. She is so methodical and her actions are smooth, proving she's done this hundreds of times.

Birdie removes her reading glasses and stretches her arms above her head and twists her torso. It has to be rough sitting in the same position for so long.

"Do you want a snack?" I ask her.

"A snack would be excellent. I'm going to the bathroom and then I'll be out."

She stands up and I hear her knees crack. "Damn, are you going to make it?" I ask with a chuckle.

"Yeah, I just get stiff," she calls over her shoulder as she walks to the bedroom to go to the adjoining bathroom.

While she's in there, I fix her a bit of cottage cheese and mandarin oranges, which I know is one of her favorite go-to meals. I know she likes to eat this on her breaks while tattooing. *I know because I'm her stalker*, I smile to myself.

Birdie comes out of the bedroom and sits down on the couch, covering a yawn with her hand. I don't know if it's just she's tired, or she truly is at peace in this moment, but she looks so serene and content I hate to intrude on her bubble. I don't have to decide because she turns her head and says, "What are we eating for snacky snack?"

Bringing over her snack, I ask her if she wants to eat and go to bed or watch a little TV. She's so tired she wants to eat and go to bed, and I agree, she needs rest. This is supposed to be her pseudo vacation and one day off will recharge her enough for me to ravish her again. I can't keep my hands off of her. "Thank you for putting your mark on me. I can't wait to see what you come up with tomorrow."

Watching her slowly eat her cottage cheese, I see how tired she is and vow silently not to ravish her tonight and let her sleep. *Goddammit man, stay off of her for a few hours.*

One thing I admire about Birdie is how hardworking she is. Her attention to detail and ability to keep a level head in situations makes my chest puff up with pride. She's truly amazing. The more I get from her, the more I love her.

After putting her paper plate in the trash, she tells me she's going to get ready for bed.

"I'm going to check a few things on my laptop, then I'll be in." Surprisingly, she comes over and leans down to where I sit on the couch to kiss me.

"Don't be long."

Her husky voice makes me shiver. God damn, I love her voice. First, I check the cameras in her apartment and see no one else there. I heard from Pierre earlier today, he went upstairs and made sure her door wasn't left wide open, and he went in to make sure everything was normal. They didn't tear through her drawers or closet, just looked for her and left.

Pierre said no one suspicious had been in the shop but that doesn't mean they weren't there. Only two guys have come in asking about Birdie. They were interested in big color portraits and agreed to come back next week to talk to her then.

He said there was no reason to suspect them. He told them she was on vacation in Chicago. They bought it and left.

I check the cameras in her studio next. Nothing seems out of place there. After that I check the camera I have stashed in a tree right in front of her studio and apartment entrance.

There's a guy standing there smoking a cigarette, leaning up against the building. I'm not sure if he's a normal Quarter wanderer, tourist, or he's there to snatch Birdie. I watch a few more minutes and see another guy come up to him, back to the camera where I can't see his face. They exchange words and the first guy moves off and the second guy stands there.

Shift change.

They're waiting on Birdie. I know in my cold, black soul, these fuckers are there for my girl.

I pick up my phone and call Rock. He answers on the second ring. I can tell he's tired.

"Yeah, Danger?"

"New development. I'm watching the cameras outside of her studio, there are men waiting by the entrance. It looks like they just had a shift change. They're just hanging out. I'm going to send a couple of guys over and see if we can spook them off. Or kill them. Haven't decided yet."

"Thanks for the update. I figured they would be hanging around the Quarter to grab her when they could." He sighs, the kind that comes from bone deep exhaustion. Rock's burning the candle at both ends trying to keep her safe. "How's she doing?"

I move to go outside to the deck once I hear the water in the bathroom shut off. She doesn't need to overhear more than she needs to.

"Shockingly, she's doing good. She doesn't put up too much of an argument. Birdie is well aware of the danger she's in. She knows the reputation of LSS is based on fact not myth. She's prepared to stay here as long as it takes."

"Good. I'm glad to hear she's calmed down and going along with the plan. What do y'all fill the day with?"

Oh, a little of nothing besides disrespectfully fucking your daughter and rutting into her as much as humanly possible. "She loves riding my bike, with a helmet of course, and she's been swimming at my mom's and hanging out with her learning to cook Cajun foods."

"You know, I kept her off bikes for a reason, right?" I hear the disappointment in his tone.

"Yes, I do know, but I feel the safest person she can ride with, besides you, is me. Plus, she begged."

He laughs and says, "And we know you cave at anything she wants. Well good, I'm glad she's not just sitting around, afraid and paranoid. Thanks for taking care of my little girl."

The dagger of deception twists in my heart.

"You're welcome, sir." I hang up with a heaviness in my chest. After I set the security alarm, I make my way to her room, which is where she's chosen to sleep tonight. She's already snuggled under the comforter with her hair bonnet on, little puffs of air pushing through her perfectly pouty lips. I don't want to wake her, but I'll be damned if I'm sleeping away from her.

I strip naked and slide in behind her, wrapping my arm around her middle and pulling her close to me. I bury my face in her neck and inhale her scent. "I love you," I whisper across her skin, and she snuggles harder back into me and sighs in her sleep.

I dreaded this week when I was ordered to take her away, but it ended up turning out to be the best week of my life so far.

Chapter 25 – Birdie

I kiss up his chest as he sleeps peacefully, hopefully dreaming of me. In his sleep, he's holding my body close to him with his large arm.

Curled up next to him, breathing in his energy is my favoritest place to be now. I'm so happy with him I could squeal.

His chest rumbles as he stirs awake groaning and it's the sexiest sound. I could get used to this. Guys make some of the sexiest rumbling noises, but Linx's send tingles straight to my clit.

He pulls me on top of him and opens his beautiful hazel eyes with a lopsided grin. "Fuck, what a beautiful sight to wake up to." He stretches with me on top straddling his morning wood. I feel him making it pulse under my bare pussy. As requested, I went to sleep in his Army shirt and no panties so there's nothing in between us.

Which was a great plan because about four this morning he slipped inside me from behind and slowly made love to me in the darkness while our hearts thudded in our chests for each other. He whispered to me about how beautiful I am, and how much he wants me and worships me, and wants to spend the rest of his life showing me how to be loved properly.

"Good morning, baby," I sweetly say to him. His answer is to pull my hips down harder on his erection. "Linx, it's only been a few hours since the last time." I swear he's insatiable. He just chuckles and continues touching me, smoothing his large, warm hands all over me, up under my shirt.

He always has to be within reach of me or watching me. My bodyguard-stalker is obsessed with me. I'm strangely ok with that. Like I'm strongly flattered. Am I deranged if I like it a lot and think it's sexy?

He softly rolls me over to my back with him on top of me and gazes down at me. I look up into his starburst, forest in the fall eyes and see nothing but love for me. His every move, every word, every action is out of love for me. More times than I care to admit, I wish I would have known sooner.

Somehow in a few short days I've managed to fall for the guy I hate. Oh god, I'm a victim of instalove. How the fuck does that even happen?

He thawed the ice queen with kindness and safety, that's how he did it. I don't even care if I make it out of this unscathed, it was worth every second with him.

His magic fingers find my wet crease and he gently massages my little nub of nerves.

"Linx," I breathlessly moan and lean forward, placing my hands by his head.

His moves grow more intense and fucking hell, it feels so good. "Yeah, baby?" he asks with his face buried between my tits, nipping and breathing across my nipples. "You want it nice and slow, or rough and hard?" His tongue runs across the swell of my left breast.

"Nice and slow, I need you to tip me over the edge so I can finish falling."

His head pops up from my boobs and our eyes lock. Eager hope's written on his face. He understands exactly what I'm asking for. What I need him to do.

Promise me forever. Unleash all his love for me and let it wrap around me.

Claim me.

Take a new oath. To me.

Choose me over everything.

Show me how much you love me. Teach me.

I need him to push me over the edge fully, I want to be in love so bad, show me. Was fate making me wait for him? My body and soul begs him to show me. Gone are the concerns about surviving this man; I'm going to willingly let him sweep me away and steal my heart.

"As my princess wishes," Linx says in a gravelly voice laced with lust and love that lights up all the fireworks in my body.

He starts undressing me, taking the T-shirt off of me, leaving me naked. "You are the most beautiful woman I've ever seen."

He settles his hips into the cradle of my smooth thighs, flush up against my wet heat. Nothing feels better than Linx coming home to me.

Linx masterfully maneuvers his hips so he rubs the head of his cock up and down my dripping pussy, coating him in my wetness. His cock finds my opening on its own with no problem, like it knows the way home already. This is where it belongs.

With no hands and just a little pressure, Linx slips into me. He drags himself out slowly and pushes back in, going further inside of me each time until he hits bottom. *Yes, come home, baby.* The tingles settle over my skin and my fingers pull his body closer to mine. Right now, I can't get him close enough, I can't hold him tight enough.

"Nothing feels better than you, baby," he says, his husky, uber sexy voice makes my chest flitter.

I've been waiting to feel this connected with someone. Funny, it happened in just a few days. His whispered words in my ear caress my once closed heart and peel back the layers I've built up the past few years against him. Oh, the twists and turns of my life. "I want to give you the world." Slow, intense thrust.

"There will never be another man in here, only me, until you die." Roll of his hips. I pant out, "Yes, yes. No one else."

"You're the only woman I want." Nip on my neck, long slide out, forceful thrust in that makes my breath catch in my throat. My own growl slips from my lips, "My man, no one else's." I clench my walls to punch my words into his heart. "My Linx."

"Who do you belong to?" he growls into my neck as he picks up his pace.

My feminism flies out the window any time he asks this. "You, Linx. All yours. I belong to you." I mean it too. I'm ruined for any other man. I've waited my whole life for this.

Our heavy breathing is the music to the morning while the sunlight streams through the window, cutting across the floor to the bed. I slide my legs up his calves and thighs to spread my thighs wider for him. I settle the heels of my feet on his ass, holding him as close as I can get. I want to take him as deep as possible. Linx groans as he sinks even deeper inside of me with every hiss through his teeth.

"Trixie, baby...fuck."

My hands run over his back muscles, bunching and flexing as he fucks me so sweetly. I can't touch him enough. He's a man pouring his love out across my body and I greedily accept it.

Linx hooks his arms on my shoulders and becomes more aggressive with his thrusts, deeper, shorter. It drives me out of my mind. I feel the tingle start deep in my lower belly. He's rubbing me just right on my clit. God, I love how he makes me feel. "Lincoln," I breathe into his shoulder before I bite him. His groan tells me how much he loves it.

Linx is rutting into me, holding me tight, hitting the spot that makes me sing and I am living for it. Fuck, it feels amazing.

My chest heaves. I want to climb inside of him, take root in his chest, curl around his heart and I still won't be close enough. My skin feels like it's on fire as I let myself wrap around him.

The flutters in my walls start and I know he can feel them. "Yes, baby, come all over my cock with your pretty pussy. There's nothing as good as you coming around me, Trix."

His pace, his pressure, his voice, it all sends me tumbling into the abyss, cracking open my hardened heart and letting emotions flood my senses. I fall faster and faster as I call for him, through my body shaking and my soul locking with his.

I cradle the back of his head with my arms wrapped around him. I squeeze him tight with my thighs, my toes curling. His cock gets harder, bigger, and he thrusts one time hard enough to move me up in bed, but he pulls me back down by my shoulders. I love the feeling of him trembling in my arms as his dick quivers inside me, filling me so full of his cum.

"Trixie, fuck, baby you're perfect, I love fucking you and this perfect pussy. I love you." The words straight from his very soul. His hips slowly stop rocking, but I still feel the aftershocks fluttering around in my pussy and he chuckles, "Your butterflies down there love me fucking you, too."

"Yeah, they sure do," I reply, trying to catch my breath.

"You want breakfast now?" he asks as he pulls out and kisses me on the forehead before he's sliding out of bed, heading to the bathroom.

"Waffles again, please," I tell him as he comes back to bed with a wet cloth.

"Anything for you, Princess."

I'm drawing the next tattoo I want to put on him on my iPad. He went outside to make a call.

Suddenly the door slams open and a very mad, beet red faced Linx comes barreling in.

"Those tweaker motherfuckers," he rages.

I jump off the couch, dropping my iPad on the cushion. "What's wrong?"

He's fuming. This is the murderous side I've never seen and quite fucking frankly, this shit is scary as fuck. Linx looks downright murderous.

He comes back out of his room with a duffel bag and drops it on the kitchen table.

"Linx?" There's a panicked waver to my voice. He pulls out a belt with two holsters. Shit is getting really real. I quickly walk up to him and lay my hand on his shoulder, "Linx, you're scaring me," I say as my voice trembles. I think it was the fear in my voice that got through to him.

He takes a deep breath and pulls his hands out of the duffel bag and turns to me. He gently cups my cheeks, "I'm sorry, baby, I'm not trying to scare you. I'm trying to control myself."

I interrupt him, "Are we in danger?"

He pulls me into a hug, "No, baby. You're safe. I swear. I'm sorry I scared you. Not Grim, it's only the crackhead motherfuckers around here stole Sampson." He releases me, kisses my lips lightly and just as quickly steps back to the duffel bag, grabbing a gun and sliding it into a holster on his side. "I knew I should have left him at Mom's last night."

"Oh my god, no." I cover my mouth with my hands. "There's a tracker, two of them actually, embedded into Sampson. I know where he is and I'm going to go get him."

"I'm coming with you!!" I shriek as I run to the front door to put my sneakers on.

"The fuck you are." He loads a magazine into some kind of gun, I don't know.

I've been around guns my whole life. Shot many of them myself. My dad required it. All of dad's associates carry them. Sometimes more than one. But I sure as shit have no idea how to tell any of them apart. I can shoot, I can aim, and I can hit a chest. All of them pew-pew is all I know.

"Yeah? Who's going to drive the vehicle back when you get Sampson? Or are we walking to wherever he is?"

I finish tying my shoe and walk up to him with my hands on my hips. "Well?" with as much bratty attitude as I can muster.

His jaw works and tenses. I got him and he knows he needs my help.

"I'm not some fragile flower, Linx. I can do this. Let me help my man. All I have to do is drive the truck. Easy peasy. Who's bringing it over here from your mom's?"

"Fuck, I can't believe I'm even considering this shit." He's strapping on his Kevlar vest. Where it would say 'Police,' his says 'Danger.' I believe he's every bit as dangerous as I've heard.

He tosses a holster belt at me. "Put that on."

Linx loads another gun and passes it over to me. "It's exactly like the one we used at practice all the time. There's one in the chamber, safety's on."

I take the gun from him and feel the weight settle into my palm. Locked and loaded. This is definitely the first time I've been allowed to carry a gun around anywhere. At the lessons at the gun range, Linx never let me walk around with a gun in my hand.

Secretly, I'm giddy with the thrill right now but also terrified he's going to get killed. I'm crazy. I mean my legs are shaking but there's chills racing in my blood and freakishly, I'm aroused.

Oh god, apparently, I love more than one kind of danger.

I take a big gulp of air to steady myself and not break down in excited laughter. He looks at me, cocks an eyebrow and says, "Ready?"

I nod, even though I'm so scared I need to go poop but excited enough to need to pee.

"Wait! I have to go pee first."

"Go on, Mom will be here within two minutes."

I quickly scramble to the bathroom to get my business done.

Please don't let him die. Crackheads have guns too.

Chapter 26 – Linx

If her dad wasn't going to kill me before, he's sure as shit's going to now.

Fuck! How does she talk me into this shit?

Big blue, diamond, doe eyes. That's how.

He was right, I always let her get her way.

My mom arrives soon in her Lexus, not in my truck seeing as how Bret's not home and she's afraid to drive my truck. I assure her we will be right back, to stay put in the camp. She begged me to call the police but that's not how her boy works.

I check my phone screen again. We are getting closer. These dumb shits didn't even have the good sense to take him further than a few miles. It's probably the old Petrie's place. That place has been in disrepair for a while and last I heard no one lives there.

Birdie's hand brushes mine and I lace our fingers together in her lap. I look over and attempt an easy smile for her. I know I scared the fuck out of her back there, but I was only seeing red and didn't think it through. I'm usually better.

I should have known better, but we wanted to take a night ride after mom's dinner and came straight home. Then I didn't feel like taking him back to her garage after the tattoo.

"You look really sexy in Kevlar and a ball cap. Like a feral military guy. It's definitely working for me."

That makes me laugh and breaks a little of my tension.

"Oh yeah?"

"Yeah, it's giving fuck-me-with-guns energy. Hold me at knife point for fun while you rail me, oh, or let me give you a hummer-in-a-Hummer-on-a-secret-mission vibes."

"Are you proud of that one?"

Her cocky grin is too cute. "Yes, I am. It reminds me of all the times I'd sneak glances at you and then go home to rub one out to the memories."

Sometimes I forget I don't know her as well as I think I do, and she simply surprises me sometimes. If she only knew how many times I've jacked off to her. Thousands of times. Every time I see her.

She counts off on her fingers, "There's military camo Linx, Linx in a sexy form fitting tux, regular suit and tie Linx, by the way my favorite tie is the silk forest green one with the little birds, then there's my personal favorite—the jeans, white shirt and a ball cap Linx."

The goofy smile permanently etched on my face because of her widens. I knew she studied me right back as much as I watched her. I lift her hand and kiss it.

My eyes flit over to the phone screen again and I see we are going to be there in two minutes.

"We're almost there, baby. What are you going to do, Trixie?"

"Wait in the truck."

"And?"

"Lock the doors?"

"Good girl."

Chapter 27 – Birdie

Oh lort, the rush of heat to my genitals at those two words in his baritone voice. *Good girl.* I love when he calls me that. *Now's not the time, Birdie.*

Linx turns onto a dirt road that doesn't even look like it's on a map. Is this a driveway? Fuck, it's not even ten in the morning with this shit. I didn't even get through my second cup of coffee.

My heart starts racing as a dilapidated house comes into view once we round a curve. There're two cars in the overgrown driveway. One looks like it's been here for the past twenty years. I doubt it's the getaway car.

Linx parks the SUV blocking most of the drive. He reaches between my legs and grabs the bullhorn that he conveniently had at camp. I thought it was odd when he asked me to carry it, but I knew I would eventually find out what it was for. Now's the time. He opens the door at the same time he honks the horn for longer than two seconds. Very loudly you hear, "I want my bike. Now." I almost giggle because of the way he nonchalantly says it. He's perfectly calm now and that's the scary part.

It's a simple request that carries deadly consequences.

A woman about sixty years old comes running out with her hands up, crying, "Please don't shoot me!!"

"Is anyone else in there with you?" he yells.

Tossing the bullhorn back into the car, he pulls out his gun. I quickly toss the bullhorn into the back seat, fascinated by what's going down here. It's like a live action move and I have a front row seat. I don't even care that my mouth is hanging open.

She vehemently shakes her head, "No, no one else is here."

"If you're lying to me, I'll kill you too." He cocks his gun towards the house.

"Not lying. I have to work here to pay off debt. I'm the only one here, I swear to fucking god. Your bike is around the back. Zack and Ryan brought it here this morning. Nothing's been done to it." Linx watches the house intensely. "What's going on here?"

"Meth lab," she says with disgust. Oh god, one of these places. Holy fucking hell. I wrinkle my nose in disgust.

"Is this your car?"

"Yes, sir."

"Do you have a purse inside?"

"Yes, sir."

"Trix, climb into the driver's seat, baby." The soft manner in which he tells me sounds much better than the mad as fuck tone he's using with her.

Like any good girl would do, I obeyed the man with the gun.

He walks up to the woman and grabs her arm, and she leads him into the house. Cheese and rice! I watch him walk into the meth house and my heart is clawing its way out of my throat.

One day when I grow up, I want to be as badass as Linx.

After what feels like forever and one mini panic meltdown later, Linx comes back out with the woman and tells her, "Get in your car and run, and when they ask who I was, you don't know shit, ok

Amanda Rose Hoskins of 512 Arcadia Lane, Grand Isle. Am I clear enough?" He hands her wallet back to her.

She gulps and strangles out, "Yes, sir. Thank you." She starts jogging to her car. She gets in and thankfully the thing starts up. She turns around in the yard and flies past the SUV, driving in the grass beside the driveway.

I watch Linx walk around to the back of the house and hear Sampson start up. Oh, thank fuck.

He rides the bike to the front of the house and pulls up by the driver's door. "I'll watch you turn around in the yard and then we're heading to mom's."

"We can't leave this house operable, Linx. They'll come back and just make more drugs for the bayou. Don't you guys stop shit like this? Can't we destroy their meth making supplies or something?"

"You're fucking kidding me right now?" he deadpans.

"No, I'm not, Lincoln. You can't let this continue down here. This is in your momma's backyard."

He kills the engine and says, "Jesus fuck, ok, I'll go break some shit."

I smile and do a little dance in my seat, fully aware my decent into dark madness with him is going exceedingly well. I'm surprising myself with my little devil heart.

But seriously, fuck meth makers.

All of a sudden glass shatters and flames lick out of the far windows making me flinch and jerk. Smoke starts bellowing out and more windows break. I jump out of the SUV and stand in shock.

Linx's in there.

"LINCOLN!" I take off running up to the house and reach the edge of the garage as Linx comes rushing out of the house. "What the fuck, Birdie."

Oh shit, oh shit he's fine. And he's mad at me. He only calls me Birdie when he's mad. FUCK! *Don't you dare hyperventilate; you're supposed to be a bad bitch!*

He grabs my arm and drags me back to the SUV as I'm trying to look behind me at the burning house. He's taking huge steps, and I can barely keep up, my feet keep tripping over themselves as I twist to watch the house go up in flames. Shit is blowing up in there. Holy fuck.

Linx pushes me at the driver's door and very sternly in his don't-fucking-backtalk-me-right-now tone says, "Get in the car." Flames lick higher behind him.

I point to the house and say, "What happened to breaking a few things?"

He laughs. Actually laughs. "Seriously? Are you happy now? I'm burning down the world for you." He spreads his arms wide over his head and gestures around us as black smoke rolls off the house. "Isn't that what all the romance books you read say it's what all the girls want?" He looks like a maniac standing in front of an inferno. Mr. Danger, the guardian of hell, looks pleased with himself.

What the fuck? "You're burning a meth lab, Linx! Think of all the fucking chemicals going to the air right now!"

He throws his leg over his bike and sits down. "I don't give a fuck about EPA rules right now. Get in the fucking Lexus, Trixie." He revs Sampson and barks, "Now."

I tilt my chin up and get in the car when he says, "And you could be a little more grateful when a guy blows up buildings for you. Now turn around."

The fucking audacity of this cheeky bastard. I whip the SUV around and pull out in front of him, heading down the way we came, as he lets his hand off the brake and we rumble away from the scene of his latest crime.

Chapter 28 – Birdie

Once we drop off Sampson, then he drives the truck back over with me in Collette's Lexus, we head back to camp. I know he's going to yell at me. I know I fucked up. I got out of the car.

We enter the camp house after we see his mom off. I kick off my shoes by the front door while he unlaces his boots. I don't even know what to say or do. Am I supposed to assume a position for punishment? Do I stand and face him? Look down? I just kinda stand in the middle of the room, bracing for his anger.

"I-I'm sorry. I know you're mad so go ahead and yell at me." I look away so he can't see the tears forming in my eyes. It hurts my heart to know he's mad at me. I must take it like a big girl and face the consequences of my actions.

"Hey," he says from in front of me. He turns my head to face him, "I'm not so much mad as I was scared. And I'm most definitely not going to yell at you. That's not the kind of guy I am."

Linx wraps his arms around me and cradles me to his chest. I wind my arms around his middle and squeeze him. Kevlar doesn't feel good smashed against your boobs or cheeks but I'm not going to complain. I need this hug. I need his comfort.

"We're going to enjoy the rest of our day. It's over, done with, and we're going to move on as if nothing happened. You ok with that?" I nod into his hard chest, "Ok, I'm good."

He pulls back and looks into my eyes, "Are you sure you're good, Princess?"

"Yes, Daddy Danger, I'm ok."

"Fuck baby, you can't be dropping words like that unless you want bent over this couch."

"Jesus, you just had pussy like two hours ago. You can't even make sperm that fast. Pace yourself, big guy." I pat his chest.

"I can't help it. You're so fucking sexy, and I don't know how long this is going to last. I mean, it's my ultimate fantasy happening, but as soon as your dad finds out, I'm fucked in a different way."

"About that. Tell me more about what you see in the future if my dad says it's ok and accepts it. You heard him yourself, the only person he would even consider dating me would be you. So, I believe I've solved that problem by actually liking you." I snag a pudding cup from the fridge and grab a spoon from the drawer. "First, are you hungry? Chocolate pudding is not an acceptable meal." He comes into the kitchen area as I roll my eyes.

He grabs my chin and squeezes my cheeks, making me look up at him, "Don't mock me trying to take care of you. Ever."

Before he starts gathering bacon and the carton of eggs from the fridge, he kisses me forcefully and his tongue invades my chocolate haze. After a few quick sweeps in my mouth, he pulls back and says, "That's the best pudding I've ever tasted. I know somewhere else it can go, and I'll happily eat it up."

"Alright, horndog," I get my bearings back, because holy shit he's zero to one hundred in two seconds. "Not all of us need a manly man's breakfast. I get by with the bizarro stuff I eat." I shovel in the pudding before he can take it from me. He's right, I could use some healthier eating but that means I have to put in the effort and quite frankly, I just don't want to. "I'm still alive, aren't I?"

"Right." He cocks his eyebrow at me, and he looks like a toned-down version of The Rock with The People's Eyebrow. This fucking guy's had a poker face as long as I've known him, but when he looks at me, he drops all pretense and his genuine facial expressions shine through. I'll take this look over the one he had thirty minutes ago when I thought he was going to rip my head off. "I guess I am hungry. I mean, I could eat, if that's what you want to hear. And not dick, like real food."

"Ahh, you knew where I was headed, princess." He cocks his fingers like a gun pointed at me and clicks his tongue. Great, my new boyfriend is as cheesy as they come.

"You know I don't know how to cook, right?"

"I've noticed. I've also noticed the amount of food delivery services that come to your apartment and studio. You must spend a small fortune on fees and delivery tips."

"Hey! I'm a busy woman. Besides my mother never felt I should have to learn how to cook because obviously she was going to marry me off to a wealthy man who had a cook and maid." "Sorry to burst your bubble, Princess, I don't have a cook in my penthouse, but I do have a housekeeper." I watch him put on an apron and tie it. At least it's not one of those frilly, girly ones. It's black and says, 'Don't make me poison you.' Whatever, he still looks sexy in it.

"Will you teach me to cook?"

He looks over with a smirk, "You wanna start right now?"

"Oh. I guess so." I'm not at all prepared mentally for this. Cooking is like science to me, and I did awful at science. I was an art major for a reason. The only science I get into is color theory. Walking over to the stove beside him, he starts talking, "The key to cooking is to feel it in your soul. I'll teach you how to measure stuff, but eventually you'll get so good you won't need to. You'll be a pro and just eyeball stuff, throw it in a bowl, and call it a meal." He flips the bacon over, "Take this bacon for instance, it is on a medium to low heat, how long do you think it will take to cook?"
"I have no idea. Forty-five minutes?"

He cracks up laughing, "No, baby, definitely not that long. It'll burn up, but good guess. It should only be about ten, maybe fifteen minutes. Depends on how you like your bacon. You want chewy or crispy?"

I rub my hands together at the mouthwatering smell of bacon permeating the air, "Ohh, crispy please, but not too crispy."

"And how do you like your eggs?"

"Scrambled. With cheese. And ketchup." It tickles me to know that annoys and disgusts him. Some habits die hard.

"Jesus," he mutters under his breath, "How do you want your toast? Light, medium, or burnt?"

"Can I have in between light and medium but not too much darker after that?"

"Baby, you can have whatever you want. I'll give you anything you ask." He looks over with his pointer finger up in the air, "Within reason."

I smirk at him adding that last piece. New goal unlocked: find unreasonable stuff to ask for. "I can work the toaster. I've made it before." I didn't add that I can't figure out my fancy toaster's digital display, so nine times out of ten I end up burning it. Thankfully, this one has a lever to push down. Seems a fuckton simpler than mine.

Once we sit down to eat, I ask him if I could ask him more questions. There's one I'm dying to know the answer to. "When did I stop being your assignment and someone you love?"

"Your senior year of college." No hesitation.

"Wait, you've loved me for five years?"

"I met you when you were barely eighteen if you remember and I did a double take then, but as you grew into the woman you are now, I fell more and more under your spell in the short, special times we've spent time together. Also, in the times I'm a shadow in the background, watching you. My favorite pastime, watching you."

He reaches over and palms my left boob and then squeezes. I just shake my head. Can't. Keep. His. Hands. Off. Me.

"I really took notice when you became the woman you are today. I used to think so hard about things to say to you, just so I could hear your voice, see your reactions, be near you. And deep down, I love your fire, how flames would sizzle in your eyes and a passionate flush would come over you. Yeah, that really added fuel to my fire. I knew I got to you then. It was me giving you that reaction, no one else."

"Un-fucking-believable," I shake my head and mutter. I can't believe this fucker's level of patience. He's a bonafide saint with a big helping of devil.

"You came home more often that year and I was already moving up in the ranks, so I was in the house more often when you were home. I was always around. Your dad was my assignment then. You were a bonus to be around. Three years ago, I was assigned to you when Grim started rumbling about having you. I manipulated it so I was the best choice. I accepted the assignment because I had already been protecting you, watching over you. It never felt like an assignment, you were my girl, it was my duty to protect you, and I do my job well."

I think back and reply, "Yeah, that's the year my dad wanted me close for some reason. Now, I see why. I had to go to so many stupid charity events and art openings, and corporate dinners." I roll my eyes at the memory of all those boring events. I didn't give a flying fuck about chumming it up with a bunch of backstabbing, two-faced rich snobs.

But what does stick in my mind, I tell him while I caress his face across the table, feeling his stubble and loving how it feels against my skin, "I would sneak glances at you. At first, I would fuck myself to your devilishly handsome smile. I used to pretend it was only for me—"

He interrupts me and says, "It was, I've never smiled at another woman like that, I swear."

It touches my heart that he loves me so much and he's so devoted to me, even when I didn't like him. I continue, "It was the way your hand grazed my lower back as you put me in cars or led me to a table or into a room. The way your lips would softly brush the shell of my ear while we were dancing, and you talked to me in your soft, sexy voice. Then it was your playful voice asking me to dance or the sultry tone you used to tell me I was beautiful. You were the first person beyond my dad that I believed to be genuine in giving me compliments."

He picks up my hand and brings it to his lips, kissing my knuckles, "When did that change? What made you hate me, little bird?"

I huff out a cynical laugh while shaking my head in disbelief, "You must not have known about Troy then."

He shakes his head with a confused look and replies, "No, should I?" He finishes his meal and pushes his plate away. I've been done for a few minutes.

I pick up our paper plates and throw them in the trash and set our utensils in the sink, rinsing them off.

"Can we sit on the couch?" I ask.

"Yeah, baby, come on, I'll rub your feet." Sold, he does amazing foot massages.

Once I get comfortable on one end of the couch and put my feet in his lap, I continue, "I don't know how he flew under the radar then," I scoff, "Seems my stalker was dropping the ball there, Linxy-poo" His hands roam over my legs, leisurely massaging, with a perplexed look on his face.

I lean into his touches, loving how his hands feel on me. I look down at him and decide he needs this just as much as I do. He needs this talk. My parents didn't even know about Troy because they never said anything. But Tally, Pierre and Zhar knew, and they hated him with a passion. "He was nice at first when we started dating."

"Wait, is this the punk that was a complete dick to you? I didn't think you were dating him. It didn't even look like a real relationship. We didn't know he was such a douche until Zharia told me to get rid of him because she was concerned that he was abusing you."

"What the fuck? She never told me that!" I cry out, astonished. "Yeah, she was worried. I never told your mom or dad; I just handled it."

"Well, thanks. I wasn't sure how to get rid of him near the end. I guess Zharia hated him more than she let on." I shrug and relax into the couch more while he rubs my calves. Motherhell, this feels so good.

"Anyways, within two weeks into seeing each other is when he started putting me down, insulting me, bullying me basically. I thought he was teasing me in a flirty way. It was small things at first, but enough to make me start changing who I was and what I did. He'd say shit like 'Are you going to wear that, it looks too revealing or your kind of body?' 'That perfume smells like sweaty feet.' Or 'You're so pale you look dead.' 'Another tattoo, don't you know they make you look trashy?' 'You going to eat all that, that's a lot.' It became constant. But he would never say these things in front of Tally or Pierre or Zharia, only me, in private. It wore me down after daily non-stop 'teasing' that he claimed it to be. He said he was only helping me be a better person. I took things too personally he complained. That's what I thought it was, lovingly helping me, just teasing until it wasn't, and it started making my soul hurt. He was making all the colors drain out of my world and all that was left was shadows. That's when I vowed to be a color artist and I needed to start figuring out how to get away from him. "It was Pierre who cornered him in front of me one day, Pierre overheard him telling me I was getting too fat. Pierre told him he needed to treat me better or move the fuck on, and in a way, it helped for like a week. Anyways, then you would tease me, and it would all lump together, it was everything wrong with me, everything ugly, and no one liked me, I was nothing. I hated myself after a while."

He opens his mouth to say something, and I sit up and place my forefinger on his lips. "I need this off my chest. I *need* to clear the slate between us." I owe it to him.

I continue to explain myself, "Just let me get this out. Then the sexual comments came from you. I was told repeatedly by Troy I was good for one thing; to be someone's whore and that's the only thing men saw in me. I wasn't the marrying type; I was the mistress type. Someone they could use and discard, because all my fancy upbringing couldn't save me from men's dirty thoughts and actions. And eventually I'd come to understand, men only whisper things in my ear to own me and get in my pants, then they go home and take care of their pretty little perfect wives and spoiled children."

I can't stop the silent tears as they slowly march down my face. "I'm so sorry, Trixie, I had no idea." He reaches up to wipe my tears, so lovingly, so gently, like I'm precious to him. Like I matter to him. His face is devastated, tragically beautiful.

"I figured you didn't. In turn, I started seeing you as someone like him, one of those kinds of guys. Rubbing it in my face and mocking me. You're good looking, higher on the food chain than me, all testosterone and muscle, dangerous and alluring, the bad boy, and here I am, every man's wet dream as Troy called me, just an object no one loves. 'Daddy's Asset' is what he used to call me." I huff out a disgusted sigh.

"I was getting constantly propositioned from Troy's friends and he wanted to share me with them. It made me hate him for not caring enough about me. About my feelings. And you just compounded on it. I didn't see it as playful flirting. I saw it as the insults I was being treated daily to, the sexual comments as I tried to prove I wasn't a whore. I didn't see you. I saw my hate and anger and hurt. I'm sorry I let my anger at Troy bleed over to you. I'm sorry I let it grow into what it was."

His whole body thrums with fury as he steadily watches me crawl across the couch to him. I perch above him, straddling his lap. "I'm so sorry," he whispers, "I can see why now. Oh god, I'm so fucking sorry, Trix."

I shrug, "Hey, it's not like you knew. This is only the why of things, right? The past? We're here now, like you say. We got right now." I lightly kiss his face, his forehead, his cheeks, the tip of his nose. How many guys get the tip of their noses kissed all cute like? Because this feels very cathartic, I keep talking through this healing conversation, "It also didn't help my mother was in my head too, right alongside Troy to push the negative talk further down my throat. She told me no respectable man would want me with my tattoos. So, I kept getting more as a rebellious streak, I think. Deep down, I knew what she expected of me. I kept trying to fly under the radar, to not be noticed. When I was younger, in my teens, she told me if I wore too revealing clothes, or too tight, Dad's men would start lusting over me and try to use me, kidnap me or worse rape me. Oh, and that y'all had no respect for women," Linx snorts, "which made me a little more than afraid of you at times. She said I would just become a dried-up whore for men, and that they start by telling you how beautiful you are. Mother said that all the nice pretty things men say, they're all lies. She was very disappointed in me; in everything I did. I didn't live by her expectations."

"Jesus." He exhales a mad, angry growl as he sits up to hug me around my waist, pulling me close to him while I sit on his lap. He's holding me so tight I can't breathe, but I let him be. I'll live and this is a moment I want to see through. Lots of emotions are being worked through right now and I want to remember how tight he held me when I spilled my heart out to him.

"I forgave you for all the things you've said, and I took the wrong way." I hold him to my chest, running my fingertips over his scalp, making him shiver. I want him to know a few more things before we move forward.

He lets up on his embrace, enough for me to sit back and watch his face, "When?" he begs. "When did your heart melt?"

"It was the moment we were at the table right over there, our first night here, and I asked you to be truthful with me and tell me what kind of danger I was in. I felt it in my gut you were under orders not to tell me anything, but you did it anyways, because I have a right to know. I have the right to know there are men out there planning to steal me, rape me, and sell me. I was grateful you kept me in the loop and made me understand the threat. You gave me a choice. You could have told me it was none of my business and I would have had to accept it, but I appreciate you being real with me. That's when I knew you had my best interests at heart instead of an assignment. You went against orders for me and my walls started crumbling."

Gazing into his eyes, "It was when you told me the man was right behind me and you barely got to me in time, then thanked me for not putting up a fight. In that moment I had to trust you with my life, Linx. It had never needed to be put to the test before. My mind knew immediately to go with you. So, I followed you. I'm still following."

I lean down and he parts his lips, meeting mine and our tongues slide together. A fire stirs to life in my gut. Tendrils of the infernos raging inside us intertwine with each other as we bond on a higher level every time we touch. The truth sets us free. No one has ever made me feel like Linx does. It's like nothing worked out because it was him I was supposed to be with.

His arms hold me like a vice, like he's afraid to let me go, like his life depends on it. I love feeling sacred to him, my presence soothing to him. But right now, I feel his fear too. He almost didn't make it.

He would never stop looking for me. He'd pull all the demons from hell to help find me and then unleash his fury on whoever did it when I was found. Linx would kill anyone trying to harm me, of that, I was sure.

I'm not stupid to think they'll stop at this. They'll keep coming. My life just changed again without my permission. I'll never be safe. I'll always have to walk with one eye over my shoulder. It'll never end.

I will never be fully safe.

Linx cradles my face, and I slant my head to deepen the kiss. Fire, intense, hot and wild, burns through me when he touches me. My pussy clenches over his shorts, on top of his cock that's growing hard, and I pray he can feel it, feel my want.

He lays me over on the couch, on my back and I pull him down with me. His hands are everywhere, burning trails across my skin. I finally understand what they mean when they say their blood is on fire in my books.

Every nerve in my body is awake and sizzling. I can't get enough of him.

Nobody taught me it could be like this.

Sweet, sweet love.

Chapter 29 – Linx

Her pliant body moves exactly how I want it to. I quickly yank her shorts and underwear off. I throw one of her legs over the back of the couch and the other I spread wide so I can pepper her lower lips with tender kisses that drive her wild. Her needy cunt is seeking out my hungry mouth with her squirming.

"Please, Linx, I hate when you tease me." Her low, husky voice swirls around me like smoke, dusting across my skin, causing little shivers up my back and neck. I close my eyes and breathe in her pussy, and everything uniquely her.

"Hmm, baby I think you're lying. You love it when I'm on my knees for you." A few more well-placed kisses across her clit. "You've never been more powerful than when I'm loving on you. You own me, Trixie." I stick my tongue into her entrance and listen to the fight in her die on her moan.

The goal is to crack her heart open wide so I can step through and sit on the throne. I wasn't kidding when I said she'll fall in love with me. I was going to make it happen for real, by any means necessary. Whatever it took.

Moving my mouth up to her clit, I open my mouth and swallow her whole. My tongue laps at her clit and her fingers tangle in my hair. I hum and hold her pussy up to my mouth, hands on her ass, looking up at her.

Our eyes clash and I'm looking at passion and desire, raw in feral form, and it's all for me. Birdie's going wild, writhing under me, and pushing her needy clit up into my mouth. I'll prove to her I'm the only one for her. I'll move mountains for my baby girl.

I lick and suck her within an inch of her life and leave her panting on the edge, then remove my mouth, saliva and her juices dripping from my lips, off my chin.

"Linx, what the hell?"

"Not yet, Trix. You wanted a slow day, remember?"

Pulling my arms out from underneath her, I reach up and cup her glorious tits, rubbing my thumbs over her pebbled nipples. I love how she reacts to this, her hips seeking me out again. Her chest quivers with desire.

"But I'm so close," she whimpers and moans and it sounds heavenly.

Every stroke of my tongue claims her more and more. I dip back into devouring her pussy, bringing her to the edge again, right up to the point she growls in frustration when I pull away this time. "Please, oh god please, let me come," she pants. I grind my cock into the front of the couch hearing her beg. I have to be inside her soon.

I chuckle darkly. "Jusqu'où t'es prêt à aller pour ça, hein?" I kiss the inside of her silky thigh and nip her tender flesh.

"Translate everything. I don't want to miss any promises," she says breathlessly.

"Oh, I'm making promises now, am I?" I dip my head to run my tongue up through her lips again and I growl into her sex. "I asked how far are you willing to go for this, little bird?" I run my tongue over her clit and gently suck. "How far down can we fall together?"

"Oh, Linx, I want you so bad. I want you inside me, please. Come up here and fill me up."

I kiss her hip. "J'ai trop hâte d'être inside de toi." I kiss her lower belly, "Means, I can't wait to be inside you."

She shudders on a sigh. My French gets her wet every time. I smell her on my face as I kiss up her body, and it smells so fucking good. I kiss her ribcage, sucking softly, leaving marks on her skin. "Tellement beau," I pause long enough to say as I nose across the skin of her sternum, her boobs grazing my cheeks, roughing up her skin with my beard I have coming in now. "Is, you're so beautiful."

Running my tongue over her nipple, feeling it harden on my tongue. I slowly pull back and blow across it, "Je te promets de t'aimer pour toujours." I suck lightly, "I promise to love you forever."

"Oh, Lincoln," her little whimper slips out. She lifts her hips in frustration to glide her wet pussy over my abdomen in her desperate search for my cock. Her arms rub across my shoulders as she wiggles beneath me, searching for the release I withhold from her.

I slide over to her other breast and lavish this nipple with my tongue. "Don't want this one to feel left out." Birdie pants and whimpers, trying to pull me to her harder. Goddamn she's wound up.

"Please, Lincoln, please," she damn near sobs.

"Tu es la seule femme pour moi, toujours et à jamais." I suck the skin on the side of her breast until I faintly taste blood, she hisses through her teeth. "You're the only woman for me, always and forever."

"Oh god, Linx, that's so beautiful."

I kiss the front of her throat, "Je m'éloignerai jamais de toi." I lick underneath, up to the tip of her chin, "I'll never leave you."

Birdie whimpers with need.

Worshiping her body with my hands and mouth, I nip up the side of her neck to nibble her earlobe and let my voice softly caress her skin, "Je t'aime plus que le ciel a d'étoiles. I love you more than the sky has stars."

Birdie truly sobs and her fingers roughly rub all over me. "Oh, Linx." I yank my shorts down and free my hard cock, rubbing the head on her dripping wet slit. She bucks up trying to get more friction.

I hover over top of her, her eyes closed and her head lolling back and forth, I command her, "Look at me, Beatrix." Her beautiful blue eyes open to mine. My hips work, rubbing the crown of my dick up and down her heat. I tease her by finding her opening and pushing in a little, just the tip mind you, only to withdraw.

Leaning over, I whisper to her parted lips, "T'es à moi et j'peux jamais te laisser partir, mon amour." I lightly kiss her succulent lips that mesmerize me most days. "You're mine and I'll never let you go, my love."

Then I push my hips in to bury myself in her hot, very wet pussy. Birdie gasps and digs her nails into my shoulders. It's like coming home. Goddamn it's everything in my life that's been missing. It's every piece of shit moment I endured for this moment of goodness; every fucking time I enter her. Nothing beats that feeling.

No woman compares.

This is where I'm meant to be.

I pull out and ram into her again. She throws her head back as I work my cock inside her, and she calls for me.

Working magic with my hips, slow, sensual, sweet torture to drive her higher and higher. Lavishing attention on her clit with my fingers, rolling her bud around and around. I make love to her slowly, like it's our last time together. She smiles at me and bites her bottom lip, hissing through her teeth at me bottoming out inside her. I see what I need to see in her eyes.

Fucking god, my heart's going to explode. My Trixie loves me and there's no hiding it anymore.

"Linx, oh, right there…I'm so close, oh fuck please," Birdie begs me. She confesses on a sob in between her chest heaving from me pumping into her, forehead to forehead, "Lincoln, I love you, I do, you made me fall in love with you. Je suis à toi, je t'aime, Lincoln."

Oh, holy fuck. My heart just stopped in my chest; air caught in my lungs. Fuck, this is the best fucking day.

My heavy breathing gives way to my own loud as fuck moans, "Oh god, Trixie, I love you too, baby." I lock her clit to me and roll my hips just how she likes it. I growl by her ear, "Come for me, my little bird. Give it to me, it's all mine, Trixie." Short, deep thrusts, as deep as I can go.

Nose to nose, she breathes, "Yours," right before she takes a deep breath, holding it in to cry out and I watch the pleasure wash over her beautiful face. Her thighs clamp around my hips and her vaginal walls pulsates, milking my cock. Birdie's tight channel pulls the cum from me as she orgasms, I jerk, and my cries join hers, saying her name over and over as I worship her, my precious princess.

Our breaths mingle between us as we both pant and suspend in time together in perfect harmony, fitting together flawlessly.

"Oh god…Linx…oh fuck," Birdie says between breaths, sucking in air and coming down from her climax high.

My face is buried in the crook of her neck while I try to catch my breath.

"Mon amour, jamais j'en aurai assez de toi," I pull back enough to kiss her between gasps and softly tell her by her cheek, "I'll never get enough of you."

Pulling out I try to catch what dribbles out of her and keep it in there. There's something inside me obsessively wanting all of me to be carried around inside her. Also, obsessively wanting this woman to have my babies.

"And where did you learn to speak French from all of a sudden?"

She giggles and says, "I asked Siri how to say it."

Chapter 30 – Linx

Shutting the front door behind me and heading down the stairs, I answer Shadow's question, "That's complicated, brother."

"How complicated is yes or no?"

"I'm not answering then."

"You've either compromised your assignment or not." Reaching the bottom step to where my truck is parked, I put my hand on top of my head, "Why is this so important for you to know?"

"Dude, I just wanna know if you finally got your dick into your fantasy girl." Shadow chuckles, ribbing me, and being an all-around pain in the ass.

"I don't know who you're talking about."

Now he's full on laughing. "I know you ain't tryna play dumb with me right now, Danger. I imagine I'm one of the very, very few who knows. You didn't have to say anything before you told me eons ago; it's always been written all over your face for years. I see with my own eyes how you are with her and how she makes you light up. Good for you, man. Now, have you tapped that ass yet or not?"

"Don't talk about her like that."

"I'm gonna take that as a yes then."

"Shut up. Why did you call me again?" He's wearing on my patience.

"No, that was it. I was just checking on ya, man. Just seeing if you were still alive or if she's killed you yet."

I reply with a growl.

"Yeah, I notice her watching you right back all of the time and then play like she can't stand you. Kinda hard to ignore the man your eye-fucking all over the room."

"What?"

"You never noticed? Duh, of course you didn't notice. I forgot you had to be schmoozey, rich playboy Mr. LaFleur and shake hands and drink champagne. Meanwhile, all you can do is track your little birdie while women throw themselves at you." He continues to snicker at me. He knows how much I hate those functions. The only reason I go is for her and well, it's my job too. On the outside, I'm LaFleur, CEO, self-made multimillionaire, hotshot businessman. On the inside, and to my associates, I am Vice-President Mr. Danger, Second-in-Command, a ruthless, cold-hearted bastard who slits people's throats with a smile on his face.

And this nosy motherfucker's superior.

I snort at the phone, "You're one to talk. Have you forgotten you're always with me at these functions? You are just as tortured as I am."

"How could I forget watching all the MILFs and daddy's past season debutantes walk around flirting with me and you? I've caused more than three affairs I'll have you know," he laughs, "Women love a Native American man with a nice fat cock."

I scoff at him. "I don't want to know." He's ten times a worse manwhore than I ever was. The fact he's been dating Birdie's best friend for more than five consecutive days has been shocking to me. Shadow doesn't do relationships. He also doesn't do monogamy.

"So does she know yet?"

"Yes." I answer honestly. This man has spent many nights listening to me confess my love and heartache over Birdie. Sometimes Shadow's stayed at camp with me and Pierre when we do a guy's weekend. We usually go through a few bottles of bourbon and do the guy bonding thing.

"All of it? Your undying, unrequited love?"

"Yeah, most all of it."

"Man, I've been around you for eight years, and I've never seen a man more pussy whipped than you, and you weren't even getting the pussy! Motherfucker, do you know how fucked up that is?"

"I'm well aware, asshole. I don't need you telling me."

A healthy guffaw escapes him, but he still presses on, "God, wait until her old man figures it out."

I quickly growl, "You need to shut the fuck up about it." I grind my teeth and fist my other hand. I would probably choke him out if he was standing in front of me taunting me like this. And he knows it, that's why he's doing it.

He's proving his point. I'm usually a lot cooler than this. My feathers don't normally ruffle this fast.

"Don't you worry, big boy, I ain't saying shit about it. Simmer down. This isn't my story to tell anyone. You know I got your back, man, I've kept your secret for years. That's a long ass time to pine over a woman, hiding it in plain sight, ya sadistic fuck. I'm not about to divulge it to her dad or anyone else, ok? We got trust here, I'm in the circle of trust, ok?" I hear him moving around, "But tell me one thing, was the wait worth it, big dog?

"Yep."

He waits for me to elaborate. I hate to break it to him but I'm not giving him details. "Hmm, a man of few words. I like it. No kiss and tell for Mr. Danger."

"Nope. It's no one's business."

"No, it's not but you know Rock ain't going to see it that way, brother. He's going to kill you. I'm sure you know that already and weighed the consequences before getting your dick wet."

"Hey! Watch it," I rumble.

"I know, I know, she's your one, she's your everything. I hope she's worth it, bro, I'm glad you got this time with her, but I'm praying it's not me who has to administer the punishments. I don't know if I could do it."

"I hope he picks someone different; I don't want it to be you either, but maybe I do because you wouldn't go as hard as some would. And she's aware my patch will likely be pulled, but she's not aware of the physical punishments that comes along with it. She does know I'm most likely a dead man on borrowed time."

"Ahh, that's why you're keeping her plum full of cum. I would too if I knew I was going to die soon."

This asshole. "Is there anything else you wanted, besides annoying me?" It's too hot out for this shit.

"Naw, brother, I just called to get under your old-as-dirt grandpa skin."

"Jesus, Shadow, I'm not that fucking old. I'm only thirty-eight, man."

"To us whippersnappers in our twenties still, you are definitely grandpa," he snickers into the phone.

"You know if you were here, I'd be beating your fucking ass with your own ripped off arm, right?"

He hoots at that comment, "Yeah, I do know, that's what makes this so good right now. I was just checking on you, brother. Go back to your little birdie. Have fun being in love. See ya, wodie."

"Bye, dick."

Finding Crow's contact info, I pull him up and call. He's another probie trying to make the cut. He picks up on the third ring. I can't blame him, I know he's at work. Even though we are Enforcers and Soldiers, we still have an outside life.

The Club is a priority, but I understand some of the other guys have lives, families, and careers that take priority over Club business. Some opt to not be part of the dirty, illegal rescue missions and just want to ride and have community. We are that for them too.

I try not to promote those guys up in ranks if I'm being brutally honest about it. Nothing against them personally, but I need people who can drop what they're doing and come running. Who aren't afraid to bend the law or straight up break it.

I have that with a couple of my guys that work for my security company. Anything I ask, they are there. I founded and modeled the company based on needs from Rock. He needed round the clock security and was willing to pay top dollar for it. It grew from there and now I provide security services globally. I've made a tidy profit with my company. I've invested every dime of it too.

My guys all have nice paying positions and jump at my commands. I couldn't ask for more.

"Yo, boss," he answers.

"Crow," I smoothly say, "Anything new?"

"No, sir. There's been no one hanging around outside today. At least not the morning shift I had. The people filtering around outside of her shop all look legit."

Lone Star Saints have to know by now we've taken her away and that staking out her studio and apartment is useless. They know she's not there and she's not coming back any time soon. I'm sure they've put more focus on outside the city.

I look at my watch and see it's still early afternoon.

I may have to go back into the city and make an appearance, just to throw them off of me so as not to lead them to her. LSS knows who I am and my position in this organization. I guarantee they're looking for me too. But the camp can't point back to me.

Under no circumstances can they find me here. Not with her here. I could take them on my own, but I'd have to worry about her. Those sons-a-bitches will have to kill me to take her from me. When I get off the phone with Crow, I call Pierre.

He answers, "Hey, Small Dick, what's up?"

Something clicks in my brain. A memory flickers. Aww, hell no.

"Let me guess, you're BigDickEnergy?"

Pierre lets out a hardy laugh. I even hear him slapping his hand on something.

"Damn, boy, that took you long enough."

"Do you know how many guys I've had running through my brain trying to figure out who it is? You're a dick."

His giggling hasn't settled down, he speaks between titters, "She told me you were *very* concerned who BigDickEnergy is, and the curiosity was *killing* you."

"You know what, fuck you both." I cover my eyes and shake my head. This guy is enjoying this too much. Him and Shadow can both go fuck themselves today.

He finally stops laughing and says, "She seemed better when I talked to her earlier, big bro. Like happier and you can hear it in her voice. Good job, man. You thawed your little ice queen."

"She told me she loves me."

"Whoaa." I hear his breath escape him in astonishment. I have to remind myself he knows her on that deeper level that only best friends do, more so than me, he knows the severity of her saying that.

"Yeah," I swallow past the lump in my throat. The only man I would ever show emotion to is Pierre. He's talked me off plenty of ledges and had my back through everything in the past almost 6 years we've been brothers. When our parents married five years ago, we knew we were already brothers since that first real meeting the previous year. We'll most likely stay brothers even if their relationship doesn't work out.

When Pierre was at college with Birdie, he was on my radar but easily dismissed as the gay friend. He was safe and I never paid much attention to him or was around him. I've never had a reason to not trust him around her. Even when we became brothers and he attempted mind-fucking me, saying what if he was all of a sudden Bi and was into her? My instant fury had him quickly saying it wasn't like that, he was happily married.

Pierre and his husband, Seven, have been married for eight years. They met in college and have been inseparable since. I like Seven, he's a cool guy, I just wish he was nicer to Pierre. He seems indifferent but yet, still involved any time we have a family dinner, and he's present. Aloof is a good descriptive word for him. Of course, Pierre is head over hills with rose colored glasses on. "I bet that felt amazing. I'm happy for you, Lincoln."

I clear my throat, "Thank you."

"So, when's the wedding?"

"Ha. This afternoon if I had it my way," I joke to him.

He snorts, "Have you even asked her yet? Maybe if you return home as married, there's nothing her dad would do to you. Have you thought of that?"

"There's no way I would take away a dream wedding from her, or having her dad give her away."

"You don't even know if she wants that. I know what she wants but I'm not giving any secrets out." His voice takes on a tone like he's shrugging, "Elope, then have a wedding for everyone. She might do that. I don't know though, she's been awfully lonely lately, and you *are* too delicious for women to look at, she might marry you just to keep your dick."

"Shut up," I scoff at him, "I just got her to *like* me, loving me is the ultimate prize, but marriage might be moving too fast for her. Although I do see where being married might spare my life, but not my patch. There's no saving my patch at this point."

"I'll drop a bug of elopement in the ear of one woman of royalty. See if she brings it up to you."

"I've tried to see a way how we could leave here and still be together. Actually have a life together, you know? Picket fences and kids and all that shit. That's my biggest goal."

"You know she's terrified to be a mother, right?"

"No. Why would she be afraid? She's amazing." This is surprising for me to hear.

"Dude, she's afraid she'll end up being her mom. That was one cold-hearted bitch, as you well know. Someone told Birdie women learn their mothering skills from their own mothers, and that planted a seed of doubt in her head that she'll be an awful mom. I know she wants kids, but she's afraid."

"She'll be a great mother. For back up, Mom will help her as much as she can. You and I both know that. Mom and Trix hit it off good. I think your dad approves of her too."

"Yeah, Dad said she was cute and nice, he likes her, and he said he could see you two together even after this shit. He said he was really happy to meet the woman who would give Mr. Danger a run for his money." Pierre chuckles.

All jokes aside, that means a lot to me. Pierre's dad, Bret, is a great guy. I can't believe my mom and him went to school together and dated, then each went off and had separate lives, only to find each other again at a class reunion. The past roughly six years of them being back together has been a big change but I like it. We feel like a complete family unit now and after it being just me and Mom my whole life, it feels really nice.

The only thing that was missing from my life was her.

Chapter 31 – Birdie

Collette's warmed up etouffee was just as good as last night's
numerous platefuls and really hit the spot. I'm rinsing out my bowl
in the sink when Linx walks through the front door with a smile
and in a happy mood. Finally, some good news. He always seems
so pissed every time he gets off the phone.

"Did you have a good nap, Princess?"

Still feeling a little sluggish after a three-and-a-half-hour nap, I
nod while I yawn and giggle, "Yeah, I just need to wake up."
"You want to go flying? Will that wake you up?"

My face lights up and I bounce in place, squealing, "YES! Yes! Do
we have time?"

He laughs and says, "Yes, it's only a little after four. Go get
dressed and we'll take a ride." I run over to kiss him then excitedly
dash off to the bedroom to get changed. A ride is just what I need.
Thankfully, we took our dirty clothes over to his mom's yesterday
and washed them. I have clean riding gear now. I didn't realize

how quickly it gets stinky from being out in the open air and sweating in the sun.

Coming out in my black pants, boots and leather zip up vest, I finish braiding my hair. He finishes tying his folded bandana on his head and pulls it low on his forehead. It does tingly things to my girly parts to see him like this.

"Ready, baby?"

"Yeah," I say as I grab my wallet from my purse and slip past him out to the sunshine, shoving my phone in my vest. There's a full tube of 100 SPF sunblock in Sampson's saddle bag waiting for me, thanks to Collette, so I don't need to worry about grabbing that. My sunglasses are already on my face as the sun kisses my skin while I float down these stairs to my next flying lesson.

I had no idea how much I'd love riding Sampson with Linx. I love being on the back of a bike with him, soaring through the wind that tickles my skin. It's quickly become my favorite thing to do. Well, a close second. Fucking Linx will always be number one now.

Linx comes around me to open the truck door and then playfully slaps my ass when I climb in. I'm not sure why he needs this big ass truck while in the city. I mean, it throws off serious small dick energy vibes, but I know from first-hand experience, Linx's not small, not even close. Considering I've only ever had four dicks, him being one, I don't have a lot to base it off of, but I have watched my fair share of porn and Linx's is just a big as most of those pornstars. Like I stay sore walking around here because of his trouser snake.

He hops into his seat behind the wheel, then reaches over and pulls me to him, hand gripped on the back on my neck and slams his lips into mine. This kiss was just the surprise I needed. He steals little bits of my soul every time he kisses me breathless. When he releases me, I'm slightly dizzy and he chuckles. "I'm really happy I affect you like that." He turns over the diesel engine, smiling and turning up the radio while we head out on our fifteen-minute drive to Collette's.

Of course, now I'm horny and there's nothing I can do about it. I mean, I could totally stick my hands down my pants. That should definitely go over well with him, so yeah, I'm doing it.

There are other ways to choose violence now.

I undo my pants and stick my hand in my panties, and he stiffens and looks over. "What are you doing, little bird?"

"Fucking myself." So matter of fact.

Side eyeing me, he adjusts himself and it gives me another idea. "I want your cock in my mouth, now. Are you up for some road head, babe?"

"Fuck yes, I am. I'll even take a longer way." His pants are undone and his cock's out in record time. Undoing my seatbelt, I flip up his center console to make it a bench seat so I can sprawl out.

My pussy throbs the second my tongue touches his velvety head. Linx sucks in air through his teeth and says, "F-f-fuckkk," when I slip him through my lips and he bumps the back of my throat.

I start humming my favorite Sleep Token song that's playing on the radio and his moans grow heavier. I love making him unhinged.

"Goddamn, Trixie, it feels so fucking good. I'm trying to stay on the road, baby."

I chuckle as I bob up and down harder and diddle my clit faster. He reaches over and cups my ass cheek with his big hand and squeezes. He smacks it good, and I feel my entire backside jiggle. "Fuck, I love that jiggle. It's so fucking sexy."

I hollow out my cheeks and I'm rewarded by his precum coating my tongue.

Linx's hand slips under the waistband of my pants and he swiftly moves my thong over before his finger plows into my pussy. I moan around his cock in my mouth. I love his magic fingers.

"My baby's so wet. Goddamn, Trixie, you're soaked." Linx brings his fingers to my backdoor and slowly circles my asshole. I lift my hips slightly, pushing back. "You like that, baby, don't you? My filthy girl. I can't wait to claim this ass. Nod if you can't wait either."

I nod my head vigorously and it takes him deeper into my throat, making him hiss. I've never been fucked in the ass or have anyone play with that area. But I'm willing to try with him.

"You gonna let my finger into your perfect ass, pretty girl? Give me a color, Trix."

Muffled by a face full of dick, "Gween!"

It's a new sensation for me when he pushes his finger past the rim, although not unpleasant.

He uses my own lubrication to push his finger in and out of my asshole and I feel like I might lose my mind. Fuck, it feels so good it makes me moan harder. It's going to make me come in like three seconds.

No, faster than that. Like now.

I writhe against the truck seat, shamelessly working my hips on my hand, riding out my climax, yelling around his dick stuffed into my mouth. "Fuck yeah, that's my good girl," Linx says before he juts his hips up and spills his seed down my throat, yelling my name and grunting. Goddamn, it's so sexy when he comes. I gobble up as much of his cum as I can and swallow my love whole. I swirl my tongue around his sensitive, softening cock and he jerks with a shudder. "Damn, baby."

As I pull my mouth off of him, I tug my hand out of my pants. They're slick with my cum and I reach over and say, "Open."

His eyes flick to mine. He obeys and opens his mouth for me to stick my fingers in. His tongue wraps around my wiggling fingers, sucking them clean. I hum my approval and in a sultry voice say, "Good boy," with a satisfied smile.

His eyes cut back over to me with a scowl on his face. I giggle and pull my fingers out of his mouth. I wipe the corners of my mouth daintily. "That was fun," I say as I button myself back up.

I tuck him back in and try my hardest to button him up before we get to Collette's. He finishes it for me.

"I didn't realize you had such great tongue skills," he says as he's pushing his sunglasses back down onto his face.

"Ya know, I didn't either. I've only done it a handful of times. I just went with what felt natural. Was it good?" I hate the self-doubt. It would be different if I would have been ok with casual sleeping around, but I wasn't. I would never be that girl. I just don't work that way; I have to have a deeper connection than just body and looks. Zharia needs a yes and a hard cock then she's your girl.

I've always envied her blasé attitude towards casual hookups. Hence the reason she's far more experienced than me. Her motto is love on 'em and then leave 'em.

Honestly, a lot of my knowledge about sex comes from Zharia. She never misses an opportunity to tell me about her one-night-stands. She gets up to some weird shit. But I'm not going to yuck her yum. That's why it was a little disconcerting when she kept Shadow from me. Something more is going on there, I just know it. For one, I think it's been going on for months, not just a few weeks. She's been acting differently.

He growls at my comment, "I prefer to think of you as untouched before me. If I would have had my way, you would still be a virgin waiting on only me and only knowing my cock." He sounds like a petulant child with his unreasonable suggestion.

I throw my hands up in exasperation with his ridiculous shit, "Jesus, and I thought being twenty was a high age to lose my virginity at. You're delulu if you thought I was waiting until I was twenty-eight to lose my virginity to you while you hem-hawed around deciding to make a move after years, sir. Fucking years, *Saint Danger.*"

His shoulders shake with his suppressed laughter.

I hold up my finger, twirling it in the air and continue my tirade, "We won't even go into all the rumors of how much of a manwhore *Mr. Danger* is."

He holds up a finger, "Hey, I have to pass the time somehow. I'm not going to abstain from sex just because I wasn't allowed to have you. I pictured you through every woman, no lie. And it's not like you were waiting for me either." He blows out a breath until it's even. "So, fine, neutral territory on past sex lives, we can't get mad at each other for it." He holds out his hand with his pinky extended.

I roll my eyes and latch my pinky in with his. I narrow my eyes, and say, "You're insufferable I hope you know."

"Oh, I know, darlin', I'm only this pleasant for you," he retorts with a smile on his face. Somehow, I think that might be one of the truest statements he's ever made.

He throws the truck in park and leans over to kiss me, and I eagerly meet him halfway. After a few playful swipes of tongue, we break apart. I love his quick, intense kisses. They're just a reminder of who I belong to.

I hop down from the truck at the same time Linx steps out. I walk around the front of the truck, grasping for his outstretched hand, when suddenly a utility van races up and slams on their brakes. So many things happen simultaneously.

Men with masks pour out of the truck with weapons. Before Linx can pull his gun from his hip, one man was already on him, hitting him with a crowbar. Another man roughly yanks me from Linx, and tosses me to a different, bigger man who clamps one arm across my waist and the other on my chest, dragging me towards the van. I kick and I start screaming. Blood curling screams.

"**LINCOLN**!"

They have him on his knees and the man standing over him punches him in the face as they continue to get me under control and drag me to the back of the van, me fighting them every step of the way. I kick, I scream, I elbow, anything at this point. I try to remember all the self-defense training. I try like hell to bite his hand when he keeps trying to put it over my mouth and he smacks me in the face, enough to bring tears to my eyes.

Just like that, quick as shit, I've been kidnapped.

I scream until I can't scream anymore.

The last thing I see as I try to claw my way back to Linx is him falling forward on the concrete driveway and Collette running out the front door towards him and her screaming.

The back doors shut and the van lurches forward with me still kicking and yelling and the man holding me falls onto a bench and hauls me back against him, my back to his chest, his hard cock digging into my back. He wraps his legs around mine to subdue me and says, "Keep fighting, Princess, that's exactly how I like my whores."

My heart stops and my blood runs cold. I immediately still my movements and with a shaky, hoarse voice, ask this asshole, "What do you want?"

"Your soon-to-be husband awaits you in Texas, Princess." He inhales deeply, rudely, running his masked face up the side of my neck, "but you keep thrashing around and I'm going to make it worth my while to hold you down, all the way there, until you bleed or beg me to stop. Behave, like a good little girl."

Chapter 32 – Linx

The last thing I remember before the darkness claimed me, was my mom yelling and rolling me over to my back. I saw her terrified face pushing through my blurry, bloodied vision as pain radiated throughout my beaten body.

With what breath I could muster, I try to yell, "Call Rock, call him now, Mom."

I succumbed to the darkness with Birdie's name on my lips and her petrified face while she screamed for me in my mind. I failed her.

Chapter 33 – Birdie

I was shoved into my own seat and told to sit there and shut up. So that's what I did while observing my surroundings.

There are no windows to look out of, and I have no idea how much time has passed.

I decided within the first five minutes of sitting here and getting my hands tied in front of me with old phone wiring, that I'm not going to sit here and cry the whole time. I'm going to be brave.

And bravery needed patience.

Something else I have in spades is the blood of a malicious king running through my veins. My father will come for me. Make no mistake, these men are dead and don't even know it yet. Linx will stop at nothing to get to me if he's survived. Oh god, I only pray he's ok.

My stomach rolls at the memory of him falling onto the concrete with blood spattered everywhere. *Keep calm, Birdie.*

Tweedledumb looks over at me and whips off his mask, "I value breathing more than my fucking identity. She isn't going to talk, is she?" He puts his hand on my thigh and slides it upwards. I jerk away and the three men back here with me start laughing.

Another takes his mask off and says, "Oh, Princess, you're in for a treat. The only thing saving you right now is Grim's order you come to him unblemished by our dicks."

I watch them, memorizing every facial feature I can. These are my captors, and I want to make no mistakes when it comes to identifying their dead bodies. They'll get their comeuppance all in due time. And I hope it fucking hurts.

I lean my head back against the moving van and take a deep breath to steady my heart. All I can do now is wait. Bide my time until I get to wherever the fuck they are taking me.

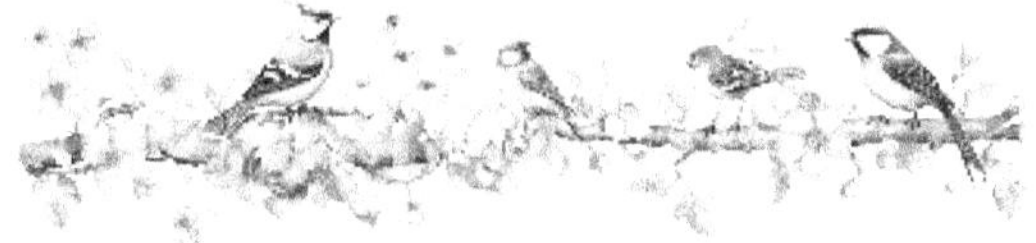

"Wakey wakey, Princess. We're home."

My eyes snap open and I jerk my body and see one of the men hovering in front of me, in my face, leering at me. I must have dozed off. I don't feel us moving anymore.

He jerks my tied hands, and I stand up on wobbly legs and follow him out of the back of the van. The first thing I notice is it's still daylight; it's dusk or early evening. I look up at the sky and see the sun is well past its zenith but not quite settled in the West. I'd say it's about six or seven, which is not nearly enough time to make the five-hour trek to Houston, where the Lone Star Saints are stationed. I'm still in Louisiana. I have to be. The timeline's not matching for being in Texas. I wasn't out that long.

I fucking hate that I can't stay awake longer than an hour in the car. Apparently not even under extreme duress. This sucks. I have no idea which direction or how long.

Of course, I don't know where at in Louisiana I am because there were no windows either. We could have driven in circles for all I know. They could have taken me in any direction, but he did say in Texas, but that didn't necessarily mean they were taking me there. I just assumed. Now I know better.

There looks like a dilapidated warehouse looming in front of me. Windows broke out, nothing around for a mile, flat land to see if anyone's coming. There will be no element of surprise here. *Just perfect*, I think as I inwardly roll my eyes.

The men yank me forward and we are walking to the door on the front of the building. The smell of death hits me first, old decay and the sickly-sweet smell of rotting flesh, like an animal's died out here. I can't dwell on it because I am hauled through the big double doors, into something that looks like a factory, definitely a production area.

One asshole pulls me further into the factory. There are big machines pushed to the sides. It's mostly cleared out. This place hasn't seen workers in at least a decade or longer. No hope in anyone coming to work to see me and save me.

In the back of this open space, at the end of the makeshift aisle, stands a sharply dressed man in an expensive suit. It looks custom made for him. He pulls his jacket sleeve down over his wrist, like he was checking the time, and clasps his hands in front of him in his shoulder's width apart stance. He just looks like a douche.

Behind him are more goons who look like defensive football players. Large men I have a snowball's chance in hell of escaping from.

Be brave, Birdie.

I'm thrust in front of this man, who I have no doubt is The Grim Reaper, leader and President of the Lone Star Saints.

He's not as good looking as he thinks he is.

His face curls into a sinister grin as he eyes me up and down with his cold, dead eyes. I barely suppress my shiver, like someone walked over my grave. I'm not giving this man an ounce of my fear.

I'm going to make Linx and my dad proud. I'm not going out groveling and crying like a bitch.

Asshole in the suit clears his throat and says, "It's a pleasure to meet you in person, Princess. I can't wait to get to know you better." His dark smirk promises some type of pain as he continues to leer at me. There will be no pleasure knowing him.

I spit at him, it lands by his feet.

"Now Beatrix, is that any way to greet your future husband?"

"Fuck you. I'll never marry you."

Before I can flinch, his hand whips up and across my face, jerking me in the goon's arms. "You don't have a choice," Grim says.

THIS MOTHERFUCKER HIT ME.

"Over my dead body."

I see his jaw ticking. "Unfortunately, that's not going to happen. You'll wish many times over that you were dead, but I can't allow my newest prized asset to die. I have many wonderful plans for you. All you have to do is stay alive, the men who will pay for your pussy will do the rest."

I have never been more grateful for my IUD than I am right now. "Bring her to the back room. I have something special I want to show her." Grim turns and starts walking further into the building, towards a wall that has two doors that have windows in their top half. There are also big windows by the doors, like this would have been a supervisor's office and he could see the day-to-day operations of the plant.

"Oh my god." The air is knocked from my lungs. Pierre, bloody and bruised, is tied to a chair, head hanging, covered in dried blood. My heart claws its way out of my chest into my throat. The little bird in my chest is frantic. I would rather them beat me than him.

"You son of a bitch, how dare you. He didn't do anything to you. It's me you want."

Grim runs his fingers down a tendril of my hair and I flinch from his touch. "He's here as reassurance you won't put up a fight. We won't kill him, but he will wish he's dead every time you fight. Remember that."

I'm led to the other door, into a darkened room with two windows, one facing out into the plant, the other is on the wall between the two rooms. I can see Pierre from my room. There's nothing in this room except an old desk and an even older, and dustier swivel chair.

"These are your new accommodations, Princess. Your father has twenty-four hours to relinquish the Florida and Caribbean ports to me, or the first bidder gets his turn at that sweet royal pussy, after me and my men, of course."

The men around him chuckle and I'm trying hard not to throw up. He walks up to me and says, "You're even more beautiful in person. They'll pay top dollar to fuck Rock's only daughter."

"Go fuck yourself."

The backhanded slap I receive is not expected right then, so it rips through my head like a hammer hitting a nail. More powerful than the previous one, it rings my bell and splits my lip. One of the men catches me and hauls me right back into Grim's face.

He's cool as a cucumber as he says, "Now, Beatrix, look what you've made me do. That wasn't nice."

THIS MOTHERFUCKER HIT ME AGAIN.

Before I can reply with some scathing remark, he slaps me again, the gaudy rings on his hands scratching my fair skin. God. Damn. It.

This fucking maniac's audacity. I narrow my eyes and just look at him, but under my skin I'm seething, furious and plotting death. My whole face throbs. I can't wait to see his head split open, chest ripped apart, bleeding out while I laugh. Linx is going to tear him apart limb from limb. I can't wait to hear him screaming.

I really hope I'm around to see his ending.

My face stings. I taste blood and swallow it down, almost making me wretch up my lunch. I'd spit it at him again but I'm afraid he'll hit me harder, and I don't think I can tolerate another blow.

"There's a camera up in the corner. The live feed has been sent to your father to watch as we dismantle his precious baby, piece by mind cracking piece." He gets in my face and hisses, "Mark my words, you're going to wish for death, but it will never come."

Grim straightens his suit and steps back, composed yet again. I see a hint of frustration ripple behind his eyes. He wasn't counting on me fighting back. He expected the pampered and spoiled daughter of Jaques Chavanet to cower and beg for leniency.

He is sorely mistaken.

"Now smile for Daddy." The guy behind me grips my hair and pulls my face up with his other hand and I see the camera with the blue light on.

I maintain my stoic attitude and give not one fucking ounce of satisfaction to this motherfucker. If Linx wouldn't have told me what Grim had planned on doing with me, I'd be going into this scary as fuck situation blind.

I make up my mind to sit here and play it cool, be the person he least expects. I can play docile for a bit. Even while this hunk of shit is right in front of me and the one bitch boy is cutting these wires off of me. *Be cool, Birdie*.

"I'll see you in," he looks at his expensive Rolex, "twenty-one hours, beautiful." He snaps his fingers and turns to leave. His fucktwits follow him out. The door slams shut and echoes through the empty plant, making Pierre lurch. I hear a lock clicking closed and I know I'm not getting out of here any time soon.

I look back up at the camera and decide to speak, just in case there's audio. "Daddy, find Linx, he's at his mom's, and make sure he's alive. I don't know where I am. The van had blacked out windows, I had no sense of direction and time. It's a warehouse or plant, a big building in the middle of nowhere. It's flat ground, no other buildings, no way to sneak in. Daddy, they have Pierre too. He's in the next room and he looks pretty beat up. Hurry."

I walk over to the window and watch the rise and fall of Pierre's labored breathing, vowing some way to get us out of here alive.

Chapter 34 – Linx

"Mr. LaFleur? Open your eyes. Come on, buddy, open your eyes."

"Lincoln, open your eyes, honey."

Mom?

There's a steady beeping penetrating through my foggy brain. The throb inside my head is enough to crack my skull open.

My eyes flutter and the bright lights make me flinch.

"Mr. LaFleur?"

I try to talk but I can't get my tongue to work. My mouth is bone dry, and I taste blood. What the fuck is happening?

"Lincoln, baby, wake up." My mom, worried, begging me on a sob, piercing my haze. The quiver in her voice puts me on alert.

I open my eyes and try to keep them open. A man leans over the bed and says, "Mr. LaFleur, can you hear me?"

All I want to do is go back to sleep. Through the fog my brain registers pain, lots of pain.

"Mom?" I croak out.

"Oh, Lincoln, I'm right here. I need you to wake up. Birdie needs you to wake up."

Suddenly it all slams back into me. Trix was taken in a hostile, planned attack at Mom's. They worked that mission like a well-oiled machine and got the jump on me. Birdie is gone.

I try my hardest to get up, pain laces through my head and ribs.

"Easy there, you're in no shape to get out of this bed."

I look over at the man and see he's wearing a tag that says *Doctor Hicks*. "Where am I?" My throat hurts from yelling, more like roaring when we were attacked. Three on one is horrible odds, especially when I didn't see it coming and they had weapons. I was distracted by her, and they were able to get the drop. My worst fear.

"I'm Doctor Hicks, your attending physician. You're in the ER and you've had a serious beat down. We have sutured the cuts on your face, stapled the laceration on your head, but I'm afraid you have a mild concussion. I'm frankly surprised it's not worse. We did a CT scan while you were knocked out and it confirmed there's no bleeding on the brain from the head trauma. Your left ulna is broken too." He lightly taps my arm, "We've set it and casted your forearm while you were under. No surgery needed. You also have two cracked ribs. Good thing you have abs of steel, it helped."

My eyes cut over to the doctor and I nod in understanding. My eyes slide over to my right, where my mom is standing, "Did you call Rock?" My voice comes out weak and raw. I try to clear my throat but it's no use, there's nothing stuck in my throat. It's just hoarse from yelling for Birdie.

"Yes, he is on his way here. I imagine he's bringing the whole club. He was very nice to me while barking orders at those around him. He should be here any minute actually."

"How long has it been?" If Rock is almost here, I know it's been well over two hours. Maybe even three. Fuck, I've been out that long? Time is precious right now.

Mom looks at her watch, "Three and a half hours."

Fuckity fuck fuck.

I close my eyes and take a deep breath. They could have gone in any direction. Anything could have happened to her by now. "Doc, when am I able to leave?"

"In an ideal situation—"

"When?" I growl.

"I'd like you to stay overnight for observation," he replies quickly. "That is not happening. My girl just got kidnapped. I have to go look for her. So, level with me, what's all wrong with me?"

"You were beaten pretty bad, horrible bruising throughout your torso and defensive marks on your hands and arms. You have two cracked ribs on the left side. I imagine the attack came from the left. As I stated before, your left ulna is broken and there's a cast on your arm already. You have a mild concussion which means you'll feel woozy and have a headache for a while. No strenuous activities. Rest as much as possible or you'll make it worse. There were a few lacerations on your head and hands, and they're also stitched and stapled up. You'll have to come back so we can remove them when it's time."

No need to remove them, Rock will kill me long before that's necessary.

A nurse knocks and pokes her head in, "Dr. Hicks, we need you in room thirteen." She scurries off in a hurry.

The doctor turns back to me and says, "Give me fifteen minutes, please. Lay here and rest until I get back and then we'll talk about discharge." He walks out of the room, and I'm left with my mom.

It's hard to focus. A million things go through my mind in the blink of a second through the horrible pounding. So many snippets of times spent with her, minutes lying in bed together, her laugh, how her eyes crinkle when she's up to no good, her silky skin next to mine.

Mom gently wipes at the corner of my wet eyes as I stare at the ceiling, "We'll get her back, mon cœur." She holds my hand and pats it as she says, "Do you want to clean the blood off your face? When you do get to her, you're going to scare her to death with how you look."

I rub my hand on my face and immediately regret it. All of it is sore. "Yeah, maman."

"You have a busted lip, black eye, and your left side of your face is swollen and bruised. There's dried blood everywhere on you," she informs me as she walks across the room to the small sink. She busies herself getting a washcloth and when I open my eyes again, she's there, handing me the hot cloth. God, it feels good on my hurt skin.

I push this bed into a sitting position and once that happens it's easier to look around and move. Definitely hurts my ribs. I don't give a fuck. I have to get up so I can go get Birdie. Time is of the essence. There's no telling what Grim or his men will do to her.

For the beating I took, I got really lucky. It's beyond me why they just didn't kill me.

Mom takes a few trips between the bed and sink, rinsing and wringing out. She helped wash as much blood off as we could get. "Mom? Did you bring my phone?" Please, all that's holy, let her have brought it and it's charged.

She pulls it from her purse as the doctor breezes back in. He rocks on his feet and says, "I'll release under one condition."

"What?" This guy's on my nerves. I'm leaving regardless if he releases me or not. He just doesn't know that yet.

"You go home and rest and let the police look for her."

Even I find his words humorous; however, the laugh from the hallway made my blood chill and made the doctor turn around. Fuck. Satan's here.

Coming through the door is none other than the man himself, Rock, looking furious, dressed out in riding gear, vest and armed to the teeth. He claps the doctor on the shoulder and says, "Well Doc, that's not going to be happening because he's going to go find my little girl, since he's the one who lost her."

Leave it to Rock to make a grand entrance. I expected nothing less. He does have a flare for the dramatic, even if he calls it confidence and swagger.

The color drains from the young doc's face. "Sir, y-you can't be in here with loaded weapons. I-I must insist you leave, right now," he stutters.

Rock still has ahold of his shoulder, and he uses that touch to swiftly turn the doctor around and head him towards the door, "Get a nurse in here and get all this shit off of him. We leave in ten minutes. Chop, chop Doc. Time's a'wastin.'" Then Rock shoves him out the door.

Rock's men station up outside my door as he shuts it behind him.

"Rock." My heart is pounding out of my chest. He wouldn't dare kill me in front of my own momma.

"Danger. How are you doing, son?" It's the son that gets me right in the heart. As of this moment, I don't know if Rock is fucking with me or if he sincerely cares. I'd like to think he's powering through his rage and actually does care about my wellbeing.

"I've seen better days." I try to sit up more, and the room spins and tilts and I collapse back onto the pillows. No time to sit here lounging around, I have to find my old lady.

After all this shit is done, I'm going to make it official with Birdie as my old lady, regardless of what Rock thinks. I'm sure she doesn't understand the reverence or even what the term means, but she will soon learn it's a high honor and requires much respect between us. She's my everything and that's the main thing about being my old lady, she's the number one, she rules my world.

I finally get sat up and the room slows down. This isn't so bad.

"You look a little beat up. How'd they get you?"

"Birdie and I was going on a ride. They caught us as we were getting out of the truck in Mom's driveway. They were watching my mom's house. I didn't even have the door all the way closed when they screeched up. Rolled up in a utility van. I counted five, four thugs and one driver. They hit me with a tire iron before I could pull my gun. This was a well-rehearsed beat and grab. One grabbed

Birdie while the three of them beat me to the ground. Look, Rock, I'm sorry. I know I failed."

Rock places his hand on my shoulder and says, "I'll admit, I didn't quite know what to expect when I got here. I knew you would fight to the death to keep her safe. And fuck yes, I'm mad as hell. You're my best man and indestructible. But seeing you now, I have a change of heart. You're damn well lucky to be alive, Lincoln. I don't know why they left you alive. Your momma told me what she saw. As mad as I want to be, I can't. You look like shit." He gives me a half ass smile full of concern.

"I feel like shit, sir." I rub the good side of my face as it throbs, "I can find her, and I guarantee I know exactly where she is," I say excitedly. I look over to Mom and ask, "Can I have my phone please?"

She already has it in her hand with a puzzled look on her face. She slips my phone into my waiting hand. A loud knock sounds at the door and a nurse pops her head into the room, "Mr. LaFleur? I'm here to get you discharged, is this a good time?"

"Yeah, it's good," I tell her. "I just need to leave as soon as possible."

She makes quick work of taking out my IV and getting all their machines off of me. My focus is taken away from my phone for a minute as she is getting me ready to leave. I swing my legs over the side of the bed. Looking around for my clothes, all I see is my boots.

"Where's my clothes?" I inquire.

"Sorry, but they're in the trash. We had to cut your shirt off of you and your jeans were soaked with blood. But we have some replacements to send you home in. It's not much but they serve a purpose." This little girl holds out a stack of folded up clothes to me and I almost laugh out loud. What in the Pulp Fiction hell is this shit?

I nod with my lips in a thin line and say a terse, "Thank you." She replies, "You're welcome. Once you're dressed, you're all set to leave."

Rock and my mom turn around while I try with all my might to quickly get dressed. Standing up was a little challenging but I finally got it. I hold up the shirt they've provided, and it has colorful hot air balloons on it and says it's the 32nd Annual Lift Off, to fight cancer. Some charity event. The shirt is baby blue, and the pants are sweatpants. Drawstring and elastic bottoms. In gray. Of course. At least they supplied a pair of boxer briefs, so my dick isn't outlined in these things.

I'm not bothered by clothes in general being thrown away; I'm bothered because it was the shirt Birdie's been sleeping in. She wanted my scent back on the shirt. That's the part that bothers me. It could have been any other shirt, and I'd give three fucks less. Now, it's all cut up, bloody, and in the trash somewhere. It makes me rage all the more inside me.

Once I'm dressed and look down at myself, I groan and tell them, "I'm ready." I hear them turn around when I pull up the app on my phone again. Rock tries to hide his snicker. I look like I'm ten. Mom brings my boots over, and I shove my feet into them.

Things have been happening so fast, I've barely had time to remember she has a tracker, a very sophisticated, precise tracker. "I've got her. Fuck," my lungs deflate with partial relief. I know where she is and that's the hardest part. Rock rushes over and looks at the screen in my hands. "Fuck yes, there she is."

"She can't be but two hours away, further over by Lake Charles. Not quite Texas."

I pull up the other tab, it gives me all her vitals. "She's still alive. Her heartbeat is steady. Doesn't seem under duress."

Rock's shoulders drop from their tense position, and I can tell he's relieved.

"Let's go," Rock gestures his arm out for my mom and I amble my way out the door after them. "When we get to the truck, I'll show you the live feed they sent us as a gift," Rock says while filling in after my mom. What the fuck?

Shit's about to get real. I'm going to get my girl, and I'm bringing Satan himself with me. And we will kill every motherfucker who gets in our way.

I walk through the door and the two guys guarding the door, Slim Jim and T-Bone, laugh behind their hands together and Slim asks, "For fuck's sake, Danger, what in the hell are you wearing?"

I keep walking in front of these two assholes. "Don't worry about it, old fuckers, let's go. Now."

Chapter 35 – Birdie

Trust me when I say being alone and held captive gives a person plenty of time to think about everything and analyze every memory that brought me to who I am today.

When I was a little girl, my dad was the light of my life. He was a very loving and giving father. He never missed an opportunity to tell me how pretty I was, or how cute my clothes were, or hang my art in his home office. He hung the moon and stars for me, and I was the center of his universe.

This angered my mother. Her jealousy of Jaques was renowned. No woman dared go near my father for fear of my mom. Even his daughter. She was just as crazy as he was. Together they ruled New Orleans as he acquired more wealth and more ports, more business and more men. My dad was building an empire.

But she never forgave me for being the only child. And a girl to boot. Not when she needed sons so desperately.

I came to be after four miscarriages. The only one to stick around. And then I had the audacity to be a girl.

I overheard my father speaking to my mother one time, he told her, "Make sure you keep the next one buried in you and it's a boy." She didn't. Two miscarriages later, they gave up.

It's no secret men always want an heir and Jaques was no different. Instead of an heir he could actually use, he got me.

As soon as I was born and handed to my mother, I was her responsibility because she failed to provide a son. I fully believe my mother resented me greatly for just existing. It's sad to say but I've made peace with it.

My father planned a Daddy & Daughter date night once a month for as long as I can remember. He carved out time in his schedule and made sure it got done. Full princess treatment, from the limo to the fancy restaurant, to the dress I could wear. He gave me his card and sent me shopping after school so I could dress shop, and I could wear whatever dress I wanted.

The dresses and styles have grown more sophisticated over the years and are a little more daring. Either way, I never wore a dress I hated. I looked stunning in each one, no matter what my mother turned her nose up at and said it was 'common' or 'trashy.' Her style of dress was anything bland and conservative in beige or black.

I remember my dad getting on to my mom for how strict she was with me. He wanted me to be a kid and get dirty. He wanted me to be an expressive teen, daring fashion and playing loud music. He indulged every whim and wish that I had.

He just didn't spend enough quality time with me. Work always came before me. I guess I should be happy with what I got. It could have always been worse. But his hugs when he had time to bestow one on me; those were the shit. Man, they felt like home. It was the way he squeezed me and rocked me, hummed and dragged out the time holding me, as if he was making up for lost time. I cherished those hugs. Lord knows my mother never gave me any.

She, on the other hand, wanted me in church service approved dresses and to learn which fork to use for the dessert and which spoon is for soup.

I have so much useless knowledge of etiquette and archaic practices. I was never going to a dinner with the Queen of England. It was beyond me why it was so important to her.

There's no way in hell I was going to marry a governor or king or high-class stuffy businessman and, in my eyes, that was going to be a living hell for me for so many reasons. I would never give up my freedom for being trapped by a powerful man. Now at twenty-eight I've nowhere to use this useless etiquette wisdom that was so important to my mother for me to know. It sure as hell wasn't helping me find a way out of this bullshit. Survival skills training would have come in handy, Mother.

I remember when I was almost twenty, I took self-defense classes with Zharia. We were on our own and I hadn't seen any of my dad's associates following me around. Zhar and I decided we needed to know how to protect ourselves.

Of course, when my dad found out a man was having his hands all over my body to practice with, he sent Linx after me and Zharia. He was to take over our self-defense training.

Zharia had a field day with it. Her sly, knowing smiles and winks every time I would catch her eye during class. She was always hoping for a love story between me and Linx. Her bleeding romantic heart wouldn't drop it. Still to this day, she insists Linx is my soulmate if I'd only give him a chance.

I'll never hear the end of her triumphant bragging.

My heart hurts so badly. What if we don't get our chance at a happily ever after? I swallow down a sob. I miss Linx.

My mind drifts to the first time I laid eyes on him. Zharia and I had just graduated from high school. Both of us a fresh and newly eighteen, ready to strike out on our own. In fact, we were moving me out of the main house and into our very first apartment near campus.

I was walking down the spiral grand staircase with boxes, and I couldn't see over top of them, and I was scared to fall down the stairs. Ya know, dangerous stuff. I was looking down to the side, towards my feet, to watch the steps because fuck all if I fall. My mother would never shut up about the blood on the carpet on the stairs if I fell.

I was concentrating hard on each measured step that I almost jerked and fell when a deeply southern, sexy voice said, "Hey, let me help you with that."

The boxes were lifted out of my arms and a sexy face appeared over the top box. A rockstar smile with straight white teeth and perfectly kissable lips. Eyes that sparkled every shade of the forest on a sunny day.

He gripped me with that killer dimpled smile, saying, "I got this, lead the way."

I was starstruck from the first time I laid eyes on him he was that beautiful. He was one of those guys off the cover of a romance novel. He straight walked off a military calendar of sexy men. He was on the list of top ten men women would like to fuck.

As I lost my lady bits over him, I remembered where I was and what we were doing. I cleared my throat and said, "Hi, yes, umm, thank you. Right this way."

Behind me I heard Zharia giggling. That bitch. Out of the two of us, she was the boy crazy one. Always has and always will be. Fuck, she still hasn't stopped her endless chase for fuckboys. She's a glutton for punishment.

I did notice he never looked at her. His gaze was solely on me.

I led him to my new SUV, a sleek gray, shiny new BMW my father gifted me for graduation. That particular day we were using it to move all of our stuff into our very own place. It was our pretend moving van. Saying we were excited was an understatement.

He walked up to the SUV with the back door up. He placed the boxes in the back, and I finally got my first good look at him and my heart stopped beating in my chest as my lungs collapsed.

He was gorgeous. A beautiful and dangerous kind of sexy. Especially as he stood there looking down at me with that cocky grin oozing sex appeal. The tight black shirt stretching over muscles and washboard abs. Green camouflage trousers tried hiding his shapely, thick legs but I could just tell, he's the whole package. Curves, cords, and bulges. Everything about him was cream your panties worthy and I stood there and did just that. It's like the earth stopped the minute he bestowed his full attention on me. And he was very focused on me.

He holds out his hand and says, "I'm Lincoln."

I take his hand and say, "Hi. I'm Birdie."

He gives me a charming smile, "So, you're my princess," He nods knowingly.

I return his smile sweetly, "And you must be Daddy's missing link."

He laughs, eyes crinkling at the corners and replies, "Good one. I guess if you put it that way, I'm just what he was missing in his army."

He still hadn't dropped my hand. Not until he heard my father boom, "Danger, I see you've met Birdie. Wonderful!"

Linx smiled at me and one last time before reluctantly letting go of my hand, he brushed his fingers over my knuckles. He turned to my dad who was walking down the front steps to the circular drive.

"Yes, sir, just now."

"Excellent." Dad walked up to me to wrap his arms around me, "I never wanted to see this day come, when my little princess grows up and moves out."

My dad was truly hurt when I wanted to move out. He said I could live at home to save money, and he would still be able to see me every day. He says save money like I don't have tens of millions in a trust fund.

I maintained I needed independence. I fought for my freedom. Eventually he relented after I threatened not to come back or move across the country in the middle of the night.

Plus, I had to get the fuck away from my mother. That bitch was smothering me.

After he feels like he's properly squeezed me enough, he steps to the side, leaving his arm around me.

"Birdie, this is Danger. He's new, but you mark my words kiddo, one day he's going to do great things, climb so many heights, devouring anything in his path."

Lincoln has the grace to actually blush and say, "Thank you, sir. I better get in shape for all that hard work."

My father chuckled and said, "If only we were all in as good as shape as you are, kid." This struck me as odd because my father was a very nice looking, fit man in his late forties. My dad was a striking silver fox, even I knew that. Well, only because Zharia pointed it out all the time to me.

Still does, because now present day my dad has aged gracefully into a man near sixty and still goes to the gym every day. Zharia has seriously told me Jaques is lucky he's my dad because she would make a move on him and become my stepmommy. Bitch better not. I notice women turning their heads when we go out on our Daddy & Daughter dates. Especially since mother died.

Linx finished helping us carry the rest of my stuff down. "I'll have to get a real truck to get my dresser and bed over there. I appreciate the help with the boxes and my clothes."

He dipped his chin with that sexy, panty melting smile and said, "I have a truck. I can run it over to your place. Let me go grab my truck and another associate and we'll get it loaded."

I smile really big, "Oh my god, that would be amazing. I'd appreciate it so much. As you can see, it wasn't fitting into this thing," I pointed at the SUV.

"I got you, Princess."

I blinked up at him, breath caught in my throat. That was the first time he actually used the title to address me. He made it sound seductive, sexy.

I knew my blush was making me bright red, all I could do was smile back at him, "Let me go make sure nothing embarrassing is under my bed." I turned and damn near bounced up the stairs back into the house.

Lincoln was the first man who made butterflies twirl their dance in my belly and I have never forgotten how he made me feel that day. Because I've felt it every time he's been near me, or I hear his voice. Such a visceral and beautiful feeling, lethal to my heart.

My heart has always secretly wanted Linx, even as I tried to bury it, and I knew I would be settling for less with any other man. I knew it on a cellular level.

Waiting in the foyer for me was my dad. "Beatrix," I blinked up at him. Only when my father needs to deliver something permanent, authoritative, some law he's made up, does he use my corporate slash government name, "I feel I need to remind you all of my associates are off limits to you. They are not allowed to make advances towards you or touch you in any way without my permission. Don't lose your heart to one of my men because you can never have him. They'll never go against my word. I own them. I don't want you getting ideas, darlin'."

I blinked at him a few times, I knew confusion was written on my features. "Daddy, I don't want a boyfriend right now. I don't want that much responsibility." You have to feed and water them, and I can barely keep up with myself. At that time this was very true. Even for a gorgeous man in camo with the most devilish grin, I couldn't let him deter me from my goals. I had no time for boys or relationships. Art school was going to be my dream come true.

Sitting in the shadows, I scoff at myself. I just didn't know at the time that owning my own studio, working a long side my best friend Pierre, both of us world-renowned, wildly successful tattoo artists, was my ultimate dream. That, all of that, was actually the dream coming true and I am utterly grateful every single day I get to live it.

I remember my dad actually laughing at me when I said I wanted to tattoo, like me being serious was such a silly affair. Then pulled me in for another hug, clapping me on my back. What my mother lacked in physical affection; my father made up for with his hugs. He had a hug for every occasion and mood but as I got older, they became fewer. I imagine because I left home, but even as a teenager they became sporadic. Hugging my dad will forever feel like home to me.

Someone else is starting to feel that way to me too, I admit.

My daddy is coming for me.

My boyfriend is coming for me.

And all the hounds of hell have gathered, and my demon army is being unleashed in their full glory at our enemy. I almost feel sorry for Grim.

Almost.

Sit tight, little bird, I'm coming, I can almost feel Linx whisper to my heart.

Within fifteen minutes of being kidnapped, as I'm begging and fighting my body not to go into shock, I remembered the teeny, tiny tracker imbedded into my flesh placed by none other than the man who's going to save me. The tracker that broke my heart. That I thought stole my freedom. The tracker that assures me and calms me now.

The tracker that's going to set me free.

I know, bone deep, Linx is coming for me if he survived. Lucifer himself cannot hold me from him, and all the devils are loose and riding with my father and Linx to come get me and kill any Lone Star Saint who gets in the way.

Only this knowledge is what has kept me calm all this time locked in this room. Once I was properly threatened and smacked, I laid low to wait out the danger to come.

And there's danger coming, I'm sure he will have guns ablazin' too.

I have to be the brave and courageous woman that Linx deserves. I've been thrust into the biker lifestyle within a few short days and I'm learning quickly. I've got no choice. I'm starting to see the type of life my mom sheltered me from and I begin to understand more and more every hour.

I'm not sure how many hours have passed though. I've watched the shadows grow thicker and thicker out in the production area of this abandoned shop.

I've cataloged every item in this room while I could see with whatever dying light I had left. There's nothing of use to escape with. Now I don't have to worry about just me escaping, I'm not leaving Pierre here while I save my own ass. Not happening. I'm not that shitty of a friend and I know damn sure Pierre would do the same for me.

I don't leave here without Pierre.

Looking up at the camera, I notice the blue light on, still recording me, still sending a live feed. I'm sure that camera is equipped with night vision and they can see me. I'm still not certain about audio.

The walk over to the window between these rooms is one of dread. I hate seeing Pierre like this. Pretty soon I won't be able to see Pierre at all; it will be too dark. He's hurt badly and needs medical care like now, and it's twisting my guts knowing he's in pain and I can't stop it; I can't help.

The many searches of this room were fruitless. It's like they stuck me in one of those escape rooms but neglected to put any clues out, or any props. It's going to be impossible to escape this room. And that scares me. I can't pick up a desk or filing cabinet to hit them with.

Not shitting anyone here, I'm terrified and running on pure spite and adrenaline. Somehow, I have to come up with a plan. I refuse to die or surrender without thinking of a plan.

I hang my head in my hands in the encroaching darkness and decide to pray.

To anyone. Any gods or deities.

I don't care if it's the god of hotdogs, I need some divine intervention here. Pronto. In the name of all holy condiments, mustard amen.

As if a miracle was being dished out immediately, lights come on out in the plant. One by one they clicked on like floodlights.

My head jerks to the right to see what's happening out there, I have no idea what to expect. I look over at Pierre and he's awake and looking at me. His face is bruised and swollen, but stony, impassive. My eyes tear up and I raise my hand up to my lips and the other hand is placed flat against the glass, trying to reach for him. He subtly shakes his head no.

I practically hear his soothing voice in my head, '*Don't give them the reaction they desire.*' It's been his go-to affirmation with me about my mother, and it works in this situation too.

I nod slightly to him and take a deep breath, wiggling my fingers, my chest rising, and I exhale, nodding my head. *We'll survive this.* If given a choice, I will fight so hard they will have to kill me.

I turn my body towards the door and watch the approaching silhouettes walk ominously towards the offices where we are. Something pivotal is about to happen. I feel it in my bones.

I look up at the camera and say, "Here we go, Daddy, they're coming for me. I plan to fight. I love you." My eyes seek out the shadows coming towards me again and I face the enemy headed right for me.

Fuck you.

Chapter 36 – Linx

Thank fuck I always carry a duffel of riding gear in my truck. I can change into them at my mom's and get out of here and get my girl. I have a one-track mind right now, getting to her and killing who took her is topmost priority.

Through the bathroom door, Mom is busy begging me to be careful and not to overdo it. She stood outside the bathroom while Rock gave me five minutes to dress for the ride, prattling on about what the doctor said.

I'm well-fuckin-aware of what he said, Mother. I splashed water on my sore and bloodied face and hoped like hell Birdie doesn't notice when she sees me again. Yeah, she's going to freak when she sees my face.

Now Mom's standing here by Sampson as I get my gloves on. There's still dried blood all over the driveway. My blood. It fuels my rage. I don't see any where Trix was or where they dragged her off to. Thank fuck. I'm already murderous, I'm not sure if there's a level above that.

I plan on riding Sampson to the location of the pretty blue beeping light on my phone screen that I keep obsessively staring at. The probie, Dobby, will be driving my truck over, leading the head of the procession so he can blast through any barriers or gates. I outfitted him in a Kevlar vest and helmet I have stashed in the truck for this very reason.

There must be a hundred bikes lining my mom's subdivision. Some of them even parked out on the highway. Some are sitting at the parking lot of the church beside the neighborhood. Bikers are everywhere and they've heeded the call to save their princess. To save a woman from disgusting men. To stop and hopefully kill peddlers of flesh.

I'm sure Mom's nosy ass fucking neighbors that complain about my bike noise are having a real conniption fit right about now. I smirk and think, *Fuck you stuffy bitches*.

It makes my petty ass smile to myself as I don my cut, my patched vest. *Daddy Danger's coming, baby girl, and he's bringing your other daddy with him.*

After I saw the live feeds of Birdie and Pierre in those rooms, I saw red. No white. Beyond red. Into darkness. Murderous hot rage.

Those motherfuckers.

I hope Trix remembers her excruciating self-defense lessons. I hope she remembers how to throw a punch, how to block, how to strike when they least expect it. I have faith in her. She's never been one to freak out, so I don't expect her to start now. My girl was always focused and calm in training. Zeroed in on a kill shot. Even when I had her pinned to the mat or up against the wall. Man, those times, fuck, I wanted her so bad back then.

I've watched her live feed on my screen for a while now. She keeps walking around the room, looking in all the drawers and under things, studying the ceiling and walls. Occasionally looking up at the camera. My little bird's looking for anything to help her escape or defend herself with. Good girl.

"Mom, I love you and I'll be safe, now kiss me so I can go." I jut out my cheek for her. She throws her arms around my neck and sobs. I hold her little shaking body and crush her to me.

"Bring her home, mon cœur," she quietly says for my ears only, then kisses my cheek again and steps back, wrapping her arms around herself.

Once Rock hugs my mother on the way to his bike, and she makes him promise to look out for me and to call her if something happens, she finally lets him mount his bike. He gives me side-eye, and I smirk, knowing he damn well likes my fussy mother and he ain't mad one tiny bit.

I have my phone propped on my dash and plugged into my USB for charging. One half of the screen is Birdie's room; the other side is Pierre. I toggle to look at the tracking app.

Birdie is an hour and a half away from us. Looking at the dying sky, I estimate we'll arrive with the cover of darkness, a hundred deep, and armed to our teeth.

Game on, motherfuckers.

A mile away from the blinking dot, we pull over to regroup. Each man cuts their engine and forms lines down the center of this deserted highway.

It brings me pride to see my men, the courageous and loyal men that I've trained, fall into formation. Not a lot of organized crime is this organized.

Rock stands at the front of the line, me to his right, Shadow to his left. All of us in our esteemed place of power.

Taking over some of the blind rage I feel, guilt cuts a jagged hole in that anger and slips through like a thief in the night.

I've betrayed every single one of these men.

My brothers.

My friends.

My father figure.

All for her. My l'âme sœur. Soulmate. For everything she is and will be, I fall at her feet.

I regret nothing.

I can regret nothing and still feel guilty.

"Men, I appreciate your sacrifice and loyalty. It's time to put a stop to the Lone Star Saints once and for all. Enough is enough," Rock growls and a few men grumble agreement. "This is kill on sight. None of them leave this property. Is that clear?"

All the men yell as one, "Yes, sir."

"Grim is to be left for me!" he yells. Rock puts up his fist, "Ride or die!" he roars.

"RIDE OR DIE!" the brothers roar our club motto.

My heart thumps in my chest like a drum, hard and loud. It's been this way since I woke up in the hospital. It won't settle until she's in my arms, alive and safe.

"Danger."

"Yes, sir."

Rock walks over to me with Shadow. "I want you to hang back to the rear."

"Sir."

"Don't argue with me, Lincoln, you're in no position to. You're a liability right now, son. You could barely ride that bike here. Keep your earpiece on." Rock turns to Shadow, "You're on point. You two are a well-oiled machine working together. I have absolute faith in you both." He claps Shadow on his shoulder, then me and he walks away to his bike.

Shadow sticks his knuckles out and I knuckle bump him and we both nod. He's a good dude and I hope nothing happens to him. But he knows I'm not hanging back.

My skin feels prickly and cold sweat pumps out of me. I'm so close to getting her back. Once I have arms around her again, I'm never letting her go.

We take off and my adrenaline spikes. Nerves and confidence clash.

As instructed through hours of practices of formations, thirty riders pull out ahead of us. That's the first line. They secure the outside.

Rock and Shadow take off with another twenty flying with them. As much as he wanted me to hang back, I respectively decline that order and follow right behind those two. Apparently, I'm not good at taking orders anymore.

The remaining band of brothers slide in behind me a split second after I take off. Second line of defense. They'll come around to the back of the building and secure it there.

The roar is deafening as we approach the blinking dot.

Three helicopters race past us, flying low overhead to provide ground cover while we pull in. Rock spared no expense and left no stone unturned. He brought out the big guns. We even have our own squad at the very back of the group.

Dobby in my truck will take care of any barriers. He's already ahead of us, taking out any obstacles such as a guard shack or gates or any foot soldiers. The helicopters will provide a good cover for us to roar into the grounds, hopefully unnoticed until it's too late.

I'm just coming up to the gate when I clearly hear the gunfire erupting over my bike and the wind in my ears. The outside perimeter is clear as I barely get Sampson parked and kickstand down by the main entrance. Swinging my leg over and grabbing my guns out of their holsters from my sides and my aching fucking ribs, I take off running right behind Rock and Shadow.

Fuck waiting and hanging back. That's my baby in there.

Chapter 37 - Birdie

Grim stands in the clearing outside the offices, in the middle of the main aisle, dressed in a nice black suit. His short dark hair is slicked back like the gangster he thinks he is, and his shiny watch glints light off its face like a homing beacon. The way the lights are strategically set in this building, it appears like he's standing in a spotlight. I'm sure he's noticed and is thrilled with the added attention.

In the light, arms crossed in front of him, staring at me, a wicked smile starts to unfurl on his face. It's like nails on chalkboard. My stomach sours and I want to throw up.

I don't think it's been twenty-one hours, liar face. I'm not kidding this time when I think it, *I truly hope your pants catch on fire, along with the rest of you.*

I see out of the corner of my eye two goons dragging Pierre out of the room, just as my door opens and two other men grab my arms and haul me out to the clearing.

Pierre is put on his knees, and I'm brought over by Grim. Good, I need to size this S.O.B. up anyways.

I'm five-eight and this guy isn't even six foot I don't think. I guess they don't go on size matters for their club president. My dad's Linx's size.

This is going to be too easy. I've taken down Linx before.

Underestimating me is his fatal flaw.

Stroke your brave little lady balls, Birdie, it's almost go time.

I take a good look around the factory. Most all the of the machinery has been taken out. Armed men are standing everywhere. There's a second level catwalk surrounding the far walls, men with rifles stationed up there. So much for running. The four guards he brought with him stand around with their hands at the ready. Two of the tense, bunched muscled henchmen train their eyes to the entrance. The other stand staring at us with hard as stone looks.

One walks over to hand Grim a rod. He turns to me with that shitty, evil smile and hits the button. Electricity sizzled at the end, cracking and snapping making my asshole pucker in fear.

Be brave. Be brave. Be brave.

"So, the fun begins. I'm going to need you to light your boyfriend up here until he passes out. Just to start this adventure with you, I've made the first task simple." This idiot thinks my gay best friend is my boyfriend.

I just stare at him with what I hope is an emotionless face. However, inside I'm horrified. I'm fighting down the bile creeping up my esophagus.

I really fucking hate this guy. "And if I don't?" Neutral tone.

His evil smirk turns the air in my lungs to lead. He leans into my space, "If you don't, I bend you over this spool of wire and force myself into that sweet princess cunt. And I'll make damn sure it hurts."

Zero to a thousand.

I stare defiantly at him. I hope he can read the giant 'fuck you' on my face because that's exactly how I feel.

"No thanks."

His eyes narrow on me, his chest puffs up trying to intimidate me.

I immediately channel my inner beast Linx instilled in me during my many, many hours of climbing his huge body to practice taking down a grown ass man. My eyes stay locked on his.

Staring into his eyes, I tell this asshole, "You'll have to rape me before I hurt him."

Pierre starts screaming. I see the pain in his eyes, but I've made my choice.

"So be it," Grim says and reaches for me as the sounds of a thousand roaring beasts beat down on our ears.

I look at him and say, "I can't wait to watch my real boyfriend, and my daddy kill you."

Within a nanosecond of that falling from my lips, Grim smacks the shit out of me. A-FUCKING-GAIN.

FUCKING HELL, that hurt.

I admit, it shocked me as I didn't see it coming.

All my training never prepared me for what an actual hit would feel like.

Shouts and gunfire blast off all around us.

The calvary has come.

Once I get my bearings again, I see Grim look at me with true fear in his eyes. He is a piss poor leader.

My father's men are infiltrating the open space and bullets are whizzing. All the burly Tweedle Dumbs are charging their way down the main aisle, getting picked off one by one. Good.

Grim's team of LSS sucks. They are slow on the uptake, like they thought it was their own brothers rolling up. They are quickly killed off.

Knowing my father, he's going to come straight through the front door like the king he is.

Fighting ensues everywhere. It's chaos. Mass chaos. Grim tries to pull us over by the back door. He really thinks he's going to make a run for it.

He digs into my arm and tries to haul me close to him. I see it in his eyes; he plans to flee and take me with him. I'm his bargaining chip. To hell with that shit.

He's the first rat to jump ship and swim to safety. The kind of leader who leaves his men to perish in vain. The worst of the lowest type of man.

It's now or never Birdie. You will never be free as long as this man breathes. You will always look behind you because of him. He'll never stop coming for you. He must die.

Linx be with me. I take a deep breath, make a fist like properly trained and drop back my foot to push off and I right hook this motherfucker right in the fucking face, breaking his nose as I hear the victorious crunch and pain blooms throughout my hand.

Element of surprise, bitch.

Chapter 38 – Linx

As soon as I hit the open doors, gunfire booms so loud and men yell, and bodies drop. I see Rock up ahead of me in the aisle seeing the same damn thing I just saw. Birdie giving Grim a mean knuckle sandwich. Her right hook is painful, I should know, she's hit me and Shadow with it many times in training.

That's my girl!

As soon as Grim is knocked off kelter, she doesn't miss a second to hit him with a left uppercut at the second his arm releases her. She jerks around while he's surprised and lands a blow to his balls with her knee, doubling him over in pain. Birdie, in a quick as shit move, reaches under his jacket and snatches his gun from his chest holster. Grim grabs his balls and falls to his knees in front of her. She holds the barrel of the gun to his forehead, point blank when he drops to his knees. Oh fuck.

My god, she's glorious.

My very own demoness.

I can't possibly fall more in love with her, but here's me digging deeper.

"Tell them to stop, right now, cease fire!"

"CEASE FIRE! STOP! STOP!" Grim booms. I wish I could watch him piss himself with fear.

"Stop!" Rock also yells. It's not as if there's many LSS men still standing. I stop, along with Rock, about halfway up the aisle. He puts out his arm to his side to hold me back as I come up running beside him.

Men stop fighting here inside, gunfire has already ceased outside since that area's been cleared of Grim's men. An eerie hush falls over the place. You only hear heavy breathing of men fighting, groans of the wounded, guns of Grim's men falling to the ground.

"Hands behind your back." Grim's not moving as fast as she likes. "Move you piece of shit!" She moves closer to him, repeatedly hitting his forehead with the muzzle of the gun to prod him quicker. She pulls back a little so he can't grab her. "How dare you. That ball pain you feel is for Pierre," my little bird yells at him. Grim puts his arms behind his back.

"Did you really think you'd get away with this? Are you insane? Both of them will destroy the universe to find me." She shoves the gun closer to his face. I admit, seeing the furious, evil leader of the Lone Star Saints on his knees in front of my woman, cowering, is getting my dick hard. She's breathtaking. I'm still scared for her but she's managing on her own so fucking well. I'm so proud of her.

"You were so worried about my Daddy, but you should have been worried about his little girl the entire time. I'll never be free as long as you're alive."

"Because you belong to me!" Grim yells at her, the vein breaking out on his forehead, neck muscles corded.

Birdie keeps her eyes trained on Grim, her hand never shakes. My girl is calm and collected, as I knew she would be. But me, I want to rip this motherfucker's skin off while he screams for me to stop.

"I belong to one man and it sure as fuck ain't you, asshole. Now, any last words?" I hold my breath at her words. I can't say if she will go through with this or not. If she shoots him, she unknowingly starts a war. I mean, we're basically at war already with her kidnapping, so fuck it, do it baby doll. Grim made the first move. Rock will annihilate every LSS member after this for retaliation.

"You don't have the guts to do it, you little bitch," he roars at her. My hands flex, busting up my stitches, I'm sure. She calmly juts her chin out and smiles her beautiful, sweet southern girl smile at him.

"I see." She nods in a sarcastic manner with that killer smile; her eyes never leaving his face. "Welllll…in that case, I want you to know this is for my boyfriend and leaving him for dead at his momma's house and taking me from him. You thought him or my dad was gonna kill ya, didn't you?" *My boyfriend*. She fucking giggles. *Giggles*. Shaking her head like she's entertained, she tsks him and says, "You ruined a perfectly good flying day with your bullshit. See you in hell when I return to my throne."

Then she pulls the trigger.

She pulls the fucking trigger.

And the deafening roar of a gunshot fills the quiet building, the casing falling to the concrete bouncing on the ground, echoing tink…tink…tink…then Grim's body slumping over to the ground. Holy fuck, oh fuck.

Chapter 39 – Birdie

"TRIXIE!"

I hear Linx screaming my name through the bloodlust haze I've slipped into out of desperation and defense. I see blood splatter everywhere. Oh god, it's on me.

What the hell am I doing? I guess if push comes to shove, I'll pull the trigger.

I look up to see Linx sprinting at me, running past my dad who takes off too. I drop the gun and run to him. My Linx! He's alive! When I reach him, I jump into his arms and wrap my legs and arms around him and start crying. He grunts in pain but tightens his grip.

"Oh my god, Linx, you're ok," I sob. My heart does leaps and my butterflies are dancing to techno music in my stomach.

"Trix, fuck baby, I thought I lost you. Oh god," Linx moans in a voice full of emotion while he has a death grip on me, holding me to him and rocking me, fingers twisting in my hair. Fuck, it feels so good. All the emotions I was holding at bay are breaking through the levy as I clutch him to me and shake.

"Oh my god Lincoln," I'm sobbing. My hands are on his face looking at all the cuts and swelling and bruising. I want to kiss this all away, I can't, so I kiss his forehead and cheeks, any spot that isn't injured, really.

"Trixie, baby, thank fuck, thank fuck," his hands are all over me too, in my hair, on my ass, on my face, as he tries to kiss me with his busted lips.

"Linx...I'm so happy you're alive," I say breathlessly. I'm so ecstatic to be in his arms again.

I hear men running up to us and hear my father's anguished cry as he reaches us, "Birdie!" I pull my lips off Linx, and I drop my legs from around him. As I shimmy out of his grasp to launch myself towards my daddy, I vaguely take in the number of men surrounding us, watching. I wrap my arms around my dad's middle, but not before I catch the shocked, then the angered face he makes upon seeing Linx and I embrace.

Linx runs over to Pierre to check on him. A couple of my dad's members have him braced between them, trying to walk with him to the door.

My dad almost suffocates me and damn near dislocates my shoulder with how tight he holds me. I don't care. This man can hold me as tight as he wants to. He rallied the troops and came for me.

"Jesus fuck, are you ok, baby girl?" He holds my cheeks in his hands, turning my head this way and that, checking for injuries. I most likely have a bruised cheek from Grim's slaps. I know for a fact my lips are busted, and I feel my eye swelling. Or maybe he's looking at the blood splatter all over me. I mean, I did just blow somebody's brains out at point blank range.

Oh god, I'm a murderer.

I feel no remorse. Zilch.

It does run in the family; I giggle like a loon in my head. I think shock might be setting in.

Either way I feel like a badass. A very tired badass bitch but still powerful and strong. Grim's dead by my hand. Sometimes the victim becomes the hero and sometimes all the good girls have to do very bad things to survive.

My heart is starting to calm down and I'm shaking from the surges of adrenaline. "Yeah, Daddy, I'm fine. I'm more worried about Pierre and Linx."

"Yeah, we'll talk about that later." He gives me a hard look, "I have been so worried and scared. Jesus, Birdie, I'm so happy you're ok." He pulls me to his chest again and squeezes.

I knew he would say that. I was so excited and grateful to see Linx, I didn't care who saw what. Apparently, neither did Linx. When Dad releases me, I step back and Linx is there, hands on my waist to usher me away. I try to look over my shoulder as we walk, and I say, "But Pierre…"

"Taken care of, love, let's get you out of here." Linx maneuvers me through the main doors into the night while my dad's crew watches us leave.

He walks me to his truck, and I turn and wrap my arms around his neck, "I knew you'd come for me. I knew it in my soul."

"Not even the Devil could keep me from you, little bird. No one." He crushes me to his chest as he cradles the back of my head.

Linx feels like coming home. I feel safe. I feel loved. I feel everything when I'm with him.

Goddamn, it's been a long day.

"Just take me home, Lincoln."

Chapter 40 – Birdie

After Linx made me get out of my bloody clothes and change into another one of his oversized motorcycle shirts from the toolbox in the bed of the truck; he made a space for me in the back seat with the blanket he keeps stashed on the floorboard. The plan was to drop me and Linx off at camp and have Collette and Bret meet the ambulance and my dad at the hospital emergency room entrance. I assured them I didn't need medical care and that I had gunshot residue on me and there's a whole factory full of dead people close enough for me to have killed. Hard pass on the hospital collecting evidence off me. Yes, to paranoia.

My father and Linx relented and agreed it might not be a good idea to take me, but it was imperative Pierre went. Pierre was in no shape to argue. He passed out as soon as Linx made sure he was stable enough for the ride. The lights on top of the ambulance came on and they took off into the dark night headed to the hospital. I was so grateful to see him getting immediate medical care and my shoulders relaxed. All the way home Linx held me. His hands constantly rubbing on me, running through my tangled mess of hair, making sure I'm still here and I'm safe.

While I was in the shower, my dad showed up. I walked out and seen him standing in the middle of the living room area, hands on his hips, red faced.

Ut oh, I think words were exchanged.

Linx is in the kitchenette making me something to eat or trying to with his poor casted arm. Bless his heart. I could wrestle one of these bayou gators and take a bite out of it, I'm that hungry.

I don't know what my dad plans on doing with dozens of dead bodies, but I guess that's not for me to worry about. I never thought it would be something I'd even have to think about. But here I am, living that biker lady life.

The deeper I sink into it, the more I understand my mother. And that alone just pisses me off.

"Daddy? Is everything ok?"

He comes over and snuggles me up with another dad-hug, swaying us back and forth with his head resting on top of my wet hair. When he feels like enough time has passed, I remove my arms from around his waist and let him move to the side of me, and his hand still on my shoulders.

"Are you ok?"

"Yeah. I really am, Daddy. I killed someone but I honestly don't feel bad about it. I feel vindicated for every girl out there he's kidnapped and forced into trafficking. I feel powerful and like a vessel and outlet for all the lost little girls' stolen innocence and power. I stopped a monster, Daddy, he's not going to hurt anyone else, and I still have my freedom. He was never going to leave me alone. I'm not living a life of fear. He had to die and good riddance to him."

I mean every word I said.

After the initial shock, Dad chuckles and squeezes me, "That's my little warrior." He shakes me slightly, then says, "Where did you learn that right hook left uppercut combo, hellion?"

I huff out laughter. Whatever words were being spoken when I came out here has dissipated between them.

"Linx taught me when I was in college."

"Hmm. Did he now?"

"Yeah, he taught me and Zharia how to fight. I've never forgotten it. I finally got to use some of it."

My eyes swing over to Linx, "Was that the correct form to use?" I give him a shit-eating grin. I know it was spot on. I was a good student.

"Trix, you know you were bad ass, baby. I'm so proud of you."

My father drops his arms, and a low growl escapes his chest. "Yes, well, I'll see you both in my study at two PM tomorrow. Have a pleasant evening. Love you, Birdie."

Oh, ok. "Love you too, Daddy."

As soon as the door is shut, I whirl on Linx but he's already coming out of the kitchen to grab me up. He holds me in an embrace so full of love and softness and everything I ever wanted.

"Fuucckk, Trixie," he groans into my hair.

"Lincoln," I whisper through my tears, body shaking, allowing me to process what I've been through, "I was so scared."

He cradles my head in his large hand, I hear his chest rumble under my cheek, "You did great, baby, such a good girl, the bestest. I watched your live feed the whole time. I'm so fucking proud of you. Really, I am."

This makes me blush, and I feel a rush of pride zing throughout my body. I guess I didn't do half bad. "I learned from the best."

I run my hands on his chest while I pull away. "Are we in trouble?" He leaves his hands on the swell of my ass while he talks, "Yes, I believe so. Me more than you, though. I reckon we'll find out tomorrow, âme sœur."

"Mmm," I sigh, "What's that mean?"

"Soul mate," he rumbles.

"I'll face the firing squad with you."

"The fuck you will," Linx says firmly, aggressively.

My temper instantly flaring, I shove his chest, hard, and open my mouth to argue.

His fingers lay across my mouth, effectively silencing me. The inner feminist part inside me wants to revolt and bite his fingers. "Trixie, we're not arguing about this right now. We're both exhausted. Come on, baby, don't fight with me. Let's eat something, you're hangry."

I stop squirming to get loose because he's right, absolutely right, as much as I hate to admit it; we don't need to fight over this. It can be dealt with tomorrow. Tonight, we just need to be grateful and happy.

Chapter 40 – Linx

Birdie looks magnificent lying beside me as the predawn light filters in through the blinds. It's just light enough to make out her curves under the blanket. Shadows dip and pull over the contours of her face. She's still just as stunning in sleep. I try not to let my blood boil at her bruised cheek, black eye, and busted lip.

I woke up hard for her, so very hard. We fell into a peaceful sleep last night just holding each other.

But this morning, I can't hold back. I reach for her, running my hand up her hip to her breasts. I cup her exquisite tit and brush her nipples with my fingertips, making them bead up perfectly. She starts moving in her sleep.

I gently pull her back against my chest, my cock nestled in between her smooth and plump ass cheeks. My good girl didn't wear panties to bed.

Throwing her leg over my hip, I reach between her legs. God, I just know her pussy will be wet. My baby stays wet for me, just the way I like her. Maybe it's all the cum I keep her full of. A day she's not dripping my cum out of her hole is a wasted day.

She's been whimpering in her sleep, pressing her thighs together all morning while I lay here and think. It better be me she's dreaming of. I was afraid she was going to have nightmares. Slowly my hand slides down between us, brushing my fingers across her clit. I lazily rub her slick bundle of nerves. I'm notching the head of my cock at her opening when she sleepily says on a sigh, "Linxy."

I murmur by her ear, "Good morning, Trixie, I can't get enough of you, baby. I have to fill you with my cum again."

She hums her assent while tilting her ass up for better access, and it's so fucking sexy. Fuck, I love the sound of her moans.

I slowly trail my fingertips up her calf, up the silky inside of her thigh, and across her mound. My breath brushes across her neck, "So beautiful." Being near her, loving her like this makes my heart race. I sweetly suck on her earlobe and lick behind her ear.

God, the promise in that lick. Her thighs start to tremble with arousal and she's sopping wet. I was right, she was dreaming of sex.

I want deep inside her, quenching my thirst for every bit of attention she lavishes on me. Every squeeze and gush of cum she can give me, I want it all.

I rub the tip of my dick over her asshole while I slid two fingers into her wet opening, "You have the prettiest pussy, baby."

Half asleep, she softly says, "Lincoln, don't tease me."

I'm like a back-alley cat in heat, so I notch my crown to her hot entrance and push into her. "You take my cock so good, baby." I push in more and splay my hand on her lower stomach, pulling her back, seating her further back on my cock. Yess, now we've hit bottom.

I pull my dick out and slide back home with as much gentleness as I can, stretching her velvet heat, using long strokes, making her body break out in goosebumps.

"I love you so much, Trixie," I whisper in her ear making her whimper with arousal. There's no better spot to kiss on her, in order to turn her on more than anything, is to kiss up the nape of her neck to right up behind her ear. It drives my baby wild.

"I was dreaming of you," she says in a breathy, dreamy voice. "I could tell. My little bird is already slippery before I even touched her." I roll her engorged clit around with my fingertips. This makes her wiggle and push back on me, squeezing me harder in her channel. Fucking hell.

At this point, I can't live the rest of my life without her, no matter what. There's no way, not since I've had a taste of what it can be like. I will beg her father to keep her. Living here with her in our love bubble was my every dream come true.

"Linx, I'm so close…"

"I feel your pussy tightening up on my fat cock. My beautiful birdie. Give it to me, baby."

She whimpers and whines. I've learned this week that means she needs something more, more to send her over the edge.

I slide my other hand under her body and bring it up around her neck. As I pinch her nipples, her breath catches in her throat, and she leans her head back.

"This is where you belong, Trix, in my arms, riding my cock. Me, deep inside you, planting my seed. Tell me who you belong to, baby. Tell Daddy Danger."

"You, Lincoln, only you…forever."

"Yes, baby, that's right, only me. You love this dick. Are you going to be a good girl for me and come on my cock?"

"Yes, please, oh god, I need more," she pants.

I tighten my grip on her chest and work my hips faster up into her while I handle her clit, disrespectfully. Her moans grow in intensity and soon, she stiffens and lets out the most beautiful shudder and loud broken moans, yelling my name like a banshee as the climax overtakes her. Her pussy convulses around my cock, and I talk her through it as my balls tighten, and my release is pulled from me, spilling into her.

"Yes, Trixie, just like that baby." I groan to her, "Fuck. You're so beautiful when you come….so beautiful, mon amour…Y a rien que j'ferais pas pour toi," I softly say to her between my own moans and catching breaths.

She's trying to catch her breath when she asks, "What's that?" I nuzzle in her shoulder and tell her, "We really need to work on your French, femme."

"Ugh, what's that now?"

"First one, I told you there's nothing I wouldn't do for you. The other one you'll have to figure out on your own."

She playfully slaps behind her looking for any piece of me she can hit. I pull my dick out to get away from her and chuckle as I get out of bed. I snag a towel from the bathroom and wipe the cum off of me on my way back over to her.

"Spread 'em."

"Linx. You don't have to be crude."

"Trixie, I'm a biker, I do crude very well."

"Don't I know it now. I especially like the moments you whisper French to me and kiss me silly, or say such filthy, dirty things to me to make my clit throb." She smiles at me with her heavy-lidded sleepy eyes, but I still see the sparkle in them.

"I love those moments too, mon amour."

I try to help clean her up but apparently, I don't do it good enough, so she took over, saying she had to pee anyways.

Alright. What I can do very well is cook her breakfast. We need to eat up everything in the fridge, which is not going to happen, but I can use whatever I can to make a big boy breakfast.

First thing I have to do though, is make some damn coffee before she turns into her morning rabid bear persona. Straight up grouchy ass bitch when she has not had her coffee, I chuckle to myself, she thinks I don't know that part about her. I don't think coffee is enough anymore, she just needs to stick a fork in an electrical outlet, enough that she wakes up and is her charming warm and friendly self.

She's friendly-ish. Sometimes. Here's to hoping she's much friendlier to me going forward.

"Can we do more bad things together today?" she says as she comes out of her bedroom wearing this flouncy, cute as fuck sundress. It has light and dark blue flowers with a white background. She's got the sweet and innocent look going for her today. "But first coffee, then chaos, my love."

Shit, she's so cute in it I'm mesmerized. My dick is never going down today.

I've seen her hundreds of times and each time I don't think she could get prettier. I'm always mistaken. Sometimes I have to remind myself to close my mouth just in time to catch the drool. "Well, mon amour, I would love to get into some trouble with you later on," I hand her the precious cup of coffee, "but we have to eat, clean up, take the left-over food to mom's and head to the city. Your father wants to see us at two, remember?"

Her shoulders drop, "Oh. Right."

"Sit down, baby. Let me feed you. Oh! First, tell me how you're feeling."

"I feel alright, I guess. I'm sore as hell from them ripping me away from you then manhandling me. Then that bastard slapping me all those fucking times. I'm so glad he's dead."

I look to the floor and nod my head. I don't want her to see the guilt or rage in my eyes. I wanted to rip those men apart with my bare hands. I'm still so fucking pissed about it.

Her hand settles gently on my arm, "Hey."

By the time I look into her eyes, I have myself under control. She doesn't need a man that falls apart with emotions when she needs support. Besides, that's not me. I appear to have tons of stronger feelings where she's concerned. Some of them are new and all of them are intense.

It's a fuckton more feelings than I had last week, that's for sure, and she's the cause. I had no idea this would evolve to this level and I'm wholly unprepared for the rush of feelings it's bringing out in me.

"Hey," I reply.

"Are you ok, Lincoln?" She cocks her head at me and even though I brace for it, I thought I was prepared for her puppy dog slash doe eyes. I was not.

They hit me right in the chest, right in my murderous, guilt-ridden heart.

I close my eyes and inhale. Fuck it, I try out her breathing exercise she does in times of great emotion. Find calming smells. I smell her perfume and lotion and sunshine. Her very essence wraps around me.

Guilt constricts my heart, but then I feel her warm hand on me, and it's like she's trying to soothe away the irregular heartbeat and mend the gaping wound in my pride.

I open my eyes and look into her bright blue eyes. "No, Trix. I'm not. I'm not sure how I feel, honestly. I feel guilty for not stopping them, for them taking you, them getting past me to you."

"Oh, Linx!" she cries, "Please don't. It was four against one. There's no way you could have taken on that many, plus they had weapons. I don't think it's your fault. There's nothing to feel guilty about. Absolutely nothing. I don't hold you at fault."

I shake my head. She should be mad at me.

She makes a playfully frustrated face because I won't listen to her. Using her hands on both sides of my face to smooth my beard, "You know, not to take away from your pity party happening right now, but I really like this beard. Please don't shave it off. It makes me feel like I'm being possessed and ravished by a burly mountain man, oh, or a wild bayou swamp man, which is not far from the truth now that I think about it." She screws up her face in thought.

My lips twitch as I try to hold back a grin at her remarks. Pity party, my ass.

She continues, "I know you feel guilty but please don't. He was the only one to hurt me, he just hit me a few times. It could have been much worse. I refuse to blame you for anything."

I slowly pull her to me, and she naturally gravitates to my embrace. Her hands come to rest on my poor broken sides.

Arms around her, I say, "I'm not having a pity party." Jesus, even hearing it come out of my mouth with no emotion still sounds like whining. *Get a grip, big man.*

"Ok, not a pity party then, more like an emotionally charged thought process, and mood, heaping tons of negative feelings on top of your head." Tears fill her eyes, "I could never blame you. Please never think that. You shouldn't blame yourself either. I knew with certainty you would come for me. That comforted me more than you'll ever know, to be so loved, so coveted and cherished, I was able to sit quietly and observe, and think, so so much thinking."

"What did you think of, Trix?"

"Regret. I thought of regret. I beat myself up over it."

I open my mouth to say something, and she does my action back to me, placing her finger across my lips.

"It's my turn. I wish I could go back in time and fix what there was between us, but I don't think it was time for us to be. Maybe it was but it definitely is now and it's not too late to have our happily ever after. You're all I thought about on the way to wherever I was being taken to, and being trapped in that room for hours, I swore on my life when I made it out, I would change things between us for there to be an *us* right now. I couldn't do it before but instead I'll spend every day showing you and telling you how much I love you for as long as you'll have me."

In a not so manly way, my heart is in my throat and I'm afraid to speak. There might be an onion under my nose too. She makes me feel so many emotions at one time. She confuses my senses by overloading me with sappy not-so-manly feelings. She's more dangerous than me, with using words as emotional triggers and getting my insides all riled up. Making me tear up and stand in awe at her bravery.

She leans back and cocks her head looking up at me with a cute little grin, fun and playfulness sparking in her eyes, "Are you about to say something that's gonna make my butterflies flitter and my clit twitch?"

I chuckle and she pulls a smile out of me, "Yes." I gather her in my arms and rub her face with one hand, pushing her head back. Gently, the caress of a feather, I lightly kiss up her neck to her jawbone with my bruised and busted lips. "Mon amour, y'a pas de mots assez forts te dire combien je t'aime."

My hot breath moves across her skin making her shiver as I continue, "My love, there are no words strong enough to tell you how much I love you."

"Oh Linx…" she breathes.

"Je t'aime plus qu'ma propre vie," I whisper in her ear as I tug her lobe with my teeth. Just a little nibble. "I love you more than my own life." She sighs and I know she believes me. "That's so very true, baby."

Her throaty moan vibrates her neck as I kiss down to her collarbone. She loves when I do this.

I slide my hand down the front of her dress and find her pussy so very wet for me, the both of us leaking out of her. The insides of her thighs, near the crease, are slick with our cum and it's so fucking hot.

I finger fuck her until she starts panting, rubbing my thumb on her swollen clit. "Does my greedy little baby want more? Do you want more fucking, little bird? Mmhmm, you always want my cock stuffed in you, don't you?"

A knock at the door interrupts her whimper and makes us freeze in our spots, both looking towards the door. She starts to giggle, "We can't just pretend we aren't here, Linx." She tries to stand up and I have to pull my finger out of her pussy, which I'm not happy about. That little hole is my happy place.

I suck on my finger while she straightens her dress and opens the door.

"Daddy! What are you doing here? Come in."

And this is me hiding my boner from my boss aka my girlfriend's dad and high lord of the crime bosses circuit on the East Coast.

"I enjoyed Bret and Collette's hospitality last night and I'm stopping in before I head home. Wanted to make sure my little girl was doing alright."

I wonder if he can smell the sex in the air, because I sure do. I try to be a good man, and sometimes I fall short, like now, as I smile a hello, but it's really because not thirty seconds ago I was knuckle deep in his daughter's snatch.

She smiles big at him, maybe thinking of the same thing I am, and replies, "I'm great, Dad. I have no regrets about what I did. I just need you to tell me I'm not going to prison, and nothing can be pinned on me. Reassure me Dad, because I'm worried."

Chapter 41 – Birdie

Dad grips my upper arms and in his super serious voice says, "Please don't worry about that. I would never allow that to happen. Never. You're in the clear."

The elephant that's been sitting on my chest since I shot a man dead finally stands up and gets the fuck out of here. I lay my hand over my heart and say, "Whew, ok then," with a half-hearted weak smile.

"Don't worry about it, honeybee. As far as I'm concerned, you did us all a favor. It might be a little fucked up to say, but I'm so fucking proud of you Birdie. You handled yourself well, better than I thought you would."

"Um, thanks, Dad."

He drops his hands off of me and looks at Linx. He takes a few steps and puts his hand out to shake Linx's hand. Oh, holy fuck. It's the hand that was just all up in my cooch. Fucking perfect. I hope his hand is dry.

Linx catches my eye and smiles. He's awful. Jesus, I know I'm beet red from embarrassment. It's a good thing my dad's attention is on Linx and not me.

"How you doing today?"

"Sore. Head's not pounding, arm throbs but other than being sore from taking a beating, I think I'm good."

"Well, you still look like hell," Dad chuckles, "but the bruising will fade, and the swelling will go down. I imagine your pride's hurt the most."

Linx's lips press into a thin line as he nods, and he says, "Yes, sir."

"Well, I won't keep you waiting. I know you need to pack up. I'll see you both at the meeting at two."

He turns back to me and stops long enough to kiss me on the forehead and out the door he goes.

"That's a man with a plan, Trixie. Just be prepared, ok?"

"How can you tell? What plan?"

He wipes a hand across his face, "I broke my vows. He can't let that slide. I'll be punished and there's nothing you can do to stop it. I don't want you to stop it. I regret nothing about our time here." I'm afraid if I go over to him, we'll end up in bed again and we don't have time for that, so I opt for, "We'll see."

He just blinks at me.

"Soo, breakfast?" I hedge.

I hated saying goodbye to his mom. I promised her I would be back. When Linx helped me up into the truck, he wiped a stray tear off my cheek, but he had a smile on his face when he shut the door. I've quickly fallen in love with his mom too, she's incredibly nice and so easy to talk to. At least I'll have a great mother-in-law. Fuck. What is wrong with me? Next, I'll be picking out dresses. And then my mind was occupied with our fake engagement photos and poses all the way to the hospital to see Pierre before we went back to the city.

I'm positive if I asked him to take me to the courthouse and marry me after this meeting he sure as fuck would. No hesitation. Bret was in Pierre's room napping in a chair when we arrived. I guess we crossed paths with Pierre's husband, Seven, as he was taking a break and was driving home to Collette's to shower and reset with a homecooked meal.

Pierre has a concussion, three broken ribs, severely bruised kidneys, two broken fingers, and tons of scratches, scrapes and cuts. The bruising and swelling is so horrible, it's worse than Linx's. Many of Pierre's cuts required stitches.

They've been keeping him pretty drugged. I would hate for him to be awake for all this. Fuck, he looks so awful in that hospital bed. I waited until I left his room to start crying.

He wouldn't be in pain if it weren't for me and Grim's revenge plot. He wouldn't have been mistaken for my boyfriend.

I tried to be quiet on the ride home, but Linx was not allowing it. When I didn't want to talk about feelings, he made me talk about my goals, my art, my passions and my favorites. In turn, I asked everything I could think of about him that I didn't know already. I learned a great deal more about him. Like how he supports the battered women's shelter and provides a local animal rescue with needed supplies each month.

It really does make sense for us to be together. The age difference isn't even thought of. We've learned—
wait, he probably already knew with his ninja bullshit skills—we are highly compatible. Love the same foods, same restaurants, same music.

I was absolutely floored when he said he's read dark romances for pointers.

I've learned Linx is my dream guy.

I'm taking all the energy I used to hate him with and complain about him and channeling it into loving him and seeing our relationship grow. Goddamn, this could be a beautiful thing.

This could be my happily ever after.

I decided somewhere in between laughing happily with him and fighting tears of regret, that I'm just going to start loving who I want and how I want, like it's my last day on Earth. As he says, we're here now, moving forward. This is our beginning.

And I'm diving in headfirst. Because that's the kind of love I want, and that's the kind Linx is offering.

Chapter 42 – Birdie

On our way to my dad's house for the meeting, Linx gets a text from my dad asking us to meet him at the clubhouse instead.
"I got a bad feeling about this, baby girl."
"Why are we going to the clubhouse now?"
"Because your dad has called church."
"Those meetings y'all have are called church, right?"
"Yes, and they are very important. Odd that he's calling one at this time of day. Even odder is him having me bring you."
"Alright, so we can collectively agree this is probably something fucked up. But then again, define fucked up for me because I've had a pretty fucked up past twenty-four hours. I doubt it'll surprise me at this point."
He nods his head and says, "Fair enough."
When we reach the clubhouse, which is a giant building in the warehouse district. Upon seeing the shit ton of bikes and vehicles in the fenced in, guarded parking area, it's safe to assume, there's a lot of members here right now.

This can't be good.

Linx ushers me into the forbidden building. I say it's forbidden because I'm not allowed in it.

I feel like I'm walking into Mount Doom.

Chapter 43 – Linx

I hold Birdie's hand while I bring her into the clubhouse. I note how her hand trembles in mine, so I give it a little reassuring squeeze. As we come through the door, I nod to Gas Pedal Fred and T-Bone who are guarding the door. Slim Jim is sitting in a chair by the table where the sign in sheet is.

I must say, I'm kinda dreading this. Rock doesn't call church for no silly reasons. Especially not in the middle of a workday. And he doesn't invite non-members to be present that's for fucking sure. I never would have guessed he'd invite his daughter to a meeting.

Then it dawns on me.

Rock isn't going to wait until I heal. He's going to make an example out of me today. Right now.

And he's going to make Birdie watch.

Son of a bitch.

Turning back to her as we walk in the door, I lean down to her ear and try to quickly convey to her, "Baby, your dad's going to make you watch me be punished for breaking my oath. I need you to find a far-off happy place in your head and go sit there until it's done. Please, Trix, tune it out and whatever it is, I can take it. I can handle it. Do not interfere. Anything to be with you." Her mouth is open in a shocked 'O' face, and she looks stunned, almost like she can't believe what she's hearing. *I know baby girl, it's a lot to take in*. Something tells me she's about to learn what type of man her daddy dearest really is.

I hope she got all that in the fifteen seconds I had to say it because her face is not reassuring me she caught it.

"Are our lovebirds having a meeting without us?" Rock teases from the stage. I know that tone. I know it well. I've watched over plenty of punishment sessions, participated and even been on the receiving end once.

Once was all it took.

A chorus of guffaws and chuckles can be heard at his flippant, condescending tone.

I know that they all know, even the ones who weren't there last night. They know.

She yanks my hand, and I look back at her, she whispers, "Anything, I'll do anything for you."

That's my ride or die girl. Part of me is glad she doesn't know what to expect. I'm not sure how she's going to handle the brutality of it, but then again, she did just blow a man's head off last night, so there's that. My girl is strong and brave. She's a gift bag full of surprises. Most women would be a mess. Birdie acts like killing a man was just as easy as painting her nails and she needs zero coping skills for that. Maybe I shouldn't worry about her.

Perhaps I should give her more credit and realize she's not as fragile as I think she is.

Rock stands on the stage waiting for us and gestures to the stairs. I walk over to the stairs leading up to the stage and hold her hand as I climb them right behind her. If I had known we were going to be on the stage, I would have nixed the dress idea on her. These ornery bastards don't need to see nothing of mine up a skirt!

"Danger! So good of you to join us. You still look like you went ten rounds with Rocky Balboa." Rock has his lethal smile on when he looks over his shoulder at the gathered men. Something's up. He shakes my hand and then turns and hugs Birdie. He gestures out into the crowd of at least fifty men and says into the mic propped on stage, "Everyone, this is my beautiful daughter, Birdie. You know, the one in your vows that you swore to protect and honor. Oh, and there's also that little caveat where it says no advances or relationships with her. Can't forget that important part. The daughter-is-off-limits clause."

More chuckling and snickering.

He holds up one finger, "But one of us didn't heed to that rule." There are grumbles in the audience. Rock continues, "They disregarded it for their own satisfaction. They broke their vow and in turn became an oath breaker, betraying everyone in this brotherhood."

Birdie opens her mouth to speak. I hold my breath because she doesn't understand what's happening. This is official club business at this point. I don't think Rock will slap her for speaking out of turn, but I've seen a lot of shit in the past twenty-four hours. Who knows. He's definitely up to something and I know the anger is simmering below the surface.

Rock levels a look at her and this shuts her up immediately. All her thoughts of speaking, they stopped and locked up right in her head because she knows not to test her father's tolerance right now. I can feel his fury palpitating the air as I'm sure she can too.

Rock feels betrayed.

I lied to him.

I hurt him.

It dawns on me; he doesn't know the depth of my love for her. Or how long I've abided by his rule, lost in my own personal hell watching her day in and day out not be mine. Maybe Rock thinks she's my flavor of the month and I'm going to leave his little girl broken hearted.

Fuck if I know what he's thinking.

Rarely have I ever seen him this pissed off as he is currently.

"Joker, Shadow, if you please."

Fuck.

Rock guides Birdie away, only backing up a few steps. Shadow comes to rest in front of me and quickly lets me know with his eyes he doesn't know what's exactly being played out here. He's on the edge. Which doesn't help my fucking mood one bit.

I've worked with this guy for eight years and the only person he's ever shown emotion to is me and Pierre. And I see worry in his somber eyes. It's the only thing he'll give me. As soon as he looks away, his eyes are shuttered again. I get it, I really do. I hate that I've put him in this position.

Shadow's my best friend, my brother. He's worried Rock's going to make him punish me. I know Shadow would hate it, but he'll do it, because what's a brotherhood without rules and consequences.

"Even The Right Hand of God must face the consequences of his actions," Rock taunts.

"Hear, hear!" echoes around the room.

"Shirt off, Danger."

I shuck my shirt off and toss it on the floor. I hold my wrists out, waiting on Shadow to buckle the leather cuffs on...the ones that have chains attached to them. He has a hard time putting the one over my cast, but it finally buckles. The chains are used to hang the associate up from the rafter so they can receive physical punishment in the form of a whipping. It's nifty because it's on a swivel and they can be turned at any angle you need them to be in.

Not so nifty that it's me on the receiving end this time.

I grind my molars and try to keep my anger in check. Whatever Rock dishes out, I have to accept. This is my penitence. I failed, and betrayed my patch, I am due some sort of suffering.

"Dad?"

Rock gives her another look, and she shuts up and doesn't try again.

Shadow and Joker secure the chains overhead. It kills my arm, but I just bear it. I hang here with my arms up, facing Birdie and Rock. Her eyes tear up when our eyes lock. I try to tell her with my eyes that it will be fine.

"Shadow."

Shadow appears and hands Rock the whip. It's a rough piece of leather, about eight feet long and its lashes feel like razor blades. This particular punishment is reserved for grievous fuck ups.

My only and last whipping prior to this was because I fucked up and let two of our guys die during a raid. I was to have their backs, I was responsible for them, and I was careless. That was nine years ago. It didn't happen again.

Rock takes the whip and snaps it onto the floor. It makes a god-awful cracking noise, so loud it sets my teeth on edge.

Birdie jumps at the noise. I bet this is the first time she's heard the crack of a whip.

With my tongue rolling on the inside of my cheek, I can only stand here and look at Rock. My anxiety is through the roof. Rock grabs the mic and starts in, "Daughter, how many nights were you together?"

Birdie looks at me and then her eyes flit over to her dad, who's standing there looking at her like a shark circling for blood. "Um, five days."

"Yes, impressive. You went from bitching and complaining about a man you claim to hate to falling in love in a matter of five days, is that correct?"

Birdie narrows her eyes at him, but he doesn't budge.

"Yes, that's correct. Funny how love works, huh?"

Oh, baby girl, don't push him, please, for all that's holy.

"I see. So, five nights. That's how many lashes Danger's going to get."

Some men cheer.

"No!" Birdie yells through the hollering of men.

"Men, do we agree, that's fair?" Rock asks the cheering crowd. *"Add in one more extra for breaking his fucking oath,"* comes from somewhere in the middle. I don't recognize the voice.

"Alright," Rock's face unfurls in a truly malevolent smile and he's positively glowing with excitement.

"Six it is." Then he turns to Birdie and holds out the whip, "You'll do the honors."

My chest seizes as the air is sucked from my lungs.

Chapter 44 – Birdie

Surely, I heard that wrong. I'm sure my puzzled face slashed with disgust clearly speaks to my flat-out rejection of his request. Like what in the ever-loving fuck?

"Fuck that, Rock, this is bullshit," Linx says hotly.

I look my father in the eye and say, "And if I don't do this?"

He chuckles darkly, "See that's the thing, sweetheart, if you want to be with my second-in-command, I won't stand in your way, but you're going to earn it. You just have to give him six lashes. If you don't, I'll send him away and you'll never see him again."

"You can't do this!" I cry, horrified.

The room is quiet now. Dead quiet. No one dares raise their voice at this man standing in front of me. Especially not in front of his associates.

"Yes, I can, and I will. If you don't do this, I'll make his best friend do it and then I'll send him away. Either way, Danger is getting his punishment," Rock says in a voice brooking no argument, deadly serious.

"Trixie, look at me," Linx instructs me from across the stage. I can't. I can't do this. I can't hurt him. I won't. *Do not hyperventilate.*

I stand here shaking my head, my eyes filling with tears. When I look over at my dad, I ask, "Why are you doing this?"

"Birdie, this is the way men handle business. This is the way our brotherhood is run. You want to be part of this life by being with him, then I will gladly shove your face into the ugly of it. This is club business and it's not for you to question," Rock says with an air of finality.

"Beatrix, look at me now," Linx commands. "Look over here." My body and mind are already conditioned to react to his authoritative tone; I take a step towards Linx and look up into his eyes. I see the sheen of tears in his own eyes that he's trying to hide. It cracks my heart. This is breaking his heart as much as mine. I can't hurt him.

"Do this," he says to me, certain I will obey his command.

My eyes drop to the ground as the big, fat, hot tears fall from my anguished eyes.

"No! No, no, don't look away from me. Look at me. Right now." I meet his gaze again.

"It's only six, baby, I'll be fine. Then we can do all the things we planned. Please, Trix, just do it," Linx begs.

"I can't," I whisper, "I don't want to hurt you." A sob escapes me and that is the moment the first inkling of hatred for my father enters my heart. It took twenty-eight years for hate to enter my heart where he's concerned.

I can only imagine the things he made my mother do and suddenly, I understand her a little bit better.

The father I know would never make me do this. But this is not the father I know, this is the other side of the coin. The President. The head dickhead in charge. The dark, relentless, brutal world of motorcycle clubs, and pact mentality, the whole loyalty game where death reigns and the Gulf trade is the reward. The part of his life I was kept well away from, sheltered, and I'm starting to see why because I hate this world right now.

"Do it, Birdie!" Linx urges firmly through clenched teeth, rattling the chains above him with his insistence. I know he's losing his patience.

Would my father really send him away?

I can't live without Linx.

He loosens a breath of frustration, "I need you to take a deep breath, baby girl. Go on." I do as Linx says. "Good girl." My body flushes at his praise but it doesn't ease the tension.

"Rock, can she come over here so I can talk to her?" Linx asks my dad.

"She has one minute."

"Com'mere, *mon amour*."

I obey immediately just to be near him. The whole environment around here sucks and I really need the comfort and safety he offers. I lay my hands flat against his abdomen, and I put my cheek next to his. The sweat lodged in his beard wets my cheek and mingles with my tears.

He doesn't waste a second. "I need you to do this. Put your big girl panties on and just do it. Get it over with. I'll never be mad at you for it. Never, because it's going to give me everything I've ever dreamed of. I'm begging Trix, do it, please, God fuck, please, just do it. Six lashes. I know your heart hurts, so does mine, but I can't live without you, I can't, so I need you to do this baby. Just go over there and get it done. Ride or die, little bird, be my ride or die. Be my brave girl."

He turns his head and captures my mouth with a fierce kiss that kindles the flames in my soul for him.

"Ok, her minute's up."

I step back and look into Linx's eyes. I remember my promise to pay for our sins right alongside of him, no matter what the price. What better way to do that than at my father's church, upon his makeshift altar.

Squaring my shoulders and stiffening my spine, I walk up to my father and say, "If I do this, we'll be left in peace for the rest of our lives to do whatever? Punishment one and done?"

"Yes, you have my word, Princess."

I sneer at the endearment.

I yank the whip out of his hand and turn to face Linx. His lips curl up into his signature wolfish smile as he watches me through his lashes and nods to me. That's the reassurance I need.

Let's fucking do this then.

I crack the whip on the ground to get a feel for it. It's a powerful tool of pain and quite intimidating.

You killed a man, Birdie, just pretend this is one of the fuckfaces that stole you.

Shadow turns Linx away from me so his back is facing me.

My father, ever the compassionate man -eye roll-, leans forward with a finger up in pause and says, "Try to keep it to his back, you don't want that little baby wrapping around to the front or on his face." He steps back away from me, but says, "Oh! And one more thing, make them count, Beatrix. I won't have some pussy ass, weak hits counting as a full lashing. You'll do them over if they aren't good enough."

I wish I could hit my father with this whip right now. Punch him straight in his jeering mouth. By the smile on his face, he knows this.

"Come on baby, hit me, let's get this shit over with so we can leave," Linx yells from where he hangs. "Here's your chance to get back at me for all the bullshit I put you through." That makes me chuckle a little, "Six good cracks and then let's go home and fuck. You're due for a good cum dumping anyways."

Men huff out laughter and good-natured chuckles. I turn to look at my father, with a smirk I say, "Yes, Daddy Danger, I can't wait to go home and fuck you again."

My father immediately turns red, fists his hands in rage, and stands there seething under his leather vest.

Turning my attention back to the task at hand, I walk up by Linx and Shadow directs me where to stand. I've had very few interactions with Shadow but he's always around too. He comes to all those stupid events and usually does hang out in the shadows, always watching, doing the bodyguard thing. I see why Zharia is interested in him. He's quite handsome in that dark, mysterious, brooding kind of way.

I give him a small smile in gratitude. I know enough to know this is Linx's best friend alongside Pierre, and Shadow doesn't want this to happen as much as me.

"Ready," I say with a little conviction and a nod. I arch my arm up and the whip sails through the air, landing on Linx's back with a loud crack and thud as it meets flesh.

He stiffens and grunts and that's the only reaction he gives. My dad gleefully yells, "One."

I'm dizzy with disgust. Another part of my heart shatters. With this demonstration, I reckon my rose-colored glasses are being crushed under my father's biker boots. Good. I needed a reality check of the world I'm willingly jumping into by being with Lincoln. The whip cracks for the second time across his skin.

"Two."

For the next three hits my heart hardens. Every jerk of his body when the leather hits him, I want to punch my dad more and more. This life they lead, full of violence and blood, is just another day for them, whereas I only believed shit like this happened in movies and books. This is insane.

Thanks for the wakeup call, Dad! Asshole.

Linx's head hangs for a moment after the fifth hit, shoulders heaving, breathing through the pain, and it almost makes me drop the whip and run to him. His held his head high the entire time through this; *don't show him weakness, Linxy.* I can't let it buckle my resolve. We've come this far. Woman up, bitch.

"*Je suis à toi, je t'aime,*" I say to Linx, loud enough for my French speaking father to hear, right before I let loose the whip on his back for the very last time. When it hits his skin, he lets out a mighty roar and shakes the chains. The soundwaves of the crack haven't even dissipated before I drop the whip and run to Linx.

His face is covered in sweat and it's dripping down his back and chest. He quickly turns around and I hold his face up to look at me, "Are you ok? Jesus fuck, tell me you're ok?"

"I'm fine, baby, I'm ok, good girl," he takes a deep breath, he's breathing like he just ran a marathon, "My good girl, thank you," he says trying to catch his breath.

The red welts are standing angrily up off his skin. I don't want to imagine how bad it stings and burns. I didn't see any blood as I ran over here.

The chains are released and his arms come down around me. He stands here holding me, my head cradled in his hand he holds me to his sweaty chest. My cheek rests on his tattooed pec, and I hear his rapid heartbeat.

Quickly, I come to my senses and break away from him.

We can hold each other at home.

I twist my head over to look at my dad's smug face, "Are we done here?" I almost snarl at him.

My dad's shitty smile is disappearing. He didn't think I had it in me, he didn't think I wanted to be with Lincoln that much; he thought I'd walk away.

Checkmate.

"Yes, we are, Princess." Mentally I'm gouging my dad's eyes out. I scoff and tell him, "You can take that princess shit and shove it up your ass. Don't call me, I'll call you, *Dad*." I let him know the disgust I feel in the tone of voice I use with him.

Shadow has the shackles off of Linx and he's waiting for me to finish with my dad.

My dad growls at me and grinds his teeth in a snarl, but I keep talking, not giving one fuck now. Daddy's little girl grew up tonight. "If we're done here, I'm going to take my boyfriend home and plan our wedding that you won't be invited to."

At that, I spin on my heel and reach for Linx's hand.

"I forbid you to marry him!" my dad practically screams.

I turn back and laugh at his continued audacity, "I don't need your permission, old man, and I don't give a fuck if you like it or not, not after this." I twirl my fingers, encompassing the whole area of fuckery that just happened. "A deal's a deal, witnessed by all these other fucked up men. See ya sometime, none too soon, Daddio."

I grab Linx's hand and drag him down the stairs and make haste towards the door.

The clubhouse is eerily silent as I escort their Vice President out of the building.

Fuck this shit. And fuck my dad with a red-hot poker.

Chapter 45 – Birdie

"How long does an uncooked lasagna stay good in the fridge?" I give it a good sniff; it's a little iffy. We got back to my apartment after dropping off his truck and grabbing a rideshare here. I wanted the comfort of my own place, and he wasn't about to let me out of his sight. Linx headed off to the shower while I said I'd come up with something for dinner.

"How long's it been in there, *cher*?" Collette asks.

"Umm, it was left in the fridge on Saturday and it's Thursday now. Is that too long?" I'm super thankful I have a woman in my life as a mother figure that I can call and ask shit like this now. My mother wouldn't know this, she would say '*Go ask the cook.*' It's laughable to think of my mother putting a casserole in the oven. I don't even think she knew how to turn the damn thing on.

I'm not much better so stay humble.

"Yeah, you might want to throw that out. I wouldn't chance a bout of food poisoning."

"Thanks, Collette, I will definitely be ordering take out then. I appreciate it." I scrape the lasagna out of the dish into the trash and soak the dish in the sink to wash for later so my housekeeper can have it back.

"Anytime. How's my boy?" I forget she doesn't know about me killing a man and then what just transpired not more than an hour ago.

I debate on how much to tell her, when I settle on, "As good as can be. He's in the shower right now, then he plans to lay down and rest."

"Hmm, you need to rest too bébé. Grab a bite and then go lay down."

After I get off the phone with her and order some po-boys on the delivery app, I find Linx in the bathroom, arms braced on the vanity, looking in the mirror.

I lean up against the door jamb with my arms crossed. I'm not sure how to approach him. I softly say, "Hey."

"Hey."

I try not to retch at the sight of the swollen lash marks. If his back wasn't tattooed, I'm sure it'd be a very angry red. It makes for a vivid vision, the tattoo on his back is a woman on a cross.

She's tied to the cross, naked. She has jet black hair, bright blue eyes and a lovely ball gag in her mouth with ruby red lips wrapped around the ball.

Linx doesn't even deny it when I ask if it's me. It very much so resembles me. Almost like Pierre tattooed a picture of me onto Linx.

He looks at me in the mirror with a painfilled gaze.

He spent the ride here to my apartment being very quiet. Somber. Stone-faced. Fists clenched and jaw working. I just prayed he wouldn't crack a tooth with how hard he was gnashing his teeth.

I know he's upset and he's guilt-ridden and he's steaming fucking mad, but I'm not sure how to move through this with him. "I ordered us some food."

Linx turns around and beckons me over to him. Of course, I rush over to where he stands by the bathroom sink. *Oh, how the mighty ice princess has fallen. At your beck and call, Daddy Danger.*

His eyes are filled with so many warring emotions. I'm not even sure he could land on just one they are so jumbled. Just like mine. "I love you," he says, pulling me to him.

"I love you too. But I'm worried."

"You wouldn't be you if you weren't worrying about something," he says playfully in an exhausted tone. I mean, he's not wrong. I'm a chronic worrier and I know it's a useless habit, but it doesn't stop it from happening.

In this relationship, I can see I'm going to have to do all the worrying for the both of us.

"Ok," he nods, "let me get dressed and we'll sit down and talk about this. It needs to be discussed. Then we don't have to speak of it again if you don't want to," he offers.

"Yeah, ok, we can do that."

He comes out of the bedroom fully dressed in some mouthwatering thin pajama pants and a black v-neck t-shirt. Goddamn there goes my ovaries again. I think he put on baby makin' pants to distract me.

The delivery service just dropped off our shrimp po-boys. Best damn sandwich, hands down.

We eat in silence, both focused on eating our first good meal after the fiasco of the past two days. These two days can get fucked. Tomorrow has to be better.

He finishes his sandwich and wipes his mouth. It's not so much the action as it's how slow, deliberate, calculated it is because of his pain. He has a ton of stuff occupying his mind, mixed with the exhaustion of being wounded, he really needs to rest.

"We can talk tomorrow. I think you really should be in bed right now, resting." I caress the back of his hand. The same beautiful hand that brings me so much comfort and pleasure.

Linx raises his head and his beautiful hazel eyes hold so much sadness. An angry father I can handle. A sad and devastated

Lincoln—no clue how to deal with that. I guess approach with extreme caution.

"I'm sorry, Birdie."

"That's not my name," I whisper with a small smile.

His lips press into a thin line as he simply sits there looking at me.

"I'm sorry, Trixie."

I nod my approval. "What's there to be sorry about?"

"Dragging you into this. Causing you trauma. Fuck," he blows out air and rolls his eyes, "Trauma after trauma." When his eyes reach mine again, he leans forward slightly, "Trix, you're like the bravest person I know. You're like the most badass woman I've ever met. I'm so proud of you. I sure as fuck don't deserve you."

I feel my cheeks and ears heating up at his compliments. I'd like to think every woman would kill the man who kidnapped them and planned such atrocities. But I know deep down, not every woman would be able to do it.

Those of us born with blood tainted by darkness have no remorse.

He must think I do. About which part though is the million-dollar question.

He rubs his face and says, "Look Trix, I know how hard that was for you, and I want you to know I'll spend the rest of my life making sure that trauma was worth it."

Ahh, this is about me whipping him.

"I know you will and I'm looking forward to it. But you don't have to beat yourself up. The past two days have been seriously eye opening for me. I did what I had to do in order to have the life I want and deserve."

I slip my hand into his, "I refuse to allow myself to have one tiny morsel of regret for killing that piece of shit. I'm good with that decision, Lincoln, trust me when I say I'm ok with that. Now about whipping you, I did what I knew you wanted. So we can have the life we deserve. We deserve our happily ever after."

His lips pull into a sexy slow grin, "You did look extremely hot killing our number one enemy. I was so proud of you at that moment and more turned on than I've ever been in my life. Fucking scared out of my mind but rock hard."

I can't help but laugh. I should have known murder and unhinged fuckery would turn him on.

"Especially when you used perfect form to throw that punch and then comboed it with the ball smash. Damn, baby. I know not to piss you off now."

"Yeah, *Mr. Danger*, some little girl paid attention in training besides drooling over the instructor all the time."

His eyebrows raise, "You were drooling over me?"

"Maybe a little." Dammit, I feel myself blushing again.

"We'll circle back around to that tidbit." He brushes his thumb over my knuckles. "How do you feel about your dad now?"

I roll my eyes and blow out some steam, "I'm so fucking mad at him."

"Baby, you know your dad has always been this way. The only person he is nice to is you. He wasn't even that nice to your mom behind closed doors. Fuck, me and Shadow are about second place to you for his niceness. You don't get to be the King of the Gulf by being a softie."

"I kinda figured he was an asshole, but I didn't know how much of one. That was some pretty fucked up shit he did."

"I agree. Any other time Shadow would have done it, but he wanted to punish both of us. There are other ways to fuck up a person without laying a hand on them and that's what I'm most worried about. How fucked up are you from it? Let's talk about that." He licks his lips and nods, "Yeah, that's what I want to talk about."

"There's not a lot to talk about. I did what I had to do, Linx. Simple as that. I did it for us and our future, whatever that future holds. I want to find out, I want to see where this goes between us. In case you haven't noticed, I've fallen pretty hard...in five days like my father pointed out."

I flip my hair over my shoulder and look at him with a serene expression, "Lincoln, I am fine, ok? I'm a little angry and a lot of worried. I'm more concerned with how you're feeling. Spill it, biker."

He drags his bear paw through his hair and lets out a growl. At another time I need to let him know what his growls do to my lady bits. I didn't even know men really did growl in real life. Books made it seem like it was a made-up thing. Whatever, I love it. He can keep doing it.

"It's all fucked up, Trix. I have so many feelings about it. I'm so fucking worried you're going to have a delayed meltdown over the bullshit from the past few days and I—"

I interrupt him holding my hand up, "I swear I'm ok and if I weren't I'd tell you right away. Promise." I pull my right hand out of his and hold up my pinky to promise with.

He chuckles, "Is this the form of promissory we're using?"

"Yep. The most sacred of them all." I wave my hand with my pinky out in his space. "If you are not ok, you'll tell me. In turn, I'll tell you if it gets to be too much, too heavy to carry."

"Deal, little bird," he vows as his pinky wraps around mine and squeezes.

"So, are you ok now?" I ask hesitantly.

"Yeah baby, I'll be fine. It's been a roller coaster of a week. I'm just processing. Fuck, I don't even know if I have a job still. But I gained a girlfriend and she's the love of my life."

Jesus. Stop blushing already.

"I think you're pretty great too, ya know." I bite my lip to keep from smiling so big. He's everything I never knew I needed wrapped in one big, beautiful package.

Linx shakes his head in disbelief, "Rock acted out of character today, you need to know that. He's not usually ruled by emotions like he was earlier. That's how I knew how pissed off he was. I've never seen him like that. But then again, no one's ever dared fuck his daughter."

I sigh. "We need to all just face it, no one was ever going to be good enough for his little girl, not even his favorite guy. I'm a grown ass woman. I will argue till I'm blue in the face, if you're good enough to be second, why can't you be good enough for me? I want to understand the rationale for his thought process. But I'm probably never getting that, and I'm ok with it. I have what I want. I fought for it."

He leans forward and pulls me onto his lap. I loop my arms around his neck.

"Me too, baby, I'll be alright, I'm just a little overwhelmed right now. Tomorrow's a new day, right?" His lips seek out mine and my mouth naturally opens for him. Our kisses are soft, light in touch since our lips are busted.

His choice of sleepwear is driving me crazy, those are baby making loungers and I...oh my god, I just felt his dick twitch under my thigh. Does he want to try to have sex?

He nuzzles into my chest then looks up at me, "So, uh, what's this I hear about you planning our wedding? Did I propose and not know it?"

"Yeah, about that. Sorry, I just said that to hurt him. It was just me lashing out. But I loved the look on his face."

He palms my face and kisses my jaw over to my lips. His other arm pulls me closer to him. His voice turning husky, "You know that's where this is headed, right?"

I nod my head slowly and a smile spreads across my mouth, "Can I at least have a few months before you ask? Can you woo me for a while?"

"I reckon, *mon amour*. Let the wooing commence."

Epilogue – Linx

Ten Weeks Later

I shut the lid of the smoker and reach over to check the other one. All's good. Just another hour while I shred this pork butt and we'll be set on meat for the annual Labor Day Smoke 'n Ride Family Supper. This is the day everyone brings their family to eat dinner with all of us associates after a charity bike run. Everyone is on their best behaviors. Sometimes.

There's a few dozen pork butts smoking and just as many briskets. It's a sight to see actually. Every associate with a smoker brings theirs down to the clubhouse and we park them out in the parking lot and start smoking early in the morning. We drink beer, play cornhole or horseshoes, and keep watch over the meats. There's usually a dozen of us or more.

It's a very sacred job. I was surprised when they asked me to be a cook again. I'm humbled to still be considered a member after everything that's went down, let alone have the honor of being a cook.

I got to keep my second-in-command position. The Elder Board voted, my vote was nullified. They convinced Rock to let me keep my balls and my rank. He's come around more, but he's still mad at me. He'll trust me with his life but fuck all for anything involving his daughter—no matter how happy she is, she's so flipping excited and happy to be together.

The rest of the club is due in around two and supper is at three. This year's benefit ride will go to one of the homeless shelters and to a couple of food banks around here. I think last year we raised slightly over ten grand with over one hundred and twenty riders. There's even more this year.

I love being a cook, but I also love being on the runs. I love being at each bar and holding up our bags to ask the patrons for donations while we drink a beer. Riders are broken up into groups of twenty and are assigned areas of New Orleans and surrounding areas to go to which bars are participating.

It's only about one thirty right now. Birdie said she was running late but she would be here by four. She was tattooing a client she had to reschedule from our wild week in the bayou.

I'm cutting up the last of the briskets and making sure the smokers are good when the thought drifts in, I haven't seen Trixie in a while. Earlier I noticed she was really hitting it off with the Old Ladies and girlfriends crowd. That made me hella happy.

Right beside her has been her trusty sidekicks, Pierre and Zharia. They're family, which means they got to come. My mom and Bret are here too. Mom surprised me and brought Uncle Pup also. The more the merrier.

My mind starts drifting again while I hum one of her Sleep Token songs. She's got me hooked. I can see at our wedding Pierre and

Shadow standing up with me, and Zharia and Tally up with Trix, and her picking a Sleep Token song as her bride march.

I have pictured our wedding so many times. What? Guys can think about marrying their girl and it not be weird.

I like to think of all the things Trixie would pick out and plan. Yep. Just me over here biding my time until she gives any indication whatsoever that she's ready for the proposal. I bought the ring over a year ago. Yeah, before we were even together I designed her wedding set and had it custom made. I know it sounds stupid, but I knew I was never marrying anyone else but her, and if I bought it, maybe one day by some miracle, it would come true.

Honestly, I feel like I got a pretty good start on that miracle already. I grin to myself, oh yeah, she definitely likes me now. Full on in love with me even. Ha-Cha! I feel a little smug at that, fuck, I waited like a goddamn saint to have her. I smile to myself.

Shadow comes walking up to me. More like sauntering up. Cocky bastard. I lift an eyebrow at him as he comes to a stop. "Sup, brother?" I greet him.

"You about done?"

"Yeah man, these are the last bits; all the smokers are shut off." I put the last morsels in the foil pan and ask, "What're you doing out here?"

"I came to see if you needed help. I'm going to get you cleaned up because you smell like a barbeque sandwich and I'm sure Birdie doesn't want to smell that sitting next to you all night," he claps me on the shoulder with an amused chuckle.

"So, are you saying I need to go hose off before joining the party?" Genuinely curious here.

"I'm just saying it wouldn't hurt, and she would be grateful."

"Fine. I'll get cleaned up for her. You still cutting out of here in an hour or so?"

"Yep. Got a date."

"Someone new?" I prod. Him and Zharia were an item for a while, but they've been off and on for what seems like forever.

They'll go for days no contact, then one will cave and the other comes running. I can't decide if they're toxic for one another or perfect for each other. They've been apart for two weeks this time. I know he's hardcore hung up on her. I've never seen him fall faster or harder for a girl than he did with Zharia.

"Yeah, she's new."

"Good for you, man. I hope it works out." Jesus fuck, do I ever hope it works out so Trix and I will stop being put in the middle. "When are you popping the question to your girl?"

"I don't know. I think she might be ready. She did ask for a few months and I've been trying to be patient, but it's so hard, man. Fuck, I just want to wife her up and keep her belly plump with my babies. Is that a lot to ask for?" I smile at him, because I know that truly is my goal. I think he knows too.

He laughs, "No, bro, that's a great plan. I love that for you." We reach the door to the clubhouse and when I walk in a few guys high five me and grunt, "Meat." I swear, men get around some good smoked meat and turn back into cavemen.

I scan the place for my woman, but I don't see her. That doesn't mean she's not outside in the courtyard.

I sneak a sniff on my clothes, and I don't smell anything. "You're nose blind right now, bro. Go get in the shower. Use the soap and wash your nacky ass." Shadow appears beside me with his nose wrinkled, like a ghost materialized.

"Goddamn. Hurt a bro's feelings why don't ya?"

"Just keeping it real with you, Mr. Danger."

I huff on towards the steps leading up to the apartment bathroom. I take the stairs two at a time. I need arms around my woman soon.

Shadow comes running behind me, "Hey man, I had some extra clothes in my saddlebag. Figured you shouldn't put the stinky clothes back on and Birdie just said you don't have extras here."

I didn't even think of that. Good thing me and him are the same size and have the same taste in clothes.

Black. And blacker. "Thanks, man."

After my shower, I throw on the boxer briefs, pants and socks. I hold up the shirt and it's a black button-up dress shirt. The fabric is butter soft and I really like the cut of it. Shadow has good taste. Probably some of his date night shit. Fuck it, it will work. I roll the sleeves up to my elbows and leave the top three buttons undone. I slip on my leather vest with my cut.

I look in the linen closet and see deodorant and a wide selection of colognes available for use by anyone. I put on some Armani Code that I always wear, and the deodorant then look at myself in the mirror. I don't look half bad.

I rub my hands together and lightly clap, *let's go get our woman, it's been far too long since I've had my hands on her.*

Rejoining the party, I search for her in the mingling people from the view point up here. I still don't see her when I reach the bottom step.

Shadow pops up out of nowhere with Pierre right beside me. The guy's a fucking phantom, I swear. He's like one of those shadow daddies Trix was telling me about from her books. He fits the descriptions.

"Hey brother, there's something on the stage I need your help with. Will you come look at it right quick? I think the audio is messed up and you know how dramatic Rock is if his mic isn't working properly."

They pull me away, but my mind is still occupied with 'where's my little bird.'

Pierre and Shadow lead me to the stage, to where the audio system sits off to the side. I crouch down and start looking at the wires.

"Here's the problem, this aux cord goes over here. Someone set it up wrong." I switch them out and say, "It should be good now." I stand up and turn around.

What I see shocks the shit out of me.

The clubhouse lights have been dimmed. Everyone is standing out front of the stage, with a center aisle between the two crowds, holding what looks like candles. My head jerks over to Shadow and he's got a shit-eating grin, raising up to the balls of his feet in excitement. I look over at Pierre and he's got hearts in his eyes and the same grin, pulling his boutonniere out of his pocket and putting it on his deep red dress shirt.

'I Get To Love You' by Ruelle plays over the speakers. My eyes narrow and I look for Trixie. The front door opens, and Zharia comes walking in with a cute blond woman, Tally. They come up on stage and stand on the other side.

Something's happening. My chest is fluttering and then the rear door opens and the most beautiful sight I've ever seen comes floating through.

My little bird, on the arm of her daddy, wearing the most beautiful black lace and satin dress, sparkling in the candlelight that's bouncing around everywhere.

But when she looks at me, her beautiful red lips pull into a smile so big and I just know, today's the day I get to say 'I do.'

I've waited for this day for so long.

Epilogue – Birdie

He looks so dashing up on that stage. It feels like the little bird that lives inside my chest is struggling to break free and fly to him. My butterflies are bouncing around in my stomach, fluttering strongly.

Soon, little darlings. We gotta pull off one helluva miracle first. For one, everyone BUT Lincoln knows about his surprise wedding. This took weeks of plotting. As soon as I knew he was staying in dad's little club, I started laying out a plan with Zharia and Pierre. Tally helped by video chats. Eventually I had to rope in Shadow, which was nice getting to know him more. Shadow roped in the rest of the club for me. I had to talk to my dad, and he didn't go as far as admitting he was wrong, but he did apologize to me in private. He's come around and allowed all this to happen in his clubhouse. He's even footed the bill for most of the food we've catered in for the event plus wedding.

There's no way Linx is saying no. I would never have planned this if there were any doubts.

This is Linx we're talking about. Come on. I'm the center of his universe. I know my place in his life.

Also, I found the rings. A whole matching set, bride and groom, in a purple velvet box. Just in my size too, surprisingly; no, not really. The guy has proven to be a first-class stalker of the highest degree. And honestly, I don't mind, no matter how fucked up that sounds.

These are the most beautiful rings I've ever seen. Linx put a lot of thought into picking these. Frankly, I think he hacked my Pinterest boards and took everything into consideration on my Dream Wedding board.

I turn my head and look at my dad. He's really struggling but he's fighting a losing battle. He has a hanky wiping away at any tears that fall. He's all red faced and snotty from seeing me earlier when he came to get me.

He told me how beautiful I looked, and he really wished my mom could see me now.

I ended up forgiving my father because I kinda feel like that was the wake up call I needed to understand what kind of life I was signing up for. I needed to learn who my dad really is.

We walk down the makeshift aisle, towards the stage. A tingly sensation stirs in my body. So close to having it all, a few more steps.

Pierre moves to the other side of Shadow, who stands to Linx's left. Zharia stands on the other side of the stage, on the bride's side. My eyes pop damn near out of my head.

Right beside her is one of my most favoritest people, our other best friend Tally. How the hell did they manage to get Tally away from New York during prep for fashion week? Ohmigod! I knew when Pierre and Zhar disappeared earlier something was up. They deviated from the plan.

My eyes are drawn back to my man up there waiting on me. He's waited so long.

I thank whatever higher power out there that he waited for me.

I got halfway down the aisle before Linx started choking up. The way his eyes continuously stayed on me, I have no doubt his heart is thudding as hard as mine is. The way his heart is on his sleeve for everyone to see, it endears me to him more.

Shadow gave him the black hanky I bought just for this moment. I knew he would lose it.

I spent so much time searching for the perfect dress. I always knew I would never wear white. I would never want a poofy Cinderella dress.

I found this extraordinarily talented lady in the Quarter who makes custom wedding dresses for the right clientele. Together we came up with my dress for a tidy price. Worth every penny.

The dress is a flowy black satin with an overlay of black lace that has thousands of sparkling beads imbedded in the lace. The top covers my sizable boobs but has a plunge halfway to my bellybutton. Pierre and Zharia about lost it when we went for the final fitting last week at the seamstress's house. They assured me he would love it and yes, he would cry.

They also raved about how sparkly in the candlelight the dress would be. I take a quick look down, yes! It's sparkling!

Back to Linx, always back to Linx. I walk up the stairs and my father follows me up. I only have eyes for Linx though.

My dad hands me the mic and I look at Linx with a wide smile and say, "Hi. Welcome to your wedding."

There's a round of hearty laughter out in the clubhouse. Linx's lips curve into a bright smile, revealing a flash of white teeth.

I see Linx's throat working against his emotions. My love, if he speaks right now, it will turn to sobs. Tears already coat his cheeks.

"There's something I have to ask first." I drop down to one knee, looking up at Linx smiling. He laughs and grabs his stomach. Everyone out in the crowd is amused.

Into the mic, "Will you marry me, Lincoln?"

"Yes!" he replies, reaching for my hands and pulling me up.

"Whew. It's a good thing you said yes, or this woulda got mighty awkward fast," I say. Whistles and laughter fill up the space.

I hand the mic back to my dad and he says, "Let's get this show on the road."

"Can you help me out of this dress?"

I turn around as he comes into the master bedroom.

"Can I fuck you in it first?"

I turn back around and look up at him with a grin, "I thought you'd never ask."

I love when he rushes at me, when his hands are flying all over my body, on my face, in my hair. When he's out of control. Desire for me overtakes his brain and all he thinks about is me. I love those moments.

He wraps his strong arms around me and swings me around while kissing me, making me dizzy. I giggle into his mouth. He backs me to the bed, and I fall back in a flurry of sparkles and swishing satin on a throaty laugh.

Linx growls and quickly dives under my wedding dress and pops his head up with a shocked look.

"Babe, where are your panties?"

I giggle and lift my head to look at him between my thighs, "I didn't wear any. I wanted to make it easy for you."

"Holy fuck, Trix. You're gonna kill me." He undoes his pants and pulls out his hard cock, rubbing the liquid gathering at the seam over the head. I can see the precum glistening in the low lights. It makes me smile. Feline. Like a bitch in heat.

Mine.

I start yanking up yards of satin and lace until he sees my pussy framed by a garter belt and fishnet hose.

He makes a painful noise, biting his knuckle. He whispers reverently, "Oh god, I gotta remember this for the rest of my life. This is the hottest thing I've ever seen."

He bends down and licks up my wet heat. When he pulls his tongue away, he groans, "Fuck, Trixie."

He positions himself at my entrance, with my high-heeled feet up on his shoulders and starts pushing into me.

God, I love when he first enters me. That first stretch, the nice burn as my body accepts him. The anticipation until he bottoms out in there, the shivers as my body accommodates him.

"Husband," I call to him in a husky, aroused voice.

He almost loses his shit, the shiver works through him, "Oh god, Trixie, baby." He growls, "Wife. *My* wife. Mine."

"Fuck me, husband."

His moan is to die for. The sweetest sound I know.

He does just that. He slams in and out of me as I open my legs as wide as they'll go for him.

Linx releases my legs but wraps them around his waist as his pants fall to his ankles. He leans over me, putting his hands by my head.

"Oh fuck, Linx, right there, I'm so close already. I've been waiting all day for this moment."

His hips press harder into me, doing that rotation I love so much, rubbing his bone on my clit, hitting my magic spot inside. He reaches between us and drags his hand up my satin covered stomach, over my tits and encircles my throat, then applies pressure.

Holy fuck. I love it when he does this. It's one of my favoritest things, for sure.

I love this man so much.

I love how he fucks me and knows exactly what my body needs.

"Come for me, Wife, clamp that pussy down on my cock and milk every drop out of me," Linx's raspy voice swirls in the lust and love induced haze in my head.

The familiar tingling spirals out of my core, down my legs, through my torso and out my hands. My voice is loud as I yell for him. Colors splash across my vision.

My little bird is happily soaring throughout my body.

"Are you ready, baby? I'm going to fill you up, I'm gonna put my baby in there, fuck, Trixie!" Linx's beautiful cock pumps stream after stream of cum inside of me. My pussy is gripping him so tight he can barely move. I feel every pulse of his orgasm.

I'll tell him later on that I had my birth control removed last week, after weeks of him asking me if it was time to get pregnant yet. He'll be pleased, but how wonderful it would be to create a child on our wedding night. Made out of pure love.

He raises his head and looks at me. There's nothing but adoration, love, and a dash of obsession written in his gorgeous eyes.

"Je te promets de t'aimer pour toujours," he whispers to me as his eyes fill. He says this particular phrase to me every day. *I promise to love you forever.*

I raise up to kiss him, "Je suis à toi, je t'aime."

'I'm yours, I love you' is always my reply. It will continue to be my reply until the day I die.

As fucked up as it sounds, I'm grateful for Grim's dumbass plan, it threw me and Linx together and I'm forever grateful for those first days in the camp house. Some of my heart's most cherished moments were lived there.

But something tells me, the best is yet to come.

He's the missing link to my soul and I'm never letting him go now that I'm complete.

The End.

I hope you enjoyed Danger and Birdie's love story. Join me for the next sinful installment of the Southern Devils Society where Shadow tries to win Zharia back, by all means necessary, while waging a war. Fuck you LSS!

A few thanks are in order.

Thank you to my readers! Y'all make it worthwhile, I tell ya. I love doing this and you help keep my spirit alive. I love telling stories and there are small tidbits of me in every book.

Did you know I am the daughter of Slim Jim, (Gone but Not Forgotten,) former Ohio President of the notorious motorcycle club, the Outlaws and later he took over the Ohio chapter of The Black Pistons. I do know bikers by these road names, however this isn't about them and this story doesn't represent them in any way. I only used handles/road names. Except my dad, he is wrote exactly like he was.

Our house out in the country was the clubhouse and church was held there once a month. My mother was the head Ole Lady, and she reigned well. My dad had a bar built into the family room to accommodate the associates and shenanigans that were done.

I am a Biker Princess and that influenced me to write this book. My Daddy and Uncle Rock (GBNF) would get a kick out of being in a spicy romance novel if they were still here with us. My Uncle Mike is in here too, T-Bone, he did find it amusing when I called to tell him.

I'd like to thank my husband who really doesn't care about smut or spicy books, but he cares about me and the things that make me happy. He does a great job being my sounding board, brainstorming partner and my snacky snack go-getter. Without his support I don't think I'd be brave enough to put myself and my stories out there. ilu

I want to thank Collin Foster, the wizard behind the cover. He does an amazing job at anything I throw at him, and he is so patient with all the changes I make. Thank you, Collin!

A big thank you goes to Sleep Token and Spotify who help your girl get through the self-doubt and creative process. To my Oldies but Goodies playlist and my Taylor Swift collection of my favorite songs by her. I sit here and listen to music the entire time I write and sometimes you might see the influence in the story.

I would give y'all a hug if I could. Thank you!

9 798999 302809